AMONG THIEVES

Douglas Hulick has been reading fantasy literature for almost as long as he can remember. He suspects this penchant for far-away lands of yore led, in part, to his acquiring a BA and MA in Medieval History, and likewise to his subsequent study and teaching of European Historical Martial Arts. It most certainly resulted in his authoring several short stories, as well as, now, a novel. Douglas reads and writes and plays with a rapier in Minnesota, where he is often surprisingly tolerated by his wife (who also fences) and two sons (who do not). All of them read.

AMONG THIEVES

A TALE OF THE KIN

DOUGLAS HULICK

TOR

First published in the US 2011 by New American Library,
a division of Penguin Group (USA) Inc.

This edition published in Great Britain 2011 by Tor
an imprint of Pan Macmillan, a division of Macmillan Publishers Limited
Pan Macmillan, 20 New Wharf Road, London N1 9RR
Basingstoke and Oxford
Associated companies throughout the world
www.panmacmillan.com

ISBN 978-0-330-53620-2

3 5 7 9 8 6 4

A CIP catalogue record for this book is available from
the British Library.

Printed and bound by CPI Group (UK) Ltd, Croydon, CR0 4YY

Visit **www.panmacmillan.com** to read more about all our books
and to buy them. You will also find features, author interviews and
news of any author events, and you can sign up for e-newsletters
so that you're always first to hear about our new releases.

For Jamie, who always believed, even when I didn't.

*In memory of my father, Nicholas Hulick,
who read to me and never said no when it came to
getting another book. I miss you, Dad.*

A Brief Note on the Use of
Cant in this Book

The various forms of "cant," or thieves' argot, in this book are inspired by records of actual use from various places and times throughout history, from Elizabethan England to twentieth-century American-underworld slang, and many places in between. I have been liberal with both the meaning and forms of many of these words, changing them as I deemed necessary for the story and world. In some places, I have altered either the definition or use of a term; in others, I have left them much as they were historically used. And, not surprisingly, I have also made up certain canting terms from the whole cloth.

So, in short, you will find cant both correct and incorrect, documentable and fanciful, in the following pages. For those who know nothing of the *patter flash*, I hope it adds to the story; for those who are familiar with it, I hope any creative license on my part doesn't prove too distracting.

AMONG THIEVES

Chapter One

Athel the Grinner wasn't grinning. In fact, he didn't look that good at all. A long night of torture will do that to a person.

I knelt beside him. He was naked, his arms lashed across the top of a barrel, the rest of him collapsed behind. I avoided looking at the bloody mess that had once been his hands and feet.

"Athel," I said. Nothing. I slapped the smuggler lightly on his sweaty cheek. "Hey, Athel." His eyelids fluttered once. I wove my fingers into his hair, took hold, and raised his head so he could see me. If any of the sympathy or pity I felt showed on my face, so be it. I don't have to like what I do sometimes. I said his name again.

Athel's eyes opened and began wandering around the shadowed room. I waited for him to notice me in the candlelight. He did.

"Drothe?" he said. His voice was slow and rusty as he spoke my name. I could tell he was having trouble focusing on me in the flickering light.

"Grinner," I replied, "want to tell me something?"

"Wha ... ?" His eyes began to close.

I gave his head a shake. "Athel!" His dark eyes snapped open, feverish in their intensity. I leaned forward and locked my gaze with his, trying to hold his attention by force of will.

"Where's the reliquary?" I said.

Athel tried to swallow, but coughed instead. "Already told you it's coming. I just . . ."

"If it's coming," I said, "why did I have to chase you halfway across the city? Why did I have to drag you off that skiff as it was launching into the bay? Doesn't seem like you've been playing straight with me, Grinner."

Athel shook his head, his hair tugging gently in my hand, and grinned weakly. "Wouldn't cross you, Drothe—you know that."

"But you did," I said. I tapped one of his ruined fingers, making him gasp. "You told me earlier, remember?" I let him think back on the pain and remember why he had decided to talk the first time. "You've put me in an awkward position, Athel. I have a buyer and no reliquary for him. That undercuts my reputation. That makes me unhappy. So, either you tell me where to find that reliquary, or I come back after my people have done some more persuading."

I could tell he was thinking about it. His eyes glassed over, and his jaw wobbled softly as he argued it over inside. If the Angels had any mercy, they would let him crack the rest of the way right now. I knelt next to what was left of him and waited, hoping it would end here.

When Athel finally came back up from wherever he had been, I could see the Angels weren't on my side tonight. Despite all he had gone through, he was still able to summon up a piercing look and give me the weakest shake of his head.

I placed his head gently back on top of the barrel and stood.

"I need to know who he sold it to," I said. "I need a name."

"I'll get you one. Don't worry," said a voice from the darkened warehouse around us.

Shatters came walking into the candle's circle of light, his two assistants behind him. One was carrying a bucket of seawater.

The Agonyman was small, even shorter than I, with broad shoulders and no neck to speak of. His hands were long and expressive, like an artist's, and he was constantly cracking his knuckles as he walked. Shatters stopped beside me and smiled a cruel, hungry smile. "He's close to the edge now. Won't take much more to get him babbling like a drunken whore." He popped a thumb joint for emphasis.

The assistant with the bucket stepped forward and emptied it over Athel. The smuggler sputtered, then howled as the salt water reached his ravaged hands. I turned away as the other assistant began sorting through the torturer's tools that had been set aside during my interview.

"Let me know when he's ready." My voice came out thick. "I'll be outside." Shatters's laughter followed me through the shuttered warehouse until I opened the door and stepped outside.

I blinked in surprise at the sunlight that struck me in the face. Dawn already? I squinted at the soft glow that seemed to suffuse every tower and building of the Imperial capital. Ildrecca tried its hardest to look peaceful and serene in that light, but I've known the city too long to be fooled so easily. Nice try, old friend.

Bronze Degan was across the street, leaning in a doorway. I went over.

"Anything?" he asked.

"Not since the last time I went in." I gestured to the sun in the east. "When did that happen?"

"Not too long ago." He yawned. "How much longer?"

I felt myself yawn in return. I hated that. "Hell if I know," I said.

Degan grunted and rearranged himself in the doorway. Half again as tall as me, with fair hair and skin, broad shoulders, and a lean build, he seemed to fill the entire space on his own. Some of that came from the cut of his clothes—the flowing, long green linen coat, left open to show off the copper-colored doublet beneath, the matching full-cut breeches, the wide-brimmed hat—but just as much came from the man himself. He had an air of easy, capable confidence about him that caused people to give him a healthy berth even in the most crowded city streets. Of course, it didn't hurt that a bronze-chased sword hung at his side, either—a sword that marked him as a member of the Order of the Degans, an old mercenary order in an even older city. No one entered into that select brotherhood of sell-swords without plenty of personal cachet to begin with.

I slid into the doorway beside Degan, sat down on the stoop, and dug out two ahrami seeds from the pouch around my neck. They were small and oval, the size of my largest knuckle, and darkly roasted. I rubbed them between my palms to let them absorb some sweat. A sharp, acrid smell, with subtle hints of cinnamon, earth, and smoke, rose up from my hands. I felt my pulse quicken at the aroma.

"Breakfast," announced Degan.

I looked up. "What?"

"I've decided you owe me breakfast."

"Oh?"

Degan gave me a wry look as he silently counted off three fingers.

"Ah," I said. "Well, I suppose you earned it."

Degan snorted. There had been three men with Athel the Grinner when I'd finally tracked him down—three very large men. For me, they would have been an impossible barrier; for Degan, they were little more than an inconvenience. If not for him, I'd never have made it out of that plaza, and Athel would still be grinning.

"Thanks," I added. It was something I didn't say to my friend nearly enough, and something he didn't worry about hearing. We'd been running the streets together long enough to have moved past words and gestures like that.

Degan shrugged. "Slow night. I needed something to do."

I smiled and was just slipping the ahrami seeds into my mouth when a muffled scream came out of the warehouse. Degan and I looked up and down the street, but there was no one to hear Athel's cries—or, at least, no one who felt inclined to investigate. I shuddered in the silence that followed.

I had been planning on letting the seeds sit in my mouth for a while, to savor the quickening of my pulse in anticipation. Now, I simply bit down. The ahrami filled my mouth with smoky, bittersweet flavor. I chewed quickly, swallowed, and waited for them to hit.

They came on fast, as the straight seeds always do. One moment I was tired and half asleep; the next, I felt revitalized. The cobwebs that had been draping themselves across my mind for the last several hours receded, replaced with a sense of alertness. I could feel the worst of the tension drain out of me. My back loosened, and the pressure that had been building behind my eyes faded away. The fatigue was still there—I wasn't going to be running across the city again any time soon—but I didn't feel as raw as I had a few moments ago.

I sat up a little straighter and worked the kinks from my shoulders. My mind was settled, my pulse was steady, and my eyes were sharp once more.

I shook the bag around my neck before slipping it back under my shirt. Only a few seeds left. I'd have to restock soon.

We settled back and waited. I thought I heard a few more screams, but the city was coming alive by then and the yells seemed softer than before, so it was hard to tell.

One of Shatters's men came out to get me just as the ahrami was starting to wear off. By the time I made it back into the warehouse and stood at the Agonyman's side, the rush had faded completely, leaving me in a less than charitable mood.

"Well?" I said.

Shatters was rinsing his hands and forearms in a large bucket of water that had been set atop a crate. "Gotcher name."

"And?" I said.

"Amazing how good this feels after a long night," he said, nodding toward the water. "Ya get warm, working on a man that long." Shatters glanced at me sideways. "Makes you appreciate the simple things, you know?"

I stayed silent. I suspected I knew where this was going, but I wanted to let him get there on his own.

"Like hawks," said Shatters. "Hawks are simple things."

"Oh?"

He nodded. "You want something, you give a person hawks and he gives it to ya. The more you want it, the more money you give him."

I nodded. This was going where I had thought it would: Shatters was trying to shake me down.

"Pretty simple," I said. "Except we already agreed on a price."

Shatters paused as he leaned over the bucket. I noticed that the water had taken on a reddish tint. "This took longer than I expected," he said flatly. "I figure if something takes that long to get, it's worth a higher price. A man don't hold out like Athel did for sheer stubbornness." He ran a finger through the water. "You want to hear what he had to say, you'll hatch some more hawks."

"Or?"

"Or he won't be telling no one nothing ever again, and the name walks with me."

"I see."

Shatters grinned. "Smart lad." He bent down to rinse his face.

"Smart," I agreed as I grabbed the back of his neck and shoved his head down into the water. I shifted my weight to keep him there, steadying the bucket with my other hand as he struggled.

As a rule, I don't mind renegotiating—hell, it's part of doing business with people like Shatters. Kin are always trying to line their pockets with a few extra hawks. But there's a right way and a wrong way to do it. The right way involves respect and a little give and take from both sides; the wrong way usually involves demanding more money "or else." Unless I'm the one offering it, I hate "or else."

Even underwater, Shatters was loud. His assistants came running. I barely glanced up as they came into sight.

"First one of you raises a hand goes dustmans," I said. They both skidded to a stop, torn between my threat to kill them and their duty to their master. They eyed me, Shatters, and each other in turn.

I knew I had them the moment they hesitated. "Fade," I said. Still, they stood there. I looked up from Shatters's flailing and met the larger man's eyes. "What are you, a couple of Eriffs? Don't you know who I *am*? I said, *fade!*"

The larger man ducked his head and turned away. The smaller one paused and eyed the distance between us, considering. I showed my teeth.

"Come on, pup. Try me."

He left.

Shatters's struggles had begun to weaken by then. I raised his head out of the water long enough for him to get half a breath, then shoved it back under. Pause, repeat, and again. Near the end of the fourth dunking, I let go and stepped away.

Shatters fell sideways with his head still in the bucket, spilling water over himself and the floor. He lay there, coughing violently, his body convulsing with the effort. I knelt down and relieved him of his dagger as he vomited up water and bile.

"The name," I said when he was done.

Shatters spit. "Screw," he said.

"That's not a name," I said. I stood and pushed his face into his own vomit with my foot, crushing his nose against the floor in the process. "Try again."

Shatters gagged and tried to wrench his head up. I let him after a moment.

"Ioclaudia," he gasped. "The name's Ioclaudia."

I arched an eyebrow. It was an old-fashioned name; certainly one I wasn't familiar with on the street. "Who is . . . ?" I asked.

Shatters started on another coughing fit. I nudged him with the toe of my boot.

"Who is?"

"Don't know. Athel wouldn't say."

"What's her connection with Athel? Was she his buyer?"

"I don't know. Maybe."

"Where is she?"

Shatters shook his head.

"What about the reliquary?" I said. "Did you find out where it is?"

Shatters was rising to his hands and knees now, arms trembling but getting stronger every moment. "All he said was he needed to make some kind of swap. It sounded as if it came up suddenlike."

"And he used *my* reliquary?"

Shatters nodded.

Bastard. "What did he swap it for?"

"How the hell should I know?" Anger had found its way back into his voice. "Shit," he said, looking up at me. "You little shit. Do you know what my brothers will do to you for this?"

I reached out and put his own dagger against his cheek. Shatters froze, staring at the steel. It was sharp; a rivulet of blood appeared without any effort on my part.

"Don't even *think* about making this personal," I said. "You tried to shake me down, and I called you on it. It's business. It's over." I moved the blade down, letting it linger beside his neck. "But if you insist on bringing in your fellow Agonymen, not only will I take it poorly, but Nicco probably won't be too pleased, either. And I *know* you don't want *him* mad at you."

Shatters paled at the mention of Nicco's name. Niccodemus Alludrus was well-known for his temper, especially when he thought he was being crossed. Trying to cheat me was not automatically the same as trying to cross Nicco, but there were times when the lines between his and my interests blurred. This wasn't one of them, but I wasn't about to let Shatters know that.

"Do we have an understanding?" I said. Shatters nodded his head as gently as he could, given the dagger at his throat.

"Good." I withdrew the blade and turned away, leaving Shatters to gather himself while I went to see Athel the Grinner.

If I had had any second thoughts about treating Shatters roughly, they vanished as soon as I saw what was left of the Grinner. The Agonyman and his boys had moved on from Athel's hands and feet after I'd left; now, there was precious little left on the smuggler that was not torn, cut, or mutilated in some way. Just seeing him hurt. Worst of all, he was still conscious . . . and looking at me.

I kept my bile down, not for Athel's sake, but because I wasn't about to give Shatters the satisfaction. I took a deep breath, ran a hand down my mustache and goatee, and stepped over to the barrel.

Athel's breathing was ragged and wet sounding. One eye was swollen shut, but the other managed to keep me in sight as I came up beside him. I expected hatred there, or anger, or madness—anything but what I seemed to see: calm. Not the false serenity brought on by shock, or the stillness of exhaustion, but a quiet, almost-composed ease. I felt myself shudder beneath that placid gaze.

Athel the Grinner, I realized as I met his eye, was done. There was nothing more we could do to make him talk; nothing left he was willing to tell us before he died. Letting Ioclaudia's name out had probably been an accident, or a gift, and he wasn't about to let that happen again—his gaze told me as much.

I crouched down beside him, keeping my knees out of the blood that covered the floor. He blinked his good eye slowly, briefly. After a moment, I realized he was winking.

I reached for my own blade and found I still had Shatters's knife in my hand. Athel followed my look, then turned his lone eye back to me. He grinned as I cut his throat.

When I came walking back from the barrel, Shatters and his two boys were waiting. One of the apprentices had refilled the bucket. Shatters's vomit-stained shirt was gone, revealing a mixture of knobby muscles and old scars scattered across his torso. Water still clung to his head and chest from where he had rinsed himself off.

"That was stupid," Shatters said. A knuckle popped.

I didn't say anything—I just rested my hand on the blued steel of my rapier guard and turned it to catch the light. It was sheer bravado; I wasn't nearly good enough to take three of them at once. With luck, I might hold them off while I yelled to Degan for help.

Shatters followed my movement and smiled. "Jumpy? Ought to be, but I ain't talking about my bath." He gestured behind me. "I meant your meat back there. You shouldn't have dusted him—I could have gotten more."

"He was done talking."

"So you say. I say he had more in him." Shatters *tsk*ed and laid a thumb across one of his fingers. "Such a waste. I could've made that meat squeal"—*pop*—"till it was music."

"Make music on your own time." I wasn't about to try to explain what I had seen in Athel's gaze—Shatters took too much joy in his work to admit anyone could outlast him. "Just clean the place up and make sure the body's found."

Shatters frowned but nodded nonetheless. When Athel's corpse turned up in a day or two, it would be missing the ring finger of each hand—street code for "This one betrayed his own." Ages ago, the empire had cut off a thief's thumb to mark him as a criminal; now, we criminals cut our own to mark them as traitors. Who says we don't learn anything from polite society?

I stepped aside as Shatters and his boys moved past on their way to the corpse. I watched them for a moment, just to be sure they weren't going to jump me, then continued back to where I had had my "conversation" with Shatters. Athel's things were still heaped in a pile on the floor. Some of the water from the spilled bucket had run over to it. Sighing, I picked up the damp mass and held it away from my body, letting it drip freely.

They had taken the lantern with them. Only a single

candle remained, perched on a nearby box. I set Athel's things on a crate and looked at the candle, considering.

It was a mixed blessing, being able to see in the dark better than anything, save maybe a cat. In alleys, on rooftops, for stalking the night, the strange gift my stepfather, Sebastian, had given me was invaluable. But at times like these, with natural light and the temporary blindness it could bring a mere glance away, my night vision was an uneasy proposition at best.

That, and the risk of discovery, gave me pause. I didn't relish trying to explain my examining Athel's things in the dark should Shatters or his assistants return. The best edge was one you kept hidden, and this was mine. I'd never met anyone else who had night vision except for Sebastian, and he had given it up the night he performed the ritual that passed it on to me. I'd shared its existence with only three people since that night decades ago, and I sure as hell wasn't about to bring Shatters into that select circle.

No. Convenient as it might have been to step off into the darkened warehouse and have Athel's belongings limn themselves in a faint amber glow, now was not the time to take chances.

I moved the candle closer to Athel's sodden possessions. I'd searched his things earlier, but not especially well. I had been counting on the questioning to give me the answers I wanted. Now, though, with nothing more than a name and a dead smuggler getting cold . . .

I started with the clothes, wringing them out and checking for hidden pockets, lined seams, or false soles on the shoes. Nothing. The purse held a few coins— three copper owls and a silver hawk—and a scarred lead lozenge. I recognized it as an old pilgrim's token from my grandfather's time. It was triple-stamped with the three symbols of the emperor, one for each of his recurring incarnations. Whoever had originally owned this had completed the imperial pilgrimage route—no small feat, given it had stretched nearly a thousand miles. A series of border wars and an imperial decree had shifted the route since then, making these tokens a rare thing. I put the coins back in the purse for Shatters's men to find, and pocketed the token.

The contents of Athel's shoulder satchel hadn't changed, either: a pipe, two thin candles (broken), a leather smoker's packet, and a wedge of moldy cheese. Feeling the need to be thorough, I broke apart the pipe, crumbled the cheese in my hands, and upended the small packet onto the crate. The pipe held nothing but char; the cheese smelled dry and old; and the packet contained some finely shredded tobacco and three long, narrow scraps of paper twisted lengthwise to form simple pipe tapers.

I turned the shoulder satchel inside out, checking the lining and cutting open the seams for good measure.

Nothing.

Hell.

I leaned against the crate and stared into the darkness of the warehouse. Back behind me, I could hear Shatters's men cursing as they moved something unwieldy—likely Athel's body. I also heard someone call my name.

"Drothe?" It was Degan.

"Here," I called.

I listened to him thread his way through the barrels and crates, then saw the glow that came with him. He must have taken one of Shatters's lanterns. I squinted and purposefully turned my back to him, but the illumination still made my eyes burn. The place must have been dim enough to start awakening my night vision after all, even with the candle.

"Anything?" he said as he came up beside me.

"A name," I said, blinking rapidly as my eyes gave one last fiery protest and then settled into normal vision. "Ioclaudia."

"Old name," observed Degan.

I nodded. "Know anyone who goes by it?"

"Nope."

I nodded again. It would have been too much to hope for, anyhow.

Degan waited. I remained silent. "Tell me that isn't all you got," he said.

"That's all I got."

Degan set the lantern down on the crate and rubbed the bridge of his nose. "Why is it always like this with you? Why is it never easy?"

"Luck?" I said. Degan didn't smile. I sighed and reached for the lantern. "Come on," I said, turning away. "The smell in here is —" I froze in midmotion. "Damn."

Degan's hand drifted ever so slightly toward his sword. "What?"

I set the lantern back down and leaned forward over the crate. There, on one of the pipe tapers, just visible among the folds and twists of the paper, was an ideograph.

I picked up the taper and carefully untwisted it. No, it hadn't been a trick of the light. The symbol *pystos*, along with a host of other random markings, had been inked on the scrap of paper. *Pystos* meant "relic." And near it, the block symbol *immus*, simple shorthand for "emperor."

Degan bent down and peered over my shoulder. He chuckled.

"Luck, indeed," he agreed.

Chapter Two

I held the slip of paper up and slightly away from me, angling it to better catch the sunlight coming over my shoulder. It was about as wide as my ring finger and a little longer than my hand. Finely inked markings—lines, dots, odd angles, and curves—ran along the left half of the paper; the rest was blank. The ideographs for *pystos* and *immus* were jumbled in among the rest of the markings. Aside from those words, though, it looked like a bunch of insect tracks set down in ink.

"Cart," said Degan from off to my right.

I looked up and found myself a step away from walking into a parked baker's cart. I sidestepped, but not fast enough to avoid catching my hip on a corner. Bread and rolls jostled from the impact, and the baker scowled as he made sure I wasn't helping myself to any of his goods.

"I'm surprised you didn't let me run into the damn thing," I said as I came alongside Degan, rubbing where I'd connected with the wood.

"I considered it," said Degan, "but it seemed a shame to ruin that baker's day just for my own amusement."

"There's a saying for friends like you, you know."

Degan laughed.

We were in Long Brick cordon now, with Little Docks and its warehouses ten blocks behind and receding. A trace of the sea still hung in the air, but it was quickly being overpowered by the earthier smells of the cordon: filthy cobbles, sweaty day laborers, busy women on their way to the public fountains, and yes, the aroma of freshly baked bread. Groups of children rushed around carts and ducked between legs, adding to the frenzy of the early-morning traffic. I figured at least a quarter of the children were on the dodge—lifting goods, cutting purses, or spying out marks for their older partners.

This was the edge of Nicco's territory—my territory—and I marked my fellow Kin as I went. A Purse Cutter here, with her small sharp knife and deft hands; a Tail Drawer there, wearing a long cloak to better hide the swords he stole from other men's belts; a Talker across the way, all fast words and plausible stories, setting up cons for the unwary; and a dozen other dodges as well. And everywhere, the Masters of the Black Art, begging bowls in hand, their faked maladies displayed for the Lighters as they walked by. A few Kin gave me discreet nods or a small signal of greeting. Most just got on with their business. I did the same.

Degan cleared his throat. "So ... ?" he said, indicating the slip of paper still in my hand.

"Beats the hell out of me." I folded it up and stuck it in my ahrami pouch. "Could be a code. Could be a cipher. Hell, it could even *be* a scrap of paper for lighting a pipe."

"A scrap of paper that just happens to mention an imperial relic?" said Degan. "Pretty convenient."

"It says 'imperial' and it says 'relic.' It doesn't say anything directly about an 'imperial relic.'"

Degan stayed eloquently silent.

"Yeah," I said, "I don't believe in coincidences like that, either, but the thing that really doesn't make sense—"

"You mean some of this makes sense?"

"The thing that *really* doesn't make sense," I continued pointedly, "is Athel. Why did he stand the knife so well?"

"Ah," said Degan. "That."

"Yes."

Relic hunting was one of the riskier dodges out there.

The empire frowned on people lightening its holy objects, let alone selling them, and they were none too gentle with those they caught in the act. It ranked somewhere below trying to actually kill the emperor, but above desecrating an imperial shrine, and the Kin who ply the trade know just what to expect if they get caught.

That was part of why I only dabbled in the trade; but Athel had made an art of it. He was famous for having hidden prayer scrolls in sausage casings, floating olive oil on top of sacred water in cooking jars, and wearing a vestment sash wrapped as a turban. But he'd also burned a four-hundred-year-old tract on imperial divinity rather than let the imperial relic trackers—the Brothers Penitent—find it on him. Athel hadn't been the kind of man to fold in the face of adversity, or to risk himself needlessly. He had known how to cut his losses, which was why it hadn't made sense for Athel to stand against Shatters for so long.

"Why would Athel keep silent?" I said out loud. "What was the point?"

"Money?" said Degan.

I shook my head. "The relic was worth a lot," I said, "but Athel knew he was dustmans from the moment I caught him. Why keep quiet if you know you aren't going to be around to enjoy the hawks?"

"Vindictive?" suggested Degan.

"How do you mean?"

"If he knew you were going to dust him, why tell you anything at all? He knew he was dead either way—maybe he just wanted to rub your nose in it one last time."

"That wasn't Athel's style," I said.

"People's styles change under a knife, Drothe."

"Maybe," I said, "but Shatters did more than enough to break a simple stubborn streak. You don't put up with that kind of pain just to be petty."

"Petty men do."

I thought back to the look in Athel's eye at the end. "He was a far cry from petty," I said.

Degan sighed. "All right—what about loyalty?"

"From one of the Kin?" I laughed out loud.

"I've known one or two to keep their word," he said, eyeing me sidelong. "Some even make a habit of it."

"Usually to their regret," I said drily. I looked around again, spotting a few of my fellow Kin on the street. Would any of them stand the knife for one of their fellows, let alone a local boss? Would any of them be able to stand it like Athel had?

Once, maybe. When there had been a Dark King. When Isidore had stood at the head of all the Kin, controlling a criminal empire that spanned the underside of the true empire. The stories told how he had formed and shaped us, turning a morass of petty criminals and local bosses into a tightly run organization. Nothing was stolen that he didn't get a cut of; no dodge pulled he couldn't get the details on; no betrayal or cross he wouldn't make someone pay for. Kin didn't prey on Kin, Isidore had said, and, for a short time, until the empire—and the emperor—had taken notice, it had even been true.

Emperor Lucien, maniacally jealous of his power in those days, couldn't abide the thought of anyone else claiming sway over a kingdom—even a dark one— within his empire. All power flowed from the imperial throne; to set up any lesser authority within the empire without his permission was a challenge to his supreme authority. And so the aging incarnation had created the White Sashes, to set his personal hunters apart from his gold-sashed house guards and the black-belted legions. They had poured through the streets of Ildrecca and beyond, those White Sashes, dragging the Imperial legions in their wake. Kin had filled the gallows like apples in autumn orchards. Those the Whites couldn't find rope for, they left lying in the streets. Entire families were cut down because one member was part of Isidore's empire within the empire. And Isidore was marched through the streets and butchered like a sheep over the course of a day and a night, kept alive by Imperial magic to make sure the message struck home.

And it had. Nearly two hundred years later, the Kin were still fractured. Where once we had a king, today small-time bosses, petty street gangs, and factional in-fighting were the norm. The closest anyone came to Isidore were the Gray Princes, and they were still a far cry away. Half-mythical crime lords who ran shadow kingdoms among the Kin, each Prince had people in dozens of different criminal organizations, reporting back and manipulating dodges to their agendas. No one knew how many jobs happened at their bidding, or what percentage of each take made it into their various coffers without anyone being the wiser; yet no one doubted they did. The Gray Princes ran no specific territories, had no bases of operation. But every Kin knew their names: Shadow, the Dance Mistress, Longreach, Soli-tude, the Piper's Son, Crook Eye, and Blazon—legends to be avoided at all costs, if you were wise.

But for all their genius and reach, the Princes were still pale, squabbling shadows of Isidore, just as we were all small reflections of them in one way or another. There was no pride, no center to the Kin anymore. I couldn't see a typical member of the Kin taking what Shatters had done to Athel and not breaking. There wouldn't be a percentage in holding out, and nowadays that was what it came down to—except, it seemed, for Athel.

"All right," I said, "even if I assume for a moment that Athel was keeping tight out of a sense of duty—which I don't—it still comes down to *who*. Who would he be loyal to? He was a smuggler. He worked for himself. Who gets a smuggler to stand up to torture like that?"

"Ioclaudia?"

Back to the one name Athel had given us. I shook my head in frustration. "Maybe," I said, "but who *is* she? She's no Boman Prig, that's for sure—otherwise one of us would have heard about her before this."

"Who says she has to be a notorious member of the Kin? Maybe Athel was doing it for some other reason."

"It'd have to be a pretty damn good reason to hold out against Shatters all night."

Degan stared off down the street for several paces. "Maybe Ioclaudia was family," he said.

"Athel's? You mean his sister or something?"

"Or a mother, or a lover."

I shook my head. "I don't see it."

"No, I don't expect you would."

I bit down on a sharp reply and managed a shrug instead. I wasn't going to let myself be baited that easily. If Degan wanted to bring up my sister, he could damn well say her name. I wasn't about to do it for him.

"Don't I owe you breakfast?" I said instead.

"Changing the subject?"

"Paying my debts."

Degan smiled. "Even better."

I did some quick mental figuring. "It's Falcon Day. That means I need to stop by Mendross's stall."

Degan glanced up at the sky. "Isn't it a little early for you to be paying calls?"

"By about eight hours," I agreed, "but I've found that it never hurts to surprise your people now and again. Keeps them on edge. Besides, his produce will be fresher this time of day."

It took us less than half an hour to make our way to Fifth Angel Square. The place was home to the A'Riif Bazaar, a maze of stalls, tents, and humanity, all crammed together in an area that should have held half as much of each. The bazaar was famed for its cheap prices, cheaper goods, and excellent street food. A perpetual haze hung over the square, made up of equal parts cooking smoke, dust, and heat. Beneath the haze, the awnings and tents of the merchants created a ragged patchwork of shade and sunlight, shadows and color, through which walked a cross section of the empire itself, from native Ildreccan bargain hunters to refugees from the Djanese frontier, and everything in between.

Presiding over it all was the square's patron, the Angel Elirokos. The statue must have been a fine representation of the old Pardoner when it went up a couple centuries ago. Now, though, the paint had peeled off nearly a quarter of his frame to reveal the dull gray stone beneath. Only one arm, the one traditionally pointing northward, remained intact; the other had been missing for decades. Without his famous handful of souls, the old boy looked like a crippled beggar trying to wave down a mark.

I'd always liked that statue.

Mendross's stall was near the base of the Angel, just beyond its shade. He was busy overcharging a woman when we walked up. As they dickered, Degan and I helped ourselves to some breakfast. Mendross took this in stride, but the woman seemed put out.

"Is this why I pay so much, eh? So your friends can eat for free, eh?"

Mendross favored us with a frown deep from within his jowls, then beamed at his customer. "Ah, no, madam! No, these fine fellows are merely sampling wares for their master, the esteemed Pandri, favored underchef to the Outer Imperial Court."

The woman looked Degan and me up and down and did not seem impressed. I couldn't blame her; even without the night we had just had, I doubt anyone would have allowed us near the Outer Court, let alone into its kitchens.

"Pah!" she concluded, and walked away.

Degan picked up a handful of brilliant mountain strawberries and sampled one. "I think our master, the underchef, would be quite pleased with these, Drothe." He popped another into his mouth. "Ought to slide down the thrice-blessed pipe quite nicely."

"Excellent timing," grumbled Mendross. "I nearly had her."

I made a dismissive gesture as I stepped up alongside the merchant, leaving only a small bushel of figs between us. "I'll give you the two damn owls you'd have made."

"Four. And you're early."

"Three, and yes I am."

"Wait here. I wasn't ready for you." The merchant lumbered to the back of his stall and made a production of rooting around. I amused myself by tossing figs to a couple of bazaar urchins. Degan ate and watched the crowd.

"Hunh, business is bad," said Mendross when he came back. He slipped a small pouch behind the bushel. I took it, making sure anyone who knew their business would catch the handoff.

"Tough all over," I said. "But it's nothing personal. . . ."

Mendross resurrected his frown. "Yeah, I know. It's just business." He spit off to one side.

The pouch was filled not with coins, but seed pits and gravel. It was a false payoff, a bogus protection dodge for the benefit of any curious Kin, as was our chatter. Mendross was an Ear—he worked for me.

I smiled at his display and sampled some nearby dates. I had noticed no one hanging around the surrounding stalls any longer than they should, so I gave Mendross a tiny nod, as if in appreciation of the fruit. He leaned forward and began rearranging a pile of oranges. It brought his face near mine.

"Niccodemus wants you," said the Ear, his lips barely moving.

"Why?"

Mendross shook his head as he set a bad orange aside. "Don't know. I only heard the call."

"Is it urgent?"

He gave a minuscule shrug.

I considered. Nicco could want me for anything, from running down a rumor to handing me a new job. And all of them would involve my going well out of my way, rather than home to bed, which was where I desperately wanted to be.

I sighed and picked up an orange. I needed sleep. I didn't want to go running down any more rumors or Kin this morning.

"Nothing about its being important?" I asked.

"Nothing."

"All right," I said, piercing the skin of the orange with my thumbnail. The sharp, sweet smell made my nose

tingle. "Get word back: I need to— No, I *have* to follow
up on something this morning. I'll see him tonight, after I've run things down." It wasn't the best answer and
wouldn't win me any points, but it would cover my ass
until I finally knocked on Nicco's door.

Mendross made a show of looking resigned, nodding
as if at the inevitable loss of the orange. Translation:
Word would get back. I suppressed a grin: Mendross had
missed a calling to the stage.

"Anything else?" I said.

"There're rumblings in Ten Ways."

I snorted. "There are always 'rumblings' in Ten
Ways." Ten Ways was a hole of a cordon that no one
truly controlled. Nicco had minor interests there, but
so did several other bosses. "Let me guess: A couple
of gangs crossed steel over their border and one of
Nicco's clients got clipped in the process. Now the client's complaining about not getting the protection he
paid for."

Mendross stopped rearranging his produce and
stared at me. "There wasn't a gang fight involved, but
yes, that's basically it. Why do I bother telling you these
things if you already know them?"

I smiled slyly. I'd come out of Ten Ways years back—I
knew how the place worked.

I separated out a section of orange. Juice trickled
down into my palm. "Next?" I said.

Mendross went back to work on a pile of dates.
"There're whispers," he said, his voice dropping. "Someone's snilching Nicco."

I stopped, the orange midway to my mouth, which
had suddenly gone dry. "Snilching?" I said. That wasn't
good. No one liked spies, but Nicco was pathological
about them. Even the hint of another crime lord's man
inside his organization would send Nicco into a rage.
And when that happened, he'd tear the place apart until
he found one, even if he had to manufacture the proof
out of rumors and suspicion.

In that kind of environment, suspicion could fall on

anyone—even on the people, like me, who were supposed to track rumors and informants.

"How loud are these whispers?" I said.

"Soft, for now."

"Any idea where they started?"

Mendross shrugged. "Someone said someone else said his uncle knows a Cutter who overheard his sister's husband talking to a guy who . . ."

"That's not soft," I said, feeling some of the tension drain out of me. "That's damn near silent."

"Call it what you want, but the whispers have been circulating for a couple days now. You know me—if something stays on the street that long, I pass it on."

I nodded in appreciation and finally slipped the orange section into my mouth. Silent or not, the rumor was still something that could grow and get back to Nicco. Having him go on a rampage wouldn't be good for any number of things, including my peace of mind. But mostly, it would be bad for business.

"Have you heard anything about anything big going down?" I said.

"No," said Mendross.

"Any important corpses turn up?"

"Nope."

"Anyone pawing at the edges of Nicco's territory?"

"Not that I've heard of."

"Me neither," I said. "Which makes me think this is nothing. Snilches are too hard to recruit to waste on something small, and from what I hear, there's nothing *but* small going down right now. There's no reason for a Snilch to do anything that might get him noticed."

"What if he made a tiny mistake and it got out?" said Mendross.

"There are no tiny mistakes when you do that kind of work," I said. "Remember, this is *Nicco's* organization we're talking about here—a spy with half a brain would bend over backward to keep this quiet. Hell, I inform for the man, and the thought of his getting wind of this makes *me* nervous."

Mendross considered it and shrugged. "You know the ins and outs better then I do," he said.

Damn straight I did. But Mendross was right in one sense: I couldn't just shrug it off. I looked out over the bazaar and decided.

"This could be nothing, or it could be a setup," I said as I took another bite of orange. "Someone might be wanting to use this as an excuse to settle some old scores." Or to start a power grab. Chaos in the ranks made for a wonderful distraction. "Put the word out that the rumors are just gutter-mumbles. If they die, so much the better. If they stick around, let me know." And I hoped like hell they did die; otherwise, I'd need to track down who was behind the rumors before they got to Nicco.

"I'll see what I can do."

We went over the rest of Mendross's news as I finished my breakfast. I filed some of what he told me away for later consideration, but ended up discarding most of it. It was a slow day on the street.

When we were finished, I made a show of wiping my fingers on a towel Mendross kept hanging on the side of his stall.

"All my best to Rizza," I said as I picked up a fig and hefted it.

Mendross nodded contentedly at his wife's name and took a step back. I cocked my arm and hurtled the fig at him, missing by inches.

"And don't even think about coming up short next time!" I snapped, my voice pitched to be heard by anyone nearby. Mendross cringed and stammered apologies as Degan and I turned and walked away. I put an arrogant swagger in my step as I left.

The moment we exited the bazaar, I let the swagger drop and surrendered to a slow, almost dragging pace.

Degan yawned and scratched at his chin. "Do you still have things to do?"

I looked up at the sky. The sun was obnoxiously high—nearly four hours past rising. I dearly wanted to crawl in out of the daylight, but I had one more person to see, and now was the best time to do it.

"Yeah," I said. "I have things."

"Do you need me for them?"

"No."

"Good, because I wasn't coming, anyhow."

"Hmm, maybe I need you after all."

"Tough." And without waiting for a reply, Degan stepped off into the crowd and headed home. I swear I could hear him whistling as he went, too. The bastard.

I watched him go for a moment, then turned in the opposite direction. I needed to talk to a man about a piece of paper.

Chapter Three

Baldezar was a Jarkman, which meant he could read and write old dialects and modern foreign tongues, as well as produce forgeries and copies when the need arose. He was also a master scribe who ran a penman's shop in the cordon next to my own. It was a big operation, with more than a dozen apprentices and journeymen working under his unforgiving eye. Baldezar would never sell you the contents of a trust, for that was what he considered the papers assigned him to be, but he'd happily knock off a forgery or copy of anything you brought to him.

The shop was bright and busy when I entered. The windows in the walls and the sliding panels on the roof had been thrown open to admit the morning sunlight. Tall, slanted desks covered the main floor. Most held an original page and the copy in progress side by side, but a select few played home to acts of individual creation. At these desks, the most skilled scribblers and illuminators plied their work. Each page, each line, was history in the making, art in progress.

I took a deep breath, savoring the smell of ink, paint, paper, and chalk. For me, this was the aroma of knowledge, of history, and I loved it. It didn't matter whether they were copying histories or inventories; as far as I was concerned, there was magic in the air.

"A bit early for you, Drothe," said a voice off to my side.

I turned to find Lyconnis coming toward me, a bundle
of parchments in his meaty hands and quiet humor in
his eyes. He was taller than I—not hard, that—and built
more like a farmer than a scribe. Broad shoulders, thick
limbs, heavy neck, and an open and trusting face that
always made me feel vaguely uneasy. I'm not used to
being around blatantly honest people.

"Late night?" asked the journeyman scribe.

"Does it show that much?"

"Afraid so." Lyconnis gestured toward the back of
the shop. "We can pull a stool over to my desk if you'd
like—I've finished another chapter of the history."

"The one on the Fourth Regency?"

"Is there any other?"

I licked my lips. It was tempting. The Fourth Regency
was one of those periods in imperial history where legend met reality; where the recurring rule of Stephen
Dorminikos was truly challenged for the first time; and
where the first subtle cracks began to show in our emperor's sanity.

By that time, the emperor had been on the throne
in one incarnation or another for more than two hundred years. True, it wasn't the six-century mark we had
recently observed in Ildrecca, but his selection by the
Angels to serve as our perpetually reincarnating emperor had been well established. He was the Triumvi-
rate Eternal, the ruler whose soul had been broken into
three parts so that he might forever be reborn as one
of three versions of himself—Markino, Theodoi, and
Lucien—each version following the next by a genera-
tion, to watch over the empire. So the Angels had de-
creed, and so it had been.

But that didn't mean everyone had to be happy about
it.

Like the rest of us, Stephen Dorminikos had started
out mortal, and that fact wasn't lost on people. If a man
could be born—and even reborn—so the reasoning
went, he could die, too. And he had—several times, in
fact. And so the emperors had created the Regencies—

appointees who ruled whenever one of the incarnations died before the next one could be found. In the case of the Second and Third Regencies, the gaps had come about through foul play and court intrigue; however, during the Fourth Regency, it had been a bout of the plague that killed off two incarnations of Stephen back to back. Innocent enough, and an eventuality the empire had long been prepared for, which was why the chaos that had followed was so surprising.

With two versions of Stephen dead, someone—no one quite knew who—had got to wondering what would happen if all three versions of the emperor were dead at once. Would he be able to come back? Save for the first time Stephen had died and gone to the Angels, there had always been at least one incarnation alive somewhere in the empire. The writings of the Imperial Cult hinted at dire consequences if no emperor strode the earth, but no one knew if the warnings were apocryphal or prophetic.

Of course, someone decided to find out. Unfortunately for Stephen, it had been his own Regents.

And so had begun the Regency Wars: eighty-one years of cat and mouse between the usurpers and the incarnations of Stephen Dorminikos. Lucien died twice, once to plague, and once to a dagger in the back. Markino passed from the same plague as Lucien while still a babe in arms. Theodoi was butchered leading an army against the walls of Ildrecca. In the sixty-fourth year of the Fourth Regency, the Regents declared there were no incarnations of Dorminikos left on this earth, let alone on the throne.

The emperors were dead.

And then, seventeen years later, Markino proved them wrong and emerged from hiding at the head of an army out of, of all places, Djan. Things had gotten interesting after that.

"Are you to the Cleansings yet?" I asked. On the march from Djan to Ildrecca, Markino had ordered his troops to deface every depiction of his former incarnations they came across. He claimed he was "cleansing" the temples and promoting a fresh start after the Regency; his other selves had had other opinions. They didn't like being erased when they weren't around. And so had begun the centuries-long, ongoing spat among the incarnations of the emperor. Lyconnis had hinted that he had found a new source on the topic, but he hadn't been willing to elaborate on it.

Today was no different. Lyconnis smiled a crafty smile — or, at least, he tried to; it didn't really fit his face. "I'm not telling," he said.

"You wouldn't be." I considered pressing him — he loved to talk about his work, and it wouldn't be hard to get him to relent — but sighed instead. "No, as much as I'd love to read it, I have to see your master on business."

Lyconnis's face clouded over. "Ah. I'll leave you be, then." He didn't know the specifics of my relationship with Baldezar, but he was smart enough to realize it was something he would rather stay ignorant about.

I walked to the back of the shop and climbed the narrow circular stairs to the gallery. Baldezar was waiting for me at the top.

"Young Lyconnis does not seem to appreciate your trade as much as you do his." The sentence rasped out of Baldezar's mouth, his words dry and brittle as the parchments that surrounded us.

"I think it's your business with me he disapproves of," I said.

"Most likely." The master scribe turned away and paced slowly toward his office. "But since the opinions of my lessers matter nothing to me . . ." He let the sentence drift to the floor, stepped past it.

I let my eyes brush the works that resided here. Books and scrolls filled the narrow spaces between the windows in the gallery, the shelves running floor to ceiling. Many were of little use to anyone except the scribes, but there were enough histories and collected tales here to keep me busy for ages. Baldezar consented to rent some out to me now and again, but only grudgingly, and always at a high price.

"No touching or taking," he warned over his shoulder. There was no humor in the tone.

I bristled at the implication. "Mind your words, Jarkman."

"It's my trade—how can I not? You just mind your trade, burglar."

"I haven't cracked a den in years," I said.

Baldezar sniffed but otherwise stayed silent.

We stepped into his office. The master scribe arranged himself like a potentate behind his reading table. I took the narrow seat across from him. The shutters to the room had been thrown back for light, but the glass windows themselves were closed against the dust and noise of the street. It made the space feel tight and bright and warm. I fought a yawn and sneezed instead.

For most people, such a basking would have made them appear healthy, or at least alive; but all it did for Baldezar was highlight the sharp crags of his face. I could make out a similar collection of jutting angles and projections beneath the ink-stained tunic, which hinted at the sparseness of his frame. He let his eyelids droop halfway closed as he regarded me.

"I hope you are not here for the work you commissioned," he said. "I told you it would not be ready until next week. I've not even received the proper linen paper from the presser yet."

I waved my hand. "No, no rush on that. Take your time." I was having him do a bit of forgery for my sister, but it wouldn't hurt to let her wait a bit. It might even teach her some patience, though I had my doubts. "I've come here for your opinion on something."

The scribe nodded as if this made perfect and natural sense, which I'm sure it did to him. He was Baldezar, after all.

I reached into my ahrami pouch and drew out the piece of paper I had taken from Athel.

Baldezar's eyebrows formed themselves into a brief

pair of peaks, then settled down again. "May I?" He held out his reedlike fingers. I obliged, and he held the strip of paper up to the light.

"And what are you looking for here?" he asked after a long moment.

Even after giving him the paper, I hesitated. My instincts were to keep as many people out of my business as possible. I had to remind myself why I had come here in the first place.

"I'm hoping it's a cipher you might recognize," I said.

"As in a coded message?"

I nodded.

"Where did you get it?"

I regarded the Jarkman silently.

"I only ask," he said, "because the provenance might help me to—"

"It doesn't matter where I got it," I said sharply, my fatigue getting the better of my patience. "What matters is what you can tell me about it."

"I see." Baldezar rubbed the paper between his fingers. "Do you know what it pertains to?"

"This is dusty stuff, Jarkman—don't play the Boman."

Baldezar lifted the side of his mouth in distaste. "I may understand your canting, Drothe, but it doesn't mean I enjoy hearing it. Use the imperial tongue in my presence, or get out."

I snapped forward in my chair, stopping myself just before I came out of it. Baldezar's eyes went wide as he almost fell back in his own.

I took a long, slow breath.

"All right," I grated. "In plain Imperial, I'm not happy about what that paper implies. In fact, I'm downright pissed. I'm having a bad day because of what's on that paper, and I don't expect I'll be the only one. Now, we both know what that means, so my advice is to tell me what you see here. Otherwise, my using the cant won't be the only thing you don't enjoy."

Baldezar opened his mouth, shut it, and cleared his throat. "A code, you say? Intriguing." He laid the strip out on his desk, studying it. After a minute or so, his hands stopped shaking. Baldezar rotated the strip a few times, looking at the markings from all angles, and then turned it blank side up. He ran his fingers over the paper and hemmed to himself. Then he sat back.

"I don't know."

"What?"

Baldezar held up his hands placatingly. "It's not any language I recognize, if it is a language at all. There seems to be no rhyme or reason to the markings. Nothing indicates a code or message of any sort."

I stood up and leaned over the table. "There're *pystos* and *immus* right there," I said, pointing. "And what about the repeating marks . . . here . . . and here, and here again? And these two here and here. Those might be fragments of common cephta."

"Not everyone uses imperial ideographs for writing, Drothe."

No, just most of the people in the empire. "Okay, so maybe they're those things the western Client Kingdoms use for writing. . . ."

"Letters?"

"Right, letters."

Baldezar let out a long sigh. "Perhaps. Or they might be a portion of an illumination exercise. Or unsanded errors. Or an attempt to use one of those useless new printing machines. But I see no traces of any cipher here, Drothe. What you have is a scrap from some scribe's rubbish." He flicked the paper. "Hardly worth threatening anyone over," he added as he began to crumple the slip into a ball.

I held out my hand. "All the same . . ."

Baldezar stopped, looked at the paper, and then held it out in his palm. I took the slip and put it back into my ahrami pouch. When I looked up, he was studying me.

"You're convinced the paper is that important?" said Baldezar.

Hell, no. It could have been a scrap, a pipe taper, even a bit of trash that had fallen to the bottom of Athel's bag.

But it was also the only thing I had gotten from Athel that hadn't come to me under duress. Even with his last breath, Athel could have lied, and I needed something to confirm or deny his story. The paper was the best lead I had, no matter how pathetic that lead might be.

So naturally, when Baldezar questioned the paper's importance, I lied.

"Positive," I said.

The scribe began drumming his fingers on the table. "It occurs to me," he said slowly, "that I may be able to impose on one of my colleagues who know more about these things than I. It would cost a bit, and I would need the 'document' in question to show him, of course, but it might provide you with some answers."

I could tell it pained him to admit anyone might know more about a subject than he did, let alone that he needed to consult them. Good.

"Tempting, but no," I said. "The paper stays with me." A thought stuck me. "Who is this 'colleague'?"

He hesitated a moment too long before answering. "No one you would know."

I regarded the Jarkman, smiling slightly as I did so. Was he trying to keep me from going to his friend on my own, or had he been hoping to up the price for the consultation and take a cut of the profits himself? Either way, I'd likely end up paying a steep price for little gain.

"Nice try," I said. Baldezar's eyebrows rose in surprise. I waved away the beginnings of his protestations, yawned and stretched in the chair. "No games," I said. "I'm too tired for games. Either you help me or you don't."

Baldezar stared at me for a long, hard moment. Then, without taking his eyes off me, he called out, "Lyconnis!"

I heard the large scribe thumping quickly up the steps and along the walkway to his master's office. He wasn't quite breathing heavily when he entered the room.

"Yes?" he said, ducking his head toward Baldezar.

"Drothe has some garbage he wants you to look at. He thinks it may be a cipher of some sort."

"A cipher?" said the scribe. If his master hadn't been here, I expect he would have rubbed his hands together in delight; as it was, the excitement that came over him was practically tangible. "May I?"

I sent a quizzical look at Baldezar even as I pulled out the strip and handed it to Lyconnis.

"Lyconnis here has made a study of secret messages and early imperial spymasters," said Baldezar drily. He sniffed. "Imagine my surprise at it suddenly proving useful."

Lyconnis bit his lip at his master's rebuke and bent over the slip of paper. He manipulated and examined it in a manner that was fast becoming familiar to me. He frowned. "Where did you get this?"

I crossed my arms and stayed silent.

Lyconnis blushed. "Of course. Excuse me for asking. You noticed the cephta for *pystos* and *immus*, I take it?" he said. I nodded. Lyconnis held the paper up to the light again, then shrugged and handed it back to me. "There might be something there, but I think it's more likely a bit of scrap of some sort. Is it important?"

"Life and death," I said, thinking of Athel. Lyconnis's face became solemn. I smiled despite myself at that, wondering if the scribe was more worried for me, or for the person who had had the paper. Likely both.

"How about someone named Ioclaudia?" I said.

"Who?" said Baldezar.

I turned back to the master scribe. Had he been peering at me? "Ioclaudia," I repeated.

"Outside of some of the more obscure histories, no, I've never heard of anyone by that name. Lyconnis?"

Lyconnis shook his head. "No," he said. He smiled timidly at me. "Not anyone living in the last three centuries, anyhow."

"The way my morning has been going," I said as I rose, "that doesn't surprise me." I nodded to Baldezar, gave a respectful bow to Lyconnis—mainly to irritate his master—and headed out of the shop.

On a normal day, it was a short walk from Baldezar's

to my home; today, it took just as long, but felt like five times the distance. The sun seemed brighter, the crowds denser, the streets dirtier. I didn't have the energy to deal with any of them.

By the time I arrived at the apothecary's shop I lived above, I was little more than a shambling mass of dulled senses. I let out a small sigh of relief. For a moment, I considered going into the shop to pester Eppyris for some ahrami, but the thought of my disheveled, lumpy mattress won out. I began moving toward the stairwell.

"Nose."

The voice came from somewhere far, far away— maybe ten whole feet behind me. Turn around? No, ignore him instead; he'd go away.

"Hey, Nose!"

Still there? Angels, this person couldn't take a hint! I made an eloquent, sincere, and highly profane gesture without turning, and continued on my shuffling way.

"Dammit," said the voice. Something heavy laid itself on my shoulder and spun me around.

Habit and adrenaline kicked in. As I turned, I let the small dagger (the poisoned one) drop from my wrist sheath into my left palm. At the same time, my right hand sought out my rapier.

There were two of them and they were big—obelisk big, blot-out-the-sun big—and they were good.

One blocked my left arm and took away my dagger, a bored look on his face. The other put his hand on my right wrist and stopped the rapier in middraw.

I knew them.

"Niccodemus wants to see you, Nose," said Salt Eye. "Now."

Chapter Four

In the "argot of the underworld," as Baldezar would no doubt call it, I am what is referred to as a Nose. This means I make a living by sticking myself in where I don't belong, sniffing around for dirt, and generally making a nuisance of myself. I'm an information broker, and I gather what I can by almost any means I can: paid informants, bribes, eavesdropping, blackmail, burglary, frame-ups ... and even, on rare occasions, torture — whatever it takes to get the story.

That's what sets a Nose apart from a run-of-the-mill rumormonger: We not only collect the pieces; we also put them together. Any Mumbler can sell you a rumor for the right price; but if you want to know the why behind the rumor, when and where things are coming together, and how it got started in the first place, you go to a Nose. Noses don't just gather whispers off the street — we sift and assemble them, putting together the pieces most Kin miss. We don't just find out something is happening — we find out *why* it's happening in the first place.

And then, we sell the information.

Whom you sell it to depends on what kind of Nose you are. If you're a Wide Nose, you work the street and sell what you learn to the highest bidder, pure and simple. It's dangerous work, since not everyone wants you sharing what you learn, but a smart Nose knows how to hold just enough information back to keep people from bothering him.

Long Noses, on the other hand, keep their heads down and their information tight. They ply their trade by infiltrating a rival crime lord's organization and feeding information back to their real boss. Being a Long Nose takes that special mixture of guts and stupidity usually reserved for mongooses and imperial tax collectors. You typically don't find out someone's doing the Long Nose until he turns up floating in the harbor.

The third kind of Nose is the Narrow Nose. That's what I do for Nicco—keep tabs on his people, find out who is or isn't cheating him, and generally solve minor problems before they get big. It doesn't exactly make me popular with my fellow Kin, but it does give me something the other two types of Noses don't have— backing. If anyone wants to come after me, he has to think about what Nicco will do to him in return. That's not a bad place to be. However, like everything else, it has its trade-offs, one of which is that I have to answer to Nicco—a lot.

It's that last part that comes back to haunt me, usually at the worst possible times.

The door at the top of the stairs opened, and I was ushered into the office by the two Arms. It was a bare-bones affair: a desk, two chairs, four blank walls, and a small window looking out onto the street. A wooden platter with the remnants of Nicco's breakfast sat on the desk, giving the room a greasy, meaty smell. Two men were waiting in that smell.

Nicco was standing at the window, heavy hands clasped behind him. I blinked at the beam of sunlight streaming in, but didn't look away. That would have been disrespectful.

In his prime, Nicco had been a slab of bone and muscle, easily big enough to make two of me. Now, he was a late-afternoon shadow of himself—still big, still strong, but losing some of his harder edges. Jowls were beginning to gather under his jaw, and more of the meat on his frame came from food than from fight. Gray smudges had settled under his eyes, making them look haggard in the wrong light. His hair was thinning. But even aging, Niccodemus Alludrus was harder than most men. He'd proved as much three months ago, when he broke an assassin's back even as the garrote had tightened around his neck. No one questioned whether Nicco still had what it took.

The other man in the room stood leaning against the far wall, arms crossed, silver rings glittering on his hands and in his ears. Long and thin, he had a sharpness about him—in his face, his clothes, his mind. His name was Rambles, and he was one of Nicco's senior street bosses. But whereas Nicco favored the lead pipe when it came to solving problems, Rambles took after the stiletto. By all accounts, Rambles and I should have gotten along famously—similar approaches, kindred spirits, and all that crap. Instead, we managed to make oil and water look tight.

Neither man seemed in a particularly good mood. I made it unanimous.

Nicco spoke without turning toward me. "Drothe, good of you to come. Sit down."

I sat. Behind me, I could hear the Arms taking up positions on either side of the door. Between them and Rambles, this wasn't a good sign. Nicco and I usually met alone; he didn't believe in anyone getting information before he did.

"I'm not used to waiting two days for people," said Nicco.

I sat up straighter. Two days? Shit. Mendross hadn't mentioned the call had come *yesterday*. I rubbed my eyes, trying to wake up. I slid a seed into my mouth.

"I was in the middle of another dodge when I got word," I said. "I didn't realize you'd been waiting."

"Way I hear it, you were already done with the smuggler when you got word."

I blinked. How the hell did Nicco know about Athel? I'd gone to a lot of trouble to keep that job hush.

Oh. Of course.

"Shatters," I said.

"That Agonyman had a few things to say about you," said Nicco, still looking out the window. "None of them good."

"That sadistic bastard is just mad because I . . ."

Nicco held up his meaty hand. "I don't give a crap about your side work, Drothe. As long as I get my cut, I'm happy. What I *do* give a crap about is my people not doing their job."

It wasn't hard to figure out that "people" meant me. "Look," I said, "I'm late and I apologize. Sincerely. I didn't know you'd been waiting—"

Nicco spun toward me. "Screw the waiting!" he bellowed. "I shouldn't have needed to call you in, Drothe. If you'd been doing your job, instead of dicking around after relics, I'd have heard about Ten Ways two days ago. As it is, I've been having to get word from the street. *I* shouldn't have to listen to the fucking street, Drothe— that's what I pay *you* to do."

"Ten Ways?" I said. I sucked on the seed in my mouth and ran through everything Mendross had told me about the cordon earlier, then through everything I'd heard about it in the last two months. Nothing important surfaced. "Why the hell are you worried about what's happening in Ten Ways?"

"The street," said Rambles.

I looked over at him. "Was I talking to you?"

Rambles smiled coolly. "The street says someone's planning on making a move against Nicco down in Ten Ways."

"'The street'?" I said. "What the hell do you know about listening to the street?"

"I have ears," said Rambles.

"Yeah, I can see them from here. Nice jingle."

"Word is it's serious."

"Serious," I said. "All right. Then answer me a couple of questions, O Sage of the Streets. Did you run this by anyone else? Maybe another Nose, or someone in the cordon? Did you drag your ass down there and check it yourself? Did you stop to consider this might just *be* a rumor? Or did you come running the moment you heard it?"

Rambles pushed himself away from the wall. "I don't need a Nose to tell me how to work the street!" he snarled.

"Of course you don't," I said. I turned back to Nicco. "He's full of crap."

"Why?" said Rambles. "Because you don't agree with me?"

I made a show of crossing my arms and leaning back in my chair. The light from the window was playing hell with my exhausted eyes, and I could feel a nasty headache coming on, but I smiled benignly nonetheless.

"Answer him," said Nicco.

"Why?" I said. "If Rambles wants to believe everything he hears on the street, that's his business. I don't give free lessons to the help."

Nicco took a step. The floor creaked beneath him. "I said, answer him."

I bit down hard on the ahrami in my mouth. The *crack* of the seed was audible in the room.

"Listen," I said, starting to get annoyed. I'd been dragged in here for *this*? "This is bullshit. One person gets leaned on, and suddenly it's a move against you? Think about it. This is how Ten Ways works. Anyone who says otherwise is a fool. If Rambles wants to—"

For a big man, Nicco could move fast. I didn't have time to flinch before he'd taken a step and backhanded me across the face.

The blow sent me halfway out of my chair and filled my head with a ringing sound. For a moment, my cheek was numb—then the pain made its way inside. I felt hands grab my shoulders and haul me back into the chair. At first I thought it was Nicco, but when I saw him standing in front of me, I realized the two Arms at the door hadn't stayed in the room for show. They were behind me, leaning down on my shoulders, holding me in place.

I worked my jaw, tasted blood. I could feel the liquid starting to slip out of my mouth and into my beard. My cheek felt half the size of my face. If that weren't enough, the headache that had been threatening moments ago was now in full, agonizing bloom.

Out of habit, my hand reached for the herb wallet at my belt. There would be painkillers there—waxed packets full of powders and leaves and unguents, maybe a little Saint's Balm for my cheek. . . .

One of the Arms stopped me before I could reach it.

"Careful," said Nicco. He was rubbing the hand that had hit me. "Be careful here, Drothe." He leaned forward, putting his face close to mine. I noticed he had had onions with breakfast. "You know why you got that?"

I nodded and slowly retrieved my hand.

"Because you agree with Rambles?" I said.

"In part. And?"

"And because I indirectly called you a fool?"

Nicco's fist drove into my stomach. I started to double over, but the Arms hauled back on my shoulders, arresting the movement. I sat there, gulping for air, my body trying to convulse in on itself. I decided that if I threw up, I was going to aim for Nicco's shoes.

"I hadn't thought of that," said Nicco, straightening up. "And?"

He waited while I gasped and gagged. Finally, when I could move enough air to talk, I said, "And because I didn't answer him the first time you told me to."

"The first *two* times I told you," corrected Nicco. "You don't want to go for three."

I nodded weakly and took a deep, ragged breath. There was definitely something going on here—Nicco might be a violent bastard, but he didn't usually knock me around for arguing with him. Something was bothering him.

I blinked and tried to clear my head. Between the pain and my lack of sleep, I wasn't exactly putting the pieces together as well as I might.

"It's all about how Ten Ways works," I said, trying to

buy some time. My voice came out far steadier than I expected. I credited the ahrami. "The place is a hole. The cordon's full of thugs and petty bosses. Almost every one of them is making a move at some time or another. It's how a person establishes himself, and it's how you get out. If you make enough things happen, or pull off a big enough dodge, you can use it to leverage your way into better things.

"That's what's happening here," I said. "Someone's trying to look tough by seeing how far he can push you in the cordon. We're not exactly big in Ten Ways, so we're a prime target. Send in a couple of Cutters, have them hand out some bruises, maybe make a corpse or two, and the Kin down there will get the message."

"I already sent people," snarled Nicco.

"Good," I said.

"They didn't come back."

"Oh."

Nicco walked over and sat down behind his desk. "Tell him," he said to Rambles.

"Three Cutters went in," said Rambles. "None came out. That was two days ago. Last night we sent two Arms in with four more Cutters. One of the Arms staggered out this morning, cut up. He died an hour later."

I whistled softly. The Cutters I could almost see. They were decent enforcers, but you could find free-lance toughs who were just as good if you looked. Arms, though, were another matter. They were the best the Kin had to offer, the select muscle in an organization. For a boss like Nicco to lose two Arms and twice as many Cutters in a pissant cordon like Ten Ways wasn't just a bad sign—it was downright embarrassing.

Now I understood why Nicco wasn't happy. He needed to pay back whoever was responsible, fast, or risk losing face among the Kin. Lose enough, and he might find other Upright Men sniffing around his turf, deciding which portions they could carve off for themselves. Top dogs didn't stay on top in this business if they let the smaller dogs get away with pissing on them.

"I hadn't heard any of this yet," I said, "which is good." Both men stared at me. "Not hearing anything means our people have been able to keep it quiet. That gives us some breathing room."

"I don't give a crap about 'breathing room,'" said Nicco. "If people are complaining on the street, then someone is talking." He scowled at Rambles. "That's not supposed to be happening."

Rambles shrugged, and suddenly I understood. Rambles had been put in charge of Ten Ways. I almost laughed out loud. I couldn't think of anyone I'd rather see consigned to that gutter of a territory.

Nicco looked over at me. "What the fuck are you grinning at?"

"Uh . . . " I said.

"You walk in two days late, you argue, you give me information I needed to know yesterday, and then you sit there smiling?"

"Well . . ."

"Shut the fuck up."

I did.

Nicco smeared a scrap of bread through the drippings on the plate and put it in his mouth. "I'll keep this short," he said, his mouth working around the bread. He pointed at Rambles. "I want the bastards behind this to pay—hard. No one fucks with me, no matter where they are. You remind those bastards in Ten Ways of that."

Rambles considered for a moment. "How far do you want me to go?"

"As far as you need to. But," Nicco said, pausing to swallow, "I don't want the whole damn cordon coming down around my ears, got it?"

Rambles seemed mildly disappointed, but he nodded, anyhow.

I nodded as well. Nicco was being smart. Ten Ways may be a hellhole, but it was a proud hellhole. Outside bosses were barely tolerated, and then usually at the fringes. Hell, even the city guard garrisoned the men stationed there outside the cordon. If Rambles went in looking for serious trouble, he'd end up with most of the Kin in Ten Ways lining up against him in a matter of days.

"Good," said Nicco. He flicked his fingers at Rambles. "Now, get the hell out of here."

Rambles bowed slightly in Nicco's direction, smirked at me, and left. Since the Arms were still looming behind me, I took the hint and stayed.

Nicco took a sip of whatever was left in his cup, made a face, and set it aside. "You're going, too."

I sat up straighter. "What?"

"To Ten Ways. You're going in."

Shit. That was what I'd been afraid of. I'd spent five years in that pit before finally clawing my way out. The climb hadn't been easy or pretty, and I'd sworn I wouldn't go back. Besides, if I was busy in there, I wouldn't be able to track Ioclaudia or my relic out here.

I wet my lips and thought fast.

"I don't know if I'm the best person for this job," I said. "I have history down there."

"I figured that would help—you know the cordon."

"*Knew* it," I said. "That was a long time ago. And if anyone does remember me, they're as likely to stab me as talk to me. I didn't leave a lot of friends in my wake when I left."

"So take some Cutters in with you."

"You know that's not how I work," I said. I ran a hand through my beard. "Dammit, Nicco, I—"

Nicco snapped his fingers. Hands clamped down on my shoulders. The Arms behind me bore down so hard, I thought they were going to push me through the chair. I winced and tried to look unfazed. I doubted I fooled anyone.

Nicco leaned back in his chair and examined his fingers. "Are we having another disagreement, Drothe?"

"No," I said. "I just—"

"I said, *are we having a disagreement*?"

The Arms put their full weight into it. I heard something creak dangerously. Probably the chair, but I could have sworn it was my spine.

"No," I gasped. "Absolutely not!"

"Good." Nicco gave a nod, and the pressure went away. "Leave."

The two Arms walked out of the room and closed the door behind them. Nicco waited for the sound of their shoes on the stairs to fade before he spoke.

"You're lucky I like you, Drothe."

"Yeah," I said, rubbing at my shoulders. Everything still seemed to be where it belonged. "Lucky."

"Damn it, Drothe!" Nicco pointed past me to where the Arms had been. "I should have had them beat the living crap out of you. What the hell were you thinking? Arguing with me in front of them, in front of Rambles? Shit." He sat back in his chair and glared at me. "Sometimes I think I give you too much freedom, even for a Nose. You forget your place."

"Believe me," I said. "I never forget my place."

"Don't give me lip, Drothe. Not right now."

I held up my hands. "I get it—no squabbles in front of the help." Or at all, at the moment. Even my tired brain could read that one. Right now, I needed to play along. "So what do you want me to do in Ten Ways?"

"I want you to find out what the hell's going on."

I frowned. I had expected to be told to shadow Rambles's efforts and report back. "Isn't that Rambles's job? He's in charge down there now."

"Rambles can kick ass and take names with the best of them, but he'll miss things. You won't—that's why I want you Nosing down there. And I don't want you sharing what you find with anyone but me."

"You don't trust him?"

"Trust has nothing to do with it: I want to compare what you say to what he says."

Ah. He didn't trust either of us. Wonderful.

I scratched at my beard. It was still damp with blood. "Rambles won't like my nosing around down there if he's not in the loop." Actually, he wouldn't like my nosing around there even if he *was* in the loop, but that was beside the point.

"Tough shit for him," said Nicco. He got up and walked back over to the window. "He doesn't need to know everything to do his part of the job."

I looked up at that. "He doesn't know everything *now*, does he?" I said. "You have something else."

Nicco didn't look at me. Instead, he ran his finger along the window frame, holding it up to study the dust it had collected. "The Arm who made it out of Ten Ways lived long enough to give us two names. One of them was 'Fedim.'"

I shook my head. "Don't know it."

"He's the Dealer who's been complaining about protection." Nicco blew the dust off his fingertip. "Things are bad enough in Ten Ways without some cut-rate fence mouthing off. It makes me look bad. Talk to him, find out what he knows. Then dust him."

I grimaced but didn't argue.

"And the other name?" I said.

Nicco stared at his finger so long, I thought he wasn't going to tell me. Then he rubbed it with his thumb and smiled. It wasn't a pleasant smile.

"Kells," he said.

If I hadn't had a chair beneath me, I would have been on the floor. As it was, I nearly grabbed the sides for support, anyhow.

"Kells?" I said. Well, shit.

Chapter Five

I stepped out onto the street in a daze. Kells? In Ten Ways?

Hell. This was all I needed. Having Kells's name turn up where Nicco was concerned was like trying to put out a fire with naphtha.

I started walking.

Back in the day, before the feud, before the countless border fights, before they had both become Upright Men, Nicco and Kells had been tight. They had run under the same boss, worked the same cordon, shared in the same dodges—right up to the point where they threw down their old boss, Rigga, and carved up her territory. Turns out that was the worst thing they could have done to each other.

Each side had a story about how it went bad, of course. Nicco's centered around respect and dishonesty: He claimed Kells had conned him out of the richest portions of Rigga's turf, even though Nicco had ended up with the bigger share of territory. Worse, he said, Kells had used the money to lure his best people away after the split. Nicco being Nicco, he'd gone for the throat.

As for Kells, the argument went that he hadn't bought Nicco's people—he'd just offered them a better deal. Instead of relying on fear and fists to keep his organization running, Kells used careful planning and cunning to make sure things ran smoothly. That was why his smaller territory had done better, and why people had left Nicco after Rigga's organization broke up. When Nicco had gone after Kells, it looked like spite.

Both arguments made sense for the men involved, and I expect each tale had a degree of truth to it. If there's one thing I've learned as a Nose, it's that every story changes with the person telling it, no matter how close the person thinks he's holding to the truth. And even though I tended to lean toward the version of the story that favored Kells, the fact of the matter was that Nicco looked to be the wronged party this time around. If Kells *was* in Ten Ways, and he *could* be linked to what had happened to Nicco's people . . .

I shook my head. It didn't make sense. Dusting six of Nicco's people out of the blue, in Nicco's own territory, wasn't Kells's style. If it had been the other way around, I could see it, but not like this. Kells was too subtle for this kind of a play. At least, he always had been up until now.

But if there was a link, or even the hint of one, Nicco would be on it. He'd go after Kells hard. And that would put me in the middle of it, in Ten Ways, in the fighting.

I groaned. Maybe it was best that Nicco was sending me in there to figure it out after all. Maybe I could even avert the looming disaster. But that didn't mean I had to like it.

I shambled the rest of the way home in the early-afternoon light and collapsed into a dreamless sleep. I awoke sometime after midnight, chewed a seed, and dragged myself out into the streets long enough to scare up a late meal. I returned and slept some more.

Late-morning sunlight was pushing its way in past the edges of my room's shutters when I woke again. Someone was knocking on my door.

I lay in bed for a moment, hoping the caller would think I was out.

He kept knocking.

Hell, might as well get up. I had to piss, anyhow.

"Bide a moment!" I yelled as I got out of bed and padded across the room.

Downstairs, beneath the sound of the knocking, I could hear the squeals and shouts of two little girls at play — Renna and Sophia. I smiled at the noise as I slipped on yesterday's shirt and picked up my sword belt, the rapier still in its scabbard.

I put my eye to the peephole and looked into the hall. A clean-shaven face, framed by perfumed blond curls, sat atop a carefully embroidered jacket and half cloak. I recognized the livery badge on his chest and groaned.

"My Lord Drothe?" asked the messenger to the peephole. He sounded unsure of the question, and I found myself wanting to lie. But there would only be another flunky like him at my door tomorrow if I did.

I disarmed the spring trap, undid the double lock, and cracked the door open a finger's width.

"Yes to the Drothe part," I said, "no to the 'lord.' I'm not noble, and I didn't marry into the blood like your mistress." He looked startled at that last part, no doubt surprised by my audacity. Well, let him be. His mistress might be the Baroness Christiana Sephada, Lady of Lythos, but she was also my sister. The fact that only a handful of people besides her and me knew about our relationship didn't change how I dealt with "her ladyship."

I glanced past the messenger to the man who loomed behind him. His name was Ruggero, and he worked for me. He gave a brief nod, indicating he'd searched the messenger. I nodded back, and Ruggero retreated silently down the stairs. I looked back to the messenger.

"You're new, aren't you?" I said. "She's never sent you before."

"Yes, uh, no ... I mean, I've never had the honor before, sir, no."

"It's no honor, believe me," I said. I opened the door and waved the young man in. "What's your name?"

"Tamas, my lord." He remained in the hallway. I could tell by the look on his face he was unsure what to do next. I was probably violating every nicety of court protocol imaginable. While the poor kid had been trained to handle everything from sycophants to haughty nobles, it was clear no one had instructed him on the finer points of dealing with a thief who has just answered the door wearing nothing more than a shirt that barely reached his knees and a sword.

"The family downstairs has children, Tamas," I explained, tossing my sword belt and blade onto the bed to make him more at ease. "I don't want their mother after me in case their eldest daughter happens by and catches a view up my shirt. Understand?"

The messenger glanced over his shoulder at the stairwell as if I had prophetic powers, then stepped quickly into the room. I shut the door.

"So, what does she want this time?" I asked as I pulled down a pair of paned slops from a wall peg and sniffed them. Definitely cleaner than the ones I had been wearing since taking after Athel. I put them on.

"My lord?"

"The baroness," I said. "Christiana didn't send you here to help me dress, did she?"

"No!"

I smiled as he caught himself.

"Relax. Just answer the question."

Tamas's smile faded. He nodded. His hand moved. He reached under his jacket.

I dived.

I went for the bed, where I had carelessly tossed my rapier moments ago. When I hit the mattress, the blade gave a small bounce and skipped off the other side. I heard it clatter on the floor. I was dead.

Out of desperation, I continued after the sword. Maybe Tamas's first thrust would be off center; maybe I could finish him and get to Eppyris downstairs before whatever poison the assassin used took effect; maybe an Angel would manifest itself right now and save my careless ass.

Amazingly, I made it over the bed and got a hand on the sword. What the hell was this assassin doing, forging the weapon right here? No one took this long!

Oh, hell. He was a Mouth. I was being spelled.

Christiana must really be pissed if she was laying out that kind of money.

Stupid, Drothe! Never let Christiana's people in your place, no matter how well you've been getting along; no matter how many years it's been since the last attempt.

I didn't bother to draw my rapier—either the blade would never clear the scabbard in time, or it was a moot point from the start. I simply rolled once along the floor and came up in a crouch, sheathed weapon held out in front of me like a staff, both hands grasping the scabbard.

Tamas was where I had left him, eyes wide, mouth empty. In his hand was a folded piece of parchment. On the parchment were a seal and a ribbon.

We stayed like that, staring at each other, for a good ten heartbeats. Tamas broke the standoff.

"I—I'm—I'm to wait for a reply."

"No reply at present."

"Very good." And he ran out the door and down the stairs. The parchment floated through the air to land where Tamas had stood.

I don't think I stopped laughing for five minutes.

The first assassin ever to come after me was a tall fellow who smelled of fish and cheap wine. I was eighteen at the time and stabbed him more out of luck than skill as he tried to garrote me in an alley.

The second Blade had a name: Gray Lark. She had mixed a measure of ground glass into one of my meals. Ironically, it was during a particularly low point in my life, when I was using the smoke. The drug had been more important than food that night, and I ended up giving my plate to another addict. I watched him scream and cough up blood for hours. The next day, I hunted down Gray Lark and force-fed her the same meal. It was the only good the smoke ever did me, and I haven't touched it since.

The third try was three years ago. His name was Hyrnos, and he tried to put a knife in my back in a dark alley—a traditionalist. The only thing that had saved me was my catching him out of the corner of my eye with my night vision. The running fight we carried out across the ice-slicked roofs of Ildrecca that winter's eve nearly did us both in. In the end, I stayed on the roofs while he ended up on the street four stories down, but it had been a close thing.

Three months after Hyrnos tried and failed, Alden came after me. It's strange, having a knife fight in your bedroom with a woman you've known for years. I'd always known she was a professional, though, so I couldn't really hold it against her, even if she was trying to dust me.

Of the four Blades who have come after me, I know one was hired by my sister, and I suspect a second. Both times, I have taken the assassin's weapons and left them in her bed. Needless to say, this has done nothing to make amends between us.

The reasons behind both attempts were different, but the underlying motive was the same: fear. Christiana fears I will reveal myself and the favors I have done for her in the past and thus ruin her at court. That she is a former courtesan and the widow of a baron means nothing in that world—or rather, if anything, they help her. Status and political influence are measured differently in the Imperial Court, and I don't pretend to understand the games involved in determining that pecking order. But I do know that, of the many things that can ruin you, bringing in outside influences, especially criminal ones, is tantamount to cutting your political throat. Assuming you get caught at it, of course. But if you *do*, and your brother is a member of the Kin as well?

Well . . .

The thing is, despite all our differences and history, I wouldn't undercut her like that. Family is family. But Christiana can't understand that, and so we've had our differences in the past, the worst being punctuated by my killing someone and delivering the weapons to her chambers.

Perhaps I shouldn't be so vindictive. After all, my first display only made her hire a better assassin the next time around. If I keep this up, she may finally find one good enough to finish the job.

But I do so enjoy teasing my little sister.

I sat on the stoop beside the entrance to the apothecary's shop and sipped my tea. It was my third cup, and by then the brew had become lukewarm, dark, and bitter despite the honey I had added. It fit my mood.

I set the tea down and took out the message Tamas had brought me.

The paper of Christiana's letter was of good quality—dry and heavy to the touch. I knew I could sell it to Baldezar, who would happily scrape it down and reuse the sheet—could, but would not. This letter would be put away with all her others, both the pleasant and the vicious, in the hidden compartment at the bottom of my clothes chest.

I read its contents again, then watched the paper as it shivered in the breeze.

A meeting. This evening. She needed to talk to me. Important matters. Her safety at stake.

The usual.

In other words, she needed a favor from her brother, the former burglar. Either that, or she was getting impatient for the forgery I was having done for her.

I ran my finger over the hard wax of the seal on the back of the letter and felt the raised image of her widow's chop. Audacity there, to display her mark so openly, so proudly, after what she had done to get it. She called me dark, but at least I only killed when it was business. I had liked her husband, Nestor, too.

A body shifted in the doorway behind me. I turned around, found Cosima looking down at me.

"Bad news?" she asked. Then, more mischievously, "Lose your sweetheart?"

I smiled up at the small woman even as I folded Christiana's letter and slipped it up an unlaced sleeve.

"Left me for a baron. What could he offer her that I can't?"

"Peace and quiet?" said the apothecary's wife as she sat down beside me. "Emperor forgive me, I sometimes wish Eppyris would drug those two girls so I could have half a day to myself."

"I hardly notice them," I said, just as Renna and Sophia came rushing around the corner and bolted into the house. Renna, the six-year-old, was laughing, but eight-year-old Sophia looked far less amused. The door slammed, followed by shrieks and the sound of feet thumping on wooden floors.

"Liar," said Cosima. She watched the door until the noises quieted; then she relaxed.

Cosima, with her raven hair, her deep brown eyes, and a face that was a near-perfect mixture of clean planes and sculpted curves, must have been stunning when Eppyris had first married her. Even after two children and years of caring for them and her husband, she still drew looks from men on the street, me included. How Eppyris won her, I have no idea, but her presence in their home has earned the apothecary a fair measure of respect in my eyes. My respect for Cosima herself is without measure.

Today, her hair was tied back, her face flushed, and the front of her apron damp—wash day, then.

"So, was it bad news?" she asked, pointing at the sleeve where I had secreted the letter.

"No more than usual."

"Who from?"

I met her eyes, but kept silent.

"Fine," she said. "Be that way."

"I explained things to you and Eppyris when I moved in."

"And I didn't like it then."

I smiled. This was an old battle between us. Cosima didn't believe in secrets; I didn't believe in not keeping them.

"My building, my rules," I said.

"Humph."

I'd acquired the two-story brick and timber building a couple of years ago from a Kin named Clyther, along with the note to a loan he held on Eppyris. Clyther hadn't exactly wanted to sell, but the property and arrangement appealed to me, and I had enough on Clyther to change his mind. Once in, I had forgiven the apothecary's debt in exchange for a silent partnership in his business and had moved into the rooms upstairs. My plan had been to live here just long enough to ensure I was getting my fair cut of the profits, but, somewhere along the way, things had changed. The three rooms above the shop had become a haven from the street, and Eppyris and his family had become a welcome relief from my gritty nights. My smart investment had managed to become my home.

So much for plans.

Cosima changed tact. "Your washerwoman stopped by earlier with your clothes," she said.

"I saw them at the foot of the stairs. Thanks."

"The least you could do is let me bring them up, seeing how you refuse to let me wash them for you."

I had a brief image of Cosima lying just inside the door to my rooms, the traps having sprung, her blood and my laundry mingling on the floor.

"No."

"You know I'm going to see that mysterious apartment of yours someday, Drothe."

"Mm-hmm."

"What are you hiding up there, anyhow?"

"One of the emperor's consorts. She's pregnant, you know—doesn't want her little royal bastard killed." Any heir born to the emperor was killed outright. There could be no claimant to the imperial throne, save one of the three incarnations of the emperor himself.

Cosima elbowed me in the ribs. "Don't even joke about that. Next thing you know, we'll have imperial guards tearing the place apart."

"They're not allowed in my rooms, either."

Cosima gave a small laugh and pointed at my cup. "You want me to brew you up some fresh? I make it better than Eppyris. Angels, *anyone* makes it better than that man!" She laughed again. It was an exceptionally good laugh.

"No, thanks. I've had enough."

"How about something more to eat? I saw that pear you had—not enough for a mouse."

"I manage."

"Well, maybe I could—"

"Cosima," I said, "I'm fine."

She paused, then took a small breath. "That bruise on your face says otherwise."

I reached up and gingerly felt the place where Nicco had struck me. "A reminder."

"Well, I certainly hope you don't forget whatever it is next time."

"I won't."

We sat in silence for a while, then; me watching the passing traffic on Echelon Way without seeing it, her running through conversations without saying them. Finally, Cosima leaned forward and wrung out the bottom of her skirt.

"It's not his fault, Drothe."

Ah, here it was. I'd been wondering.

"I'm not mad at Eppyris," I said.

"Nor he at you."

"I know," I lied.

"It's just that . . . he's proud, Drothe. And it's not as if you've demanded anything of us. A little medicine, some herbs now and then—what's that? I keep telling him he'd be hobbling around on crutches, selling poultices in the street, if you hadn't gotten Clyther to—"

"Cosima," I said, "leave it be."

She bit her lip, and looked wonderful doing it.

"He's not an angry man, Drothe. Just . . ." She let the sentence trail off.

Just unhappy having a criminal as a landlord. And a neighbor. And a friend to his wife.

I took a sip of my cold bitter tea. I was just beginning to frame a reply when I noticed a familiar figure coming down the street. I poured the rest of the liquid out on the cobbles and handed the empty cup to Cosima. "Sorry," I said, my eyes tracking Degan as he approached. "I have to go."

Cosima looked from the cup to me, and then followed my gaze down Echelon Way. I saw her shoulders tense.

"I have to see to the girls, anyway," she said, standing.

I laid my hand on her forearm. "It's all right," I said. "He's a friend."

"For you, maybe." Cosima summoned a feeble smile and shuddered. "I'm sorry," she said, and turned back toward the shop. Even after all this time, any other Kin besides me made Cosima nervous—shades of Clyther.

I stepped out into Echelon Way and waited for Degan. Behind me, I heard the door shut.

"You busy?" I asked as he came up.

"Hello to you, too. And, no," said Degan.

The question was a courtesy on my part. You could always tell when Bronze Degan was working—he vanished. One day here, the next day gone. A week, two weeks, sometimes a month. And then, just as suddenly, he would be back, laughing, gambling, and wasting time as if nothing had happened. I had made some inquiries early on in our friendship, both of him and others, to find out where he disappeared to, what he was doing—and gotten nothing. I, the Nose, came up empty, and Degan had just smiled at my complaints.

Damn his sense of humor, anyhow.

"What did you have in mind?" asked Degan.

"I need someone to watch my blinders tonight."

"*There's* a surprise."

"This is a bit tougher," I said. Degan raised an eyebrow, still smiling.

"I need to go into Ten Ways."

The smile faltered. "Ah." He considered a moment. "Death wish?"

"Hardly."

Degan nodded. "Just checking."

Chapter Six

"Looks the same," said Degan. "Smells worse."

"This is rose hips and perfume compared to the summer," I said, "and we're not even inside yet."

"Don't remind me."

We stood at the edge of Ten Ways. Before us, the scarred archway that led into the cordon stood gaping, its doors long ago torn down and carted off. To either side, the walls of the cordon stretched off into the distance, separating Ten Ways from the city, or the city from Ten Ways, depending on your point of view.

Ten Ways is an old cordon in an even older city. Ildrecca dates back more than a millennium, the center of kingdoms and empires long before the line of Dorminikos made it its own. It is a city of growing palaces and crumbling temples, worked stone and shattered ruins, where you can jump over a wall at street level and end up in a private sunken garden or on someone's laundry-covered roof. Dig down and you find the broken fragments of history; look up, and you see the growing glory of the future.

There are any number of stories about why Ten Ways is called Ten Ways: because on every block there are ten ways to die; because there are only ten safe ways out of the cordon; because every person in the cordon knows at least ten ways to rob you; and so on. The best one I've heard is that it was named after a whore who . . . Well, let's just say she was imaginative when it came to keeping multiple clients pleased at the same time.

Charming anecdotes aside, the cordon is one of the oldest of the old. Search through ancient maps and records of the city and you find incarnations of Ten Ways running back to the well before the reign of the Undying Dorminikos, when it was the cordon of choice for the wealthy and learned. Almost all of the buildings are much more recent, of course, but there were times late at night, in the cellars that passed for wine dens here, I'd have sworn I heard the voices of eight hundred years of history dripping from the walls. Maybe it was the cheap vintages combined with the smoke, but I can't believe that so much time, and so many souls, can pass through a place and not leave bits and pieces of themselves behind.

"Do you know where to find this Dealer?" asked Degan. I had told him I was looking for a fence named Fedim, but not why.

"Not yet," I said. "Right now, we walk and watch. I need to relearn the lay of the land. If we're lucky, some of my old contacts may still be around."

"And if we're not lucky?"

"Some of my old contacts may still be around."

"Why do I have the feeling that it's going to end up being an unlucky night?" said Degan.

I ignored him.

Much of the cordon was as I remembered it. The main thoroughfare, Solace Way, was broad for Ten Ways and narrow for any other part of Ildrecca. Nearly half of its cobbles were missing, and the rest were covered over with mud and refuse, making the footing tricky. Side streets were little more than alleys, and the alleys little more than near-accidental spaces between buildings. What little sky we could see was smudged over with smoke, hiding the stars.

The buildings themselves were a jumble of old and not as old, all running to ruin. Roughly one in five was missing a roof, walls, or some other critical portion of architecture. Here and there, I saw a flower box, a tiny garden, a newly painted lintel—attempts by the Lighters to make their fragment of the cordon more respectable, more homey. While it might have made them feel better, to me it only underscored the desolation of the place.

I felt eyes upon us the whole time. We needed no sign, had to speak no word to be spotted as outsiders by the Kin of Ten Ways. Street traffic was low this time of afternoon. I saw no one following us, but I didn't believe that to be true for a moment.

I paused on corners and in doorways, asking after old names, slipping the occasional coin to jog memories. Most of my former contacts had either vanished or become tight-lipped. I wasn't local anymore, and that meant I wasn't to be trusted. I couldn't turn up anything on Nicco, or Kells, or even on the Dealer I had been sent to find, Fedim.

Finally, when I had paid three different Kin to track down one of my more reliable sources from a decade back—a Whisperer named Elek—only to find he had died six months ago, I lost my temper.

"So who the hell has taken over for him?" I demanded of the ragpicker who had informed me of Elek's demise—*after* I had paid her for the privilege.

"That'd be, ah . . . ah . . . " she began, before breaking into a nervous coughing fit.

"Eliza," said a dark voice off to the side.

I looked over and saw a cloaked figure sitting in a doorway. His outline was barely visible, so well did his clothing match the shadows.

"*Silent* Eliza?" I asked.

The man nodded, or should I say, the cowl of his hood did.

"Where is she standing now?" I asked.

"Rose and Castle."

I knew the tavern. I tossed a copper owl his way, saw him pluck it out of the air. He chuckled as I walked off down the street. Degan eyed me as we went, but he refrained from saying anything.

Silent Eliza was anything but; she was loud, raucous, and still one of the best Ears there was in Ten Ways. When people think you are too busy talking to listen, they let things slip. It cost me more than I would have liked to get the information from her, but a jug of wine and a handful of hawks passed under the table got us directions after an hour or so of listening to her go on about . . . everything.

The sun was just beginning to edge below the horizon when we left the Rose and Castle. We had only gone a few blocks before Degan nudged my arm.

"That's the third one in as many blocks," he said.

"What?" I said.

"Ahrami."

I looked down and found myself slipping the pouch back beneath my shirt. Sure enough, I could feel a seed under my tongue, softening.

"And?" I said.

Degan shrugged. "Nothing."

"It's not as if I enjoy being here," I said.

"Of course not."

"I worked my ass off getting out of this damn place. Coming back is the last thing I wanted to do."

"Mm-hmm."

"And then being charged four damn hawks by 'Liza for the location of Fedim's shop?" I said. "That's just insulting."

"I didn't say it wasn't."

We walked on, turned a corner.

"So, what's bothering you?" asked Degan.

"I just told you," I said.

Degan nodded. "So you did."

"Then leave off."

"Of course."

We cut down another alley. It was darker than the others we had been taking, the buildings closer on either side. My night vision began to awaken, highlighting the squalor around us in deep amber. The smell of urine and rotting meat grew stronger.

"So," said Degan.

I kept silent, instead eyeing the shadows as we walked.

"So," he said again.

Damn!

"Look, I'm here to lean on a Dealer for Nicco, all right?" I said. "Let's just focus on that and get it done. The sooner I'm out of this hellhole, the better!"

"I just—" began Degan, but he stopped as a shape slid out of a doorway farther down the alley. A moment later, three more forms bled from the shadows to join it. Behind us, someone cleared his throat.

We were surrounded.

Degan didn't hesitate. He stepped forward, his sword sliding from its scabbard in easy time with his movement. "Front," he said as he moved to meet the four figures lined up across the alley.

"Be my guest," I said as I turned and lugged out my own sword and dagger. Thankfully, there were only two coming from behind.

My night vision showed one of the men to be carrying a heavy-looking club, its end studded with broken glass and metal; the other held a pair of knives. They came forward carefully, moving to bracket me in the narrow space.

Behind me, I heard the first songs of steel on steel as Degan met his four. He was taking the fight to them, making them react instead of deciding how to best surround him. I needed to do the same, but I didn't relish the idea. I was no degan.

I edged toward the one with the knives, my rapier held out before me, my dagger low at my left side. His weapons had the speed, mine the reach. If he came into my range, I had first strike; if he stayed out, I had to deal not only with him, but eventually with his friend as well. Time was on his side.

He stepped back a pace, smiling, his knives flickering dully in my night vision. No dummy there. I took another step. He retreated again. I took one more. When he retreated for the third time, instead of following, I pivoted and launched myself at his friend with the club.

Neither of them had been expecting it, least of all the man with the club. His eyes grew wide as I came in, and he took an involuntary step back. Bad idea. By the time he had his weight resettled and was starting to swing, I was already inside.

I ducked in under his arm as the club came down, my sword raised to ward off the blow. Wood met the steel of my guard, sending shock waves down my right arm. Even as my grip on the sword wavered, I brought my left around and buried the dagger up to the cross-guard in his right kidney. He grunted. I twisted the blade inside him. He grunted again. Then he began to fall forward.

I pulled on my dagger. It wouldn't budge. Leaving it, I stepped to the side, only to find the Cutter with the daggers closing on me, fast.

One slash passed inches from my face, and I felt another pluck at a fold in my shirt. I leapt back and just managed to dodge a thrust to my left side.

Too close, too close, too damn close!

There was no room to bring my rapier up, no way to back up faster than he could come forward. I pointed the tip of my sword down, brought the guard up, and made a moving vertical bar of steel between us, frantically blocking his thrusts and slashes. It was good in the short term, but, sooner or later, he would get past it.

The Cutter came on, pressing me hard. I blocked once, twice, and then punched at his face with the guard of my sword. I managed light contact—nothing solid—but it surprised him. He hesitated, and that was all I needed.

In an instant, I had my wrist knife in my left hand. I lashed out, not worrying about hitting him so much as letting him know it was there. He took a hasty step back.

I let out a shallow breath. I was at sword range again. I took my own step back and brought my rapier in line.

The Cutter was still busy scowling at this latest development when Degan spoke up from behind me.

"Are you almost done?" he said.

"Let me check," I said. I smiled at the man with the knives. "Are we done?"

He looked at me, then past me into the growing darkness. I saw his eyes go wide. Then he was running away.

"I'm done," I said, and turned around.

Degan stood amid four corpses. Not one of the bodies had more than a single fatal wound. All things considered, I couldn't blame the Cutter for running.

"Just here to lean on someone, then?" said Degan, picking up the conversation where we had left off.

I came over and looked at the bodies. "This is local color," I said. "They're too rough to be any of 'Liza's brood, and no one else I've talked to has the clout to gather up this many Kin on short notice."

"Just a robbery, then?" said Degan.

"Yes."

"You're positive of that?"

"Yes," I said.

Degan eyed me across the corpses.

"It was a damn robbery!" I said.

"I stand reassured."

We began moving down the alley again.

"Of course," said Degan, "if it *wasn't* a robbery, things could get worse. And if that happens and I get pulled in ..."

"You're too smart for that."

Degan tipped the brim of his hat in mock salute. "Of course. But if I should go temporarily insane ..."

"Fine," I said. "If that happens, I'll pay for your time. Standard rate."

Degan shook his head. "Not this one, Drothe. If the job gets you back into Ten Ways, it's deeper than I'd like. Hawks won't cover it."

I looked over at my friend. "You can't be talking about an Oath?"

Degan blinked in surprise. "Hardly," he said. "It's not *that* dire."

I let out a sigh of relief.

For all the years I had known Bronze Degan, and for all the things I had heard about degans as a whole, there were still things I did not understand about them as a group. That they were the best Arms you could get, there was no doubt. Nor did you have to worry about a degan turning on you once you paid him. But sometimes, they took the legends about their group's origins a little too seriously, even to the point of assuming the first degans' names. The man standing next to me in the alley was not the first, nor would he be the last, to be called Bronze Degan.

The Oath was another holdover from when the degans had been a potent force in the Dark World. Back then, an Oath had bound them to you and you to them, with the degan being able to call on you at any time to pay off your portion of the promise. And repayment could be anything the degan named. The oldest Kin, repeating the tales of their grandfathers, tell how the power of the Oath was so strong that promisers turned on their own families rather than risk the consequences.

Nowadays, the Oath was a formality, a shadow of the original degans' prowess, just as Bronze Degan was a distant reflection of the first man to bear his name. But the Oath was still not lightly given, or taken. After all, who wanted a degan pissed at him if he decided he didn't want to fulfill his end of the bargain?

"No," said Degan, smiling. "A night out with your sister would be enough. Along with the standard rate, of course."

I glowered at my friend. Degan had had an eye for Christiana since the first time he'd met her. And while Christiana might have turned her nose up at any of my other associates, I knew that when it came to Degan, she would make an exception. It had been that obvious. The sheer idea of my sister—who had tried to have me killed—and my best friend together not only terrified me; it made my skin crawl on a more personal level. I just couldn't tell if that sensation came out of brotherly concern for Christiana or friendly concern for Degan.

"I'll pay you triple," I growled. Degan laughed again.

A few turns later we were at Fedim's.

Fedim's place fronted as a pottery shop. A few unimpressive jugs and goblets had been set on a table near the door. I resisted the urge to turn the table over, mainly because I doubted it would draw more than a shrug from the Dealer. Most fences at least make an effort to appear legitimate, but, given the quality of what he had out, it was obvious Fedim had given up that pretense long ago.

I wondered briefly what I would do if the Dealer wasn't in. It had taken the better part of a day just to find his shop. What if word had gotten to him ahead of us and he had gone to ground? I didn't relish the thought of having to spend more time looking for him.

As it turned out, Fedim was easy to find—his entrails led from just inside the door, straight to his belly, ten feet away.

Chapter Seven

No money was missing, either from Fedim's purse or from the cash box behind the counter. The back room was empty, save for a bed and the Dealer's personal effects.

"Must keep the swag somewhere else," I said as I came back into the front of the shop.

"Either that, or it was taken." Degan was standing near the entrance, peering out through a gap in the curtain that served as a door.

"And the hawks were left? No, this is a message."

"From?"

"From whoever I'm supposed to find."

"I thought you were supposed to find Fedim."

"Change in plan," I said.

I stepped over to Fedim and looked down at him. As Kin went, he was fairly unremarkable with his olive complexion, thinning hair, and long nose. Acne scars covered the left half of his face. If he hadn't been lying dead on the floor, I doubt I would have remarked on him at all.

"This is bad," I said.

"What a surprise," said Degan.

"No." I nudged Fedim's lifeless form with my foot. "It's worse. I was supposed to do this after I was done with him."

Degan nodded. "You're right," he said, "this is bad." Then a wry smile slid onto his face. "Still, it's ironic, no?"

"Yeah," I said. "Ironic."

Before we had found him, Fedim was a minor problem that needed solving. Now that he was dead, he was a big embarrassment. That was the first little bit of irony: If I killed Fedim, it was business; if someone else dusted him, it was an insult to Nicco's strength.

The galling part was, no matter what I did, word would get out: *Nicco couldn't shield his clients. Open season on Nicco in Ten Ways.* This was exactly what he had been trying to avoid, exactly what I had been sent to prevent. If the person or persons responsible weren't brought down hard and fast, Nicco's reputation would fall instead—and so would my head.

That was the other piece of irony: Since I was supposed to have killed Fedim, it was my responsibility to track down whoever had dusted the Dealer and return the favor.

Drothe, the Avenging Angel—I didn't care for the sound of that.

I was staring at Fedim, wishing his soul a long, frustrating journey to the Hosting Grounds, when Degan snapped his fingers twice. I looked up to see him flatten himself against the wall beside the doorway. He held up a single finger, then pointed toward the door.

Translation: a visitor.

I looked around for somewhere to hide, then thought better of it. Instead, I sat myself on a table in easy view a few feet past Fedim's body. I drew my rapier and placed it across my lap for effect.

The sound of leather scuffing on dirt came from beyond the curtain. A throat cleared.

"Fedim?" It was a male voice, half whispering. "Fedim?"

The curtain moved aside to admit the craning head of a young-looking man. What little hair he had was in full retreat from his forehead and shaved down to a thin black stubble. His narrow features were screwed up into a squint that quickly collapsed when he spied the body on the floor. He looked at me and made to bolt, but Degan already had hold of the man's neck.

Degan dragged the man the rest of the way inside. To his credit, the man didn't cry out—not that it would have done him any good. Screams were almost as common as cockroaches around here.

Our visitor was small, though still slightly taller than I, and thin. No, not thin—lean. There was strength beneath those baggy clothes and ill-fitting belt—Degan actually had to work to keep his hold on the man. He had a cloth satchel in one hand that he clutched to himself.

"I didn't see anything!" the man said quickly. "You weren't here."

"That's too bad," I said.

He stopped his struggling and tilted his head as far to the side as Degan's hold would allow. Already, there was the beginnings of an opportunistic, almost carnal gleam in his eyes.

"Huh?" he said.

"I need someone who's seen something," I explained. He looked down at Fedim, licked his lips.

"Such as?" he asked.

"Such as who dusted the Dealer, here."

"Not you?"

"Not me. Or him." I indicated Degan with my sword.

"Truth?" the man asked.

I smiled. "It'd be nice."

"I don't know."

"Not the answer I was looking for."

He shrugged. "Sorry."

I lifted my jaw. Degan squeezed.

"Wait!" yelled the man. "I can find out. I can find out!"

"How?"

"I can play Ear."

"Got local Ears," I lied.

His eyes flicked around the room. "But I know—knew Fedim. I know who to ask, where to listen."

I nodded, as if considering his offer. "How'd you know the Dealer?"

"He holds—uh, held my swag for me."

I raised my eyebrows. "He *held* your swag? Don't you mean he moved it?" Fences didn't hold on to stolen property; they sold it, usually as quickly as possible.

"No, he held it."

I must not have looked convinced, because Degan began squeezing again. The man hunched his shoulders against the pain.

"I'm a Whipjack!" he gasped. "Fedim held my stuff for a cut of the profits."

"Ah," I said. Now it made sense.

Whipjacks did "turn around" thefts—stealing from one person, selling to another, then stealing it back again and returning it to the original owner once a reward had been offered. The idea was that, besides making twice the profit off a single piece of swag, the Whipjack couldn't be caught with the valuables in hand since he moved it between marks so fast.

Fedim must have been this Whipjack's middleman, selling the swag and then leading the thief back when it was time to steal it again. It was a relationship that required trust on both ends; either man could sell the other out for a quick profit. And trust, I've found, breeds reliance, which leads to shared confidences. It was those confidences I needed to know about.

I indicated a three-legged stool in the corner.

"Sit," I said.

The Whipjack obeyed. Degan resumed his post at the curtained doorway.

"What's your name, Whipjack?" I asked.

"Larrios."

"Tell me about Fedim, Larrios."

He shrugged. "Fedim was a Dealer. We got along all right."

"Did he specialize in anything?"

"Not really. He took almost anything from anyone—coin, jewelry, cloth, steel, books, beer ... anything. He used to say that being in Ten Ways, he had to make up for quality with quantity."

"Did he have anyone he unloaded to regularly?"

"I don't know, but he always found someone to buy."

"He ever cheat anyone?"

Larrios snorted.

"All right," I said. "Had he cheated anyone *recently* that you knew about?" If I could find out who Fedim had dealt with, I might be able to get a line on who wanted him dead; or on who had been leaning on him to make Nicco look bad; or both.

Larrios leaned back against the wall behind the stool. "Not that he mentioned. I know he'd been talking to this one man, I think. He never said his name, but he referred to 'him' a lot."

"Any idea what about?"

"Swag, I'd guess."

"Makes sense." I pointed at his satchel. "What's in the bag, Larrios?"

He smiled thinly. "Swag, I'd guess."

"Is that why you were here?" I said. "To move your swag?"

Larrios's smile grew strained. "I didn't catch your name?"

"That's right. You didn't."

His face curled itself up into another squint. "You're not from here—you're from outside the Ten. What're cousins from the outside doing in the cordon?"

"Slumming," said Degan from the doorway.

I shot Degan a glare.

"Looking for Fedim," I said sharply. "Only now, we're looking for whoever dusted him."

"That, too," said Degan.

"Mind if I ask why?" said Larrios.

I ignored the question. "What did you want with Fedim?" I asked again.

Larrios regarded me through narrowed eyes. "Fedim was yours, wasn't he?" he said after a moment. "They beat you to him."

"'They'?" I said.

This time Larrios ignored my question. He looked across the room at Fedim's body. "You're more important dead than alive," he told the corpse, grinning. "And you can't make a single hawk from it. Serves you right."

I reached out and tapped Larrios with my rapier, letting the point linger on his chest. "You mentioned 'they.'"

He looked down at the blade, then back up at me. His voice tried for flippant but failed. "'They' depends on who *you* are."

"*I'm* the man with the sword who's losing his patience."

"Good . . . uh, point." Larrios' eyes flicked around the room once more, then came back to me. "Fedim had been complaining about someone putting pressure on him. He kept saying he didn't know why he was paying for protection when anyone could put the rough on him night and day."

"Any idea who?"

"You mean who was putting on the rough? I don't know—this is a pretty open cordon, you know? I just remember Fedim's saying they laughed in his face when he threatened to go to Nicco about it."

Great. Not only were people leaning on and crossing Kin, but they were also laughing at the Upright Men who controlled them. If Nicco got wind of this . . . No, I didn't want to think about that at the moment. One disaster at a time.

"All I know," continued Larrios, "is that there had to be some serious pull behind those guys."

"Why do you say that?"

"Are you kidding? Nicco isn't the only one getting snubbed around here: Nijjan Red Nails, the Five Ears gang, maybe some others. Hell, I even heard that Kells's operation over on the west side has—"

"Wait a minute," I said, my mind skidding to a sudden halt. "*Kells* actually has people in Ten Ways?" What in the hell was he doing here? I'd been hoping it was just a bad rumor.

Larrios shrugged. "Well—"

"Company," announced Degan.

"What?" I said, turning toward the door.

"Cutters," he said, drawing his sword. The hiss of the steel clearing the scabbard only emphasized the statement.

I looked back to Larrios.

He shook his head. "Don't look at me: I work alone." He seemed worried.

"How many?" I called to Degan.

"Enough."

"Enough what? Enough to make it interesting, enough to work up a sweat, enough to dig us each a grave? What?"

"Enough to consider the back door."

I pictured Fedim's back room in my mind. "There isn't one."

"Unfortunate, that."

I prodded Larrios. "Who are they?"

"How the hell should I know?"

I kicked the stool out from under him, sending Larrios sprawling on the floor. I was crouching beside him in an instant, the edge of my blade against his throat.

"If I find out you planned this party," I said, "I'll make sure it's slow and painful before you die."

"We don't have time for this," called Degan.

"I swear," said Larrios. He was sweating—a lot. "I came alone. I just wanted to get some swag Fedim was holding. I swear."

I stared at Larrios for a long moment. Two choices: kill him or trust him.

Ah, hell. Degan was right. We didn't have time for this. Besides, if there were as many as Degan said, they didn't need a man on the inside. Nor would they move if we had him.

I leaned back, indicating the long knife on Larrios's belt with my chin. "You any good with that?"

Larrios put his hand on the blade and smiled. It wasn't a pleasant thing to see. "I manage."

"Now that we're all friends," said Degan from the doorway, "I can die a happy man. Alone, defending a curtain, but a happy man."

"You're not dead yet," I said. I stood up and walked

over to Degan, leaving Larrios to pick himself up off the floor.

"They haven't begun closing in," said Degan. He was standing away from the curtain now, looking through the space where it failed to meet with the doorway. He stepped aside as I moved up and put my eye to the fading daylight.

The easiest way to tell when something is going down on the street is to watch the locals. They don't run or shout or make a fuss, at least not in the parts of town I'm used to—they just slowly fade and vanish. It's a sort of sixth sense for crowds, a survival instinct. And right now, that instinct was hard at work, because the street out front was empty of any sort of normal early-evening traffic.

Instead, I saw three men lounging on the corner across the street and two to our right. On our left, a man and woman were taking turns tossing coins against a wall. Three more men were standing in a doorway directly ahead. I could just make out the bows leaned up against the door behind them. All of them were looking at Fedim's shop far too frequently.

"Four more on this side of the street," said Degan as I stepped back from the curtain. "They slipped into a couple doorways before you came up."

I gave a soft whistle. "Twelve? Just for us?"

A caustic grin formed on Degan's face. "Flattering in a disturbing sort of way, isn't it?"

Frightening, more like it. Who spends a dozen blades on two? The odds were obscene, unnecessary, even with Degan in the equation. Someone wanted us beyond dead—someone wanted to erase us.

"You didn't see them coming before they were in position?" I asked.

Degan shrugged. "Their turf."

I tapped my rapier against my boot. Maybe they were just holding us for someone. After all, they hadn't started to—

"Here we go," said Degan.

I flipped a small bit of curtain back with my sword. The five up and down the street were starting to move our way, slowly. The three in the doorway seemed to be staying put.

"They won't rush until they're close," said Degan. "They're hoping we panic and make a break for it. Easier for them to take us in the open."

"Good thing we don't panic," I said.

Degan smiled. "Good thing."

"Got anything to throw?"

He gestured at a shelf on the wall. "Vases."

I drew the knife from my boot and held it up for Degan. I had the one in my wrist sheath for myself.

Degan shook his head. "More your style than mine."

I turned around to Larrios. "Can you throw a—"

He was gone. Of course. Damn. Damndamndamn.

Chapter Eight

"**P**roblem," I said.

Degan glanced back over his shoulder, saw the empty room. He didn't even blink.

"If he got out ..." said Degan.

"So can we." I ran toward the back room. There was no time to be subtle, no way to play it safe and still see what Larrios was up to. Two paces from the doorway to the back room, I planted my feet and leapt. I crossed my arms above and behind my head, hoping the rapier and boot dagger would deflect any attack Larrios tried as I sailed into the room. Odds were, though, if he did swing, I was dead.

I hit the floor in the back room, rolled awkwardly. The dagger skipped from my hand. I put my sword through three parries before I took a single breath.

No one.

No light, either, except for sunset's dirty leftovers coming in from the front room. Not enough to see by, but too much for my night vision to help.

I stood and scanned the room. Woven mats on the floor prevented footprints. No walls appeared out of place, no hole made itself invitingly apparent in the ceiling. I stamped the floor. Dirt beneath the mats.

"Larrios!" I called.

No answer. No surprise.

"Well?" yelled Degan.

"Hold on."

Degan mumbled something I couldn't catch.

I ran a circuit of the room, four paces for each wall, striking the plaster with my blade. Everything sounded equally solid. I guessed where I might put a concealed door and threw my weight against the spot. The wall surrendered a thin snow of dust, but nothing more.

I looked over the rest of the room, taking in its dim shapes, grainy textures, hints of a shadow here and there. Why the hell couldn't it be darker out?

There was nothing beneath Fedim's bed but dirt, same for the lone table.

I threw myself at another spot on the wall in desperation, bounced off it. As I staggered back, my heel caught on the hard corner of a mat and sent me over. I scrambled back up, wondering how fast I could cut through the weathered lumber of the ceiling. Then it hit me.

Hard corner of a woven mat?

I dropped to my knees and pulled the mat away. Or rather, I tried to, since it was attached to the floor by long pegs that ran into the dirt.

I ran my fingers around the edges, felt a sunken wooden frame beneath it. There were two rope handles tucked beneath the mat. Grabbing one in each hand, I crouched and lifted.

It was heavy.

"Ah, Angels!" I gasped as the trapdoor slowly came up out of the ground.

"Door" was generous; it was a nothing more than a wooden box filled with dirt, placed in a shaped recess in the floor. Unwieldy, but it would sound as solid as the rest of the floor to anyone walking on it.

Beneath, there was a crude shaft running straight down into darkness. A horrible, familiar stench rose from the hole—sewage.

Suddenly, staying here and dying didn't seem like such a bad option.

Nevertheless, I yelled, "Degan! Let's go!"

Degan came running into the room, sword in one hand, a hefty-looking vase in the other.

"They'll rush soon," he said. "The pots slowed them down, but not enough." He looked at the hole and moved toward it. Then the smell reached him.

"Ugh!" Degan wrinkled his nose and looked at me pointedly. "You always manage to find a sewer, don't you?"

"Only when you're around," I said.

Pushing his hat down more firmly on his head, Degan climbed into the shaft. Grumbling something about Noses liking the worst scents, he disappeared into the darkness below.

I set the "door" near the edge of the hole, sat down, and swung my legs in.

The stench was nauseating, ten times worse than anything we'd encountered in Ten Ways that night. As I slid into the hole, I heard a yell from outside. The Cutters were coming.

I pulled on the box of dirt, trying to shift it back into place as I sank the last few feet into the hole. My feet met round, slippery resistance: a peg or spike of some sort set into the shaft wall. The box moved two fingers' breadth, then stopped. I tugged at it again. Nothing. Larrios *had* been stronger than he looked to move this thing by himself. Then again, he hadn't had ten Cutters breathing down his neck, either.

I gave up on the box and started climbing down the peg ladder set in the shaft wall. I hoped the smell would be enough to keep the Cutters off our blinds.

The darkness was thick with moisture and odor. After eight pegs, my foot met nothing but air.

I shifted in the hole, trying to find the next peg, and something poked me in the shoulder. I felt behind me, found a niche dug out of the earth. In the niche was a long, thin object, like a small case of some sort. So, this was where Fedim had kept his swag. Clever bastard. Larrios must not have known it was here; otherwise I doubted he would have left it behind. I pulled the object out and tucked it between my back and my belt. Damned if I was going to leave this place empty-handed.

"Degan?" I called.

His voice rose up from below. "It's a short drop. Just let go." His voice echoed and reechoed.

I went down to the last peg and hung by my hands. Dropping off into darkness is always an unnerving proposition, but twice so when you're used to being able to see in the stuff. I was tempted to hang and wait for my night vision to adapt, but I could hear Degan splashing about below. He had no such advantage to wait for; for him, the darkness was there to stay. Every moment I held on was another he had to spend listening and groping and wondering at every sound and sensation.

I let go and fell.

Darkness and the rush of air. My feet hit light resistance, then firmer, slicker stuff. Sewage and then the bottom of the sewage tunnel, respectively. I staggered, legs wide, and went to one knee and a hand to keep from falling over completely. The sewage would have come up high on my calf if I had been standing. As it was, I could feel the muck at my hips and past my left elbow.

The stench! My stomach started rolling over and over within me. I felt my throat tighten, my guts lurch, and I tasted bile. Force of will kept everything else down, but there was no telling how long that would last.

"Larrios," I said, gasping, "is a dead man." I stood and shook off my left arm. "You hear that, Larrios?" I yelled. "A dead man!"

I heard my own voice echo and reecho down the sewers. I couldn't be sure, but I thought I caught the faintest hint of laughter from far away. It was hard to tell in that place.

Bastard.

"You all right?" said Degan from off to my right.

"Superb." I spit to clear my mouth, slogging toward his voice. "What kind of idiot has a rabbit hole that drops him into the middle of a sewer?"

"One who'd rather smell bad than die."

"Uhm." I had taken to the sewers for much the same reason a few years ago, although it had been out of desperation. But the idea of anyone choosing to dig into the streams and pools of filth that ran beneath Ildrecca of his own accord—*that* was beyond me.

The thrum of a bowstring and thwack of something striking water came to us out of the darkness. Another whoosh and splash followed moments later.

"Arrows," said Degan. "They're shooting down the shaft."

I smiled and put my clean hand to the side of my mouth.

"Bene!" I yelled at the ceiling. "You just skewered a piece of shit." Unless we were standing directly beneath the shaft, there was no way they could hit us.

"Then we got you!" a voice called back.

I barked a laugh. "Come down and try me, Eriff."

The sound of voices drifted down. Another arrow hissed through the darkness into the slop. If they were dumb enough to follow us down, we could wait beneath the hole and cut them down as they landed. I doubted they were that stupid, but one could always hope.

"Another time, cousin," called the voice from above.

There was a dragging sound, followed by a thud. They had put Fedim's "door" back in place.

"Well?" said Degan.

"Almost," I said.

We stood in the darkness. To my right, I could hear Degan breathing through his mouth, just as I was. It only helped foil the smell a little, and I knew we would start tasting the air after a while. I didn't want to be down here that long.

I stood still and let my eyes slowly roam the blackness around us, looking for the first hint of amber that would mean my gift was beginning to work. It was not long in coming.

The first thing I picked out was a jutting brick in the far wall, showing dark red against the black. Next came the crimson and yellow flecked surface of the sewage, sluggish in some spots, fluid in others. I had forgotten how strangely serene it could look this way, a slow dance of colors that would have disgusted me in the light of day.

Degan appeared next, rapidly followed by the arching walls and ceiling. I looked overhead and saw Fedim's shaft closer than I had expected it to be. A true trapdoor was hanging open above the sewer from it. Larrios had neglected to shut it in his haste to escape. Good thing, too; otherwise Degan and I would be a pair of arrow-riddled corpses by now.

To the side of the trapdoor, a rope ran along the ceiling to a stone walkway. Anyone knowing what they were about would be able to shinny along the rope and land, dry and filth-free, on the pathway the imperial engineers used to inspect and repair the city's sewers.

I considered climbing back up for a moment, then considered the ambush that might very well be waiting for us on the other side of the trap box.

"There's a causeway to our left," I said. I didn't have the heart to tell Degan our dunking could have been avoided.

I led him over to the causeway and helped him find footing to climb out. I followed.

"Recognize anything?" he asked, crouching to avoid the arch of the wall as it rose toward the ceiling.

I looked up and down the tunnel. There was an empty torch bracket nearby. I suspected the torch had made its way out with Larrios.

"I'm not sure," I said. "I don't think I ever made it this far in."

"Any sign of Larrios?"

"None."

"There must be a way out nearby. I can't imagine he came down here just to stumble around in the dark."

I nodded, then remembered Degan couldn't see me. "Probably a drainage shaft or access tunnel," I said.

"Lead on."

I placed Degan's hand on my shoulder and headed to our right. It seemed as good a direction as any.

The stones of the walkway were slicked over with slime

and rat droppings. In one spot, the edge of the causeway had crumbled away, forcing us to sidle past, our backs against the wall. Rats confronted us continually along the path, and I soon had my rapier out before me, sweeping the more belligerent rodents into the river of waste that flowed beside us. The rats squeaked in protest, and their cries formed a sharp counterpoint to the otherwise soft sounds of dripping and squelching that surrounded us.

It was a short time later, while I was leaning over the sewage, emptying what little remained in my stomach for the second time, that Degan's grip tightened on my arm.

"Feel that?" he asked.

I spit, stood up, and leaned back against the wall as best I could. The damn smell—it had always gotten to me.

"What?" I gasped as I fumbled at my herb wallet with my cleaner hand. Thank the Angels, the oiled lining had kept the water out.

"Cross breeze," said Degan.

I lifted my head and waited.

"I don't feel anything," I said.

I returned my attention to my herb wallet and managed to pull out two small parchment packets. One held echember roots, the other ground mysennius seeds. I ripped open the first with my teeth. Half of the echember fell out before I got the packet to my mouth. The powder was easier, and I poured what I hoped was half of it in with the roots. I chewed. The echember wasn't bad, but the mysennius tasted awful without wine to mix it in. With any luck, my stomach would settle down soon and my senses would become sufficiently dulled to keep the stench from getting to me further.

"There it is again," said Degan, more excited now.

This time I felt it, too—the lightest brush of air across my face.

"Yes," I said.

Air movement meant ventilation. Ventilation meant a way out.

We tracked the breeze to a side tunnel. Fresh air, or at least the ghost of it, met our nostrils.

I went first. The tunnel had a low ceiling, forcing me to hunch my shoulders and Degan to bend nearly double. As we slopped along, I began to see a brighter patch of amber ahead—starlight and the smallest hint of moon glow coming in from above.

"Something up ahead," I said. "Either a grate or a small cave-in."

Degan made no response.

After ten paces, the smell began to lessen. After another five, I allowed myself a small smile of relief. It was a sewer grate, set in the ceiling of the tunnel. Despite the drugs, I could even hear voices coming from the street above us.

"It's a gra—" I began to whisper, but Degan suddenly grabbed me and shoved me against the tunnel wall. He put a warning hand over my mouth.

"Hsst!" he whispered through clenched teeth.

I fell silent. Degan held me a moment longer, then released me. I turned to him for an explanation, but his attention was elsewhere. He had his head cocked, eyes staring off into the darkness. I realized he was trying to listen to the voices coming down the tunnel. After a moment, he shook his head in frustration.

"Closer," he whispered, his voice so faint it was almost lost in the few inches that separated us.

We crept forward, one soggy, sucking pace at a time. When we were practically beneath the grate, we stopped again. The voices were still there.

" . . . found nothing?" said a female voice from above us.

"No swag worth taking, no," replied a man.

They couldn't have been more than five paces from the grate, by the sound of it.

"And the book?"

"No sign of it."

The woman swore—proficiently.

"All the payoffs," she said, "All the damn planning, and we miss it by minutes!" Someone kicked something.

"It wasn't a total loss," observed the man. Gravel being ground under a boulder, that voice.

I looked at Degan. He put a hand on my shoulder to stop me from moving even that much. I could tell by the set of his jaw that he was clenching his teeth.

"Finding out the book isn't here is *not* the same as finding it," the woman said.

"Maybe," said the man. "Maybe not. It depends on who got away with it."

The woman grunted. "My money's on Larrios."

Degan's hand tightened on my shoulder. I leaned toward the glow that marked the grate.

"And the other two?" said the man again.

"Hard to say," said the woman. I realized suddenly that she had the smallest of lisps—hardly there, but alluring in its own way. "From what you told me, they weren't there to see Larrios—otherwise, they wouldn't have grabbed him. Does anyone know who they were?"

The man's voice turned carefully neutral as he said, "One might have been a degan."

There was a pause. I could imagine the woman staring at the man, waiting for him to continue.

"And?" she said at last.

"I don't know—I wasn't there, remember? Urios says he saw the degan's sword. He says the other one was small, dark, and moved like a thief."

"A degan and a thief," said the woman thoughtfully. I felt a sudden chill go down my spine. There was something about the way she said it . . . as if she could sense us below her in the tunnels. The owner of that voice seemed too confident, too knowing for my liking.

The man cleared his throat. "About Fedim . . ."

"Yes," said the woman. "Any number of people are going to be upset about that. And it's going to play hell with my timetable." She fell silent for a long moment. "Clean it up," she said finally. "Dump the body somewhere and spread enough hawks around to keep people from getting too curious. I don't want us associated with it."

"For how long? It's only a matter of time before tongues begin to wag."

"For as long as we can afford it. In the meantime, find Larrios."

I heard footsteps beginning to move away. A soft jingling, like the music of tiny bells, or loose jewelry, accompanied them.

"What about the degan and the other one?" said the man, his voice pitched to carry a short distance.

The jingling stopped. "Let me worry about them," said the woman, her voice farther away from us. "You just get me Larrios and that book."

Her footsteps began again, and now I could hear the man moving away from us as well. Soon, the only sounds we heard were the distant drips and squeaks of the sewer behind us.

"How did you know?" I asked as I moved forward to inspect the grate. It was set solidly in the ceiling.

"Know what?" said Degan.

"Don't insult me."

He moved up next to me. "I didn't 'know' anything. I suspected."

I drew my boot dagger and began working at the mortar around the grate. "Like hell," I said. "You don't almost shove me through a wall on a hunch."

"You don't know how close I've come to shoving you through one for less."

"Ha-ha," I said.

There must have been enough light seeping in, since Degan pulled a small knife from his belt and began working beside me.

"I figured there would be people looking for us," he said after a moment. "After all, they knew we were in the sewers and had enough men to cover a good-sized area."

Mortar dust was falling onto my face. I looked down, shaking my head to get rid of it.

"But when we first heard them," I said, "you couldn't have known they were talking about what happened at Fedim's place."

"Seemed possible. You yourself said there was no swag in the shop."

"Bullshit," I said.

Degan paused to wipe some mortar from his own face, then kept scraping.

I regarded him for a long moment. "You're not going to tell me, are you?"

He pushed on the grate. "I think this end is coming loose—how about yours?"

"Degan—" I began.

"I thought I recognized one of the voices," he said.

"And?" I prompted.

"And I was right."

"And?"

"And I can't tell you any more."

I lowered my arm. "What do you mean, you can't tell me any more?"

Degan lowered his own knife and looked at me in the light of the sewer grate. "I can't. I'd like to, but I can't."

"Can't, or won't?" I said.

"*Can't*," said Degan. "If it were just about friendship, I'd tell you, but . . ." He turned back to the grate and resumed scraping.

I stared at him for a long moment there in that small patch of starlight.

"It's about being a degan, isn't it?" I said.

Degan kept working.

I swallowed. "It's about the fucking Oath, isn't it?"

The scraping stopped. Degan lowered his head. He didn't have to say anything after that.

"Well, hell," I said.

Chapter Nine

When we climbed out of the sewer, the street was empty. No trace remained of the man or the woman we had overheard. Above, a narrow strip of sky stood black against the copper-amber tint my night vision lent the roofs. The moon was still up, so it wasn't too late yet.

Degan took a deep breath. "Who knew Ten Ways could smell so sweet?" he said.

I didn't reply. I was too busy trying to make sense of what had just happened in the tunnel.

The Oath—Degan had brought up the Oath with *me*, which meant something had changed down there—something stemming from the conversation we had overheard, something about him and me and Ten Ways. And he wasn't telling—couldn't, according to him, because he was a degan, not that he could tell me why *that* made a difference all of a sudden, either.

If I hadn't known him better . . . but I did. I didn't understand what had changed, or why, but I did know this much: If whatever he knew would make the difference between my living and dying, Degan would tell me. I had to believe in that, had to believe in him; otherwise, there wasn't much point. You have to be able to trust someone—at least one person—with your life if it's going to be at all worth living. Degan had earned that trust from me over and over again, just as I had earned it from him.

The only thing Degan *had* said about the Oath was

that, even if I'd wanted to give it to him, he wouldn't accept it. That was fine by me, since I hadn't wanted to give it in the first place—not over a dead Dealer and an ambush in Ten Ways. If I were going to put our friendship to that kind of a test, it would have to be for stakes a hell of a lot bigger than those.

I followed Degan's example and took a deep breath of the night's offerings—not bad at all.

"So," I said, thinking back over the conversation we had overheard. "Any ideas about this book they seem to be looking for? Or can't you talk about that, either?"

"No, and yes I can," said Degan. "Whatever it is, someone wants it pretty bad—bad enough to send a dozen Cutters after Fedim."

"Or worry about someone showing up to take it away from him."

"I hadn't thought of that." Degan pursed his lips. "Do you think whoever killed Fedim was there for the same reason as everyone else?"

"You mean, did whoever it was show up, not find what he wanted, and then dust Fedim out of frustration? Maybe. But it's not the best way to track something down. Still, there're plenty of Kin out there who cut first and think later." I shook my head. "I had thought Fedim's getting dusted was a message from whoever had been leaning on him. Now, I'm not so sure. There are too many paths crossing here, which reminds me . . ."

I reached back behind my belt and drew out the case I had found in Fedim's escape shaft. A little longer than my hand and about as wide, it was a rectangular box with a curved top and a flat bottom.

"What's that?"

"Something I found at Fedim's."

"You think it's the swag Larrios was looking for?"

"I think it's whatever Larrios was planning to trade the book for."

"He had the book?"

"He had something in his satchel, and he sure as hell didn't want to share it. It might have been the book, might not." I waggled the case in the air. "Either way, I'm betting this was his payoff."

Degan looked at the case, then at me. "Well?"

I placed my hand on the hasp and brought it closer to my face. Degan leaned in beside me. The case was covered with filth and sewage, but I could make out traces of rosewood around the edges and a bit of ivory inlay in the cover.

"No," I said suddenly, lowering the case and tucking it back behind me. "No, I think this should wait until we're out of Ten Ways. They may still be looking for us, after all."

Degan straightened and looked down at me. "This is because of the Oath, isn't it? You're getting me back for the Oath."

I began walking away down the street, mainly so he couldn't see my grin. "Never!"

"Uh-huh. Well, you'd just better hope we don't meet another dozen Cutters."

We headed out of Ten Ways, watching our blinds all the while. If anyone was looking for us, they didn't find us. As for the local talent, I suspect our looking, and smelling, like a pair of Dredgers kept them from bothering us. No one rolls sewer crawlers.

By the time we were back in Nicco's territory, we had discovered that not only did the Kin avoid us—Lighters and even the city watch quickly found someplace else to be when we came into range.

"That's one way to avoid the Rags," I said, indicating the retreating red sashes of another Watch patrol.

"Nah. Too easy to track you by smell." Degan scratched absently at his pants leg. Like mine, his clothes were beginning to dry out, making them stiff and itchy.

"Moriarty's?" he suggested.

"Do we have a choice?"

Degan chuckled. "I'll meet you there."

We parted company. I headed home to get a clean change of clothes to wear after the bathhouse did its work.

A long evening at Moriarty's—the idea hung before me like an illicit fantasy as I turned onto Echelon Way. A hot bath to wash away the filth; a cold one to shock the system back to some semblance of normalcy; and then a warm tub to enjoy the feeling of being human again. And after that, maybe one of Moriarty's girls ...

Yes. Yes, that would work just fine. There would be time enough afterward to wade back into Ten Ways, to cross palms and crack heads. Time enough to gather rumors and run down Kin—including Larrios.

But right now, all I wanted was to get clean.

The apothecary's shop was dark when I arrived, both above and below. I paused in the arch that led to the stairway, looking around the street and along the roofs. No one. Good. If I couldn't see the people I paid to watch my place, no one with normal vision was going to spot them, either.

My laundry was still at the foot of the stairs. True to her word, Cosima had left it. I stuffed a stray shirtsleeve into the basket and crept softly up the stairs, avoiding the three steps I intentionally left squeaky.

In the end, it was the laundry that saved my life.

I was on the top step when the assassin came at me, slipping around the banister and thrusting hard before I could react. It was a good move; my back was to open space, my footing uneven, with no place for me to retreat. Plus, I had my hands full. All I could do was stare as he pushed the stiletto into my chest—or, rather, into the basket of laundry I was holding in front of my chest.

I heard the wicker of the basket crack and start to give way. I felt the weight of his body behind the blow, pushing the steel into the basket, the basket into me, me into the open air behind. The dispassion on his face told me he was a deep-file Blade—not hating, not caring, just killing.

He looked vaguely familiar.

As I tipped backward, my feet scrambling for ground that wasn't there, a sweet, lingering scent came to me through the odor of sewage. Perfume—I knew that perfume!

And that face . . .

My sister's messenger.

"Tamas," I said as my laundry flew up in the air and I went down.

In the brief instant I was airborne, I had enough time to feel a dark, cold fury settle upon me. Christiana—again. Then I hit the steps, and anger was replaced by pain.

I half rolled, half slid down the stairs. Sharp edges, hollow thuds, bright bursts of agony. I think I went head over heels at least once. I know I yelled and tasted blood on the way down.

The ride ended with me in a heap at the bottom of the steps, Tamas still standing at the top. Clothing lay scattered on the stairs between us.

I saw the assassin put his foot on the first step.

Time to go, Drothe. I needed to get out of there—get onto the street and into the night where I could lose him.

I pushed myself up off the floor. The world tilted. A sharp throbbing singled itself out from the rest of my new aches; one of the steps had introduced itself to the back of my head on the way down.

I staggered out onto the street and let myself drift right. I needed to go right, I realized, but why? Something was there . . . something important.

There were voices coming from Eppyris's now. Crying, yelling. A faint light flared behind the shutters. Oh no, Eppyris, don't bring a light out here. I need to see to get away, damn it.

I put a hand on my rapier, drew it. The steel gleamed bloody gold in my eyes. I put the tip to the ground and used it as a feeble cane.

Despite the blood, my mouth felt dry. I tried to spit. I failed.

To the right. Keep going right.

More voices now. Thuds inside the building. Stay inside, apothecary! I opened my mouth to yell a warning, barely managed a thick squawk.

"You missed your appointment," said a voice from the stairwell. Tamas. "That's not polite, Nose."

I blinked. Appointment? Oh, right—Christiana's letter. I had forgotten her request to meet with me tonight. Nothing like getting a man to show up for his own assassination.

"Frankly, I didn't expect you to put rolling in a dung heap before seeing a baroness," said Tamas. "Still, I suppose there's no accounting for taste."

He sounded close. No more running, then, if you could even call it that. I turned, straightened, and edged farther to what had been my right. I'd remembered why I wanted to go there now. I may not have gotten close enough, but this would have to do.

I extended my rapier on a line with him, held out straight, pointed at his eyes. The tip of the sword wavered more than I would have liked.

Tamas had just stepped out of the archway at the bottom of the stairs. His movements were fluid, his manner relaxed. All traces of the nervous, uncertain messenger were gone. The slightest hint of a sneer hung about his lips. He had a broad, double-edged blade, halfway between a long dagger and a short sword, in his left hand. In his right, he held a four-foot length of rope. The rope was broken up by a regular series of knots, and each knot looked to have a small piece of cloth or paper tied into it. He swung the rope in a lazy circle at his side.

I was in trouble.

He came on and I slid back, maintaining my guard before me. I could see better in the dark, but he hadn't just fallen down a flight of stairs. I would have called us even for that, except for the piece of knotted magic he was swinging in his right hand.

I heard a door open in the shop, saw a light shine into the stairwell. Eppyris called my name.

"Back inside!" I yelled. "Lock the door!"

The light vanished as the door slammed.

Tamas flicked his eyes toward the shop, back to me.

"Don't worry," he said. "I've only been paid to clean you."

I edged another step away, drew the dagger at my belt with my left hand. Getting close, now.

"She didn't pay you enough," I said.

Tamas smiled, then shrugged. The cord moved faster. Then he did, too.

He closed quickly, thrusting with his sword. I dropped my own point and turned my rapier through a downward arc, catching his blade and driving the attack off to my right. At the same time, I stepped forward with my left foot to fill the opening I had just created. With my body blocking his right arm and my rapier engaging his left, I was hoping to use my dagger to carve his guts at my leisure.

It was a good plan. Unfortunately, Tamas didn't cooperate. As soon as I moved in, he stepped back and away to my right, out of dagger range. At the same time, he lashed out with the rope. There was no time for me to get out of the way, so I put my dagger out to try to catch the attack. I missed.

The cord caught me along the left arm and swung around to connect with my back. I heard three soft pops, felt three sharp points of pain where the rope hit.

It was as bad as I'd feared—there were runes tied into the knots.

I leapt back, flicking a cut at his face with my sword to keep him from following. He blocked the feint, then smiled. Three of the knots on his rope were smoking and glowing like embers.

I realized I had been only half wrong when I suspected him of being a Mouth up in my rooms. The only problem was, this was worse. He didn't have to say a thing to make the magic work—all he had to do was hit me.

I switched to a more traditional guard, right hand before me, weight back, rapier held just above waist level. I turned my body sideways and let my left arm drop down behind me, ready to throw the dagger underhand across my body.

Or so I wanted him to think. Truth be told, my left arm was already beginning to feel numb from the runes. I wasn't even sure I'd be able to keep hold of the dagger, let alone throw it.

The rope was spinning in Tamas's hand again. He beat my blade with his own once, twice, then stepped in, trying for the bind. At the same time, the cord snaked out again, heading for my groin.

I tried to disengage my rapier from his attack by bringing its tip underneath his and back in line between us. I needed the sword to block the rope. I had no idea if the steel could stand up to his magic, but it seemed as good a time as any to find out. The question quickly became academic, though. My sword didn't make it around in time, and I barely managed to bring my left hand forward to catch the tip of the rope across the knuckles.

Pop. Pain. My dagger fell to the street.

I withdrew again. My disengage had worked well enough that I was in position to slip by his blade and score a light chest slash on the way out.

Tamas rolled his shoulders once and kept smiling.

I took another step back. There was an alley near my left now.

Someone yelled for the Watch from down the street. The sound of our steel had raised the alarm. Knowing the local Rags, they would arrive in time to find a few spots of blood on the cobbles and scratch their heads. After all, that was what Nicco paid them to do.

I feinted at Tamas's head, then dropped into a crouch and went for his groin when he moved to parry. He swung the rope at the same time. The cord passed over my head. I missed his crotch by a finger's breadth, my point passing between his legs.

"You fight better than you dust," I said as I scrambled upright and back into guard.

Tamas pushed his lower lip out in a dismissive manner. "You got lucky."

It was my turn to shrug. I backed away again.

"Trying for the alley?" he asked, following my retreat.

Before I could answer, Tamas swung the rope at the side of my head, forcing me to my right. At the same time, he stepped to his own right, placing himself between me and the alley mouth.

Tamas *tsk*ed.

"And here you're supposed to be such a Boman Prig," he said, shaking his head in mock pity. "I didn't think you'd be so easy to beat."

"Finish it," I said.

Tamas swung his rope faster. "With pleasure."

I smiled. "I wasn't talking to you, Blade."

I'll say this: He was quick. Tamas was already turning when one of my Oaks stepped from the alley and ran him through. The rope was still spinning when he hit the ground.

I let my guard drop and tried to make a fist with my left hand. The entire arm just hung there, limp and full of pain.

"What the hell were you waiting for?" I snapped.

The Oak, a big stone-faced cove named Scratch, put his foot on the body and wrenched his blade free. "Just got here," he said.

"What the hell do you mean, you just got here?"

"Ran my ass off from my post over there," he said, pointing at a roof halfway down the street. "Alley was faster, so I came out here."

"Then who was supposed to be here?"

Scratch wrinkled his nose and moved a step away from me. "Roma."

"Where is she?"

Scratch shrugged.

"Signal Fowler," I said.

"Expect she's already coming."

"Just do it."

Scratch let out a long, wavering whistle as I knelt down next to Tamas. Bloody bubbles were coming from where the sword had exited the front of his chest. His eyes were half closed, already glazing over. He wouldn't be answering any questions.

I gave the Blade a quick roll, coming up with a handful of hawks, two more daggers, and not much else. I left the cutlery, tossed the coins to Scratch, and looped the rope into a coil on the ground, careful not to touch any of the knots. I could already feel the results of my trip down the stairs coming back, now that the excitement was over.

"Get rid of him," I said, standing, rope held between my thumb and forefinger. Scratch picked up Tamas's sword, stuffed it through the man's belt, and dragged the whole mess away.

I headed back to the shop. Eppyris was waiting in the doorway to his family's apartments, framed by candlelight from behind. The light burned my night vision, bringing tears to my eyes. I wanted to look away, toward the cooling, dark shadows of the ground; instead, I stared straight ahead and gritted my teeth.

Eppyris remained silent as I walked up. Straightbacked, square-shouldered, with a hard jaw and high forehead, Eppyris is one of those men who comes across taller than he actually is. In truth, he barely has three hands on me, but, between his iron posture on the outside and solid demeanor within, it's hard to see him as a little man.

Behind him, I could hear Cosima's voice, talking softly to their two girls.

"Something for the pain," I said. I was wincing with every step now, and limping every other. "Lots of something."

He nodded once. "In the shop. We'll talk there."

Before I could answer, he had shut the door in my face.

It was shaping up to be a wonderful evening all the way around.

I blinked in the semidarkness, waiting for my eyes to recover from Eppyris's candle. I knew if I concentrated hard enough, I could hasten the recovery, but I just didn't have the will right now. Instead, I walked over to the stairs.

There was laundry everywhere. I bent down, picked

up the laundry basket, and looked at the knife lodged in it.

A throat cleared itself behind me. I turned to find Fowler Jess standing in the arched doorway to the street.

"Let me start," she said, "by saying that I don't know how he got in."

"Through the door you're standing in, I imagine," I said, setting the basket down. "Funny thing is, someone's supposed to be *watching* that door."

The Oak Mistress put her hands behind her back and looked up at me from beneath blond brows. She had a thick, flowing mane to match, but right now it was tied back and hidden beneath a floppy green cap. The cap was big, making her delicate face and fine shoulders seem even smaller than usual. A bit of dirty lace showed at her neck, escaping from beneath the green doublet she wore. Her skirt was a deep brown, but beneath it, I knew, were green stockings. She was all of nineteen summers, maybe, and if I weren't so furious, I would have taken her upstairs right then.

"We never saw him," she said.

"'We'?"

"All right, I. But I was on rover, so I can't be sure. Sylos was watching the front. I'll check with him and see what the problem was."

"The problem," I said, my voice rising, "is that I was almost dusted in my own hallway! I got shoved down the stairs, chased into the street, and all your people did was watch! If I hadn't drawn the Blade over to that alley, Scratch would still be picking lice out of his hair and I'd be dead."

"I was coming."

"When?"

"It takes time to get down off a roof, Drothe."

"And Roma?"

Fowler cocked her head, brows knitting together. "What about her?"

"To hear Scratch tell it, she was supposed to be on the alley he came out of, only she wasn't."

Fowler looked over her shoulder in the direction of the alley.

"You'd better check on your people, Fowler," I said. "You might find one's been bought out from under you."

Fowler's head whipped back around. "My people don't sell out," she snapped. "I don't do the cross, and neither do they. That's why you hired me, and that's why I hire them. I'll talk to Roma and see what happened, but I know her. She wouldn't give you up like that."

"You'd better do more than talk," I said, "or I know some people who aren't going to be happy."

Fowler's hands came forward to rest on her hips. "Look, Drothe, I botched it, all right? You almost died, and I'm supposed to stop that from happening, so yeah, I botched it. Be mad, but be mad at *me*. Scratch, Roma, Sylos, and the rest are *my* worry. If there's a problem, I'll take care of it. Don't be threatening to put weight on my coves — I can do that myself."

I reached out with my right hand and laid it where her shoulder and neck met. She flinched but didn't move away.

"Listen up," I said. "Anyone leaves my blinds open when they should be shut, I take it badly. And personally. You talk to those Eriffs you call Oaks and get things straight. But tell them this, too: Any more problems and I deal with them myself."

Fowler's jaw set, pushing her lower lip out. Anyone who didn't know her would think she was pouting, instead of barely keeping her hands from my throat.

"My people, Drothe," she said. "My problem."

"My neck takes precedence over your people," I said. "Just remember that."

Fowler clenched her jaw some more. "Like you'll . . . Oh, to hell with this!" Fowler gagged and took two quick steps back, waving her hand in front of her face. "I can't argue with you when you smell like that. What did that Blade attack you with, anyhow—a chamber pot?"

I resisted the urge to look down at my clothes. "It's a long story."

"Then tell it to me after a long bath," she said. "I'm going to try and figure out what went wrong before I lose my dinner. Do you need to yell at me about anything else before I go?"

"No." I waved a hand. The adrenaline was finally starting to wear off, and I could feel the fatigue setting in. "Wait—yes."

Fowler stopped just beyond the archway and turned back, the setting moon turning the hair at the nape of her neck into fine silver. "What?" she said.

"Send someone to find Jelem the Sly. He'll either be in Brass Street or Quarters cordons this time of night."

Fowler nodded. "It may take a while." She waved up and down the street. "I have a few things to do here, first."

"You'll find me."

"Damn straight I will," she said. Then she was off, jaw set, steps fast. I didn't envy her people the grilling they were about to receive.

I sat down on the steps. I knew Eppyris was waiting on me, but I didn't have the energy for another argument right now. I needed five minutes—just five minutes of no motion.

I leaned back on the steps and winced as something shifted and poked into the small of my back. Oh, right.

I reached behind me and pulled out the case—or rather, its broken remains. The fall down the stairs had split its top nearly in two, and the fine hinges and clasp that held it closed were a twisted and buckled mess.

The filth from the sewers was dry now, and some of it had flaked away. I could see more of the inlay and make out hints of gold wire along with the ivory—even a few glints that might have been precious stone. It looked for all the world like the box a person would . . .

"Son of a bitch," I said as I carefully lifted the broken lid. Inside the battered case, on a bed of padded velvet scented with myrrh, rested a narrow crystal tube. Gold filigree scrolled around it, forming artful flowers and intricate symbols, almost hiding the crystal itself. I didn't need to look in the small window that had been left in the filigree to know what was inside the tube, but I did anyhow, and saw an old, faded, slightly dirty quill pen, its end feathers nearly gone.

I knew it; or rather, knew of it. It was the pen the emperor Theodoi had used to write the Second Apologia in an attempt to make amends with his other incarnations almost two centuries ago. By all accounts, he was still the most consistently sane of the three, but that hadn't stopped him from writing far less placating tracts to his various selves in later incarnations.

I resisted the urge to bow to the quill three times, then three more, then three again. I've handled enough purloined relics to know my obeisance wasn't going to make a difference to the Angels anymore—I was damned a couple times over, by that reckoning.

"Son of a bitch," I said again as I examined the gold-wrapped tube. "What the hell were you doing with my relic, Fedim?"

Chapter Ten

I sat at the bottom of the steps, trying to put things together. Nothing fit.

Athel and Fedim, Fedim and Athel—was there a direct connection between the two, or had the relic passed through more hands on the way to the Dealer's shop in Ten Ways? And what was it *doing* in Ten Ways, for that matter? Imperial relics meant money and powerful interests—neither of which frequented Ten Ways, and certainly not a Dealer of Fedim's status.

The book—somehow, I suspected, this all had to do with the book the Cutters and their employers had been looking for; a book they thought Fedim had had, and Larrios might have right now; a book I was suddenly starting to get interested in despite myself.

I pulled the slip of paper out of my ahrami pouch and ran it through my fingers. *Imperial* and *relic*, it said—but what else? If there was a connection between Athel and Fedim, the relic and the book, I was in deeper than I'd thought and against people even Degan wanted to leave alone, barring an Oath.

Shit. I needed to get my hands on Larrios and squeeze some answers out of him.

I stood up and gingerly made my way upstairs, every ache and bruise I'd gathered making itself felt along the way. My left arm still wasn't working, so getting into my rooms was a challenge, but I managed it without setting anything off. I deposited the reliquary and Tamas's rope underneath a loose floorboard, then made my way back down the stairs and to the front door of Eppyris's shop.

The apothecary had a brazier glowing and was adding a pinch of something or other to a mortar when I opened the door. He didn't look up. I shaded my eyes against the light coming from the lamp, and entered.

I took a deep breath as I waited for my eyes to adjust. As always, a riot of smells greeted me, and, as always, they seemed just a little different from the last time. There was a dark, almost roasted smell in the shop tonight, mixed with a hint of spice, riding on a wave of smoke and oil and lampblack. Nothing was brewing or steeping overnight, which left a vacancy usually filled by some sharp, caustic, or musty odor.

My vision began to adjust, and I got a better view of Eppyris seated at one of the two massive tables that played host to an assortment of bottles, mortars, cups, scales, and loose ingredients. The walls to either side were covered with row upon row of shelves, each crammed with the raw ingredients of Eppyris's trade: jars of oils, boxes of fine powders, sheaves of dried herbs, and the occasional jug or sealed pot marked with the strange script Eppyris refused to translate for me.

Eppyris put pestle to mortar and gave a few quick, well-practiced grinds. As I walked over, he pulled a small box down from a shelf, removed a dried sprig of something, and sniffed it.

"Separate the flowers," he said, handing me the delicate bit of branch. I moved to join him at the table. "Over there." He pointed to the far end of the room. "And burn this beside you."

I took the proffered incense, went to another brazier at the far end of the room, and tossed in the scented nugget. The heavy odor of the incense mingled with the smell of sewage that clung about me, but did little to hide it.

I sat down and lit a candle from the brazier. Feeling was starting to creep back into my left arm and hand — along with the occasional flash fire of pain — so I was actually able to strip the flowers. The petals were tiny purple-and-yellow things the shape of tears, their colors faded from drying. They felt like fly wings beneath my fingers.

"Are you all right?" asked Eppyris after several minutes of silence.

"Bruised, mainly. Nothing broken that I can tell."

"And the filth you're wearing?"

"Long story."

Eppyris grunted. He shook the contents of the mortar into a cup, added two pinches of something from a shallow bowl, and poured boiling water over the whole thing.

I held up the nearly naked branch. "You need this?"

The apothecary shook his head and pointed at the cup. "Has to steep. We've time. What are you handling?"

I tasted the dust on my fingers—sweet, heavy, with a bit of burning at the back of the throat. "Harlock?"

"Yes. Good. But you should use your nose before your tongue, and your eyes before either. The flowers might have been poisonous."

"I know what can kill me in that small a dose."

"Of that, I have no doubt." Eppyris picked up the steaming cup and gave it a practiced swirl. "What about the other man?" he said.

"The one who was on the stairs? He didn't fare as well as I."

"What did he want?"

"I missed an appointment. He was upset."

"So he came for you."

"More or less."

Eppyris set the cup down, then put both hands on the table. "I thought they weren't supposed to be able to get in the building. You said it was taken care of."

"It was a mistake," I said. "It won't happen again."

"He got in the *building*, Drothe." Eppyris's voice began to rise. "On the stairs." He stood and pointed toward the entryway beyond the wall. "One door away from my family!"

"He wouldn't have come after you or Cosima or the girls."

"No?"

"No. He was deep fi— He was professional. He was here for me, no one else."

"And what if I had walked out into the stairwell when he was there, Drothe? What if Cosima had come up to ask you down for tea? What if one of us had found him by accident?"

I stood up and walked the petals over to him. I set them down carefully, then stared up into his face.

"He was a *professional*, Eppyris. That means you wouldn't have seen him. Even if any of you *had* been up four hours before sunrise."

Eppyris scowled. "Don't patronize me. You know what I mean." He swept up the petals and crumbled them between his fingers, letting them fall into the cup.

"So what happens the next time?" he said more softly. "What happens if the next one isn't as 'professional'? What do you do then?"

The next time—there was the problem. Would there be a next time? Would I allow her another chance?

I didn't doubt my sister was behind this; there was precedent, after all. Besides, no one knew to use her livery, let alone to make an appointment with me, like that. I couldn't figure exactly what I had done to bring this latest attempt down on me, but that didn't matter. I've found you don't have to know why someone is trying to kill you; you just have to know that they are.

I thought of the rope upstairs, its knots as dark as charcoal. That was the part that bothered me the most. Hiring a Mouth to speak a spell is one thing; spoken magic is hard to trace, difficult for the empire to come down on. But portable glimmer like Tamas's rope was another thing entirely; magic of that sort had been outlawed by the empire three centuries ago. It was still around, of course; it just cost—a lot. More than I had thought I was worth.

But if she was now willing to go that far . . .

If.

"There won't be a next time," I said.

Eppyris grunted.

I looked up, meeting his eyes. "There won't."

We stared at each other for a long moment, both of us feeling righteous, or just right, or stubborn, I'm not sure which. Finally, Eppyris sighed and rubbed his eyes.

"My shop is here," he said. "I'll stay for now. But Cosima, Alarenna, and Sophia will go to her mother's tomorrow."

"Eppyris, they don't have to."

"Yes, they do," he said.

I wanted to argue, but didn't. I wasn't about to put my pride above his family.

"Here," he said, setting the steaming cup before me. "This should be ready. I'll prepare a salve and set it on the stairs for you. Do you need more ahrami?"

"Yes." I picked up the cup. The brew was hot and bitter and scorched my throat on the way down.

I heard the click of a lock, the soft rattle of a latch being turned. A male voice spoke; it was Josef, my sister's butler. The words were muffled by the double doors leading from the hallway to her parlor. I was in a room farther beyond, in Christiana's bedroom, but I could still make them out.

"Will you be needing Sara tonight, madam?"

"No, thank you, Josef. It's late. Let her sleep. I can manage."

"As you will, madam."

I heard the outer chamber doors open, then close, saw the flicker of approaching candlelight reflected on the marble floor. I had left the doors between the bedroom and parlor ajar.

I bit down on the seed in my mouth, worked it for a moment, swallowed. It had little effect, as the painkilling potion Eppyris had given me also dulled the ahrami. Still, it tasted good, and after my argument at the baths with Degan, I'd take whatever solace the night was willing to offer.

He had wanted to come with me; I had refused—not because I didn't want a sword at my back after Tamas's attempt, but because I didn't trust him when it came to Christiana. I'd seen the way Degan looked at my sister, and the way her eyes played over him. It wasn't that I thought he would harm me when it came to her; it was just that I wasn't sure he would let me harm her.

And I wouldn't brook outsiders—not even Degan—interfering in family matters.

I sat in a high-backed chair in a corner of the bedroom. Behind me, the window I had entered through let in a soft breath of air, sending the flame of the single candle I had lit to flickering. The candle was on the far side of the room, letting me remain in shadow while still putting my night vision to sleep. When the bedroom doors opened fully, I was ready for the light.

Christiana entered, all grace and ease, the skirts of her emerald and almond gown flowing with her every movement. The neckline had slipped, revealing a smooth shoulder among the chestnut avalanche of her hair. In her left hand was a candelabra with three buds of flame growing from silver and wax stems. Her pale eyes were distant, her brows drawn slightly down, her lips pursed. Weighing the implications and innuendos of the evening, no doubt. After two steps, she smiled to herself, then nodded; someone at court, I knew, was doomed.

Then she noticed the lone candle. She noticed me. The candelabra almost fell out of her hand.

"Bastard!" she gasped. "You nearly scared the life out of me!"

"Can't have that," I said.

Christiana glared at me for a moment, then relinquished a darkly playful smile.

"Still don't know how to use a door, I see," she said as she continued into the room.

"I find it best to avoid your servants."

"Always the cautious one."

"You should talk," I said.

My sister gave a thoughtful smile. "I suppose. He *did* teach us both well, after all."

He. Sebastian. Our stepfather.

He had come striding out of Balsturan Forest three years after my father's death. I had been seven at the time; Christiana four. Our mother had kept him at arm's length at first, but time had won her over, and the trapper had become our second father.

It quickly became clear, however, that Sebastian had once been more than a trapper. Trappers didn't know how to pick a lock and evaluate a fine wine, how to fight with a rapier and dance a galliard, how to speak the thieves' cant and practice court manners. Sebastian had known all this and more, and he'd spent as much time teaching these things to Christiana and me as he had maintaining his trap lines and repairing our home. Our educations had been distinctly divided, with Christiana learning the courtly graces (mostly) and myself learning the darker skills (again, mostly). I could cavort my way through a pavane if necessary, and Christiana was an acceptable hand with a small rapier, but our familiarity with each other's studies had crossed only when Sebastian needed an extra set of hands to help teach something.

My mother hadn't understood why he insisted on teaching us all of these things, since we lived in the wilds and not the city, but Sebastian had only smiled his slippery smile and said—as he always had—that there was more than one kind of education. Besides, if our chores got done, who was to care? Our mother had merely shaken her head and made sure we got time for ourselves.

She had died six years later, and Sebastian had been killed a handful after that. Left with a two-room cottage in the woods and little desire to stay, Christiana and I had eventually found our way to Ildrecca and put what Sebastian had taught us to use.

Unfortunately, we've gotten into the habit of using our educations against one another in the intervening years. I doubt it was what Sebastian had had in mind.

Christiana set the candelabra on a small table in the middle of the room, then moved over to her bed, placing its richly covered expanse between us. She began removing her rings, setting them on a bedside table.

"I was beginning to think your man would never get that forgery done," she said. "What kept you?"

"Business."

"A poor excuse, but typical. Still, I'm glad you're here."

I let out a single, dry laugh.

Christiana looked at me askance. She had turned away, placing herself in profile. "You're in a splendid mood tonight, I see."

"I get that way when people try to kill me."

"I thought that was an occupational hazard for you."

My voice caught in my throat. "Sometimes. But this wasn't Kin business."

She had begun removing a web of gems and silver thread from around her neck but stopped when she heard the change in my voice. She turned, and the look of aristocratic indulgence faded from her face. Christiana's eyes became sharp. Languid grace turned into steeled suspicion.

"Drothe?" Her voice dropped a notch and slid to the back of her throat. "Why *are* you here?"

I gave no answer, since I wasn't all that sure myself. All I knew was that the rage inside me was demanding action—vengeance. I stood up and began moving toward her.

"I suggest," she said, "you sit back down and we talk about this."

I shook my head. "Not this time, Ana. We talk my way."

One of her fine eyebrows went up. "I see," was all she said. As I came around the corner of the bed, Christiana began edging back.

I laid my hand on my rapier. I was only a handful of paces from her now. "This has to end," I said.

"Same as always, dear brother." The corner of her fine, painted mouth turned up. Christiana raised her voice. "Josef!"

I was moving before she got to the second syllable, had my left hand to her throat just as she finished. I shoved Christiana back over the night table and up against the wall. By the time the doors to the bedroom opened, I had the dagger from my forearm sheath at her cheek.

"Mistress!" Josef shouted. It didn't sound like he was alone.

Christiana and I were close, nearly pressed up against each other. The heady smell of perfume filled the air between us, her own spicy scent just discernible beneath it. I could feel the vein in her neck pulsing fast beneath my palm, see the flush as it spread across her skin. My own heart was pounding in my ears.

"Tell them to leave," I said, my voice almost a gasp.

Christiana locked her gold and blue eyes with mine, set her shoulders against the wall, and straightened her back as best she could. She did not struggle. Instead, I felt something sharp against my stomach.

"No," she said.

I glanced down and saw a dagger in her left hand. Its handle looked remarkably like part of the decorative carving on her headboard. A quick glance to my right showed me where the disguised blade had been moments before.

I put enough pressure on my own knife to dent her skin, but not to cut. "Send them away, Ana."

She glanced at my dagger. "Poisoned?" I turned up a corner of my mouth in answer. "I think I'd like them to stay," she said.

I heard hushed voices talking behind me.

"Best get out, Josef," I said, my eyes still on my sister. "Unless you want to be looking for a new position come morning."

Christiana let out a light laugh. "You wouldn't," she said to me. "You never could."

My grip on her throat tightened. She gave a small cough, but the mocking light in her eyes remained.

"And you," I said, "always would. Without a second thought."

Her shoulders rose, fell. "What can I say? I'm a bad girl. I never listened to Sebastian."

"Your loss," I said.

"Maybe." Then some of the steel faded from Christiana's eyes. "But not this time, Drothe. Whatever you're thinking, you're wrong."

"I doubt it," I said, sounding more certain than I suddenly felt.

"Fine," said Christiana. I felt her dagger move away from my stomach, saw Christiana toss it on the bed. "Fine. If you want to kill me, get it over with. I'm tired of waiting on you — either do it or take your hands off me."

Her face was set, her chin raised in defiance. But I could feel her trembling, see the soft edge of doubt that marred her iron stare. She was afraid. And that was when I knew; Christiana was too good a liar to let weakness show through her facade — only the truth could cause the cracks I saw there. If she'd sent Tamas after me, she would have anticipated this possibility and been ready with a better lie, a better excuse. And she damn well wouldn't have given me the satisfaction of seeing her afraid at the end.

I looked from the dagger on the bed back to my sister. It had been too easy; too obvious. That wasn't Christiana's style — we were too much alike in that regard. And the magic — even she knew better than that. . . .

"Decide, Drothe," said Christiana.

I still had my hand on her throat and a frown on my face when someone put a sword to my back. I let them pull me away from her.

My sister's eyes turned soft in that moment. "Sometimes," she said, "you're incredibly stupid, Drothe."

I had to agree with her.

*   *   *

"How dare you!" shouted Christiana.

I winced at the noise. My head had begun hurting again shortly after the guards pulled me away from her. Each word caused an accompanying throb at the base of my skull.

"How *dare* you think me so simple, so naive, so ... unskilled as to have an assassin come after you in my own livery?"

"I've already apologized," I said. "Now, will you stop yelling?"

"I'll yell all I want!"

I pinched the bridge of my nose with one hand even as I wrapped the fingers of my other around the chair arm to keep from throttling my little sister. All of a sudden, not killing her seemed like the wrong choice.

I was in the high-backed chair again. After disarming me and piling my weapons on the bed, the guards — excuse me, "footmen," as my sister preferred to call them — had all but thrown me into the seat. Christiana had then dismissed them. She didn't want the hired help hearing what came next.

Josef, knowing about Christiana's and my relationship, was allowed to stay. He had listened attentively to my explanation until I came to the part about Christiana's letter; after that, he took himself and the letter off to one side. Now he sat at my sister's writing desk, his prodigious nose bent over the piece of paper.

Christiana herself was pacing back and forth in front of the bed. Her skirts whispered and snapped as she turned at the end of each circuit. She was not pleased with my explanation.

"The Blade wasn't wearing your livery when he tried to dust me," I said, "only when he arrived with the letter."

Christiana paused midstep, raising her chin in that haughty way she's always had. "And you naturally assumed I was behind it." She actually had the audacity to sound indignant.

I lowered my hand and looked her in the eye. "You've got to be joking," I said. "The livery, the letter, the setup—what would *you* think? It's not as if I don't have history to fall back on here."

"We reached an agreement about that, Drothe. I gave you my word!"

I snorted. "I know the worth of your word," I said. "Don't forget, I've paid visits to people you've given your 'word' to in the past—all at your request. I know better than to trust your word, Ana."

Christiana waved a dismissive hand. "That was just blackmail and politics. This is different."

"Yes," I said. "It's me. It's personal. Even less reason to trust you."

"So then, why didn't you kill me? You had your chance."

I almost told her it was because I hadn't liked the odds of getting out alive, that I had better things to do. Instead, I told the truth.

"Like you said," I told her, leaning back into the chair and slipping a seed into my mouth, "it was too straight-forward. The messenger to the letter to the assassin to you—you'd never leave a trail that broad for me to follow. If I hadn't been so tired, so angry, I might have even realized that first. As it was . . ." I shrugged.

Christiana raised an eyebrow. "Why Drothe, that's almost a compliment. You *do* appreciate me."

"What I'd appreciate," I said, "is getting some answers. Stroke your ego on your own time, Ana. I have other things to worry about."

Christiana pursed her lips. "Ooh, poor Drothepholous. With me out of the picture, you don't know whom to kill now, do you?"

"I can always make an exception," I said pointedly.

She dismissed my threat with a sniff. "I don't suppose you have any idea who might want you dead—besides me after tonight, that is?"

"No." I had already been considering the question myself. The number of people I had crossed recently was small; the number who could afford a Blade of Tamas's ability, even smaller; and the number who were power-

ful, or desperate, enough to use magic made it, well . . .
zero. Except someone *had* hired the Blade, given him a
piece of glimmer, and sent him after me.

I slumped down farther in the chair. One of the
bruises Tamas had given me found a hard edge somewhere and began protesting. I grimaced, then shifted
slightly—no good.

"Drothe . . . " said Christiana.

"Ana," I said, "if you warn me about dirtying the up-
holstery one more time . . ."

"I don't give a damn about the chair, Drothe." There
was iron in her tone. I stopped shifting around and
looked up.

"How did the assassin know to wear my livery?" she
said. "*Mine.* To get to *you*?"

I blinked at her implication. If they knew to put Tamas
in her livery, they knew about our relationship and knew
to send me a letter under her name.

I began mentally kicking myself. That I had missed
this was bad enough; that Christiana had had to point
it out was even worse. Now I'd never hear the end of it.

"Who knows about us, Drothe?"

"I . . . No one." I shook my head, thinking. "The two
of us, Degan, Josef. Maybe someone who remembers
when we first got to Ildrecca, but I doubt it. It's been too
long—they would have acted on it before this."

"So, whoever hired the assassin just got lucky and
guessed I'm your sister? With no help from you?"

I sat up straighter, not liking what she was implying.
"I don't know," I said. "You're the ex-courtesan. You
know more about people getting lucky than I do."

It was a cheap shot and we both knew it. I deserved
the kick she launched at my shin. That still didn't mean
I let her land it, though.

"You bastard!" she yelled. "You know I don't talk
about family. I was a *courtesan*, not a whore like you're
used to. I catered to my patrons' minds as well as their
bodies, and as hard as it might be for you to believe, talking about my brother the criminal was never a part of

that. Do you honestly think I'd risk what I have here and at court just to talk about *you*?"

I was opening my mouth to make things worse when Josef cleared his throat.

"Ah, if I may ... " he said.

"Yes?" said Christiana as she and I continued to glare at each other.

"You're both assuming whoever is behind this knows about your ... relationship," he said. He tapped the letter I had handed him earlier. "This doesn't mention that at all. If anything, it reads more formally than most of the baroness's correspondence with you, sir. More of a summons than a letter, if you will."

"There's a difference between the two when it comes to my sister?" I said.

Josef coughed discreetly.

"So they may not know anything about our blood," said Christiana.

"Just our business," I concluded.

"Which is bad enough for me, but still more manageable."

"Oh, thank the Angels for that!" I said caustically as I got out of the chair and walked across the room. I rested a hand on the back of Josef's chair and looked over his shoulder. Christiana glided over to his other side.

"What else can you tell me about that letter?" I said.

Josef had three pieces of paper before him on the desk: my letter and two other crisp, clean documents.

"I'm no expert, to be sure," said Josef, pointing to the letter Tamas had delivered, "but it seems to me that someone went to a good deal of effort to produce this forgery."

"So it *is* a forgery?" I said.

"Drothe!" said Christiana. "How many times do I have to tell you I didn't write that letter?"

"You haven't denied it until now," I pointed out. "Besides, it's easy enough to ambush a messenger, then alter the letter." I stared down at the letter, then at the other two documents. The hand looked identical on each page.

"How can you tell?" I asked Josef.

"It's small things," he said. "Most of it is very well-done, but you can see errors in the characters for distinction and address. Here, in *iro* and *mneios*, and, let's see ... Oh, and there, in *phai*—far too light a hand. The style is close, but the calligraphy is from a different school than madam's or my own."

I looked where he indicated. I thought I saw a difference but couldn't be sure. I nodded knowingly, nonetheless.

"What else?" I asked.

"Well, the chop is flawed; or rather, it's not flawed." Josef flipped my letter and one of the adjacent documents over. Each had a red blob of sealing wax impressed with a copy of Christiana's baronial widow's chop.

"The chop on your letter is false," said Josef. "The baroness's has a chip missing in the lower-right corner. There is no such flaw in the other seal."

"A flaw in my sister's seal?" I said, bending closer to see it. "I'm surprised you haven't been flogged, Josef."

"It was done on purpose," said Christiana. "To prevent problems like this."

I gave a slight bow of my head—leave it to Christiana to think of something like that.

"And then there's the paper," said Josef. "It's, well, too fine." He said it almost apologetically.

"Too fine?" said Christiana and I, almost in unison. Her voice was incredulous, while mine was full of amusement.

"For this type of missive," said Josef quickly. "It's too good for ... That is to say, the paper is not what ..."

Christiana's eyes narrowed. "Ye-es?"

Josef took a deep breath and started over. "This isn't the type of paper a person would use for simple correspondence. Its texture and weight are too good. This is the kind of paper used for fine volumes, or maybe imperial documents. It's far too valuable to be, uh, well, wasted on a simple invitation."

I reached down and felt one of the clean sheets of paper, then my own. It was hard to tell because of all the wear and tear, but the stuff of my letter did seem weightier. Christiana did the same, nodding her agreement with Josef's conclusion.

I straightened up, taking my letter and refolding it. I put it back in my sleeve.

Christiana was studying me. "You know who did this?"

"No. But I know where to start." Baldezar—damn that arrogant scribe, anyhow.

"I want them dead, Drothe. All of them."

"Of course you do," I said. Whoever was behind this knew about Christiana and me, at least on some level. Any threat to her reputation was a threat to her status, and I was one of the bigger threats her reputation faced. "But it's not that easy."

Christiana crossed her arms and arched an eyebrow at me. "Really? And why not?"

"Because whoever sent Tamas—the assassin—gave him glimmer. Magic. That means money and connections. That means they're willing to risk the empire sniffing around if their man gets caught." I shook my head. "Frankly, I'm not worth that kind of risk."

"I could have told you that."

"Notice I'm not arguing. But my point is, the person I have in mind doesn't have the resources or clout to hire someone of Tamas's caliber, let alone hand him a piece of glimmer."

Christiana shrugged, her shoulders rising and falling in the curtain of her hair. "So just hold the forger's feet in a. . . ." She stopped, and I could almost hear the pieces clicking together in her head. "It's that *scribe* of yours, isn't it? The one you've had doing the documents for me. Damn it, Drothe! I told you to find someone you could trust."

I had to laugh at that. "You expected me to find a *trustworthy* forger? Ana, listen to yourself. I found someone who's reliable and good at what he does; that's as good as you're going to get with a Jarkman. And because he's reliable, he's going to be hard to crack. He doesn't give up his clients easily."

"He didn't seem to have a problem giving you up."

I nodded. "I know, which is what is going to make this interesting."

Chapter Eleven

The sun was tinting the east with purple and pink when
Baldezar arrived at his shop. Some of his younger
apprentices had been there for an hour already, grinding
pigments, sorting papers, and gathering glair from the
egg whites they had wrung through sponges the night
before. I had waited across the street beneath a book-
binder's eaves. I'd nearly nodded off twice, and had only
managed to stay awake by chewing a handful of ahrami.
Now, though, just the sight of the scribe was enough to
quicken my heart.

I stepped across the street and slipped up behind Baldezar as he opened the door to his shop.

"Bene lightmans, Jarkman," I said as I put a hand between his shoulders and shoved. He stumbled across the
threshold and fell to his knees. I stepped in behind him
and shut the door. Throughout the shop, the apprentices
froze, their eyes wide.

Baldezar spun around on the floor. His face was already turning red, both from anger and embarrassment.
His mouth was a dark scowl.

"How dare you!" he said as he began to gather his
feet beneath him. "What do—"

I stepped forward and kicked out, catching him just
inside the left shoulder with my foot. I held back on purpose, not wanting to break anything at this point. Right
now, I was just setting the tone.

Baldezar went over backward. I heard his head strike

the floor with a hollow *thunk*. He relaxed but didn't go entirely limp. Dazed but not unconscious—good.

I reached behind me and locked the door to the street. "The shop is closed," I said to the apprentices. "No one comes or goes until I'm finished. Is that clear?" They all nodded. I pointed to a corner. "Sit there. Don't move." They didn't quite fall over themselves getting to the corner, but it was close.

I bent down and pulled Baldezar to his feet. "We need to have a talk," I told him as he shook his head, trying to clear it. "Upstairs."

Baldezar turned and walked unsteadily toward the steps. I followed behind, a hand on his back to steady him as much as to reinforce the threat.

He fumbled briefly with the latch before opening the door to his office. Baldezar settled in heavily behind his reading table, rubbing at the back of his head. I stood, hand on the back of the chair that faced him. One of the apprentices had opened the shutters earlier in preparation for their master's arrival. The room was a strange mixture of gentle morning light and leftover shadows.

"This had better be good," he said, managing to summon a sliver of his normally imperious tone.

"Yes," I said, taking the forged letter out of my sleeve. I unfolded it and set it on the table in front of him. "It had better be."

He stared down at it for a long moment. Finally, he picked up the paper, holding it gently between his thumbs and forefingers.

"I take it," he said dourly, "you think I did this."

"The thought had occurred, yes."

"Then the thought would be wrong."

I leaned on the chair. It creaked under my weight. "I'm not in the mood for hints and vagaries, Jarkman."

Baldezar touched the back of his head gently. "I'd gathered as much." He wet his lips, then set the letter back down. "Since I don't know the context of this forgery, I can only guess it was used to get you somewhere for some reason. The text is clear on that much. But the reason you're here is because whoever wrote the letter used the name, writing, and chop of a certain noble-woman with whom we both know you do business."

"Which puts the person behind the letter into a very small circle of someones."

Baldezar nodded. "Yes. And my having done work for both you and her in the past, and having access to her writing through you" — he shook his head — "a very neat line, I admit."

"But?" I said.

"But I'm not stupid. That's the key." Baldezar eased gently back in his chair. "I've been forging documents for decades, Drothe. Bills of lading, imperial trade waiv-ers, letters of passage, contracts, tax stamps, diplomatic negotiations . . . More documents than I can name, and most of them far more dangerous than a simple letter of summons. If I've been able to keep nobles, ambassadors, tax masters, and imperial ministers from tracing things back to me, do you really think I would make it this easy for you? Forgers die if they give people easy trails to follow."

"Normally, yes," I said. "Except when they expect the recipient of the forgery to end up dead."

"Murder? Is *that* it?" Baldezar shook his head. "I'm surprised you settled for knocking me down. The more traditional response would have been to run me through, would it not?"

"Dusting people is easy," I said. "Getting answers is a bit more tricky. Corpses make it even harder."

"Very pragmatic," observed Baldezar. "But I'm prag-matic as well. By all accounts, you're a hard man to kill, Drothe. How many attempts now — two, three?"

"More," I said.

Baldezar nodded. "Precisely. And I'm to think I will be the exception? I would have to consider the possibil-ity you might live, and that you might get your hands on this letter. That's too clear a road back to me."

"Unless you were in a hurry. People make mistakes when they're rushed."

"True, but what's the hurry? Why would I even want to kill you in the first place?"

"It wouldn't have to be you," I said. I pointed at my sister's forged signature. "You do this kind of thing for hire."

"Yes. And I like to be able to spend the money I get for it, too. Besides," he said, flicking at the paper, "this is substandard workmanship. I wouldn't turn out something this poorly done, no matter whether my life were on the line or no."

I thought back to what Josef had said about the letter. "The flaws were minor at best," I said, "and damn hard to find."

"But you *found* them," said Baldezar. "A good forgery should be able to withstand an amateur's scrutiny. This did not." He pointed at various spots on the page. "Improper forms here, here, and here. Inconsistent pen strokes on the third and fifth lines. And at least two scraped and redone stylistic errors I can see at a glance. This is beginner's work. Forging is as much art as it is duplication; whoever did this was a copyist, not an artist."

"Whoever it was had access to Baroness Sephada's letters," I pointed out. "And he knew about our business arrangement. That still points to you."

Baldezar nodded. "Yes, and that's what troubles me. It means someone either gained access to my office, or someone in my shop is involved. Either way, I'm not pleased. But I have no reason to want you dead."

Baldezar studied the letter again, then held it out to me. "I've explained to you why I wouldn't have done this, Drothe, but I can't prove it to you. It's a forgery, and that's what I do. But I'm an excellent forger, and this *isn't* an excellent forgery."

If it had been anyone besides Baldezar, I would have laughed in his face at that explanation. But it *was* Baldezar, and I had been dealing with him long enough to know he was right; he couldn't put out a bad document even if he wanted to. His ego wouldn't allow it.

I took the letter from his hands and leaned in close.

"All right," I said. "Even if you didn't do it, I'm thinking the information about the baroness and me came from here. Find out how they got it and who they are, or I might be less 'pragmatic' my next visit."

"Not to worry," said Baldezar. "We're both victims in this. I want whoever did this as much as you do."

I grinned darkly. "I doubt that very much, Jarkman. Very much, indeed."

The sun was a good two hand spans above the horizon when I finally made it home and crawled into bed. Ideally, I could have used ten hours or so of sleep, but my brain was having none of it. Dreams of fighting, falling, sewers, and giant pen-wielding Angels filled my head. By midafternoon, I decided to cut my losses and crawl back out into the day.

I had a quick bite at Prospo's, checked for messages with three of my usual drops, and began working the streets. Not surprisingly, half of the rumors I gathered in the first two hours dealt with me—or, more specifically, with Tamas's attempt on me, and what it had meant. When you have a running fight in your own front yard, the locals are going to notice. Little of what I heard was accurate, some was downright wrong, and a few people even seemed surprised to see me alive.

I wrote that last reaction off to overblown accounts of the fight—until I ran into Betriz. Like me, Betriz was a Nose, Wide to my Narrow, and like most Noses, she told me something I didn't want to hear.

"Street says you're holding out on Nicco." She said it matter-of-factly as she popped an olive into her mouth. She had six more on the tips of her fingers—the easiest way to carry the snack she had purchased moments before.

"*What?*" I said. "Holding out how?"

Betriz was a long, lean woman, with deep brown eyes and the knowing smile of a Nose. She swallowed her olive and showed me that smile now.

"Whispers are you found a Snilch in Nicco's house

and haven't told him," she said, licking the brine from her lips. "That true?"

I stared at her, my face impassive even as my mind raced. The Snilch rumor was supposed to be soft, dying — not making the circuit with other information brokers. I'd had Mendross put out the word to kill it. What in the hell was Betriz doing with it?

"You're a fool," she said, reading my silence. "You, of all people, should know better than to hold out on Nicco, Drothe."

"I'm not . . ." I began, then stopped. I took a deep breath and started over. "I'm doing my damn job, which you, of all people, should understand: I'm separating the bull from the shit. I'm keeping Nicco from tearing his own organization apart to look for something that isn't there. There's nothing solid on this. The last thing I need is for him to start swinging ham-handedly at anything that catches his suspicion."

Betriz arched a sun-faded eyebrow. "The last thing *you* need?"

"Me, the organization, everyone."

"Uh-huh." She didn't sound completely convinced.

"Where'd you hear this?" I said.

"Oh, you know . . ." Betriz gestured vaguely with an olive-tipped finger. "Around."

"Mm-hmm," I said. "How much?"

Betriz beamed down at me. "That's what I love about you, Drothe — you know how to cut through the bullshit."

I paid Betriz, got a handful of names, and spent the rest of the afternoon tracking rumors. Fortunately, there weren't a lot to find. The rumor about me and Nicco was young yet, and the one on the Snilch still fairly mild. I talked to some people, paid off some others, and put the lean on a couple more. It wouldn't solve anything permanently, I knew, but it might give me some working room.

If I wanted to fight these rumors — if I wanted to keep Nicco from digging into his own organization, not to mention holding my feet to the fire for not telling him about the whispers—I needed to come to him with something bigger, something better. I needed to be able to stand in front of him with names and answers and maybe even a body or two, so that I could tell him that instead of chasing after rumors, I had spent my time getting results.

Success was my best argument now, but to get that success, I needed to go to back into Ten Ways.

Word of my previous visit to Ten Ways had already gotten around. The locals had tagged me as Nicco's man, and some even blamed me for Fedim's death. The irony of the latter was not lost on me.

Few of the local Kin had any interest in talking to me. Being Nicco's Nose was almost the same as being Nicco himself in that cordon, and most Tenners would rather be gut-stabbed than help a foreign boss.

Still, hawks have a way of starting conversations. And, as it turned out, so did mentioning Rambles's name.

Rambles, it seemed, had been stepping on more toes than anyone could count. According to the street, he'd come in, set up shop, and begun acting as if Nicco's tenuous holdings were a bastion of criminal strength. Sure, he needed to throw some weight around and reestablish Nicco's presence in the cordon, but that didn't mean he could roll over the native talent, push out local operators, and call the neighboring gangs to heel like a pack of misbehaving dogs. Nicco—and by extension, Rambles— didn't have the clout to pull off something like that in Ten Ways.

I needed to talk to Rambles to see what the hell was going on. Nicco hadn't wanted me to pay a call on him, but, if Rambles was going to make my job harder, I wanted to know why he was doing it in such a damn efficient manner.

Rambles's people, it turned out, were depressingly easy to find, and his base of operation not much harder. He had established himself in the back of a gaming den, one floor above a milliner's shop. The gambling room wasn't so much a cover as a source of income, I gathered, given the ready action in the place. I passed among the tables to the back of the room, where a big Cutter was busy making the door he guarded look small.

"Rambles in?" I asked as I came up. My hand went out for the handle, was engulfed by a slab of meat with fingers before it reached it.

"He's out."

I looked meaningfully at the light showing beneath the door. As I watched, a shadow passed across the sliver of illumination from the other side.

"Uh-huh," I said. I gave my hand a slight tug, but it stayed where it was. "Well, in case he isn't, you may want to tell him Drothe is here. He'll be in for me."

"He ain't, and he won't be. Not for you."

That told me something: Rambles had heard I was in Ten Ways, and had given orders that I was to be kept away. Interesting.

I tilted my head back and met the Cutter's eyes. He smiled, showing yellowed teeth. *Try me,* the smile said, *please.*

"You got a name?" I said.

More teeth.

"Any idea when he'll be back?"

Teeth again.

"Should I be talking slower?"

He scowled and squeezed my hand. I winced as I felt the bones rub together, but I met his gaze. After a long moment, he let go. I resisted the urge to snatch my hand back and instead let it fall casually to my side.

"Get out," he said.

I stood there just long enough to make him wonder if he'd have to haul me out on his own, then turned and left.

The sky was a deep blue going on black when I stepped outside. Behind me, one of Rambles's people stepped through the door and leaned against the wall beside it. Another one joined him. The second one smiled and waved good-bye. I got the message.

Four blocks later, when I was sure I wasn't being followed, I doubled back and took to the roofs. It was a clear night, with a waning moon that wouldn't be up for hours. Between the early darkness and my night vision, I wasn't worried about any high watch Rambles may have stationed above his building. As it turned out, it didn't matter—the roofs were empty all the way to the milliner's shop.

That gave me pause. Either Rambles was being incredibly confident, or incredibly stupid. And since he wasn't a stupid man, that meant he thought he was safe in Ten Ways—safe enough to not bother putting even one person on the Dancer's Way. This ran counter to the grumblings I'd heard on the street.

That, or it was a trap. Either way, though, I wasn't going to find anything out staring at his shingle-covered peak.

Six dormers, three on a side, poked out from the roofline of his building. A quick investigation showed the windows boarded up on five of the dormers. The sixth, however, had had its boards pried away. It was dark inside, and my night vision showed me signs of squatters from sometime in the past. Judging by the dust and bird nests, no one had been up here in a while.

I slipped inside and crept along carefully, worried as much about finding a rotted board as about making noise. The damp odor of mold and bitter scent of bird droppings filled the place, tickling my nose. Below me, I could hear the shouts and curses and clatter of the gaming room coming up through the floor. Farther along, the noises faded to a murmur, then a hum. I knelt and put my head close to the floor. The faint buzz of two people in conversation came to me.

It occurred to me as I knelt there, trying to make out even a fraction of what was being said, that I didn't know for sure it was Rambles in the room below. I was just going on instinct, a shadow beneath a doorframe, and the Cutter's bad attitude. And even if it was Rambles down there, he could just as easily be spending the evening with his whore as talking about anything I cared about. Hell, odds favored the former, to be honest.

I smiled to myself in the darkness. Well, it wouldn't be the first time I got a face full of dust and dried bird droppings on my clothes while Nosing. Creeping around on long shots was part of the job.

Nothing—or, more precisely, not enough of something came to me through the attic's floor. The conversation was tantalizingly distinguishable, just not understandable. I drew out the listening cup I kept in my herb wallet—a short, fluted tin tube I'd had since my days as a Wide Nose—and looked around more carefully. Seeing a faint sliver of light shining up through the floorboards, I crawled to it, then laid myself prone, my ear to the cup and the cup to the light.

Better.

"...the damn cordon," Rambles was saying. "I'm supposed to be getting things in order here, not taking them over the edge."

"Funny," said another voice. "I could have sworn you were trying for the exact opposite."

I started to take an involuntary breath, then stopped myself before I ended up with a mouth full of dust. I knew that voice—deep, gravelly, with the mildest irreverence riding beneath the surface. Last time I'd heard it, it had been coming down through a sewer grate rather than up through a crack in the ceiling. I didn't have a name or a face to put to it, but I recognized it from the conversation Degan and I had overheard beneath the street outside Fedim's.

What the hell was *he* doing here with Rambles?

I heard Rambles make a noise, maybe a laugh or a cough. "And your people have nothing to do with it, right?"

"*Her* people aren't the problem here," said the other man. "*Yours* are. They're thick on the street and leaning hard. People expected Nicco to react, yes, but not like this. Ten Ways Kin are spitting when they speak his name, lad; that, or spitting on their steel as they hone it. What you're doing, it's too—"

"Too much like him?" said Rambles.

"Too heavy, too fast."

"Then it's just what he'd want," said Rambles. "Nicco likes results, and I'm not about to put my neck on the line for your timetable. You're the ones who stirred things up in the first place—don't blame me if the locals aren't playing the tune you set out. As far as *my* boss is concerned, as long as I don't start a war, he's happy."

There was a pause. "You *do* know it might well come down to that?"

"What—my starting it, or a war happening?"

"Either way."

This time I did take an involuntary breath and barely kept from choking. A Kin war in Ten Ways? The blood would flow in rivers. In most other cordons, a gang war could be kept among the Kin, leaving the Lighters out of it. The empire might notice, but, as long as we spent our time putting knives in one another, it didn't really care.

Ten Ways, though, was a different animal. The local gangs would take a full-scale war as an excuse to settle old scores, even if they weren't directly involved. Nor would they make as fine a distinction between Kin and Lighter; any slight, real or imagined, would be cause enough for vengeance. And it would only spiral out from there.

Too many riots had begun in Ten Ways for the empire to ignore a gang war in the cordon. At the first hint of anything larger than a turf battle, the empire would send the legions in, all Black Sashes and swinging swords. And if the legions couldn't handle it, well, then the White Sashes would wade in, just as they had when they threw down Isidore, the Dark King.

I shuddered. No, best not to think about the Whites.

I let out my breath slowly, suppressing a cough. My mouth tasted like dust and bird droppings; dry, gritty, with acid and vinegar mixed in. I grimaced, tried to summon up enough spit to move some of it out, and failed. I wanted nothing so much as a long drink and a good coughing fit, but neither was an option—not while Rambles and his friend were talking below.

"I thought it wasn't supposed to come to a war," Rambles was saying. I noted he didn't sound terribly surprised at his visitor's announcement.

"Aye, well, there've been some new ... considerations ... brought into the mix. It's not just a matter of playing the locals off against one another anymore."

"You mean you aren't the only ones trying to manipulate the Kin in Ten Ways," said Rambles smugly. "You're having to deal with other players now."

"Down, lad. It's not what you think," said the other man. "We *wanted* some of the other Upright Men and Rufflers to take notice. Nothing against your boss, but even he's not a big enough threat on his own to motivate a cordon like Ten Ways. We needed the Kin here to feel threatened, to have a reason to start acting like a single entity, rather than a bunch of warring gangs. But you're going too far. Kin on the edge of Nicco's territory are getting anxious. They're looking for protection from other Uprights when we want them to come to you."

"I can't offer people protection if I don't have a stable base, damn it!" said Rambles. "Nicco has to have enough clout in the cordon to be seen as a refuge. That's what I'm working on. *You're* the ones who've been pushing Ten Ways from every direction, prodding gangs into turf wars and playing with local politics. If you hadn't put the Kin here so on edge, they wouldn't be trying to cut my damn nose off every time I stuck it out."

I chuckled silently at the analogy, appreciating it far more than Rambles ever could. It was a mistake. The sharp movement of air in my throat started it itching. My chest convulsed once, twice. I took a slow, deep breath and held it, trying to force the cough down.

"If they're that worked up, we may need to give them something else to think about," said the man.

"Such as?"

There was a pause. My chest was still convulsing. I let my breath out in slow, shallow gasps, hoping to ease the pressure.

"It may be time to see just how far an Upright Man can be pushed," said the man.

"You mean into war?" said Rambles.

"If we have—"

That was when the cough came. I clamped my mouth shut and locked my teeth together. No good. All I accomplished was to turn the cough into a snort. I quickly put a hand over my face. The listening tube shifted beneath me, tipped over. Another snort. I grabbed for the tube with my free hand and put it back over the crack.

Silence.

Then the man said, "Rats?"

"Rats don't sneeze."

More silence. Then I heard something fall to the floor, followed by a muttered curse.

"Shit!" said Rambles. "Screw sneaking up on him. Just go. Go!"

I jumped up and ran, ducking beneath beams and leaping over debris. Below, I heard voices and the sound of feet thudding on floorboards. I wasn't sure where the stairs leading up from the second floor were, but I was certain they had a quick way up here. I dodged around a portion of floor that had felt weak earlier and veered toward the window.

I was just putting a leg through when the chamber began to grow brighter behind me. I was aware of feet pounding up steps, Rambles yelling, and some sort of light source being brought up. I slipped over the sill, ducked around the edge of the dormer, and scanned the roof. No one coming up over the eaves or down from the peak.

Leaving then would have been the smart move. Instead, I scrambled partway up the roof, slipped over to the dormer, and peak-walked out to the edge. Then I sat down, straddling the dormer's ridge, and looked down at the window I had just exited. I drew my rapier.

Light shone out the window now, bright in the early-evening darkness. I blinked several times, letting my night vision settle down.

Beneath me, I heard Rambles curse again as he found the evidence of my presence left in the filth. There sounded to be at least four of them in there, maybe more.

A shadow moved across the window, and I readied my blade. I didn't want to dust anyone so much as to persuade them not to follow me. If I were lucky, it would be Rambles sticking his head out; I had some questions for him.

A head wearing a gray flat cap came out of the window, followed by a broad pair of shoulders in a tan and gold doublet. The head turned from side to side, looking along the roof. I caught glimpses of short steely gray hair.

"Anything?" called Rambles from inside.

The head began to shake, then paused. Slowly, he twisted until he was looking up at me. He had a broad nose and a prominent jaw. No obvious scars, but I could tell it was a fighter's face—hard, solid, not afraid to be hit. He saw my rapier poised above him and smiled slowly, showing small, even teeth.

"We won't be catching him tonight," he said in the deep, gravelly voice I knew from the sewers; the voice I now had a face to put to. "Not without a lot of pain and trouble, anyhow."

"Shit!" said Rambles. "We need to know how much he heard. Who he was working for."

The man raised an eyebrow. I pretended to study my rapier, then shook my head. He shrugged, glanced inside, and gave me a questioning look. Could he go back in?

I debated. I was in a good position, wanted answers, and might not get a better chance. However, I didn't know whether or not Rambles had people moving toward the roof even now. Nor could I count on Rambles's going easy on me just because we both worked for Nicco. Our mutual dislike aside, it was obvious he had a side deal going with the man below me, if not an out-right partnership. Depending on how much or how little Nicco knew about it, Rambles might not be inclined to let me walk away.

No, best to get away while I could. Sticking around, no matter how tempting, could get me in far worse trouble than I cared to court.

"Name?" I said to the man.

He considered a moment. "Ironius," he said. "You?"

I grinned and said, "Tell Rambles his favorite Nose said, 'Bene darkmans.'" Then I leaned back from the edge, vanishing from his sight, and took to the roofs. I didn't get down off them until I was safely inside Stone Arch cordon.

Chapter Twelve

I spent half the night trying to find Nicco after that, only to learn that he had left town at sunset. He had retired to his villa outside the city with a new whore and left strict instructions not to be disturbed. I had been tempted to hike out there regardless, but the off-duty bodyguard I'd spoken to had made it clear I would be wasting my time. At best, I would end up with a pair of sore feet, at worst, a mouthful of loose teeth.

No one was getting in to see Nicco; the man took his whoring seriously.

Still, if I couldn't get to him, neither could Rambles. Not the best solace, but it would have to do, at least until sunrise. And in the meantime, I could go see a man about a rope.

Entering the Raffa Na'Ir cordon is like walking into the Despotate of Djan, except you don't have to sail across the Corsian Passage or brave the wastes of the southern Imperial Frontier. In the Raffa Na'Ir, there are no carved angels watching over the squares, no temples to the three incarnations of the emperor. Instead, small rectangular plaques are set in the walls at every street corner, each depicting a member of the family of wandering gods the Djanese worship. Immigrant Djanese throng the streets, buying, trading, stealing, and living much as they would in their own land, save they are even more aware of the imperial sons and daughters who walk among them. In the camp of the enemy, one must always be vigilant.

I made my way through the darkened ways of the cordon without concern. The empire was in one of its intermittent periods of peace with the Despotate of Djan, meaning resentment toward Imperials was at a low ebb. That didn't mean I wasn't a target for theft, confidence games, or even a simple social tap across the back of my head, but no one was likely to dust me just because of my parentage. During war, the risks went up, but, even then, the locals knew it was better to dust Imperials outside the cordon rather than in it. They were here on sufferance, after all.

I found Jelem sitting in front of the Café Lumar with four of his countrymen. Lamps hung from the wooden lattices overhead, providing a patchwork of soft light and deep shadows on the patio. Each man had a small brass cup and matching pot full of coffee at hand. Two had water pipes within easy reach as well. Even from the street, I could smell the mixture of burning herbs and ghannar—a mild narcotic favored by many of the Djanese.

They were playing *aja*, a Djanese game involving marked bone chits, dice, and a complex system of betting I've never been able to get the hang of. In my opinion, there are less confusing ways to lose money.

I paused at the edge of the patio to let my eyes adjust. Jelem looked up and smiled, his teeth shining white in the walnut darkness of his face. As usual, he had an air of disinterest about him, as if nothing were quite important enough to demand his full attention. He half sat, half lay in his chair, the long, dark fingers of one hand idly playing with a chit while his other hand stroked the needlework on his crimson vest. His slippered feet, just visible beneath a long cream-colored tunic, were crossed at the ankles. Even the sharp lines of his face seemed to blur and soften in the lamplight. But for all the ease and dispassion his body implied, it was his eyes that I paid attention to—two flat, dull chips of blackness, as hard as the rest of him seemed soft; calculating eyes; magician's eyes.

"Bene darkmans, Drothe," said Jelem. "I hear you've been looking for me." The other men at the table looked at me the way they might acknowledge a cockroach that had just crawled from beneath the table.

Relations between the Kin and the *Zakur*, the Djanese underworld in Ildrecca, have always been guarded. They pay their share to us (mostly), and we leave them alone (mostly). My artifact smuggling occasionally puts me in closer dealings with the *Zakur* than most other Kin, but it doesn't mean I have any more clout with them. They're Djanese; I'm Imperial. It's a basic fact neither side forgets.

Jelem is one of the few exceptions. He'll work for anyone if the price is right.

I nodded to Jelem. "Bene darkmans," I said. "Can you drag yourself away?"

Jelem glanced down at the unclaimed pile of coins in the middle of the table, then at the chit he had placed before him a few moments ago. "Now isn't the best time, Drothe."

My face remained expressionless as I reached into the bag I was carrying and drew out the rope I had retrieved from my rooms — Tamas's rope. I tossed the coiled mass onto the table.

I hadn't known what would happen, just that I wanted to get Jelem's attention. It worked.

The rope landed on the chit in front of Jelem, shattering the bone with a loud *crack*. Pieces flew across the table, skipping off coins and sending gamblers scampering.

"*Whoreson Imperial!*" they shouted at me in Djanese. "*Camel fucker!*" "*Gods damned stealer of shit!*" Then there was the usual litany about my parentage. But none of them came at me. I was here to see Jelem, and they knew better than to cross him.

I pretended not to understand what they were saying and instead watched Jelem. Of all the men at the table, only he had remained seated during the display.

He quietly regarded the smoking rope, then reached out to gingerly pick it up between the knots.

"I'll be sitting out the next few hands," said Jelem in Djanese as he pushed out his chair and stood up.

The other men grumbled and glared at me as they returned to the table, dark eyes simmering with anger. I gave them a sneering smile in return and turned away.

Jelem and I settled in at a small table against the outside wall of the café. A boy stuck his head out of the front door to see what all the commotion was about, and I waved him over. I ordered in Djanese: a pot of coffee for myself, another for Jelem, and whatever light fare they had in the kitchen. The boy ducked back out of sight, and I let myself relax into the thin cushions of the chair.

I remained silent as Jelem examined the rope. He ran it lightly through his fingers, over and over, always avoiding the knots, whole or charred. Now and then, he mumbled something to himself, or to the rope—I wasn't sure which.

Through the wall, I could hear soft, rhythmic music and the low hum of voices coming from inside the café.

"I see some of the spells have been used," said Jelem at last.

"I can vouch for that firsthand."

Jelem glanced up at me, raising an eyebrow in appreciation. "Not Nicco's, I assume?"

"Not his style." I frowned. "Why?"

Jelem shrugged. "He's one of the few people I can see affording this. But yes, if he were after you, you'd either be dead or two days away from the city by now."

"The Blade's name was Tamas," I said.

"Any idea who hired him?"

Our coffee arrived then. Jelem and I regarded each other as the boy filled our cups and left.

"That's why I'm here," I said.

"Ah," said Jelem. He looked back down at the rope, *tsk*ed, and set it aside. Then he took a long sip of coffee. "This isn't good."

I knew he wasn't talking about the coffee.

I'm told there are a lot of different ways to categorize magic, but, when it comes to the Kin, we have only three labels that matter: legal, illegal, and imperial.

Legal glimmer is something we ignore. There's no money in it. Between the Imperial Cult, which has things like blessings, the comforting of souls, and "miraculous" salves sewn up, and the Sodality of Street Mouths, which has a lock on mending spells, wart removal, luck charms, and other day-work glimmer, there's no room to maneuver.

Illegal glimmer, though, is another story. It's been one of the monetary cornerstones of the Kin for ages. Need someone hurt without leaving a mark? A stone building fired? A rival's shipment to rot on the docks? There are people who can speak that kind of spell—for a price. A *high* price.

And for an even higher price, a piece of portable glimmer can be made—magic that anyone can use; magic that can hurt or break or kill with hardly any effort on the user's part; magic that was banned three centuries ago after the Golem Riots of Nimenia. Magic that will, in short, get you hanged if you're found with it on your person.

As for imperial glimmer, well, even we know better than that. Tweaking the imperial nose with a bit of rope like Tamas's is one thing, but playing with magic that was gifted to the emperor and his court by the Angels, magic that could level buildings or burn a forest to the ground in a matter of minutes? Let's put it this way: People who make or use portable glimmer die; people who play with imperial glimmer become examples—*lasting* examples, for decades or longer.

Tamas's rope was the portable kind of glimmer.

"I need to find out who sent the Blade after me," I said. "Finding the person who made that rope might help. You know portable glimmer, so ..." I let the sentence trail off meaningfully.

"Not possible," said Jelem, his eyes focused on the

coffee in the cup before him. "*Yazani*, or Mouths as you like to call them, don't leave their names on the things they make. At least, the smart ones don't, and I suspect whoever made this rope is smart."

"Then how do the Paragons track them down?"

Jelem shrugged. "I'm not an imperial magician: I don't know."

I poured myself another cup of coffee.

"However . . . " Jelem said.

I grinned. I had suspected there was more to it than a simple "no."

"That doesn't mean I can't take a look at the rope itself."

"For a price?" I said.

"Even so."

"How much?" I asked.

Jelem spread his hands in a single, elegant motion. "Hard to say. It will depend on how complex the magic is. Once I have a better idea of who glimmered the rope, I can better—"

"Wait a minute," I said. "I thought you said you couldn't tell who made it."

"I did."

"But—"

Jelem held up a hand. "Bide."

I leaned forward in my chair. "Don't you tell *me* to bide. If you're playing me—"

"No," said Jelem, pointing past me. "*Bide*. Your food is here."

I looked up and almost put my face into the plate coming past my shoulder. It veered away at the last moment, and the boy smiled apologetically as he adjusted his arm to place my dinner before me.

It was a salad of nuts, leafy greens, and sliced fruit, all tossed with a spiced oil. He set down a stack of flat bread beside it, along with a bowl of chopped peppers and softened beans marinated in red vinegar. Typical Djanese fare.

As the boy bowed and walked away, I suddenly realized just how hungry I was. I tore into the repast with relish. Jelem laughed indulgently, commenting on the superiority of Djanese food compared to imperial fare. I shrugged noncommittally, as my mouth was too full to answer.

After a few minutes, I slowed my pace somewhat. A new pot of coffee arrived, and I used its sharp flavor to cut the sweet heat of the salad oil. Now that I was bothering to taste it, the food was excellent. I said as much to Jelem.

"Of course," he said, smiling broadly. "You think I would frequent just any café?" He leaned in closer. "Besides, the owner is my wife's second cousin—their whole family are excellent cooks. Ahnya would never forgive me if ate anywhere else."

I smiled in turn. The image of Jelem's small, delicate, yet fiery wife, Ahnya, berating the Mouth for snubbing her family was a picture I could easily imagine.

I leaned back in my own seat, tore off a small strip of flat bread, and decided to take advantage of Jelem's relaxed frame of mind.

"You were saying," I said as I dipped the bread into the beans and peppers, "something about Tamas's rope?"

Jelem sighed and closed his eyes. "I had said I could not find out who made the item, which is true. What I can do, however, is try to find out *how* they made it. There are only so many ways to gather magic and weave it into something like this."

"And how does knowing how it was made help us?" I said.

Jelem opened his eyes and regarded me with the same expression he might use for a pheasant that had asked why it was being eaten. "'How' tells us which style of magic the maker used," he explained. "'How' tells us what degree of ability the maker had. 'How' tells us how much, roughly, someone is willing to spend on killing you. And 'how' tells me—maybe—how to make more of these charming little baubles." He tapped the rope.

"The magic is keyed to the runes. That ought to make it easier to unravel."

I looked at the pieces of paper—scraps, really—sticking out of the knots. On a hunch, I reached into my pouch and pulled out the strip of parchment I had taken off Athel the Grinner's body.

"What can you make of this?" I said.

Jelem took the battered slip of paper in his long fingers and held it up to the light of a lamp hanging above us.

"It means nothing to me," he said after a moment. "Why?"

I took back the paper. "I haven't been able to figure out what's written on it. It just occurred to me it may be some sort of notation or script used in glimmering."

"If it is, I've never seen its like before."

"I've been getting a lot of that lately," I said. I looked at the paper again in the dim light. It looked the same as before—dots, dashes, squiggles, and angles, with the hint of something legible here and there. Except for "imperial" and "relic," though, nothing on it made sense.

"Is it important?" said Jelem.

"It had better be," said a familiar voice off to my right. "Otherwise, he's been doing a lot of chasing for nothing."

I looked up to see Degan stepping onto the porch of the café. He brushed the brim of his hat in Jelem's direction; the Mouth smiled lazily in return.

"Sometimes, nothing is the best thing to chase," said Jelem.

"Drothe's 'nothings' usually carry swords," said Degan, "and come with several well-armed friends."

"Ah," said Jelem. "*That* kind of nothing." He sat up in his chair. "In that case, I think we have 'nothing' further to discuss." Jelem laid his hand on the rope. "We are agreed?" he said.

"We're agreed." I didn't have much of a choice. "Just don't screw me too bad on the price. And make it quick."

Jelem stood, sketching a graceful bow while tracing a

complex spiral pattern in the air. "As the Scions of the Great Family allow," he said. He took the rope, coiled it, and walked back over to his game.

I turned to Degan as he took Jelem's vacated seat. "I've been hoping to catch up with you," I said.

"Must be your lucky night," he said, tearing off a piece of flat bread and running it through the beans. "Or mine."

"I have a name to run by you."

"Oh?"

"'Ironius,'" I said, letting the name of the man we had heard in the sewers of Ten Ways and I had seen at Rambles's drop into the space between us.

Degan froze, the bread poised before his mouth. Without looking at me, he set it back down and stood up.

"We're leaving," he said. Before I could answer, he had turned away and begun walking. I hurried to my feet and followed.

Degan led me through Raffa Na'Ir cordon and out, then into the Hounds, all in silence. I was nearly running at points to keep up with his long, quick stride. Finally, I stopped in a small piazza and leaned a hand against the fountain in the center. I was breathing hard.

"Enough," I said. "Here is good enough."

Degan stopped and looked around, as if not realizing where he had brought me. Perhaps he hadn't. He came over and scooped up a handful of water from the basin in the fountain, sipped, then spit it out onto the bricks of the piazza.

"How'd you come by that name?" he said.

I hesitated for half a second, debating about pushing him to talk first. The hard look in his eyes persuaded me otherwise.

"He was with Rambles," I said.

"Nicco's Rambles?"

"Do you know any other Rambles?" I said. "They were in Ten Ways."

"Doing?"

I told him about the conversation I'd overheard,

about Rambles's apparent arrangement with Ironius, about my brief meeting with the latter on the roof. "Ironius and the woman are working Ten Ways," I finished. "Have been for a while. It sounds as if they're trying to unify the local gangs for some reason."

Degan scowled. "Why?"

"I don't know," I said. "To take over the cordon? No one runs the place right now. But if they're that organized, why waste time on Ten Ways? There are better cordons out there that would be easier to take over."

"Why indeed?" said Degan. He ran his hand over a carved faun's head on the fountain, letting his thumb brush the stream of water coming from it. "What makes the cordon worth going after? Is there something about Ten Ways itself, a reason they need to control the cordon?"

"You mean besides the charming atmosphere?" I said. I'd been asking myself the same question: why try to control a hellhole like Ten Ways, given how hard it would be to bring it together? *If* they could bring it together. "I suppose it would be a nice feather in someone's cap. No one's been able to unite Ten Ways since Isidore, and he went on to become the Dark King. If someone managed to do the same, it would go a long way toward making him look like . . ." I trailed off and looked over at Degan. He was staring back at me.

"That can't be it," I said, almost in a whisper. "Follow in the Dark King's footsteps? Take control of all the Kin in Ildrecca again? That can't be it." The first time had been a work of genius, a miracle, a fluke—no one could repeat that. Could they?

"It doesn't mean someone can't try," said Degan.

I nodded as I connected the dots in my head. "And a war between a couple of Upright Men—like, say Nicco and Kells—would only help. Hell, if done right, it could draw in most of the bosses and Uprights within three cordons of the place."

"That would put almost half of the Kin in Ildrecca at one another's throats," said Degan.

"And get the local element in Ten Ways up in arms, too," I said. "Having the neighbors come in to fight their war wouldn't go over too well."

"It might even be enough to get the Kin in Ten Ways to unite behind someone," said Degan.

"Someone who jingles when she walks and has Ironius in her back pocket," I said sourly. "And all they'd have to do is sit back and wait for everyone else to weaken themselves by fighting one another. Then, when things are at their worst, they step in at the head of the Kin in Ten Ways and take over."

"How very imperial," said Degan.

He was right. It had been working for the empire for centuries—get local kings or chiefs to fight one another, then step in and shore up whoever looks to make the best puppet.

And now someone wanted to do it to the Kin.

"Tell me about Ironius," I said.

"I—" Degan sighed and ran a hand over his face.

"Don't say it," I said.

"I can't."

"Damn it, Degan! How can you *not*?" My voice echoed off the buildings around us. Somewhere, a dog started barking. "This is me, for Angels' sake!"

"Yes, it is," he said, stepping closer, his voice dropping lower. I could barely hear him over the splashing of the fountain. "Which is why I'm telling you to *let this go*. Back off. Report to Nicco and be done with it."

"What?" I forced my voice down to near-normal levels. "If we're right, we're talking about someone orchestrating a Kin war in Ten Ways—maybe even throughout the whole city. And if that happens, you know what comes next."

"We don't know that the empire will step in," he said, not sounding wholly convinced.

"If it even looks like someone is trying to repeat Isidore's climb, it won't just be the Rags hassling us in the streets," I said. "It'll be the legions. The White Sashes. And I'm *not* going to let someone screw with *my* life and *my* livelihood just because he wants a midnight crown on his head."

"You don't know it will come to that," said Degan. "This could just be about Ten Ways. You said yourself it was a fluke with Isidore—that no one can unite the Kin again. Let them set up Nicco. Let *him* go to war. Let *him* die. You've never liked the bastard, anyhow. Get out now."

I looked up at my friend, seeing him, seeing his face in my night vision. I took a step back. "You're scared," I said, barely believing it. "Angels help me, *you're* scared."

Degan grimaced. "Not scared," he said. "Worried."

"About what?"

"About where it will take you. Take us."

"'Where it will take me'?" I said. I nearly laughed, only it wasn't funny. "In case you haven't noticed, things around me have been going from bad to worse over the last couple of days. I don't want your worry right now; I want your help."

Degan's head lunged forward so fast, I nearly fell back. "*I can't help you in this!*" he yelled. "Don't you understand? I *can't*! Not while . . ."

"While what?" I said. *"What?"*

Degan glared at me and turned away. I saw his shoulders rise and fall as he took a breath. "Just let it be," he said. "Please."

And then it hit me, and I got truly angry.

"This is about the Order of the Degans, isn't it?" I said. "You won't tell me anything unless I take your damn Oath!" I reached out and grabbed Degan's arm, spinning him around. He didn't resist. "Fine," I said. "I'll take the damn thing. If that's what you want me to do, I'll do it."

Degan jerked his arm out of my grasp. "It's *not* what I want you to do," he snapped. "And even if I did, that wouldn't be all of it. There are other things at play here besides my being a degan."

"Like friendship?" I said. I threw the words out, using them like a lash. "Like bleeding for each other so many times I've lost count? We've never needed an Oath for any of that!"

Degan winced. I pressed on.

"What the hell is it with you degans and your Oaths?" I said. "Secrets and silence and promises—you're a bunch of fucking Arms, Degan! You lug steel around and dust other people's enemies. If anyone ought to be demanding promises of silence, it's *me*. I'm the Nose here. What's so damn important about Ironius that you can't . . . can't . . ."

And I stopped and stared up at Degan. At *Bronze* Degan. Of course—I was too used to thinking of him as just Degan.

"It isn't 'Ironius,' is it?" I said softly. "It's 'Iron.' He's a degan. He's Iron Degan."

Degan didn't answer, but the look on his face made anything he might have said redundant. Whoever we were working against had a degan on their side. And if Bronze Degan wasn't willing to talk about it, my guess was that Iron Degan and the woman had already exchanged the Oath.

Which meant that if I wanted Degan's help against them, I would have to do the same. The only problem was, I suddenly didn't want to take the Oath anymore.

Chapter Thirteen

"You don't want to do this," said Degan.

No kidding. But it suddenly wasn't about wanting anymore; it was about needing. I needed to take the Oath.

"I have to," I said.

"No, you don't," said Degan.

"Oh?" I said. "And how do you figure that? You've as much as said you can't talk to me about Iron Degan or his business because he's under Oath to whoever that woman is. And it seemed pretty clear in the sewers that unless I'm willing to take that same step, I won't be getting any answers from you on the matter. So, yes, I'd say it's a matter of need."

"I told you before, I don't *know* what Iron or his boss are up to. Your taking the Oath won't change that."

"But you suspect," I said. "You have some ideas about what's going on."

Degan paused. "I have suspicions," he said. "But they're based on who Iron is, not on anything I know."

"And . . . ?" Degan looked down at me in silence. "My point exactly," I said. "You can't even tell me your suspicions without the Oath."

"Drothe, do you realize what taking the Oath means?" said Degan. "For you? For me?"

"It means I owe you," I said. "Big. Really big. And that you can call in your marker at any time. I also know that I get you, not just as a friend, but as a degan, working for me on my payroll. And I get what you know about Iron and his boss, even if it's just an educated guess."

"And you'd be willing to take that deal?"

"Yes," I said. Maybe. It was hard to say, not knowing what Degan knew, but I wasn't going to get anything from him if I didn't take the Oath. That much was clear.

Degan nodded thoughtfully. "And what if I told you that was the street version of the story? What if I told you there was more?"

"How much more?"

"When I say I can ask for anything," Degan said, "I mean *anything*. And I expect you to serve it up on a plate, because that's what I would do for you if I took the Oath. The Oath means I'm willing to put my life on the line, not only for you, but for your interests as declared in the Oath. I'm your man until I die or the Oath is fulfilled. And I expect the same of you when it comes time to call in my side of the bargain. You have to do what I say, without question, without hesitation, even if it goes against what you want or believe in. Even if it means you stand a good chance of being killed. Because we exchanged the Oath, and that's the burden each side carries for the other—me for you, and you for the Order."

"Wait," I said. "What do you mean, the burden I carry 'for the Order'? What do I owe them?"

A ghost of a smile touched Degan's lips. "Just this: If I complete my part of the Oath and die before calling in my 'marker,' or I die in your service, your Oath passes on to the Order of the Degans."

"The *entire* Order?" I said, feeling my insides going into a free fall. Angels, how many degans were there, anyhow?

"To the first degan who decides to call it in." Degan leaned in toward me. "Even, maybe, Iron Degan. How would that turn out, do you think?"

Not well, I realized. But that involved a lot of ifs. It also brought up another question.

"What if someone refuses to fulfill his end of the Oath?" I said. "It has to have come up."

"It has," said Degan.

"And?"

Degan straightened up. "In many ways, the Order of the Degans *is* the Oath. It's what makes us degans. Some of us have been known to give ourselves over for years in fulfilling an Oath. How do *you* think we would react if someone recanted on his end, especially if one of us had lied, cheated, killed, and maybe even died, to fulfill his part of the agreement?"

I shuddered. "That'd be a lot of pissed-off talent," I said.

"And that's only the beginning."

That didn't sound good—as if any of this could.

"We're an old order, Drothe," continued Degan. "And the Oath is an old binding."

I felt my jaw dropping open and stopped it. "Are you saying there's *glimmer* involved?" I said.

"I'm saying it's an old binding. I don't pretend to understand it, but there are stories."

"What kind of stories?"

Degan eyed me coolly and remained silent.

Son of a bitch. Half of me was worried that Degan was playing me, trying to scare me off; the other half was just as worried he wasn't.

"What's your angle in all this?" I said.

"What do you mean?"

"The degans," I said. "What's your angle? How do you come out ahead making deals like this? You said yourself, some of you spend years fulfilling your Oaths. How does getting one service in return even begin to make up for all of that?"

Degan's eyebrows crept up. "Why, we ask for the right service. From the right people."

"The right service for what?"

"The right service for the Order."

I felt my hands balling themselves into fists at my side. "Dammit, Degan!" I snapped. "No games!"

"I'm not playing any. All I can tell you is that the Order of the Degans is content with what it gets in ex-

change for its services, both when it comes to members
hiring out for money or taking an Oath." Degan paused,
then added, "We don't take Oaths from just anyone, after all."

Which hinted at volumes, but said nothing.

"Would you take an Oath from me?" I said.

"I'd rather not."

I didn't know if I was flattered or frightened by the
answer, let alone by what it implied.

Degan read my expression and nodded. "Now you
understand why I don't want you to take the Oath. Because of our friendship and what the Oath may mean to
it. Better for us both if you step away and let things in
Ten Ways—and with Iron—run themselves out."

"Except it's about more than just Ten Ways now," I
said. "There's the whole question of Larrios and Athel
and the book and my relic. Iron Degan and his boss
didn't storm Fedim's shop because they liked crappy
pottery—they wanted whatever Larrios had. And now
I find out they're trying to start a Kin war between
Nicco and Kells in Ten Ways, too? That can't just be
coincidence!"

"You don't know for certain that the two are connected," said Degan. "Larrios and the book and your
relic may have nothing to do with Ten Ways."

"You mean like the scrap of paper we pulled off
Athel?" I said.

Degan opened his mouth to speak, but I held up my
hand.

"Look," I said. "You've scared the shit out of me with
all of this about the Oath, all right? The idea of taking
the Oath, of being bound to perform a service I can't refuse . . ." I shook my head. "I don't even go that far as a
Nose—not with anybody. And then you tell me I would
have to keep the Oath with Iron Degan if you died and
he got to me first? That alone's enough to shy me away
from taking it."

"Good," said Degan, his shoulders relaxing. "Because—"

"Except," I said, "that I wouldn't be taking the Oath

with a degan—I'd be taking it with *you*. I trust you, not only to keep your end of the bargain, but to not take advantage of my end, either. Hell, you've covered my blinds so many times, if you wanted to screw me, you'd have done it by now."

A pained expression crossed Degan's face. "My covering your blinds is worlds different from calling in the Oath, Drothe."

"You've made that painfully clear," I said. "But, really, it all comes down to trust. I trust you. I trust your Oath. And if I thought there was any other way, I wouldn't ask you to do this. But whether you take the Oath with me or not, I'm going to keep pressing, and that means I'll likely come up against Iron Degan and his boss at some point. When that happens, I'd rather have you at my back than not." I held out my hand, palm up. "I want to exchange the Oath with you, Degan."

Degan stared at me so long, I thought he wasn't going to answer.

"We're both a couple of fools," he finally said. "Fools of the first order." His hand came down and clasped my forearm, even as mine closed on his. Then he let go. "Come on, then."

"Where?"

"Where we won't be interrupted when we exchange the damn Oath."

I followed Degan through the streets of Ildrecca as the sun lightened the sky in the east. He didn't seem to be searching for a specific location so much as walking off his frustration.

His disquiet almost made me want to stop, to say that we could forget the Oath, that I would manage on my own. Almost. But I didn't think I could do this without him, especially if I was going to be facing Iron Degan. And what I had said was true—I trusted Degan. I had to believe that he wouldn't let me take the Oath if it wasn't worthwhile, that he wouldn't betray me when it came time to pay. There was too much riding on it to believe otherwise.

We finally turned into a series of alleys called the Cloisters, running along the border between Stone Arch and Lady of the Roses cordons. The alleys were unique in that they had a series of peaked arches running across them at regular intervals, providing not only artistic support for the buildings on either side, but easy bridges for anyone running the roofs.

Degan led me down one alley, into another, then stopped. We stood beneath an ivy-covered arch. He turned around.

Degan drew his sword without preamble and held it by the blade, just below the guard, point down. He placed his other hand on the bronze-chased guard. I gathered I was supposed to do the same, and did so.

The metal was warmer than I expected. I wondered if it had picked up some heat from the sunlight and Degan's body, or if there was another explanation. Then again, maybe my palms were just feeling chilled from the sweat gathering on them. Either way, it didn't matter much at this point.

I looked up at Degan. He stood straight and formal, his eyes hooded in shadow. The look of near-amusement I was so used to seeing on his face was gone. Now he regarded me as he did everyone else on the street — without mercy or friendship. He was no longer my friend; he was Bronze Degan. For the first time in a long time, I remembered what that truly meant. I felt the fear he inspired in others, in those he did not call friend. I felt the weight of the Oath.

I swallowed and tried to clear my throat. It didn't help. "So, how do we do this?" I asked.

"What is the service you wish me to perform?" he said.

Into it that quickly, then. I pulled my gaze away from his and stared at the sword while I ordered my thoughts.

Up close, I could see that the bronze inlays on the guard were immaculate. There was no hint of tarnish or greening there — even around the dents and scratches it had earned in hard service. Fine swirls and broad strokes intermixed in an almost-sylvan pattern against the steel of his guard, suggesting creeping vines, or maybe wind-tossed grasses. The blade itself had a milky quality to it, as if someone had just breathed on the steel and paused before wiping off the condensation. Below the seeming haze were tiny lines and arcs, slightly darker than the rest of the steel, running throughout the blade. Black Isle steel, forged at the monastery of the same name, renowned for its strength and near-legendary ability to hold an edge. It was the best steel that money—or anything else, for that matter—could buy.

I studied the sword and noticed for the first time that a faint teardrop had been etched into the blade, just between where Degan's hand was holding it and where the steel met the guard. I looked back up at Degan.

"I need you to help me settle things in Ten Ways," I said. "No matter who is involved or what the outcome, I need you to stand beside and protect me. And I need you to tell me what you know about what's going on down there, and help me find out whatever we may not know." I paused a moment, then added, "Basically, I need you to cover my blinds and keep my best interests at heart. Again."

Degan clenched and unclenched his jaw a few times. "Is this all you require of me?" he said.

I thought about it. There was plenty more I could add, but I was afraid the more specific I got, the more limited my options might become. Better to keep things loose and mutable, rather than locking myself into something I couldn't amend later. "Yes," I said, "that's all I require of you."

Degan nodded. "Very well. I am willing to be so bound by my Oath as a degan to serve you, in faith as well as in deed. Are you willing to be bound likewise to my service, whenever I should request it and for whatever reason, unable to refuse or evade me? And will you honor this Oath with my brethren, should I perish before I am able to reclaim my payment?"

Visions of Iron Degan calling in my marker, a toothy

grin on his broad face, ran through my mind. "You'd better not die," I said to Degan. A small smile flickered onto his face, then vanished. "Yes, I'm willing to be bound by all that," I said.

Degan nodded curtly. "Since the first days of the degans, through to the present, and until our Order is broken and its members turned to dust, so will it be. As I am bound to your service, so are you bound to mine. My sword stands as a symbol of this covenant."

With that, he turned the sword in his hand so the point was facing up, brought it to his lips, and kissed the steel. Then he held it out to me. I followed suit. The metal was cool on my lips and tasted of oil.

"So be it," said Degan. He wiped his blade on a sleeve and sheathed it.

We stood in silence.

"That's it?" I said at last.

"That's it," said Degan.

"No clap of thunder, no lightning, no wailing spirits in the shadows? After all you told me, I expected something a little more dramatic."

"Sorry to disappoint you. Next time I'll hire a Mouth to fill the streets with fog and glowing lights."

"Don't worry," I said. "There won't be a next time."

"There usually isn't," said Degan.

I wiped my mouth on the back of my hand to remove the last lingering hints of honing oil. "So?" I said.

Degan turned and resumed walking down the alley, this time slowly. I fell in beside him.

"Iron Degan," he said, letting the name hang on the air for several paces. "He's proud. As a man, as a degan. He doesn't exactly cozen to the idea of some members of the Order selling their swords for coin, rather than solely for the Oath. It's something most of us have done at one point or another—you have to live, after all, and coin tends to spend better than reputation in the long run. But, except for one or two occasions, my brothers and sisters have been able to keep the distinction between paid work and the Oath separate."

"'One or two occasions'?" I said.

Degan glanced down at my rapier. "Funny," he said. "That doesn't *look* like a degan's sword in your scabbard."

I chuckled. "Right," I said. "Mind my own damn business. So what would Iron Degan have the Order do?"

"Find a cause and fight for it. Serve a worthy master or mistress. Hold ourselves above petty squabbles and enforcement-for-hire. Iron had his share of clan wars and slaughter-for-profit when he was growing up; he wants to put that behind him. He'd rather serve the goal than the man."

"So he's seeking a higher road?"

"As much as anyone can who fights and kills for a living."

"Which means he's sworn himself to an idea or a cause, and not just a person, in Ten Ways."

Degan shrugged. "It's Iron. He's given the Oath to someone he believes in. That person either *is* the cause for him, or his link to it. But whoever that is, they aren't a run-of-the-mill Kin, or even a promising Upright Man. As I said, Iron is proud, and as a degan, he wouldn't let himself serve a minor cause. Whoever he's sworn to, it's no small player."

"Bigger than an Upright Man?" I said.

We stopped short of where the Cloisters let out onto Plank Street, keeping to the shadows for a little longer. Ahead of us, the street was filling up with morning light and foot traffic.

"That's my guess," said Degan.

I leaned back against the alley wall, feeling the sudden need for support. "Degan," I said, "are you telling me we're up against a Gray Prince in Ten Ways? A fucking *Gray Prince*?"

Degan kept his eyes locked on the street as he said, "Now you understand why I wanted you to walk away."

I barely heard him. I was too busy contemplating the wall behind my head, wondering how hard, and how many times, I would need to bash my skull against it to

make this all go away. No more than five, I decided—
maybe six to be safe.

Go up against one of the Princes of the Kin? People
talked about them in whispers, spoke about them as
legends more than as flesh and blood. How the hell do
you take on a legend? Even an Upright Man like Nicco
knew better than to cross *that* line. And here was Degan, who seemed to have figured all of this out before
me, agreeing to do it, anyhow—no, not just agreeing, but
taking *an Oath* on it. My friend was insane.

But then what did that make me? Degan had been
telling me to walk away, to let it go; yet my gut still told
me to follow it through. Why?

Because of the Dark King; because if whoever was
backing Iron Degan got his way, he'd bring the empire
down on us all over again. I didn't want to have to face
the empire, to choose between fighting or hiding, to
have to look over my shoulder for White Sashes for the
next five years or give up the Kin life altogether.

And, ultimately, because I was a Nose, I wanted to
know what the hell was going on, who was trying to play
me, and make them pay. If the empire stepped in, that
might never happen.

"Any idea which Prince it might be?" I said. I thought
back to the sewers. "Was it the woman we heard with
him in Ten Ways?"

"I don't know," said Degan. "Maybe, but that could
just as easily have been a lieutenant. Gray Princes don't
usually run on raids from what I hear. But I do have a
few avenues I can follow, now that I'm committed to the
matter."

There was a resigned note to Degan's voice. I suspected he was going to tap his resources within his Order, to pry into his fellow degan's business.

I knew how he felt; as a Nose, I couldn't help but
know. But as a Nose, I also knew that no amount of
sympathy or comment on my part would make a difference. So I held my peace and instead pushed myself
away from the alley wall.

"Good hunting," I said.

"What about you?" said Degan.

I looked out on Plank Street again. More people, more light, shorter shadows; it was well into morning.

"I have to go see if I can keep my boss from being drawn into a war he can't win," I said.

"Good luck with that," said Degan drily. I shrugged and headed deeper into the Cloisters. Degan stayed where he was for a moment, then walked in the opposite direction, out onto Plank Street.

A few blocks later, I found a Dancer's Ladder—a collection of crates and refuse arranged to look like a random pile of garbage. In truth, there were hidden handholds and carefully arranged supports among the debris to allow for a quick ascent to the arches and roofs above. Even with the ladder, though, it wasn't easy—between the fall down the stairs and the deep bruises and muscle knots Tamas's rope had caused, I wasn't moving as easily as I'd like. Every reach and pull and push burned in a different part of my body. When I got to the top, I was gasping.

At least the air up here was still heavy with the smells of the sea that surrounded the city on three sides. As the day wore on, it would be replaced by smoke and dust, but, for now, I took a deep breath and reveled in its freshness. Overhead, the sky was a deep blue, with only the slightest smudge of gray far to the west—rain, but whether it would make it here or not was another matter. The sea had a habit of fighting with the land when it came to who ruled the skies over Ildrecca.

I yawned and slipped another two ahrami into my mouth. They helped, but only just. I could feel the last several days looming behind me, waiting to pounce. Yesterday's sleep had helped, but that was almost eighteen hours gone. I glanced off in the direction of Stone Arch and my home, then turned away.

One more thing, I promised myself. One more errand, and then I could sleep.

I made it across the Dancer's Highway more out of

habit than out of conscious effort. Peaks and gutters and roof gardens passed in a blur, and before I was fully aware of it, I was scrambling down a drain pipe into a back alley in Silver Disc cordon. I was sweaty, tired, and more than a little ready to say to hell with it. Except I knew I couldn't.

I wended my way to a scarred green door on a nondescript street, halfway between a sleepy neighborhood tavern on one end and a cordwainer's shop on the other. I knocked.

The door opened partway. A large hard-faced man looked out from the other side, his body blocking the entrance. He looked at me, and his eyes went wide.

"What the hell are *you* doing here?" he asked.

"Nice to see you, too, Ios," I said, pushing past him. "Now, do me a favor and run and tell Kells I need to see him immediately."

Chapter Fourteen

"We've got trouble," I told my boss. "Big trouble."
     "I suspected as much," said Kells. "Otherwise you wouldn't have come."

We were in Kells's study, a small tidy place in a small tidy building. The floors and walls and furniture were polished wood, accented by several fine tapestries. But what really grabbed your attention was the stone: marble and granite, soapstone and pumice. It was everywhere, in every shape—statues, vases, balls, and bowls, even the finely wrought fireplace—all of it done by Kells, apprentice stonemason turned crime lord.

"There's a war brewing in Ten Ways," I said.

Kells nodded but otherwise didn't react. He still looked more like a laborer than a crime lord. With his bald pate, heavy white mustache and brows, and sleeves rolled up past his thick forearms, he seemed more inclined to haggle over prices than order someone's death. I'd seen him do both, and more—the man had vaulted garden walls I could barely scramble over—but mostly, he was content to sit back, look simpler than he was, and spin his webs.

"You know?" I said.

"I can read the signs as well as the next man."

"And?"

"The next move is Nicco's." Kells ran his hand over the granite owl set in the mantel. It had been carved to appear as if it were flying out of the stone of the fireplace itself. If I looked closely, I knew, I would be able to make out individual feathers. "If Nicco wants to keep pushing in Ten Ways," said Kells, "that's his choice. But I'm not going to sit by and take it, and neither are some of the other Uprights. Blue Cloak Rhys is almost ready to go after Nicco on his own; same for Shy Meg. They both want me to wade in, and frankly, I'm tempted." Kells brushed his hand off on his shirt and glared. "If he sends even one more crew into my territory, I — "

"Wait a moment," I said. "You're saying *Nicco's* been moving against *you* in Ten Ways?"

"For more than two months," he said. "Nicco's been working through intermediaries, but the trail always leads back to him." Kells's bushy brows drew together. "Why? What have you heard?"

"The same thing you're saying, only from Nicco's end — that you've been using locals to muscle in on some of his action, as well as other parts of the cordon." Even Rambles had sounded as if he thought Kells was behind the push against Nicco. Nor, I realized, had Ironius dissuaded him from that notion.

Ironius. And his Gray Prince. Shit.

"*Has* Nicco been moving against me?" said Kells.

"Until recently? No. Now, though . . ."

Kells flexed his fingers, made a fist, then let it go. "We're being played, aren't we?"

"Like a tin whistle," I said. "You and the whole damn cordon."

"Why?"

I grinned wryly. "Because Kin wars make people nervous," I said, remembering what Ironius had said. "Because sometimes, they even make them desperate."

"How desperate?"

"Desperate enough to consider the unthinkable."

"The unthinkable," muttered Kells. Then he looked at me and seemed to see me for the first time. "Sit," he said. "You look ready to fall over."

I did as he said, turning the chair around so I could

lean forward onto its back. It felt wonderful. Kells stepped out of the room briefly, then came back in to take up his place before the fireplace again. "Food and wine are on the way," he said. "In the meantime . . ." He handed me a cup of water.

"The unthinkable," repeated Kells as I drank. "I take it you mean more than forming simple alliances, like the one I was just talking about?"

"That may be part of it," I said. "But I think there's more."

"Such as?"

"What happens if you and Nicco go to war in Ten Ways?"

I could almost hear the pieces clicking together in his head: War leading to instability leading to a power vacuum leading to opportunity.

"A new Upright Man takes control of Ten Ways and kicks us all out," he said. "He just has to wait until everyone else is reeling, then step in and do a cleanup."

"She," I said. "*She* has to wait and clean up. Except there's more to it than that."

Kells raised an eyebrow. "You mean make a push into our territories afterward? This woman doesn't think small, does she?"

"You have no idea," I said. I set my cup down and met Kells's eyes over the back of the chair. "She's eyeing all of Ildrecca. The whole thing."

"You mean like Isidore?" said Kells. He snorted. "Well, in that case, I don't think we have anything to—"

"It's a Prince," I said. "There's a Gray Prince's hand over all of this: Ten Ways, Ildrecca, the whole thing. At least, I think there is."

Kells put his own hand out toward the owl, missed, and would have stumbled into the fireplace if he hadn't caught the edge of the opening with his other hand. As he straightened up, he ran that hand over his mustache, leaving a smudge of soot in the thick whiteness.

"That . . . changes things," he said. There was the slightest quaver in his voice. Kells pulled the chair from behind his desk over to the fireplace and sat down across from me.

"Do you have any idea which Prince?" he asked.

"I'm working on it," I said.

"Tell me everything," he said. "From the beginning."

So I did—everything, that is, except my Oath with Degan. I wasn't sure yet where my duty to Kells left off and the Oath began. Given a little time, and plenty of sleep, I probably could have reasoned it out, but I wasn't trusting my judgment on the finer points right now. Kells didn't push in any case—he was too busy working through the ramifications of everything else I told him.

"It fits," he said. "Damn it, but it fits. Nicco and I are the perfect foils for this. He's been itching to come after me for years, and I'm sure as hell not about to back down if he pushes the matter. There's too much history for either of us to step away. And while we pound away at each other, whoever is behind this can sit back and gather their strength." He shook his head. "Damn sneaky, conniving Princes."

"There's one thing that bothers me, though," I said.

Kells chuckled. "I wish my list were that short, but all right, my 'optimistic' Long Nose—what's your one thorn?"

"The empire," I said. "Do you honestly think Markino is going to keep his hand, and his troops, out of this if the war gets as big as we think it will?"

Kells sat back and stroked his mustache, spreading the dark spot wider within it. "I think," he said slowly, "that whoever hatched this has already factored in the empire in some way. I can't see how—*I* certainly wouldn't want to try to play the emperor, especially Markino. He's getting older, which means he's liable to be a bit less ... understanding."

I snorted. That was putting it mildly. As each incarnation of the emperor got older, he went a little bit crazy. Paranoia, mania, and unusual obsessions weren't uncommon in the final years of the imperial life, but they were usually mild and kept within the Imperial cordon—or so the popular stories went. However, if Markino got wind of the Kin trying to play him, and he was in a vindictive, obsessive mood . . . I shuddered.

"The point is," said Kells, "you don't go to these lengths and forget about something like that. No, we may not see how the empire fits in, but I expect it has its place as well."

"We can't let it get to that point," I said. "We need to keep the war in Ten Ways from happening."

"Possibly," said Kells.

"*Possibly*?" I said. "Didn't you hear what I just said? Kin war. Gray Prince. Targeting you—targeting *us*!"

Kells stared at me coolly. "I heard you, Drothe, but I think you need to remember something: I'm not Nicco. I don't jump at the first hint of smoke. Something like this can run in any number of directions, and I don't want to end up going down a blind alley because I didn't stop to think first.

"Yes, keeping this war from happening would be the best course of action, but it may not be possible. We're talking about Nicco here. He may not listen to reason, and he certainly won't listen to it from me. If he decides I'm behind what's happening in Ten Ways, he'll see it as a personal attack and come at me with both fists cocked. And I won't back down from him, even if this *is* all a setup. I still have my organization and my people to think about."

"So you'll do what the Prince wants?" I said.

"I may not have a choice." Kells grinned. "But that doesn't mean I have to follow the script she prepared."

"Hold on," I said. "Are you telling me that you're thinking about taking on a Gray Prince?" There was a hell of a lot of difference between my going up against one and Kells's doing it. With luck, I might escape notice, but Kells didn't have that kind of option. He was too big to miss.

Kells's finger ran through his mustache again, highlighting the grin. "Tempting, isn't it? Taking on one of them at their own game? Proving you cannot only stand against them, but maybe even with them? It has its appeal."

"*You* become a Gray Prince?" I said. Was that even possible? I'd never thought about it, but they had to come from somewhere.

"What, you don't think I'd look good in the shadows?" he said. Then he sighed, and the sparkle dimmed in his eyes. "No, you're right. It's too risky to try, especially like this. The risks are too great to do it on the fly, but I *can* use what we know to manipulate things, to make sure Nicco is the more tempting target for the Prince. I might even be able to arrange it so I end up with a share of Nicco's territory myself—possibly a healthy share."

"So you don't want to take on a Gray Prince," I said drily. "You just want to manipulate one."

Kells's grin widened. "More or less."

"And if you can't?"

Kells laughed. "Hell, I haven't even figured out how to con her yet, and you want to know what I'll do if the plan falls apart. Give me some time, Drothe!" He leaned forward and pointed a finger at me. "But I do agree with you—even if we can't stop this war, we can't let it get out of hand, either. If it gets big enough to draw in the empire, like you fear . . ." He waved his hand. "*Poof!* Everything, on our level at least, goes up in smoke. The best we could hope for would be to hunker down and hope the White Sashes pass us by."

"That doesn't sound very promising," I said.

"Last resorts never are."

I yawned and rubbed at my eyes. It was midday and damn bright out. I was so fatigued that even though my night vision was dormant, the light still hurt. I added it to the list of all my other current aches and pains—pains I had managed to almost forget while sitting with Kells, but that had come back with a vengeance now that I was up and moving. Well, barely moving. As I walked, I consoled myself with visions of painkilling powders and drug-deepened sleep. I'd earned them.

Kells and I had kept at it for another couple of hours, chewing over concerns and possibilities, discarding more ideas than we kept—just like old times. I never realized how much I missed that until the rare occasions I got to see him.

Kells was the one who had brought me up within the Kin, who had spotted me in Ten Ways and decided that I could be more than a Draw Latch. He had pointed me toward Wide Nosing by asking careful questions, requesting the odd favor, and steering bits of information my way early in my career. I hadn't known it then, of course, but, over the years, I've caught enough hints here and there to piece it together: Kells had been grooming me. And not just as a Wide Nose—he'd seen Long Nose potential.

That was why I had never officially worked for him back then, even though I had asked—repeatedly. If I'd been visibly attached to him, Nicco would never have taken me. Better I appeared "independent," Kells had said. And I had listened, because he had helped me out of Ten Ways and had taught me to Nose, and because he had one of the best criminal minds I had ever encountered. But mainly I'd listened because he had stood by me and believed in me when no one else would.

And so we had hacked and kicked and spun ideas around each other in his office until he had told me to get out. I didn't doubt that Kells had the beginnings of a plan already, but he wasn't about to share it with me, which was smart. The less I knew, the less I could spill— always a wise policy with Long Noses.

As for me, my assignment was more or less what I had already been doing: try to keep Nicco from going to war in Ten Ways. I rated my chances at better than even, given what I had on Rambles, but I knew better than to assume it would be easy. As long as Nicco thought Kells was involved, his first inclination would be to wade in swinging; I needed to convince him that Rambles and Ironius were a better target for his anger.

I was cutting through an alley three blocks west of

Ten Ways, running likely scenarios through my foggy head, when a voice came to me out of the shadows.

"You're looking for Larrios." It was a rich voice, smooth as fine cognac. I instinctively dropped into a crouch, a knife in each hand. The alley walls were too close for rapier work. I scanned the shadows for the source of the voice, but there was enough sunlight seeping in from above to foil my night vision.

The voice sounded vaguely familiar.

"Rumor has it," I said. I'd put the word out two days back but hadn't expected to hear anything so soon. Larrios had struck me as the kind of Kin who could vanish when he needed to.

A figure stirred in the gloom ahead of me, seeming to materialize from the shadows. He was tall, and that was about all I could say of him. The full gray-black cloak and hood he wore hid any other features he had.

"You'd better be paying more than last time," he said.

"Last time?" I said.

He was five paces away when his gloved hand slipped out of the cloak and casually flipped something toward me. A hint of sunlight caught metal, glinting dully as the coin spun through the air. The copper owl chinked as it bounced once, twice, then rolled across two cobbles to come to rest in a slimed-over puddle of . . . something, at my feet.

The man chuckled, and my memory stirred at the sound. This was the cove that had directed Degan and me to Silent Eliza our first night back inside Ten Ways.

"If you can take me to Larrios," I said, "the pay'll be better. Much."

The cowl dipped once in acknowledgment.

"Provided," I added, "Larrios is in one piece when I get him. Finding him dustmans does me no good."

"That's your problem," he said. "I can help you find him. I can't promise what shape he'll be in."

"You know where he is?"

"Essentially."

I frowned. "That's vague. Vague lowers the price."

Shoulders shrugged beneath the cloak. "Give me a day and I'll have more details."

"What kind of details?"

"The kind you'll be happy to pay for."

I slipped my knives home and crossed my arms before me. "You're an arrogant bastard, you know that?"

I could hear the smile in his voice as he answered, "I can afford to be. Can you?"

"I'm the one with the hawks," I reminded him as he turned away.

"Hawks don't make a Kin deep-file."

"Neither does friendship with the shadows."

He chuckled again. "Don't be too sure," he said as he slipped into the dark edges of the alley. When I moved forward, he was gone.

I was still rolling the cloaked Kin's copper owl through my fingers when I turned onto Echelon Way.

Larrios. If he could get me Larrios, I could get some answers about the relic and the book. Hell, Larrios might even know something about the damn scrap of paper. At this point, I'd be surprised if he didn't. Too many paths were crossing over the book and the relic—Athel's, Larrios's, the Gray Prince's and Iron Degan's, not to mention Nicco's business and mine both touching on Fedim—to be coincidence. And even though it was a tenuous bridge, the scrap of paper in my ahrami pouch seemed to connect them all—Athel to the relic to Fedim to Larrios to the ambushers to the book, all the while bringing me along for the ride.

Yes, I definitely wanted that dark Kin to find Larrios.

I was still two doors away when I noticed Cosima standing in front of the building, shaking out a rug. She saw me at the same time, but, rather than say hello or even flash me a smile, she turned and stalked into their apartments and slammed the door.

What the . . . ?

Wait—what was she still doing here?

I walked up to the door and knocked. No answer.

"Cosima?" I said.

"I'm not leaving," she said from the other side of the door. "You can't make me leave."

"I'm not here to make you do anything," I said. "I thought Eppyris was sending you and the girls to stay with family for a while?"

"Renna and Sophia are with my mother."

"But you're still here," I observed.

"As long as Eppyris stays, I stay."

I sighed and laid my forehead against the door. "He's only looking out for your safety," I said. "Considering what happened the other night, he may be right."

There was a pause on the other side of the door. "Do *you* think he's right?"

I took a long, thoughtful breath. "I think a husband is right to worry about his wife and family."

"That's not an answer."

"It's the only answer I'm qualified to give."

The door swung open, causing me to stumble forward two steps and almost into Cosima's arms. She laid a hand on my chest, stopping me.

"You're the one that man was trying to kill," said Cosima. "If anyone's qualified to talk about it, you are."

"The only thing he's qualified to talk about," said a dour voice behind me, "is his own life." I turned to find Eppyris standing in the stairwell, his leather apothecary's apron tied around his chest. The side door to his shop stood open behind him. "Our lives are our own concern," he said. "Not his."

I bit back my words even as I stared Eppyris in the eye. They lived in my building—that *made* them my concern. Everything that happened under this roof was my business. Admitting otherwise was the same as admitting I couldn't protect my own interests, that I couldn't keep other Kin at bay.

Except Eppyris didn't see it that way. And I understood why.

"Do whatever you feel you need to do," I said to them. "Stay or go. Either way, you're safe."

I turned my back and stalked up the stairs. Behind me, I heard a pair of doors close. I didn't look back to see who had gone where.

Fowler Jess was waiting at the top of the stairs, seated on the floor beside my door.

"That went well," she said.

"Go to hell." I looked her up and down. Fowler's hair was sticking out at all angles from beneath her cap, which, judging by the grime on it, had slipped off her head more than once. The knuckles of one hand showed fresh scrapes, and I noticed a small tear in her new leggings.

"What's been running you ragged?" I asked as I put the key in the lock, turned it left half a turn, then right the same amount. It was unlocked now, but I still needed to give the key another full rotation to disarm the tension spring in the lock housing; otherwise, I'd get a handful of barbed spikes when I went to turn the door handle.

"Sylos."

I paused as I took the key out of the lock. "He was the one standing watch out front the other night, wasn't he? When Tamas came."

"Yes."

"And what did he have to say for himself?"

"Not much," said Fowler. "Considering he ran as soon as he saw me coming."

I heard the sound of my key bouncing off the floor, but I didn't remember letting go of it. "It was him? I said. "He's the one who let Tamas pass?"

Fowler nodded.

"I want to see him," I said. "Now."

"Yeah, well, good luck on that," she said, plucking my key up from the floor. "He took a slip off a roof. Went down four stories in Square Hills as fast as you can say 'splat.'" She slapped her hand on the floorboards for emphasis.

"Damn it, Fowler, I needed him breathing!"

"*You* needed him breathing?" Fowler jumped to her feet so fast I had to step back to keep from being hit in the jaw by her head. "Do you know what that bastard did, Drothe? I found three of my people dustmans after I left you the other night. *Three!* I don't know if he did the deed himself or left them to that Blade, but, either way, he crossed me and mine far worse than he did you. So don't talk to me about how much you 'needed' him alive—I wanted that bastard so bad it hurt."

I was about to argue the point when I noticed Fowler's eyes. They weren't hard or intense or raging as I had expected; they were wide, and filled with anguish. She'd lost three people—I'd only lost my peace of mind.

"Sorry," I said. "I haven't run with a crew for a long time. I . . . forgot."

Fowler nodded.

"Did he say anything?" I asked.

"You mean before or after he jumped out the window of the boardinghouse?" She shook her head. "No, he wasn't too talkative. And while I'm sure *you* could get a confession out of someone while chasing him across a roof, I'm not quite up to it."

"What about the body?"

"What about it?" said Fowler. "There were some hawks, a handful of golden falcons—at least they paid him well—and a bit of personal swag. Oh, and a pilgrim's token." Fowler snorted. "A lot of good *that* did him."

"Wait," I said. "A *pilgrim's* token? What kind?"

"Hell, I don't know. Do I look like I'd go on pilgrimage?" She reached into the small pouch on her belt, rummaged around, and brought out a lead lozenge. "Here."

I took it. It was the same. The same as the token I had found on Athel—round, triple-stamped, old.

"Paper," I said, not looking away from the token. "Were there any bits of paper on Sylos's body?"

More rummaging, and then her hand was before me, two balled-up, filthy scraps of paper in her palm. I gently picked up one of the wads and unfolded it. It had the same collection of marks I'd come to know so well from playing with Athel's strip.

"What the hell is it?" said Fowler, craning her head so much, she almost blocked my view.

"I'm not sure," I said. I removed Athel's scrap from my ahrami pouch and held it next to the one she had found on Sylos. The markings were different, but the size and overall pattern were the same. "I found this on someone who crossed me on a different dodge. He had a pilgrim's token, too."

"What's the connection?"

I shook my head. "I don't know."

I'd been toying with the idea that instead of Christiana, it could have been one of her court rivals behind Tamas's attempt—one noble trying to remove another's tool. It certainly would have explained the livery and the forged letter, as well as the money needed to lay hands on a piece of portable glimmer. Except now, it didn't fit. Sylos didn't have any connection with the relic; he didn't have any reason to have the same kind of slip on him as Athel.

Yet here they were.

I stared at the papers, trying to see the line that had to run through all of this. Athel led to Fedim led to Larrios led to Ironius and the Gray Prince. From there, the trail split, with one leading into Ten Ways, and the other following Larrios's book. On the other side of things, it looked as though things went from Sylos to the forgery to Tamas, with Christiana being used as an "in" against me.

Nothing overlapped, except the papers themselves.

I was starting to regret the moment of mercy I'd shown Athel in the warehouse.

"Damn you, Athel," I grumbled as I tucked away the slips and the token and reached out for the doorknob. "Why the hell couldn't you have given me more than a damn na—"

"Drothe!"

Fowler's yell came the same instant she launched herself into me, sending us both tumbling to the ground.

A fraction of a second later, I heard the solid *thunk* of something driving itself deep into my door.

"You moron!" she yelled into my ear, still on top of me.

"Ow," I said, feeling her on me, me on the floor, and all my bruises between the two.

"Damn straight, 'Ow'!" she said, climbing off. "What the hell were you thinking?"

"I wasn't," I said as I came up off the floor more slowly. "That's the problem. Too tired to think."

Sticking out of the door at chest level, its head buried so deep I couldn't see it, was a short crossbow bolt. It had come from the shadows above the stairwell behind us. I had positioned the firing mechanism more than a year ago and run a trip wire through the wall to the door. When I'd started to open the door without first releasing the tension on the wire, I'd set it off.

Stupid, stupid mistake.

"Damn it, Drothe!" said Fowler. "If you think I'm going to lose people just so you can dust yourself with your own fucking trap, you can find another Oak! If I hadn't been here, you'd be pinned to that door like some first-night Eriff. Angels! I've told you before that you don't need to be so damn paranoid, but will you listen? No. And now—"

I didn't bother pointing out that if she hadn't been here, I wouldn't have been distracted by thoughts of Athel and Sylos and pieces of paper. Instead, I held up a placating hand and said, "Fowler, you're right. Thank you. I owe you. More than ever. But right now, will you please just lock the inside floorboard for me? I don't trust myself at this point."

"You, either, huh?"

"Fowler . . ."

"All right, all right." She took a few deep breaths to get her own hands to stop shaking. Then she knelt, cracked the door open, and reached inside to turn the small handle on the wall that locked down the loose floorboard just past the entry. Stepping on the board without locking it would get us both a face full of quick lime from the air bladder installed underneath it.

"When's the last time you slept, anyhow?" she said as she stood up.

"A day? Two?" I said. "I don't even remember at this point."

"Well then," she said, pushing open the door. "I suggest you . . . Fuck."

Even if it had been an invitation, I doubt I would have been able to take her up on it just then. Inspiring as she could be in bed, I just didn't have it in me at the moment. But as it turned out, I didn't have to worry about coming up with an answer. The catch in her voice and way she froze in the doorway told me more than I needed to know.

I reached out without thinking, ready to pull her back and slam the door shut against whatever was waiting for us inside. Then I saw what she saw, and I froze as well.

There was a woman in my bedroom—a dead woman; a dead floating woman, held a foot off the floor by nothing I could see.

"We've got trouble," said Fowler Jess. "Big trouble."

Chapter Fifteen

"Who is she?" asked Jelem as he walked slowly around the floating corpse.

"She's a Blade named Task," I said from the edge of my bed. "A good one. A *very* good one."

"So whoever did this did you a favor," he observed.

"Lucky me."

Jelem smiled and continued to circle the dead assassin. He was still wearing the cream-colored robe from last night, but the vest had been replaced by a long, lightweight coat of blue linen. A matching cloth was wrapped around his head. Even though I was sure he had not slept, Jelem looked fresher than half the people I had seen on the street while coming home.

I had sent for Jelem immediately—this was his specialty, not mine. Besides, it had direct bearing on the matter of Tamas and his rope: Task had an identical rope hanging from her belt.

"When can we get her down?" I asked. I wanted to see what else she had on her besides the rope—like maybe some bits of paper.

"Soon," said Jelem. "The glimmer holding her up isn't impossible to unravel, but it's no simple thing, either." He pulled out a small calfskin pouch, drew an ahrami seed from it, and slipped the seed into his mouth. Jelem sucked thoughtfully as he moved. "This is well-done," he said after a moment, gesturing at Task's body. "The magic's of a higher quality than I usually see on the street. The anchors are strong, tapped directly into the Nether. That's a lot of work just to float a corpse in the air. A simple repulsion spell on the floor would have done the same thing, but it would have faded after a few days. Done this way, the body could stay here for years." Jelem looked at me meaningfully. I stared back blankly.

"I assume you're making a point besides, 'This isn't small-time,'" I said, "because I figured that much out myself."

"What I'm saying is that there is glimmer, and there is *glimmer*."

I pinched the bridge of my nose. "This isn't going to be good news, is it?"

"You can ask me that with a dead assassin floating in your bedroom?"

He had a point. "Let's hear it, then."

"How much do you know about magical theory?"

"Probably as much as you know about picking a Kettlemaker lock."

"Indeed," said Jelem. "I'll keep it brief, then.

"At its most basic," he said, "magic gets its power from what we call the Nether. Most magicians agree on this basic premise—the differences come when we start to talk about what exactly the Nether *is*. I won't bore you with all the various theories on the nature of the Nether—"

"Oh, damn," I said.

"Although if you insist on interrupting me, I could." Jelem paused to take a meaningful breath. "The main point is that while the Nether is a separate thing from our reality, some of its energy manages to cross over into our world. Whether it accumulates naturally, is drawn here by other powers, or is some sort of cosmic or religious 'gift' isn't really important for our current discussion.

"Most street magic, as you know it, is powered by energy that has already seeped into our world from the Nether of its own accord. This means the average Mouth doesn't summon the energy for his spells so much as gather up a portion of what is already here and form it to his needs. Furthermore, how he collects, channels, and forms the energy ultimately decides not only what it does, but how long it lasts."

"You make Mouths sound almost like garbage pickers," I said.

Jelem looked down his nose at me. "I prefer to think of them as tailors, taking in raw fabric and fashioning something useful with a cut here and a stitch there."

"Uh-huh," I said. "So, my good 'tailor,' what does this have to do with Task over there?"

"Ninety-nine out of one hundred Mouths would have used a basic repulsion spell to suspend her in the air, as I said. It's a straightforward enchantment that uses the available energy in a simple manner. Not to mention that it's the only way most Mouths know how to power any kind of glimmer." Jelem gestured at the dead Blade. "*This* caster, though, did something different: He opened up a small tap into the Nether and tied his spell to it. Instead of using the magical energy that has accumulated around us, he opened up a direct link to the Nether itself."

"How hard is that to do?"

"Very."

"Could *you* do it?"

"I've done it on a total of four occasions," he said. "All back in Djan. And each of those times required days of preparation, in a controlled setting. Doing it here, in someone else's home, on a tight schedule? No, I couldn't. Nor would I want to."

"But you say you can undo it," I said.

"Yes, because whoever did this also made it so that another Mouth could unravel the glimmer."

"On purpose?"

"Just so."

I looked at the Blade, and a thought occurred to me—a very bad thought. "Jelem," I said slowly, "are you trying to tell me this is *imperial* glimmer?"

"What?" said Jelem. He turned and looked at me. "By the Family, no! No. If it were, I'd be back home devising an alibi and considering the best route out of Ildrecca. This magic is very potent, but it's still street magic. Imperial glimmer is far above this. Or at least, that's what I hear—it's all rumors when it comes to the empire's magic, anyhow."

"Oh, well, as long as it's just 'very potent' then," I said sourly.

Still, despite the magic, I felt strangely calm. It was as if I had gotten to a point where, with so many things piling up around me, one more brick didn't matter anymore. The new assassin should have worried me; her presence in my rooms should have frightened me; and the unknown source of the magic used to deal with her should have scared me out of my wits. Instead, it all washed over and around me, leaving me untouched.

I suspected that things would look much worse once I got a good night's sleep.

I heard hard, measured footfalls on the stairs. A moment later, Fowler Jess came stalking into the room, her every gesture a study in rage. "My people report all clear for the entire night," she fumed. "No one saw a thing."

"Not surprising," said Jelem. He had taken a small brush from his coat and begun sweeping it through the air around the body. "The *yazani* who did this can likely come and go as he pleases, at least where your efforts are concerned." Jelem paused, wet his dark thumb, and rubbed at something on Task's corpse. "You may want to consider some glimmered defenses, Drothe," he said. "My rates are, well, let's not say reasonable; affordable, perhaps?"

"I can handle this just fine!" snapped Fowler. "I don't need some cut-rate glimmer monger throwing magic all over the place—magic that'll just end up getting in my people's way."

"Yes," said Jelem as he returned to his brushing. "You've obviously done a superb job so far. Tell me, do I need to make an appointment to try to kill Drothe, or is it simply on a first-come, first-served basis? I can never keep Kin etiquette straight."

I reached out and grabbed Fowler's arm as her long knife cleared its scabbard. Fowler glared at me, yanked against my grip. I shook my head. Jelem didn't even glance our way.

"Would your glimmer have stopped my visitor?" I asked.

Jelem sucked on his seed. "Her?" he said, pointing at the assassin. "Most likely, although I wouldn't be surprised if she was killed somewhere else and brought here afterward. It's far easier to veil corpses than it is live bodies. As for whoever put her here in the first place? No, I don't think my spells would have done anything other than annoy your anonymous benefactor."

"Like I said," said Fowler, "we can handle this." I let go of her arm. She put her knife away and moved over to one of the room's two windows. With a shove, Fowler opened the shutters the rest of the way and seated herself on the sill.

"You said 'benefactor,'" I said to Jelem.

He nodded, still circling Task. "What else? Believe me, if whoever did this wanted you dead, you'd be dead."

We all grew silent after that. Jelem continued to work on the floating corpse, pausing occasionally to mutter softly to himself in singsong Djanese. Fowler sat in the window, brooding. Every now and then, I caught her making small gestures to the world outside: signaling her people and gathering reports. Doubling the guard, more likely than not.

I turned this newest question over in my head. Why kill a Blade and go to all the trouble of suspending her in my room, when a well-thrust knife and a note under my door would have accomplished the same thing? It was, I decided, more than a warning; it was a statement. Not only was someone watching over me—they had access to the kinds of power I couldn't come close to touching.

And if they had access to this kind of power—and were willing to flaunt it—what were the odds of whoever was after me having the same level of resources? The glimmered rope had been bad enough, but what if that was only small-time for them?

I looked back up at Task. Why even bother hiring Blades at all? If the person behind Tamas and Task was as potent as my benefactor, why wasn't I dead already? And why, for that matter, was either of these people interested in *me*?

I placed my forehead in the palm of one hand and drew a seed from my pouch with the other, then stopped myself. No. Ahrami wasn't the answer now. No matter how many I ate, they would only make me alert, not awake. My mind was a jumble of questions and information, none of it fitting together well. Tackling that mess now would be like trying to find my way out of a maze wearing a blindfold. I needed sleep. Hell, I practically ached for it.

"How much longer until you have her down?" I asked Jelem, already starting to lean back onto my bed.

"Hard to say," said Jelem. "Not soon, anyhow."

"I thought you said the glimmer on her was breakable."

"And every lock is pickable, but do I stand beside you in dark hallways and shake your elbow?"

"Then where the hell am I supposed to sleep?"

"I would suggest 'not here,'" said Jelem, turning back to Task's body. "I don't want company, and you don't want to be here for some of the things I'll need to do to get her down. You find things for a living—surely you can find someplace to sleep."

Finding someplace wasn't the problem; finding someplace *safe*, though, was another matter. Still, Jelem was right—I didn't want to think about the kind of dreams I would have if I stayed here.

I looked over at Fowler Jess.

"Oh, hell no," she said. "*Hell* no!"

"Jess . . . " I began.

"You're pulling in trouble like a crooked Rag rakes in hawks, Drothe. No way I'm letting you anywhere near my place."

"It's just for one night," I said. "And besides, in a way—"

"Don't!" she said, slipping down off the windowsill. "Don't you *dare* tell me I owe you, or it's my fault you don't have a place to stay, or anything like that. Killing you would ruin my reputation, but, right now, I'd happily pay that price if you said something stupid."

Since that was exactly what I had been going to say, I shut my mouth. "I don't suppose you can spare anyone to watch me if I go to an inn?" I said instead.

Fowler leaned back against the wall. A look of pity crossed her face. Apparently, I was still being stupid.

"I'm having enough trouble keeping the Kin out of *your* place," she said. "I don't need the headache of trying to secure a public inn against another Blade, let alone a Mouth who can walk through walls. Go someplace unexpected, where people won't look for you. That'll protect you better than an army of Oaks could right now."

I nodded. She was right. Go someplace unexpected. . . .

I stood up.

"I'm off, then," I said, heading for the door.

"That quickly? Where to?" asked Fowler.

"To someplace even *I* can't believe I'm considering," I said, and closed the door behind me.

The large wooden door swung open just as I was reaching for the knocker for the second time. If Josef felt any surprise at seeing me, he hid it well. My sister's butler of the chamber merely inclined his head and stepped aside to let me in.

"Good to see you again, sir," said Josef as I crossed the threshold of my sister's house. I grunted a reply.

"Is the baroness expecting you?" he asked.

"What do you think?"

Josef smiled a bit. He closed the door. "Yes, well, I'll announce you then, shall I?"

"Yes, do," I said. "I suppose it's an occasion of sorts, isn't it?"

"Indeed," said Josef as he turned away. "And, if I may, it's a pleasure to see you entering the home this way again."

How many years had it been since I had actually used the front door to come calling? Not since before Nestor's death. It hadn't seemed right to come walking into his house after that, but it felt somehow wrong to come skulking over the garden wall tonight, too. Maybe I'd come knocking because, for the first time in a long time, I'd be asking my sister for a favor, rather than striking a bargain of necessity.

I looked around the entry foyer. Little had changed— same polished tile floor, same mosaics on the wall, same view through the archway to the garden beyond. I almost expected my brother-in-law, Nestor, to come strolling through one of the side passages, a half-unrolled scroll dangling from his hands, ready to launch into a discussion on his latest interpretation of Regency history. I smiled briefly at the thought.

Of all the men Christiana could have married, Nestor had been the most unexpected. Then again, maybe that was why they had come together. An eccentric nobleman, he hadn't cared that his wife was a former courtesan, nor, when he found out, that his brother-in-law was a criminal. If anything, he had flown in the face of court propriety and declared it "quite charming" to have a "Gentleman of the Shadows" as a relative. It had taken Christiana nearly a week to persuade Nestor that introducing me at their wedding, let alone at court, would be a disaster for them both. He had agreed in the end, but I suspect part of him had wanted to see just how the scandal would have played out.

I yawned and leaned my head back. Above me, on the wall, depicted in a mosaic of cut glass and stone and marble, stood Releskoi, Nestor's family's patron Angel.

Releskoi was tall, with the traditional blue-white skin, golden eyes, and fair hair of his kind. This version had a scar on his left cheek, marking not only the Angel but also Nestor's family as followers of the Achadean sect— those who saw the Angels as more supernatural than divine, more as the original servants of the dead gods than as the deities they had become. The traditional fox and desert lion crouched near Releskoi's feet. The Angel's symbol, a staff wrapped in a banner of holy inscriptions, floated before his chest.

I yawned again. "Fat lot of good you did Nestor," I said to the Angel.

"Releskoi is one of the Angels of Judgment," said Christiana. "I doubt he can do much when it comes to stopping poison and plots."

I sat up to find my sister framed by daylight in the garden's archway. She was wearing a simple linen morning dress, undyed, that left her arms exposed. A belt of fine silver links drew the otherwise shapeless dress in at her waist. Her hair was gathered up casually and held in place with a pair of silver pins.

"How convenient for Nestor's killer," I said.

Christiana sighed and walked into the shade of the foyer. "I hope you've haven't come here to throw that old accusation around again. If so, you know where the door—or the wall—is."

I chewed on a particularly nasty response for a moment, then swallowed it. There was no point in arguing about Nestor's death again; or at least, not right now.

"Someone tried for me again," I said. "Another Blade—I mean, assassin."

One of Christiana's eyebrows arched upward. "And you're not trying kill me as a result? How novel."

"It's worse," I said, and I told her.

By the time I was finished, she was sitting next to me on the bench, staring hard into the middle of the room.

"So whoever knows about us is a magician," said Christiana. Her voice made the stone bench we sat on seem warm and soft by comparison.

"'Us'?" I said. "Angels, Ana, this isn't about you—I'm the one they're trying to kill!"

"By using *my* livery and forging *my* name," she said. She turned and glared at me. "You weren't followed here, were you?"

"Give me *some* credit."

She nodded and turned back to the foyer. "In case you're wondering, yes, I *do* realize they're trying to kill you. But they used our connection to try to set you up the first time, so I'm involved as well."

"Only peripherally," I said.

"That makes me feel *so* much better."

"What the hell do you want me to do, Ana? I came here to warn you—what else do you want?"

"For a start? Bring me that magician's head on a platter."

I laughed harshly. "Oh, by all means—we can't have the Baroness Sephada *inconvenienced*. If I wasn't motivated before, I am now." I leapt to my feet. "Stay here and powder something while I gather up the Kin and scour the city!"

"Don't be an ass. I want whoever knows about us eliminated. That means I'll help." She held out her hand. "Give me the paper strips you were talking about."

"What?"

"I used to be a courtesan and am still a dowager baroness—I've had some experience with secret letters and messages, Drothe."

I stared at her, hesitating.

Christiana sighed. "Drothe, why did you come here?"

"To warn you," I said. "And to get some sleep."

She nodded. "Mm-hmm. And when was the last time you came through the front door?"

"I . . ."

"Drothe, you're nearly asleep on your feet. You've been going for Angels know how long, and have a dead assassin and a Djanese magician in your home. But even with all that, I know you didn't walk in here because you're too tired to climb the garden wall."

"It *is* a high wall . . . " I said.

Christiana leapt to her feet. "Fine, dammit! Go ahead and be a stubborn son of a—"

I couldn't help myself; I started laughing.

Christiana stopped and glared at me. Then she grinned just like she used to when she was eleven. It was good to see.

"You bastard," she said.

"You're still easy." I reached into the pouch and pulled out the slips of paper. Little sister or no, she had a point—she dealt with codes and ciphers more than I did.

Christiana took the scraps almost casually, but her demeanor changed as she looked them over. She held them up, frowning, and turned the papers this way and that. Finally, she went over to the entrance to the garden to stand in the sunlight.

I resumed my seat on the bench and leaned my head back, Releskoi's image perched above me. "Lay your odds on her not cracking them," I said to the Angel. He didn't take the bet. I chose to take that as a good sign.

I closed my eyes.

And awoke to Christiana kicking my foot.

"Where the hell did you get these?" she said.

I rubbed at my face, trying to wake up. The closest I managed was consciousness.

"What?" I said.

Christiana waved the slips under my nose. "*These*," she said. "Where did you get them?"

"I told you—off a smuggler and a turn-cloak. Why?"

"Is that *all* you know about them?"

I looked at the papers, then up at my sister. There was enough tension running through her for the both of us. I felt myself finally starting to wake up.

"What did you find?" I said.

"It's what I didn't find," she snapped, turning away in a swirl of linen and perfume. "No codes, no hidden sequences, no secret writing. Nothing."

I noticed the room had changed while I was asleep. A low desk had been brought in, along with a chair and a small reading table. A handful of books were scattered across the table, some open, others piled at the corner. The desk held two more books, a candle, several bowls, and a collection of small vials and bottles. Beyond them, the garden was in partial shadow.

Midafternoon, then. I'd been out for two hours at least.

"These don't make any sense," complained Christiana, waving the strips in the air. "There's not enough consistency for a code—you need actual writing, or at least repeating symbols, for that. I checked them against a mirror, in case they used a reversal or partial cipher, but that didn't show me anything, either. And none of them matches up against one another, or against any common printing type I can find, so it's not a text cipher, either."

"Invisible ink?" I said.

"I tried the four most common reagents," said Christiana, gesturing at the desk.

"What about the less common ones?" I asked.

"Poisonous, expensive, or both."

I thought back to the dead Blade floating in my bedroom. "'Too dangerous' and 'too expensive' aren't necessarily limiting factors here."

Christiana shrugged. "Fine, I can test the others later, but I don't think it will do us any good."

"Why not?"

Christiana came back and leaned down over me. Nutmeg and musk, with an mild undertone of salt from her sweat, came to my nose. "Look at the line where all the writing stops before it reaches the far edge," she said, handing me one of the slips. "That means whoever wrote this did something *to* the paper when he wrote on it, something that broke or stopped the writing at that point." She straightened up and ran a hand absently through a loose strand of her hair. "If we want to break this, we need to physically do something to the paper— manipulate it in some way."

I stared at the ideograph fragments, the dots and

lines that surrounded them, and the razor-edged strip of whiteness that ran along one edge, cutting through the marks. I could feel something trying to take shape in the back of my mind, something from long ago, but, when I reached for it, it faded away.

"Have you tried folding it?" I asked.

"More ways than you can count. You can get a few marks to match up here or there, but the rest is still gibberish."

I leaned back against the wall. My shoulders complained, but I ignored them. "We have to be missing something," I said. "These were meant for Kin, not imperial spies. If someone was sending written instructions to Athel and Sylos, I don't think he'd make the cipher more complex than the message."

Christiana grunted and straightened up. She began to chew absently on her lower lip, twisting a strand of hair around her finger as she did so.

I looked up at Releskoi. "Should have taken the bet," I murmured to him.

"What?" said Christiana.

"Nothing." I levered my way to my feet and walked over to the desk. "These other reagents for invisible ink," I said, turning around to face my sister. "How hard are they . . . ?" And I froze.

She was standing, looking at me, arms crossed. The strand of hair she had been playing with now hung beside her ear. It had curled slightly from her worrying it.

"Your hair," I said, pointing.

Christiana raised a hand self-consciously. "My *hair*? Drothe, what are you talking—"

I looked from her to the mosaic of Releskoi—at his staff with the parchment spiraling around it. At his credo written on the parchment.

Of course.

"There!" I said, pointing up at the Angel. "The staff. And your hair. And my own damn habit of wrapping the paper around my own fingers. I should have seen it!" I brandished one of the strips. "You don't fold it or hold it to a mirror or look for hidden writing," I said. "You spiral it around something so the marks match up and form ideographs!"

Christiana's eyes went wide. "A scytale cipher?" she said. "Those haven't been used in centuries."

"All the better," I said. "Who would think of using something that old? *You* didn't."

Christiana humphed but didn't argue. "It makes sense," she admitted. "All they would need is the same diameter rod, and they could wrap the paper to either write or read the messages. It's certainly simple enough for anyone to use. Did either of the corpses have a baton or rod of some sort? Something innocuous, that no one would question their keeping on them?"

I hadn't seen Sylos's body, but I'd gone over Athel's things well enough to be able to see them again in my head. "A pipe," I said. "Athel had a long-stemmed pipe. Sylos may have had the same."

"I don't suppose you still have it?"

"No," I said. "But I remember what it looked like." I began to tuck the papers away. "If I get over to Ash Street right now, I ought be able to cover at least a half-dozen pipe sellers before—"

"Nonsense," said Christiana. She clapped her hands. "You'll do nothing of the sort. And I'll not sit around waiting while you do."

Josef came gliding into the room, stopped at a respectful distance, and bowed.

"I find myself in need of tobacco pipes, Josef," Christiana pronounced. "A *wide array* of tobacco pipes."

"Very good, madam. How many tobacconists would you care to interview?"

"Start with a dozen."

"And when would madam wish them to call upon her?"

"Immediately."

Josef bowed again. "I will send runners at once. Shall I have them assemble in the solar?"

Christiana inclined her head. "Please. And inform

Cook that Drothe and I will be taking an early dinner in the garden."

Josef bobbed a third time and hurried from the room.

Christiana turned back to me and arched a satisfied smile. "And that, dear brother," she said, "is how a baroness does 'legwork.'"

Chapter Sixteen

They were just bringing down the shutters and closing the main door when I bulled my way into Baldezar's shop. One of the older scribes stepped forward and tried to cluck at me about the place being closed for the day. I gave him the back of my hand. By the time I reached the stairway to the upper level, there was a visible trail of scattering scribes and drifting paper in my wake. I took the steps two at a time, strode to the master scribe's door, and threw it open.

Desk, parchment, books, quills and ink, but no Baldezar.

I turned around and looked out over the shop, leaning on the walkway's wrought-iron railing. I'd come straight from Christiana's. The continued lack of sleep hadn't improved either my mood or my appearance. *"Where?"* I demanded.

The room fell silent. I heard a piece of paper settle to the ground. A bottle rolled off a scribe's stand and clattered on the floor.

"Where is your thrice-damned master?" I yelled.

"Gone."

Lyconnis was standing in the doorway to the palimpsest room, where they scraped and cleaned parchment for reuse. His sleeves were rolled up, displaying a pair of thick, hairy arms. His apron had done little to keep the pumice and chalk dust off his scribe's robe.

"Gone where?" I said.

Lyconnis shrugged.

"Up here," I said. "Now."

I went back into Baldezar's office. Books and scrolls filled the shelves behind the desk, along with small boxes full of penknives, sharpening stones, mortars and pestles, uncut quills, seashells for holding pigments, and ink-stained rags. Save for a neat array of sealed ink pots, the desktop was bare.

I slipped in behind and tried the two drawers in the desk—locked. I pulled my spiders from my pocket, bent down, and got to work.

Feet thumped heavily along the walkway, came into the room, and stopped. I didn't glance up.

"What are you doing?" said Lyconnis.

"Not what I was hoping to do, I can tell you that," I said. I felt the pick catch on one of the wards in the lock, then slip free. I shifted the pick slightly, felt it miss again. Wrong head, I decided. I pulled the spider out and fished for another.

Lyconnis sighed and settled into the narrow chair on the other side of the desk.

"What has Master Baldezar done?"

"Lied, for a start," I said as I selected a pick with a heavier curve and slipped it in alongside the tension wrench. "Forged a letter from my . . . patron. Set me up. Maybe even put a Blade on my trail." I felt the pick slip past the ward, tickle a tumbler, and push it home. I moved on to the next one, then the third. I turned the tension wrench, felt the lock give, and heard a scraping click. I pulled the drawer open.

I looked up to find Lyconnis staring at me.

"He tried to have you *killed*?" he said.

"He sure as hell didn't send flowers."

"But . . . he hired . . . a . . . an . . ."

"Maybe," I said, sitting down in Baldezar's desk chair. "Maybe not. I doubt he could afford the people who were sent. But he had a hand in it." I pulled the scraps of paper from my ahrami pouch, then reaching into my herb wallet, drew out the pipe Christiana and I had gotten from the sixth pipe merchant who had come calling.

"You know how a scytale cipher works?" I said as I set them on the desk. Lyconnis nodded. "Have a read."

Lyconnis wrapped, read, unwrapped, and wrapped again as I scoured the contents of the drawer. I didn't need to see his face to know what he was seeing—I'd read and reread the strips so many times at Christiana's, I'd committed them to memory.

The message from Athel's bag had been straightforward. *The thief is getting anxious,* it read. *Trade imperial relic for book. Stall the Nose until we can make other arrangements. There is new action in Ten Ways—act with haste.* Whoever Athel had been dealing with, he had decided it was better for him to trade the relic than to sell it to me. I suspected "the thief" was Larrios, and that he'd demanded payment sooner than they had expected. I didn't know if the book was supposed to be a final payment or just collateral until they could get him the hawks, but, either way, the plan had gotten Athel—and likely Fedim—killed.

Why hadn't Athel told me what he'd done with the book? Had he or his masters been afraid I would go after it? Why had it been worth dying for?

Or killing for, for that matter?

The message to Sylos had been a more hastily scrawled thing: *Jarkman says Nose got to Athel. Has made arrangements. Blade will deliver the message, arrange for cleaning. Cooperate.* I had no doubt the Jarkman in question was Baldezar, but I had been wanting to confirm it in person. That, and find out why they had felt it was necessary to dust me in the first place.

The first drawer held nothing more than a few incriminating letters on some minor gentry and a handful of falsed seals. I dumped it out on the desk, checked the bottom and sides for hidden panels, and then got to work on the second lock.

"He said it was an exercise," said Lyconnis as I tickled the second set of tumblers.

"What?" I said.

"The letter to you," said Lyconnis. "An exercise for me. And a lesson for you."

I stopped picking the lock and looked up over the desk. Lyconnis was staring down at the strips in his hand.

"*You* forged the letter to Chr— To the baroness?" I said.

"'A good scribe should be able to compose his cephta in almost any style,'" recited Lyconnis. "At least, that's what Master Baldezar says. I don't agree, but he's a master of my guild, and I'm in his shop. If I ever want to be a master in my own right, I have to heed him. So I do copies and minor forgeries from time to time."

"Didn't you wonder why he was having you forge a letter to me?"

"Yes."

"And?"

"He's a master in my guild," repeated Lyconnis, this time almost pleading. "He told me it was to show you up—to teach you a lesson. You have to believe me when I say I didn't know what it was about! If I had even thought he was capable of hiring a . . . an . . ."

"I get the idea," I said sourly. "Baldezar was covering his ass, and he used you to do it." I bent back to the lock. "If things didn't work out and I came hunting, he could point out the flaws and deny writing it." And, I thought, point to Lyconnis if I got too close. I had no doubt that if it had come to that, Baldezar would have made sure Lyconnis wasn't in a position to argue by the time I made it to him.

The second lock gave way more easily than the first. Among a collection of castings for chops and silk sealing ribbons, I found four blank strips of paper that matched my own and a narrow wooden rod. Beneath the rod was a fifth strip of paper with markings on it. I picked it up and wrapped it around the rod. The symbols lined up perfectly.

Heard the second attempt failed, it read in a shaky hand. *Nose suspects me. I need protection. I need—* The message ended in midsymbol, unfinished. That meant

Baldezar had either been in too much of a hurry to finish it, or that he had been interrupted by someone before he disappeared. I hoped it was the former, because I wanted him alive.

"Best tell your guild they need a new master here," I said, standing up.

Lyconnis stared at the slip as I unwound it and put it in my ahrami pouch.

"Is he dead?" he said.

"If he's not," I said, "he will be by the time I'm done with him."

I put the word on the street to watch for Baldezar, but I didn't hold out much hope. If he was smart, the scribe was already out of the city; if not, he was likely hiding or dead. Either way, the chances of someone spotting him in passing were slim.

Which left me Ten Ways.

Kells was right: I needed to stop Nicco from going to war, or at least delay him. Ten Ways was an avalanche waiting to happen—one that could very well sweep me along if I wasn't careful. There were too many things tying me to the cordon now, and too many ways they could go wrong. Long Nosing aside, if Kin started killing Kin down there, someone could use it as an excuse to take care of me. Loose ends and vendettas are easy to resolve when blood is already running in the gutters.

A little asking around told me Nicco had gotten back into Ildrecca earlier in the day. I found him at his favorite gymnasium on the east side of Stone Arch cordon. Stripped to his smallclothes, he was working in the sandpit with a towering slab of muscle almost half his age. I couldn't help noticing that the younger wrestler was both dirtier and bloodier than his opponent, which didn't surprise me. Even when training, Nicco made a habit of using nasty tricks whenever he could.

I approached the ring and was stopped a dozen feet away by Salt Eye. That wasn't a good sign.

"What the hell?" I said, staring up at the Arm.

"He's busy."

"And?" I said, throwing on a heavy dose of bravado.

Salt Eye hesitated. He was used to letting me pass, used to not giving me a second glance. That he now had to do both told me my status had changed. That he hesitated told me the change had happened recently.

"Screw you," I said as I feinted left and dodged right. I could hear Salt Eye spin and come after me. I sped up my pace, but not so much that I lost any dignity in the process.

"Drothe," said Nicco, not looking away from his opponent as I neared the oval pit. "Nice of you to come see me on your own for a change. Salt Eye, it's all right."

I heard Salt Eye stop, then retreat behind me.

"I tried last night, but you were out," I said.

"I heard." Nicco feinted low at his opponent, went high, and locked his arms around his neck and behind one shoulder. It didn't seem like a good hold to me, and the other man began to easily twist his way out. That was when Nicco brought his knee into the other man's midriff, lifting him off the ground. When the younger man hit the pit floor, Nicco was there in an instant, managing to kick sand in his face even as he got the pin.

Nicco rose, dusted himself off, and strolled over to the edge of the pit. He didn't spare a backward glance for the man busy trying to brush sand out of his eyes; nor for the scowling trainer who handed the Upright Man a bowl of water but kept his mouth shut. No—Nicco merely drank, spit, and stepped out of the pit. All that mattered was that he had won.

"Come with me." Nicco led me to a series of doorways on one side of the training room. He opened one and gestured for me to enter. I did.

The moist heat hit me immediately. It was a hot room—the first room of a three-room private bath, used for scrub massages and steam baths. Beyond the opposite door were the warm and cool rooms, for washing and relaxing respectively. I hoped Nicco would head to the last; instead, he sat down on one of the benches and started filling a shallow bowl from a tap beside him in the wall.

The sweat started gathering beneath my arms and along my forehead almost immediately. Nicco ignored my loosening my collar and cuffs, and instead sluiced water down his back. Then he refilled the bowl.

So, it was going to be like that.

I helped myself to one of the towels stacked in a corner, wiped my face with it, and sat on the heavy marble massage table in the middle of the room.

"You have to know you're on my shit list," said Nicco as he watched the bowl fill. "I've been hearing things about how you've been sitting on information; about how you tried to keep rumors of a Snilcher from me; about how you paid some piece of shit named Larrios to dust that Dealer for you. Hell, people are even saying you're trying to sabotage Rambles—and my operation—in Ten Ways."

"People?" I said.

Nicco shrugged. "All right, Rambles."

"You talked to him?"

"About an hour ago," said Nicco.

Shit! While I had been hunting Baldezar, Rambles had gotten to Nicco. That was exactly what I hadn't wanted to happen. I was starting to have too many balls in the air to manage.

"And you believe him?" I said.

Nicco looked at me sidelong. "Shouldn't I?"

I let out a derisive snort. "Well, if you want to listen to Rambles's fairy tales, then of course I'm going to come off as a complete—"

Nicco held up a hand. I stopped talking.

"I know how to pick through what Rambles tells me," he said, "just like I know how to pick over the information you supply. Don't look so surprised—I don't take *anyone* completely at their word, including you. But things are adding up, Drothe. You're fucking up, and it's costing you. And me."

"I . . ."

"I'm not finished," said Nicco. He paused to pour the bowl over his head and sighed. "You don't want to fall out of my good graces, Drothe," he said, "but you're damn close to doing just that."

I watched as he sat there, nearly naked, letting the water run down his face, his eyes closed. And me across from him, fully clothed—and fully armed.

It was tempting. One step, one cut, and it would be over. No Nicco meant no war in Ten Ways, or, at least, not as ruthless a war for Kells. I could live with that.

My fingers began to itch for my dagger handle.

Then I remembered the wrestling pit and Nicco's seemingly weak grab, followed by a hard kick and a footful of sand in his opponent's face. Was he setting me up? Testing me? *Me?*

I studied the Upright Man without seeming to. Yes, there—Nicco's eyelid twitched ever so slightly, revealing a sliver of color beneath it.

The son of a bitch was watching me. He was ready. Waiting. Testing.

And in that instant, I knew I was in trouble. If Nicco had to see if I would go after him, to see if I would confirm what Rambles had been saying, then I was already on my way out. Rambles had the upper hand with him now; anything I might accuse the Ruffler of would only seem petty—or defensive.

I put my hands on the massage table in easy sight and pretended not to have noticed Nicco's test. "All right," I said, "maybe I've been fucking up lately, maybe not. Either way, I'd like to think everything I've done over the years would count for something, maybe give you reason to cut me a little slack. But that's not the point right now. The point is what's been happening in Ten Ways. You're being played down there, and not just you, but the whole cordon. Someone's been setting up a war for months and—"

"I know," grated Nicco. "Kells."

"No," I said. Almost shouted. "*Not* Kells. That's what—"

Nicco's eyes snapped open.

"*Don't* tell me he isn't behind it!" yelled Nicco. "I have five people lying in the street in Ten Ways. Five, with two of their killers next to them. And do you know what those other two are wearing?"

I felt a sinking sensation inside me. "I can guess."

"Gray-and-red ribbons on their arms," said Nicco. "Kells's war colors. He's not just trying to embarrass me anymore, Drothe—he's fucking calling me out." Nicco stood and began stalking about the massage table, circling me. "War cords! I didn't think he had the balls, but if he wants to throw that glove in my face, I'll pick it up. Cord for cord, man for man."

I shook my head. A pale imitation of the colored sashes that identified the different arms of the imperial military, war cords were the closest thing we had to uniforms among the Kin. Wearing a cord was the same as declaring your allegiance. It was an invitation for attack, an excuse to let blood and take revenge. It was war among the Kin.

Except it was all a dodge. I knew firsthand that Kells hadn't put cords on anyone in Ten Ways—not yet.

"Think about this for a moment," I said, turning to follow Nicco as he paced his circles around me. "This is *Kells* we're talking about. It's not a matter of his having the balls to do something—it's a matter of his even *considering* doing this. War cords? Unannounced, and in Ten Ways? That's not his style. It's too obvious, too direct. Kells doesn't work that way."

Nicco gave me a dark look. "Since when did you become a fucking expert on Kells?"

I raised the towel and wiped at my face, hiding my expression. I was suddenly grateful Nicco had brought us into a steam bath—in here, I had every reason to be sweating.

"You forget," he continued, not noticing my reaction. "I know him. *Knew* him ... damn well. He's a cold, calculating bastard, but he's not half as smart as he'd like everyone to believe. Kells can be as hot-tempered and bloodthirsty as the next man, and there were plenty of times I *was* the next man. I wouldn't put this past him if he thought he could pull it off. Especially against me."

"But what if it's *not* personal?" I said. "What if it just looks that way? I don't think—"

"I don't give a *fuck* what you think," Nicco snarled. "I've already told Rambles to put cords on our people. We're going to war in Ten Ways, and we're going to bring that son of a bitch to his knees."

"You're going to fight him in *Ten Ways*?" I said. "You don't have the people down there to take him on!" Kells didn't have the people there, either, but I wasn't about to share that tidbit of information.

"It's taken care of," said Nicco. "If you'd been Nosing like you're supposed to, you'd know that." Nicco paused and let his breath out. He rolled his shoulders. Something popped. "Besides, we have more friends there than you think. Rambles has seen to that." Nicco grunted. "At least *someone* can do his fucking job."

So, there it was: Rambles not only had Nicco's ear; he had arranged for "friends" in Ten Ways as well. It wasn't a stretch to guess who two of them were, either. The only question left was, would Nicco believe me if I told him about Iron Degan and the Gray Prince? Would he even care?

To hell with it. The war was on, and Nicco no longer trusted me. I was a marked man, even if Nicco hadn't decided it yet. My chances of swaying him at the moment were nil. I needed to find some way to get back in his good graces, or to walk away. I couldn't do either of those dead, and that was how I would end up if I pushed him now.

I slid off the table and onto my feet. Suddenly, I felt overwhelmingly tired.

"Where the hell are you going?" said Nicco.

"To go do my fucking job," I said. "Unless Rambles has seen to that, too."

Nicco didn't answer—he just stared at me as I walked

past him and out through the other two rooms of the bath.

I didn't work the streets that night, didn't do anything except find my way home and collapse onto my bed. I vaguely recall noticing Task's body was gone from my rooms, but, to be honest, I wouldn't have cared either way at that point.

When the knock came at my door sometime later, it felt early. The muted daylight slanting in through the shutters suggested noon. After the last two days, that was early.

"Who?" I called through the door, my boot knife in my hand.

"Assassins!" called Degan cheerily. I let him in, anyhow.

Word, it seemed, had gotten out on the street about Task and her singular appearance in my rooms. As things went, it wasn't the worst rumor to have making the rounds; if nothing else, my showing that kind of backing—inadvertent or no—would make it harder for whoever was after me to recruit a replacement. My concern was they'd find a Blade who could do the job, regardless.

I washed up from a basin as Degan told me what he had been able to find out about Iron, which was little enough. Iron Degan hadn't taken a new Oath in a long time—at least several years; this suggested he had been working for his Gray Prince for a while now. Nor had Degan been able to find out which Prince Iron was working for, but that wasn't surprising. Tracking a Gray Prince was like trying to catch a bird's shadow.

During the last few years, though, Degan said, Iron had repeatedly been in and out of Ten Ways. He had also traveled across the empire three separate times. Each time had been to one of the most ancient cities of the empire—former seats of either Stephen Dorminikos, or one of his incarnations shortly after he began his cycle of resurrections. That was when the emperor had still gone on progress, surveying his nobles and lands, sometimes for years at a time — back before the walling off of the Imperial cordon and the first rumors of his rising paranoia.

"Sounds like Iron's been looking for something," I said as I pulled on a change of clothes. There were a few small spots of blood in the laundry in my hamper from Tamas's attack, but nothing so bad I couldn't wear it. "Something old, too, given where he's been hunting. Tyrogennes, Lonpo, Crosswinds and Ten Ways — all of them predate the empire."

"Something old," said Degan, "or something that talks about something old. At least two of those cities have respectable libraries."

"And libraries have books," I said. I buckled on my sword belt and put my knives back in place. "And who do we know who *has* a book, I wonder."

"Larrios," said Degan.

Which meant Ten Ways — again.

I stopped by Eppyris's shop on the way out. The apothecary didn't have more than four words for me, even when I told him about Task's body — minus the glimmer. He simply handed me a fresh supply of ahrami, closed his shop's door, and headed over to his apartments. I heard his and Cosima's voices raised in argument when I left with Degan.

Given what had happened with Task, I hoped Eppyris would persuade Cosima to leave. In fact, I decided, if he didn't, I'd make arrangements to get them both out when I returned. Cosima wouldn't like it, but it was getting to the point where I needed to cut back on my distractions and worries, and they definitely fit under both headings now.

It wasn't hard to tell that Ten Ways was on edge when we arrived. As if sensing the coming war, the city guard had put almost four dozen Rags outside the main entrance to Ten Ways. They were gathered around campaign lanterns — large iron cages on tripods, filled with fuel that could burn all night when lit — checking their

weapons and eyeing the cordon nervously. Several of
them watched Degan and me as we went into the cordon, but none moved to stop us. I suspected it would be
a different story when we tried to come out.

It was still twilight, but already the streets in Ten
Ways were emptying of Lighters. Nicco's men were in
full sight, walking in groups, gold-and-green war cords
openly displayed on their arms. A few gave me a small
nod, but most kept it to a cool eye. Rambles would have
told them about me. I wasn't wearing a cord; I wouldn't
have even if I weren't working for Kells—a Nose did
his best work unseen, or at least unmarked. Putting on
a cord would have made me an instant target outside
Nicco's territory.

There were other Cutters on the street, too—back
alley toughs who had either been bought, or who were
using the war for their own ends. This was their time—a
time of killing and rape, when atrocities could be blamed
on the war, and retribution from local bosses was less
likely. The Upright Men's soldiers and their allies would be
too busy watching out for one another—they wouldn't
bother with minor talent as long as it didn't get in their
way.

"So, what's the plan?" said Degan.

"We wander and wait," I said as two men came rolling out of a doorway in front of us, cursing and biting
and hitting each other. We stepped around them.

"Until?"

"Until the person I need to talk to finds us."

"Until *he* finds *us*?" said Degan.

"Yes."

A woman's voice joined the fray behind us. I heard
the solid *thunk* of something large and heavy hitting
something soft and breakable. One of the men screamed.

"I would have thought," said Degan, "what with your
being a Nose and all, you might go looking for *him*.
Maybe ask around."

"I'm going to," I said, "but I doubt I'll have much
luck—I don't know his name."

"No name," said Degan. A dog started barking back at the fight. "Do you know anything else about him?"

"He wears a big dark cloak."

Degan clicked his tongue. "And this unnamed man in a big dark cloak is your best lead on Larrios?"

"At the moment, yes."

"And here I was worried you didn't have a plan," said Degan.

In truth, we did more than wander. Since I didn't have a network in Ten Ways, I had to resort to the basics: eavesdropping, rumormongering, and whisper buying. We roamed the streets, loitered at corners, and crawled in and out of more basement taverns and smoke holes than I could count.

I didn't find my man right away, but I did hear any number of rumors about what was happening in the cordon. Most were more fantasy than fact, but, after a while, I was able to discern a common thread running through all of them: Everyone—in terms of local gangs and organizations—was getting hit, and most of them were blaming either Nicco or Kells. Even if there wasn't any proof of their involvement, the common wisdom on the street was that the two Upright Men were positioning themselves for a takeover of the cordon itself. And that wasn't sitting well with the local Kin.

It was exactly what Degan and I had feared, and it had the Gray Prince's fingers all over it. Not only was the Prince going to get Nicco and Kells to go to war with each other, but she was also prepping the local gangs to fight the Upright Men for her. I doubted she'd be able to call all the shots once the fighting began, but I was certain she was ready to step in and come off as the hero in the end. And, if we were right, this was only the beginning.

My one chance of preventing all this was the book. Whatever it was, she clearly wanted it. If I could find Larrios and get my hands on it, I could use the book as leverage to negotiate with the Prince. I doubted I'd be able to save Ten Ways, but maybe I could ransom the rest of the Underworld from her; or at least keep Kells and his—my—organization in one piece.

It was two hours past midnight when we came out of yet another dive. This one had smelled primarily of sweat and vomit—definitely a step up from the previous two.

"I think I'll just burn the whole damn cordon down and be done with it," I said to Degan as we took a deep breath of the night air. "Easier for everyone that way."

Degan laughed. "There'll always be a Ten Ways," he said. We started walking. "Burn it down tonight, and to-morrow morning someone will be building on the ashes."

"And *that* would only be a cover so they could dig for melted hawks," I said.

"My, but you're a pessimistic one," said a voice off to our right.

Degan had his blade out and pointed at a deep door-way in an instant. I put a restraining hand on his shoul-der but otherwise didn't move. I'd recognized the voice.

"I find that pessimism keeps me from being disap-pointed," I said.

A piece of shadow moved within the doorway and stepped out. Tall, cloaked, hooded—he could have been anyone, except for the voice.

"Prudent," said the cloaked Kin. Once again, the cowl was so far forward, and the shadows so dark, I couldn't see his face. The hood turned to face Degan and held out his hands, palms up. "Your friend and I have an ar-rangement," he said.

"Do you now?" said Degan.

"We do," I said. "He's the one who's going to lead us to Larrios." I turned to the Kin. "Assuming he's man-aged to *find* Larrios, that is."

He bowed slightly from the waist. "I can show you where he was staying as of sunset."

I nodded, then looked at Degan. He still had his sword pointed at the Kin. I was about to say something when Degan dropped the tip of his weapon and sent it home to its scabbard with a snap.

"Lead on," I said.

The cowl shook back and forth. "Payment first," he said, holding out a gloved hand.

"Not until I see Larrios," I said. Thunder rumbled overhead. I allowed myself a small smile at nature's timing.

"There are other buyers," said the smooth voice inside the hood. "Larrios is a popular man right now."

Meaning Iron Degan was likely offering a reward as well. "One half now," I said. "The rest after."

"Done."

I counted some hawks into his hands. He laughed at the amount. We dickered, finally settling on a price.

Our walking shadow led us deeper into Ten Ways. The alleys grew steadily narrower as we went, seeming to gather and condense the darkness around us. The buildings on either side went from shoddy to pathetic to practically uninhabitable. Evidence of fires marked several structures, and those that had not collapsed in on themselves looked to be seriously considering the idea. And the stench . . . It almost made me miss the sewers. Waste, rot, decay—and most of it human in origin. Somewhere along the way it began to rain, which at least reduced the smell.

The worst part, though, was that things were beginning to look familiar.

"The Barren," I said to no one in particular.

The Kin's cowl turned to face back over his shoulder. "You know it?" he asked.

"I used to live here," I said. Live? More like "survive"— that hadn't been living. "I swore I'd never return."

"Oaths are meant to be broken," said the Kin. Behind me, I heard Degan grumble deep in his throat.

The more desolate a place, the less it changes. Then again, it wasn't as if anyone was going to come running into the Barren and start fixing things up. The neighborhood was wide-open—no one ruled here—and people seldom asked, or answered, questions.

This made it all the more impressive that our guide

had managed to find Larrios here, of all places. You didn't track someone down in the Barren unless you were local, or good, or both. He didn't strike me as the former, which pointed at the latter. But if he was that good, what was he doing here?

Sometimes, the best way to get answers is to let a thing play out. I didn't expect this Kin to tell me what his game was, but that didn't mean I had to walk into it blind, either. I loosened my rapier in its sheath and let my left hand slide closer to my dagger. Degan noticed and followed suit. If anything happened, I decided, our guide would be the first to go down.

We stopped at the end of a particularly narrow alley. "There," said our guide, pointing out of the alley and down the street. "The fourth one on the left. Larrios is on the second floor."

I had to squeeze past him just to see where he was pointing. "Which room?" I asked.

The cowl turned toward me. "How should I know? You're lucky I found him at all."

I studied the building through the rain. It looked to be an old warehouse of some kind, but I couldn't be sure.

Rain has always caused problems with my night vision; looking through it is like looking through a curtain of fine beads falling from the sky. I can still make things out, but it gets disorienting now and then. This time it was worse—despite the rest I had gotten, despite all the seeds I was taking, I was still feeling the last several days weighing down on me. Fatigue was doing as much to blur my vision now as the rain.

"How do we know he's still in the building?" I asked.

"Larrios is there," said the smooth voice. "Don't worry."

"What, you made him promise to stay put?" I said.

The cowl remained pointed at me for a long moment. I gathered I was being scowled at. "He's there," repeated the Kin.

"Let's hope so," I said. "Otherwise, you owe me a fair-sized pile of hawks."

"Just worry about what you'll owe me when you're done," said the Kin.

I turned to Degan. "Ready?"

Degan had pulled his hat lower to keep the rain from his eyes. It made him look ominous. He nodded, and we headed out, leaving the cloaked Kin standing in the alley.

The top layer of dirt and refuse on the street had softened in the rain. It shifted and slid beneath our feet as we walked to the building. There was no door on the hinges. We went in.

Puddles were already beginning to form on the first floor. The sound of the water dripping from the ceiling overhead blended with the whisper of the rain to produce a constant noise that was at once both gentle and disturbing. The air was heavy with the smell of mold.

The lower level was open and empty. A small forest of posts had once held up the entire second floor, although a good third of it had fallen through at some point in the past. We were halfway to the stairway at the back of the building when we heard several loud thumps from somewhere above us.

Degan and I stopped and looked at each other. We listened. *Drip drip*, *splash splash*. Then the sounds came again. Footsteps.

"Shit!" I said. "He's moving!"

Degan and I raced for the stairs. I scrambled up as fast as I could, Degan vaulting along beside me, clearing two steps at a time. The stairs creaked and groaned, but didn't collapse beneath us.

The second floor consisted of a big main room with several large doorways to our left and right. A good half of the roof was gone up here, covering the floor with its remains. I noticed that the rain was now coming down harder. A path had been cleared in the debris, leading from the stairs to one of the doorways under the surviving portion of roof. A curtain hung across the doorway, and a feeble flicker of light showed around its edges.

We ran for the curtain without a word. I wondered if the cloaked Kin outside would stop Larrios if he made it out of the building before us. More likely he'd let the Whipjack run so he could follow him and charge me for his location all over again.

When I tossed the curtain aside, I had my rapier in one hand, dagger in the other, and Degan at my back. Larrios was empty-handed. Even better, the two men who were busy beating the crap out of him hadn't drawn their weapons.

I smiled.

"Sorry to interrupt," I said, "but I'm afraid I'll have to insist you stop kicking that Whipjack's ass—that's my job."

The man closest to us looked up almost casually from where he was kneeling, while the other didn't even pause in dealing out his punishment. Both were wearing dark, water-laden cloaks.

"Get out," said the first man. "Now."

I stepped through the doorway so Degan could come in behind me. The room was wide and deep. Toward the back, near Larrios and the men, a trio of candles flickered on the floor. My eyes ached a moment, then adjusted. I put my rapier through a small circle in the air to make sure it caught what little light there was.

"Just what I was going to suggest to you," I said.

The first man got slowly to his feet. The other slowed in his work but still kept up a rhythmic pounding of Larrios's face and body, alternating fists with each strike. Degan and I moved a step closer.

The first man studied me for a moment, then moved his shoulders forward and back, shifting his cloak so that it hung behind him.

"Mistake," he said.

I didn't answer. I was too busy staring at the white sash wrapped around his waist and the golden imperial hawk emblazoned on his breastplate.

Chapter Seventeen

White Sashes!

I froze, all my bravado gone in an instant. What the hell were two of the emperor's elites doing here, working over Larrios? Why did they want him? What the *hell* had I just walked into?

I opened my mouth to say . . . What? What do you say to men whose predecessors had nearly wiped out the Kin? Men who, if we weren't lucky, might very well try to do it again? Not a lot, I decided, especially when there were two of them and two of us.

Lousy, lousy odds.

I began to put up my sword and back away, hoping to make it out of the room in one piece. They could have Larrios; I'd find some other angle on all this. Confer with Kells, maybe even dust Rambles or Iron Degan. As long as I steered clear of the Sashes, I would be ahead.

Then Degan rushed past me and changed everything.

I watched in horror as he charged the closest Sash, his sword low, a snarl on his lips. The Sash, for his part, barely adjusted his stance. He didn't even bother to draw his sword.

Shit. Shit. Oh shit.

At the last possible moment, Degan launched himself in the air, changing his low attack into a high one. The Sash twisted and tried to pivot sideways off his front foot. The maneuver didn't quite clear him from the path of Degan's cut, but it was enough to cause Degan's blade to skip off the Sash's breastplate and strike him across the shoulder instead.

The Sash yelled out in pain even as Degan landed and planted the elbow of his free arm in the Sash's face. The Sash staggered back, blood gushing from his nose, and managed to draw his own sword and parry Degan's next thrust.

"Take this one!" yelled Degan as he stepped back, putting both Sashes in his field of vision. The second was already on his feet, his own blade out and moving, threatening Degan. There was no way Degan could finish off the first Sash without opening himself up to an attack from the second.

Take him? I thought. How? With what? I was a fucking Nose, for Angel's sake!

I looked over at Larrios. Maybe between the two of us . . . But no, he was an unmoving lump on the floor. No help there.

The second Sash advanced on Degan, his sword dancing in the candlelight. The first had regained his balance now and was wiping away the tears caused by his broken nose. He'd be back in the fight any moment.

"Drothe!" said Degan, a desperate tone creeping into his voice. "Take the wounded one, damn it!"

Well, fuck.

I ran into the room with a yell. The first Sash took another swipe at the blood on his face, then turned to face me. I was still a handful of paces away when he stepped forward and threw an incredibly fast lunge at me while I was still coming into range. I barely got my dagger up in time to parry the blow.

Damn, he was fast!

I backed off and brought my rapier back while extending my dagger forward so the tips of the two weapons nearly touched before me. The small triangle of steel was supposed to give me better protection, but I didn't feel particularly safe.

My Sash didn't look to be in great shape, what with one arm hanging limp and blood running from his nose, but neither did he seem terribly bothered by this. I decided that, barring evidence to the contrary, I was still outclassed and in trouble.

We both paused to measure each other up. He had a heavier rapier, closer to Degan's than my own, but it looked light in his hand. The breastplate would be a problem, too; the armor meant I would have to aim for extremities and his head—smaller, harder to hit targets. I wasn't used to fighting people in any kind of armor, since very few Kin or Lighters bothered with it, let alone owned it. Unless you knew you were going into a fight, it was just too uncomfortable and heavy to wear day in and day out in a crowded city. Plus, it drew far too much interest from the Rags.

Behind my opponent, I caught glimpses of furious swordplay. While I dared not follow Degan and his Sash in detail, what little I did see looked frighteningly good: blindingly fast attacks, parries that left barely a hairbreadth of room for error, body slips, and the occasional attempts at a grab or a punch with a free hand. Moves, in short, that would have left me quartered and sorted on the floor in a matter of seconds.

And if that weren't enough, Degan and the other Sash were smiling at each other. *Smiling!*

Idiots.

As for the wounded Sash, he didn't even crack a grin as he stepped forward and flicked a cut at my left hand. I moved the hand, trying to block with my dagger, and suddenly saw his sword coming right at my chest. He'd feinted and gotten me to open myself up.

I brought my sword up and across my chest even as I tried to leap back out of range. He must have been expecting that, too, since he immediately redirected his sword and buried its tip in my left thigh.

The sword had an amazingly fine edge—I hardly felt it go in. It wasn't until the Sash pulled it back out, twisting and cutting down slightly as he went, that I felt the steel dragging against my flesh. That was when I screamed.

It wasn't the pain that ripped the howl from me—it

was the sheer frustration of being stabbed so easily. Five seconds into the fight and I was already being carved up like one of Prospo's roast ducks. At this rate, Degan would be facing the both of them in less than a minute — not that I would be in a position to worry about it by then.

I backed away quickly, putting my left leg behind me, drawing my body into profile. My rapier went out before me while my dagger stayed in close to my body. I couldn't threaten with the shorter blade this way, but I could — hopefully — have a bit more time to defend with it.

I was outclassed, wounded, and on the defensive, and I let it show. If I was lucky, it could work to my advantage.

The Sash came on almost casually. I managed to parry his next three attacks — a cut, a thrust, another thrust, all in quick succession — but it was a close thing every time. I didn't even try to counterattack. The Sash grimaced at my hesitancy, rolled his bloody shoulder, and came in again. This time, I reacted.

As he thrust, I slipped my right leg back and extended my dagger out to catch his sword. I wanted to catch his blade and bind it with my dagger, even for a second, so I could follow it up with a thrust from my rapier. With his sword bound up and his left arm useless, I figured it was the best chance I'd get to put steel into him, preferably in the neighborhood of his head.

The problem was, I had to put all of my weight on my left leg to do this. I steeled myself and shifted my weight.

Fire shot through me, from leg to groin to body. I gasped at the pain, trying to ignore it as I brought my dagger and rapier forward. The dagger met his sword, but weakly and at the wrong angle — a twist of his wrist pried it out of my hand and sent it spinning off into the room. At the same time, he slipped his back leg behind him, turning his body out of the way at the last instant.

I cursed and took two quick, stumbling steps back. The Sash smiled.

"That's the best you have?" he asked. "You should've left when you had the chance."

Behind him, I caught a glimpse of Degan and his Sash—all whirling steel and blurring arms. No help from that front any time soon.

"I suppose it's too late to take you up on that now?" I said as I let my empty left hand drift back behind me. I turned my torso sideways again, trying to provide the smallest possible target.

"It was too late when you walked into the room," said the Sash.

So, Degan had been right in attacking—score another one for him.

The Sash moved forward and angled his blade across my own. I retreated, adjusting my own guard to block his line of attack. He advanced and angled again, and I responded in kind. Then a thought occurred to me.

It was risky and open to failure in any number of ways, but, at this point, I was dead no matter what I did.

I felt my left leg begin to tremble beneath me. I gritted my teeth and took another step back. Just a bit longer, I told myself. Either the Sash would fall for this or he would kill me; one way or another, it would be settled soon.

The Sash stepped forward and placed his blade over mine, just as before. As he moved, I snapped my left hand down. My wrist knife fell into my palm, the action blocked from the Sash's view by my own body. He didn't seem to notice.

I resisted the urge to smile.

I drew my body back, seemingly ready to retreat yet again. Then I let my back leg begin to fold. I yelled out in pain as my rapier's tip sank toward the floor. I was collapsing, my leg for all intents failing from the agony of the wound, and it wasn't terribly far off. In fact, I realized as the Sash grinned and began to step forward, his sword rising up for a final cut, I didn't know if I could get back up at all.

Except I didn't have a choice.

I pushed forward hard off my left leg, through the pain and the burning and the weakness, to turn my collapse into something resembling a forward lunge. At the same time, I brought my rapier up above my head, point aimed at the Sash's face, the length of the blade between me and his descending sword.

I saw his eyes go wide, saw him begin to shift his weight as he turned the cut into a parry. Let him. I didn't care about the swords, anyhow. While he was busy knocking my blade aside and saving his face, I was busy bringing my left hand around and driving my wrist knife up into him.

I felt the knife hit home just as his sword met my own. The impact of the two weapons ran down along my arm, gathering at my shoulder like a punch. Then the Sash ran into me.

The collision sent me tumbling over backward, the Sash on top of me. I screamed as both his weight and my own came down on my left leg in the tangle. Then everything went black.

I was with my late stepfather, Sebastian, standing in the clearing in front of our home in the Balsturan Forest. He was holding his sword and showing me how to false a retreat and then follow it with a counterthrust. Mother was in the doorway, watching, while Christiana sat on the ground, stacking wooden blocks. Christiana was full grown and wearing a court dress. I thought it strange that my little sister was suddenly older than I and getting her good clothes so dirty. She always got away with everything.

Sebastian called my name and tapped his sword on the ground. I nodded and tried to do what he had done, but my fingers wouldn't close on my wooden practice sword properly. I looked down to find the handle slippery with blood. I looked back up, but everyone was dead except Christiana, who was now seven. She was crying. . . .

The pain returned with a rush, and I was suddenly conscious again. I felt the Sash on top of me, trying to push himself away. His knee was in my left thigh and he was cursing, but softly. I returned the favor and tried to push him away as well. He rose up and rolled to my right; I immediately rolled left—onto my leg.

"Shit!" I yelled, and kept rolling. It was tricky with my rapier in my right hand, but I managed to get onto my back, sit up, and extend the sword toward the Sash.

I needn't have bothered. The Sash was still lying where he had rolled. My knife was sticking out of his right thigh, where the leg met the hip. A few inches higher, I realized, and my blade would have skidded off steel instead of penetrating flesh.

He was propped up on an elbow, staring at the blade, a confused look on his face. I could almost guess what he was thinking: *This is hardly anything; the arm wound is worse. So why the hell can't I move my legs? Why can't I breathe?*

I set my hands on the floor, gathered my right leg beneath me, and got to my feet as best I could. My left leg had to get in on the act near the end, and I felt myself go light-headed for a moment. No mixed-up visions of the past appeared before me, though.

By the time I was standing, the Sash had fallen back onto the floor. His lips were turning blue, and he was beginning to go through the first set of convulsions. It would get worse shortly.

I bent down and put my hand over the wound in my own thigh. My left pant leg was already soaked red, and there were smears where I had rolled across the floor. I needed stitching. I looked up to see how Degan was coming with his own battle.

They were still at it, but neither Degan nor the other Sash was smiling anymore. Degan had lost his hat somewhere along the way and had what looked like a small gash on one side of his forehead. He kept raising his free hand to wipe at the blood running toward his eyes. The other Sash was no better off. He was holding his left hand close to his chest, blood dripping from the closed fist. When he parried one of Degan's cuts, the Sash's hand moved away from his body, and I could see he was now missing a finger.

I hesitated. I didn't know if stepping in would help or hurt Degan, especially in my present condition. I might distract the Sash, but I might end up distracting Degan, too. Hell, I might just plain get in the way and get stabbed by accident.

I took a firmer grip on my rapier. Enough excuses— this was a White Sash, a man supposedly blessed by the emperor and a favorite of the Angels. Killing a White Sash was like defecating on an imperial shrine, only the shrine's buddies didn't get together and hunt you down afterward. It was too late to turn back. If that Sash got out alive, he'd report to the palace, and Degan and I would end up dead within the week—or less.

I limped toward Degan and the Sash as fast as my leg would allow. The Sash saw me coming almost immediately, saw his friend lying behind me on the floor. He wasn't stupid; he began to retreat, circling back toward the door, away from us both. Degan followed.

I changed course, hustling as best I could to block off his escape. My leg burned with every step.

I reached the doorway just as the Sash broke into a full-out run and charged at me. The move caught Degan off guard—he was a full four paces behind the Sash now, trying to catch up. It was obvious he wouldn't make it in time.

I stepped back and felt the curtain brush against me. I was squarely in the Sash's path now—there was no easy way around me. I shifted my weight back on my right leg, bracing myself even as I tried to ease the pressure on my left. Not the most solid of stances, especially against a rushing opponent, but it would have to do. As Degan liked to say, you fight the fight you get, not the fight you want. I raised my rapier, took it in both hands, and extended it before me at shoulder level. Then I angled the point across my body and settled.

I had no illusions about the Sash throwing himself on my blade—my luck hadn't been running that way for a long time. But I did hope I could slow him down long enough for Degan to catch up.

No such luck.

Instead, the Sash raised his sword and came on faster. I steadied my rapier, wondering belatedly if it would punch through his breastplate or shatter into pieces on impact. Too late to worry about it now. I let out my breath and readied myself for his blade to come crashing down on mine.

Which was exactly what he wanted. At the last possible instant, the Sash dropped his body low and came in beneath my blade, his own steel thrusting up.

I danced backward frantically, my own sword arcing down in a wild parry. I could feel the tattered curtain dragging at me as I backed into it, slowing my retreat and pulling me off balance. I sensed more than saw my sword intercept his, felt the catch of the blades followed by the finger-rattling crash of our two guards slamming into each other.

His body rose up, colliding with mine. He was trying to lift and force me out of the way. I let myself fold over him, becoming deadweight. Well, not quite dead—I managed to drive my right knee up and forward as he shifted me back. I felt it hit something hard. The Sash grunted beneath me but kept coming. A fist hit me in the ribs. I drove the pommel of my rapier into his back, trying to hit a kidney.

I felt myself going over backward. My left hand reached out, grabbing—for the Sash, for the door, for anything that could keep him from getting away. A ripping sound came to me, followed by a fall of dirty red darkness. The curtain . . . I heard the Sash cursing, felt him struggling against the fabric even as it enveloped us. Then he shuddered beside me, moved, shuddered again, and was still.

"You all right?" said Degan from beyond the darkness.

"Fine," I gasped. "You?"

"Feeling a bit inadequate, but otherwise fine." Degan pulled the curtain away from my face in a cloud of dust. I sneezed, started to push myself up, then sneezed again.

The Sash was beside and astride me, lying across my left knee and right foot. His head and shoulders were still wound in the curtain. Blood was seeping from two holes in the fabric.

Degan knelt down to check the Sash. Then he saw my leg. "What happened?" he said.

"What do you think happened?" I said. "I fought a White Sash!"

"It's more traditional to use a sword against them," said Degan. He rolled the dead Sash away and bent over my leg. I started to shift my weight to get up. Degan put a hand against my chest and shook his head.

"You need to stay put," he said. "This needs to be bound."

"Later," I said. "First we need to make sure Larrios is alive and in shape to talk."

Degan glanced back into the room at the heap that was Larrios. "He's not going anywhere," said Degan. He peeled away a blood-soaked portion of pants near the wound, ignoring my gasp of pain, and frowned. "Do you have anything in that traveling apothecary's shop of yours besides painkillers and ahrami?"

"Such as?"

"Such as a needle and thread? Or something to help pack the wound?"

I rummaged through the pouch while Degan busied himself over the Sash. The sound of ripping fabric came to my ears. I managed to find some dried wing moss and a packet of boiled lint. I also popped three seeds into my mouth, just to be safe.

"Here," I said as Degan turned back around. He had several pieces of the Sash's sash in his hands. Well, what's a little symbolic desecration when you've already killed one of the emperor's favorites?

Degan cleaned the wound as best he could with no water and poor light, packed the moss and lint into the cut, and bound a makeshift pad to it with the rest of the sash. I held still as best I could and watched him. He was quick and efficient, with no wasted motions.

"You'll need sewing up," said Degan, "but that'll have to wait." He wiped his hands on one last piece of sash, then stood. He helped me to my feet and over to Larrios. My leg held me better than I expected, as long as I went slow.

Larrios was still lying where the Sashes had left him. He was on his side, partially curled up, facing away from us. I resisted the urge to kick him, since it would have hurt me more than him at this point.

"Larrios," I said. Nothing. "Larrios, you remember me?" I cooed. "I'm the Nose from Fedim's shop—the one you lied to; the one you ducked out on." I put an edge in my voice. "And the one who's going to make you wish the Sashes were still alive if you don't tell me what I want to know."

Larrios lifted his head and rolled over onto his back. "They're dead?" he said. His upper lip was split, the lower one was swollen, and his right eye was already starting to puff shut. He'd been kicked and battered and bruised, but none of it looked old. Degan and I must have arrived just after the Sashes—they'd barely started to soften him up.

"Don't get too excited," I said. "You might be next. I took a sword in the leg to talk to you: I'm not in a generous mood."

Larrios smiled as best he could through his broken mouth. "You took a sword for me? Really?"

I turned to Degan. "Kick him for me."

Degan cocked his leg.

"Wait!" cried Larrios. "Wait—I'm serious! I owe you—those bastards were going to dust me whether I talked or not."

"Then talk to me instead," I said. "Where's the book?"

"The what?" said Larrios.

I glanced at Degan. He kicked Larrios in the side hard enough to move him two feet across the floor. I limped closer.

"I *told* you, I'm not in a generous mood," I said. "Now, where's the book?"

Larrios had his eyes squeezed shut. He was gasping for breath, arms wrapped around his ribs. He groaned.

I sighed. "Look, no one's walking out of here until I hear what I need to hear. So you can roll around and groan and bleed all you want, but we'll keep beating the crap out of you until you talk."

Larrios cracked his left eye open—the right was completely swollen shut by now. I shuddered at the image, remembering what Athel had looked like at the end, and kept my face impassive. I didn't want it to come to that again.

"I need to get out of the city," Larrios said. "There're too many people after me—I need out."

"Too many people?" I said, exchanging a glance with Degan. He didn't look reassured. "What kind of people?"

Larrios coughed and spit out a bloody gob. He levered himself slowly into a sitting position. I watched, letting the pain of his efforts do the work for me.

"Them, for one," he said, gesturing at the dead Sashes on the floor. "Then there's you; that fucking big Arm, Ironius; his Ten Ways allies; Kells; the—"

"Wait," I said, standing up straighter. "*Kells* is after you?"

Larrios nodded. "As of two days ago. He was nicer than most. He put word out that he'd pay a third of what the book's probably worth. Most people have just gone straight to the knife." Larrios shook his head. "I should have taken the offer. Fuck."

I let out my breath. My first thought had been that Larrios had somehow linked Kells and me, but that clearly wasn't the case. Still, why was Kells after the book all of a sudden? I'd only mentioned it in passing before. . . .

"Then there're all the loose Kin," continued Larrios. He looked darkly at me. "I have *you* to thank for that— they wouldn't be hunting me if you hadn't put a price on my ass."

I blinked. The room had started to lose its focus all of

a sudden. Blood loss? Fatigue? I put my hand to the wall and slowly lowered myself to the floor.

"Duck out on a Nose," I said as I leaned back against the wall, "and that's what you get." The room began to steady itself.

"Hey," said Larrios, peering at me in the dim light. "You look like shit, too. What happened?"

"The book," I said, refusing to get distracted.

"I told you, I need to get out of town."

"And I told you, no bargains."

"Then you might as well dust me right now," he said, "because I'm dead either way."

I looked up at Degan. "You heard the man."

Degan had just begun his downswing when Larrios yelled out that he'd take us to the book. The sword buried its tip in the wall three inches to the right of Larrios's ear. Degan smiled, and we all left.

I sat inside the ruined warehouse's doorway and stared out into the rain. Larrios sat behind me, hands bound, legs shanked together with a length of sash long enough to let him walk, but not run. His remaining good eye was almost completely swollen shut now, too, but I still didn't trust him not to run, even half blind and bound.

I watched as Degan came walking back through the rain. He was alone—no cloaked and hooded Kin on his trail; no guide back out of the Barren. Degan shook his head as he stepped through the door, his hat scattering drops of water in the process.

"The bastard set us up," I said.

"Maybe," said Degan, not sounding convinced. "He might have heard the yells and decided to rabbit. Or ..."

I waited. Degan remained silent and continued to stare out into the rainy night. "Or?" I said.

"Or the other White Sash got him."

I started at that. "The *other* White Sash?"

"Probably," said Degan. "They usually travel in groups of three. Or six, or nine—always a number divisible by three. It's their way of paying tribute to the three endless incarnations of the emperor."

"So why didn't the third one come and help the other two?" I said.

Degan shook his head. "I don't know—and that's what concerns me."

I peered back out into the night but saw nothing. "Let's get out of here," I said. Degan helped me to my feet. If possible, I was suddenly feeling more nervous.

The rain was worse than before, the drops having become the large, heavy sort that immediately soaked through whatever they hit. They were colder now, too; that, or I was colder. Either way, it wasn't pleasant to be out. Enough water had come down to churn up the alleys, making every step a slippery, slogging challenge. The only positive thing was that most of the stench had been washed out of the air for the moment.

The storm made the streets a distorted maze to my night vision. The shadows and shapes I usually knew so well took turns melting around the edges and springing back into focus as I limped along at Degan's side. I found myself watching my feet more and more often, hoping to banish the headache the rainy night was causing. That didn't stop the ache, but it kept it from getting worse.

We stopped often, both to rest my leg, and to let Larrios get his bearings.

"Here," I said to Larrios at one point. We were leaning up against a building, barely out of the rain beneath a narrow overhang. Degan was off scouting out the next few blocks.

I had a seed in my palm. Larrios peered at it as best he could.

"Ahrami?" he asked after a moment.

"It'll help you stay sharp," I said.

"No, thanks."

I returned the seed to the pouch around my neck. I had been taking them at regular intervals since the fight with the Sashes, and now it was close to empty. So much for this supply lasting a week.

"What do the White Sashes want with the book?" I said.

I caught the shadow of a shrug. "Same as you, I suppose."

"I doubt that." Somehow I didn't see the Sashes using the book as leverage against Ironius and his Gray Prince. As far as they were concerned, the more dead Kin, the better. No, they had been sent after the book for a different reason—I expected they wanted the book for whatever was in it, not for what it could do for them.

"You've seen the book," I said. "What's in it that's so damn important?"

"How should I know?" said Larrios. "I can barely read. Besides, it's not in any language I've ever seen." He reached up to wipe the rain from his eyes and winced when his hand brushed across the torn and swollen skin. "I should've taken Kells's money."

"How much did he offer you?"

Larrios showed me a broken grin. "Why? You thinking of selling it to him?"

"Wouldn't that be something?" I said, chuckling at the thought. Then I heard a sharp whistle. I looked up to see Degan halfway down the block, waving us forward.

Larrios guided us as best he could, but, with his damaged eyes and the rain, it was slow going. We had to backtrack twice, but eventually we arrived in front of the burned-out husk of a building. Only the back and the right side walls were still standing—the other two walls, as well as the roof, had collapsed long ago. The floor was gone, too, leaving a sodden pit that had once been a basement.

We were in the heart of the Barren.

"You hid a book in *there*?" I said, pointing at the morass before us.

"What?" said Larrios. "It's not like anyone's going to look for it there."

"It's a *book*," I said incredulously. "The weather, the

rats ... Do you know what they could do to something like that?"

"I was in a hurry," said Larrios as he walked up to the edge of the basement and looked down. "I didn't have time to be picky."

I limped up beside Larrios and squinted into the pit. It was tempting to push him in, just on principle, but I restrained myself.

The water looked to be knee deep. Tangles of blackened beams and broken stone formed islands in the dirty pond. There were weeds everywhere. A small sapling grew out of the rubble off to our right. I had a momentary sensation of dizziness and quickly moved back from the edge, nearly falling over Degan in the process.

Degan gave me a quizzical look as he helped steady me.

"I'm fine," I said. His look said he didn't believe me. Well, hell, neither did I, for that matter. I felt like shit and could barely make out the real garbage around me from the things my mind and night vision were starting to invent.

I took another seed for good measure, even though my heart was already racing.

"Where's the book?" I asked.

Larrios was at the edge of the pit, staring. "At the back."

Of course. We moved left, toward a section of the basement wall that had collapsed and formed a steep ramp down. Degan was practically carrying me by now. He set me down on a pile of bricks a little ways from the edge of the pit, and I gasped as he did so. Even though my head felt as thin as a piece of fine silk, I was still sharply aware of the throbbing in my leg. I closed my eyes and rested my face in my hands. Neither the seeds nor Eppyris's drugs were working.

I thought back to the fight with the Sashes. I could still see the blade, could still feel it twisting and pulling at the flesh of my thigh. Still see it ...

No. Think of something else. Something ...

Athel is strapped to the barrel, head hanging to one side. He's grinning his grin at me, knowing and mocking and ironic. His eyes are sharp and focused, questioning. *What are you going to do now, Drothe?* the look says. *Will you die for the book, too?* He laughs. *Are you already dying for it?*

Am I . . . ?

"Drothe!"

I jerked upright. "What?" I said, looking around for the source of the voice. I had somehow slipped back into a reclining position on the pile.

Degan was standing over me in the rain. He looked worried.

"What?" said Degan.

"Didn't you call me?" I said. "I heard my name."

Degan shook his head. "No one said anything."

I blinked the rain out of my eyes. "Oh," I said. "Fine."

"Drothe," said Degan, "maybe you—"

"Where's Larrios?" I said, suddenly noticing we were alone.

"He's getting the book," said Degan patiently. "You told him to go retrieve it."

"I did?"

Degan nodded, his hat producing a small waterfall when his head dipped. "He wanted me to go instead, since he can barely see, but you said we couldn't waste the time it would take me to search for it."

That certainly sounded like something I would say. And it was a smart decision. I decided to take Degan's word that I had actually said it.

"How long's he been gone?" I said.

"Not long." Degan knelt down next to me. "Drothe, I think we should get you out of the rain and check your leg."

"When we have the book," I said.

"There's a building across the street that still has its roof," said Degan. "We could watch for Larrios from the doorway or a window."

I mustered my concentration and stared Degan in the

eye. "I leave when I have the book," I said, "not before. Everyone wants that damn thing so bad. Well, *I'm* going to get it. It'll give me an edge in this whole mess. For the first time since this started, *I'll* have the edge. Me. Do you understand?"

Degan returned my gaze for a long moment. I could feel myself beginning to waver—being out of the rain *did* sound good, so good—but the sound of feet scrabbling on the muddy rocks of the ramp saved me.

"Hey, give me a hand!" yelled Larrios from beyond the edge of the pit.

Degan smiled and gave me a light slap on the shoulder. "Lucky."

"Stubborn," I replied.

As Degan stood and went to help Larrios, I let myself ease back on my rough seat. Bits of broken bricks and stone poked into my back, but it felt wonderful to lie back nonetheless. I shifted slightly so I could see the edge of the pit.

I was watching Degan, down on one knee and leaning forward, his arm reaching toward Larrios, when I heard a splash come from somewhere behind me. It sounded too big to be a rat or a dog, and I twisted my neck to peer into the night.

He was coming fast, sword out, cloak flying behind him. For a moment, I thought it was our dark guide, come to betray us in person, until I saw the broad swath of white around his waist.

"Degan!" I said even as I sat up and tried to push myself into a more or less standing position. "White Sash!"

It came out a little bit louder than a mumble.

Somehow, I managed to lever myself upright. I still had my rapier in my hand, but there wasn't much I was going to do with it. Nevertheless, I raised the blade's tip as best I could and staggered my way between the Sash and Degan's back.

The Sash saw me and didn't even slow down. I saw a smile form on his face, and suddenly realized this Sash was a woman.

"Degan!" I said again, "Sash!" This time it came out louder.

I heard a yell behind me and the sound of feet scrambling for purchase in the mud.

The Sash was practically on top of me. Her smile was wide and genuine and cruel, and it made her beautiful in the beaded amber of my night vision. I found myself wanting to say something to the woman who was about to kill me: to tell her how lovely she was, how graceful, how much she reminded me of my sister, but reality was working faster than my mind by that point. I was still figuring out the words when she raised her sword and swatted me aside with its guard.

The blow spun me as I fell. I caught a glimpse of Degan drawing his own blade even as his back foot slid out from under him and he began to fall down the ramp. Larrios was behind, yelling something I could no longer hear, a dripping leather sack clutched to his chest. And the Sash—she was in midleap, her sword held high, her teeth flashing in the night.

Then I was facing the ground, watching it come up toward me. I thought I heard myself say, "Ana," but it might have been my mind playing with me again. I hit the mud, and the world became a dark and quiet place.

Chapter Eighteen

I was running through the forest. Trees flashed by on either side, and I leapt over roots and rotting logs with ease. Through the leaves overhead, the sky shone the brilliant blue I remembered from my youth, and I suddenly knew where I was—home, in the Balsturan Forest.

But I was me—Drothe the Nose, older, jaded, with a rapier slapping at my side. The youth I should have been was absent, leaving me in his place. I didn't know why, but I felt that this was a good thing—that I could do something the teen could not.

Then I heard the screams and the sound of steel on steel, and I remembered. This was the day it all ended. This was the day my life became a twisted, broken thing. This was the day they killed my stepfather, Sebastian, and the day any hope I had ever had of family died.

I pushed myself harder, tried to move faster, but my left leg was suddenly filled with pain. I looked down to see blood running from it, leaving a trail of red in the forest behind me. I howled and kept going.

I limped and stumbled, ran and ducked as best I could. The cottage was too far and I was too slow. The boy I had been could run faster, but he'd be helpless once he got there. It had to be me—I could stop this. I *had* to stop this!

I burst from the trees, half running, half falling, and stumbled over my mother's grave, long overgrown with grass. My rapier fell from my hand. I pushed myself up.

I expected to see Sebastian, my stepfather, just finish-ing off one assassin as a second took careful aim with a crossbow and shot him down. I expected to see Christi-ana, thirteen years old, lying unconscious in the doorway, blood running from her head. I expected to see the agony that had seared itself into my mind all those years ago.

Instead, I saw a marble-paved courtyard, its walls covered with flowering vines. A fountain, carved from rose-colored stone and resembling a collection of those same flowers, stood in the center of the place. Water gurgled gently from each stone rose, spilling across the petals and collecting in the sunken pool at the fountain's base. Sunlight spilled in from windows cut in one of the walls, turning the puddles on the paving stones to mol-ten fire.

The place smelled green and fresh and alive; I didn't trust it.

Toward the garden's back corner stood a woman dressed in loose golden pants and a fitted brown jerkin. She was looking out the window, her back to me. Her hair was an unremarkable shade of brown, tied back in a short tail with a piece of white ribbon. Tiny silver bells hung from the end of the ribbon.

The woman didn't turn as I stood up. I scanned the ground for my sword, didn't see it. Must have left it in the other dream.

I took a step—my leg felt fine again—and another before the woman spoke.

"Why do you want the book?" she said as she reached out and plucked a white rose from a vine running up the wall.

Degan no doubt would have come back with a witty reply of some sort; Jelem would have replied with some-thing caustic enough to get himself kicked back into consciousness; me, I simply blurted out, "What the hell is it to you?"

The hand holding the rose made a dismissive ges-ture. "It would take too long to explain, and we don't have the time." She brought the flower to her face, then turned toward me. Suddenly, we were less than a foot apart. I almost fell over as I took a hasty step backward.

She breathed in over the rose, her eyes closed, and she smiled. "Memory always makes them sweeter," she said wistfully. Then she tossed the flower aside and looked at me.

Up to that point, I would have called her unremarkable—plain mouth, thin nose, small forehead, with dark brown hair tousled carelessly on top. But when she lifted her lids and displayed the gold-touched jade that resided beneath them, I knew I wouldn't be forgetting her.

"Frankly," she said, ignoring—or perhaps, counting on—the effect her eyes had on me, "I'm impressed you're still alive. It speaks well for you. But if you keep stumbling around as you have been, even that degan you have in tow won't be able to save you."

"How—" I began, but my words came out slow and muffled. The woman waved her hand impatiently, twice as fast as I knew I could move my own.

"Don't worry about the 'how,' Drothe. Focus on the 'who.' Who else knows? Who is after you? You're a popular boy lately, and I'm the least of the players in this game."

I almost laughed at that last bit. You don't step into another person's dream without being *someone*—but I knew better than to argue. If she wanted me to know who she was, she'd tell me; and if not . . . Well, there was nothing I could do to make her.

"All right," I said, each word sitting like softened lead in my mouth, "who wants the book? And why?"

Now it was her turn to stare, but only for a moment. Then she tilted her head back and laughed. The bells in her hair chimed in counterpoint to her mirth.

"You mean you don't know?" she said. "You have Ioclaudia's book, and you don't even know what this is all about?" She met my gaze, a wide smile on her face. The smile was almost as captivating as her eyes. "Oh, this is too good."

Ioclaudia's book? Athel had given me the name of the *author*? No wonder I hadn't been able to track her down—if the book was as old as I was starting to think, Ioclaudia had been dead for centuries.

I looked at the woman before me. Bells. And books. And then it hit me.

"Princess," I said, sketching a deep, ironic bow.

She'd been the one outside Fedim's shop, the one who had jingled as she walked away while I crouched in the sewer. Iron Degan was *hers*. Which meant I was talking with a Gray Prince. Princess. *The* Gray Princess.

"It's 'Prince,'" she said, sounding almost embarrassed. "And it's nice to know you can at least figure something out."

"What I've figured out," I said, my temper rising, "is that I have Cutters, White Sashes, a couple of Blades—not to mention *your* pet degan—after me. But I haven't figured out why. Now, if you think that's amusing, you can shut this garden down and find someone else to play dream games with, because I have better things to do."

I turned to walk out of the garden and suddenly found myself seated on a bench beside the fountain. There hadn't been any benches in the courtyard before. The woman was sitting next to me.

"I'm sorry," she said, looking me straight in the eye. Coming from her, the words didn't sound so much like an apology as a simple statement of fact. "I had just figured that anyone involved this deeply would know the stakes."

"That would be assuming I got involved in all this by choice," I said. "Bad assumption. Enlighten me."

A line formed between her brows as she frowned. She tilted her head to one side and stared past me. I thought I could hear a faint whisper on the air, as if the garden were speaking to her on the breeze. Then she nodded and focused on me again.

"I can't go into details right now," she said, "but I can warn you to be very careful about whom you ultimately give that book to."

"What," I said, "afraid I'll make it harder for you to get your hands on it?"

She surrendered a wry smile. "I can't say that's not part of it, but it's not my main worry. I'm more concerned abou—"

Pain erupted in my leg as the courtyard winked out of existence. I opened my eyes to see the back of a pair of boots moving beneath me. They were walking across wet and muddy cobbles. I realized by the motion I felt that I was slung over someone's shoulder and being carried through the streets. I tried to shift my weight so I could fall and get away, tried to ask who the hell was carrying me. All I managed was a weak wobble of my head and a pathetic mumble. The person carrying me readjusted my body on his frame with a grunt. The movement sent fresh fire racing up my leg. I groaned and closed my eyes, fleeing from the pain and misery into darkness.

" . . . happening?!" yelled the woman. I opened my eyes to find myself on the paved floor of the courtyard, my knees up against my chest. The woman was standing beside the bench, turned toward a shadowy, half-transparent figure that had not been there before. The figure was short—even shorter than I—but I couldn't make out any details beyond that. It gestured as if it were speaking, and I heard the whispering on the breeze again.

So, she'd contracted a Mouth to glimmer the dream for her. Good. The thought of a Gray Prince being able to walk into my dreams at will was just too much for me at the moment.

My leg still hurt, but it was not nearly as bad here. I unfolded and rolled slowly to my hands and knees. I noticed that the veins in the marble tiles seemed to shift and move of their own accord. That couldn't be a good sign.

"How long can we keep hold of him?" asked the woman. Pause. "Well, shit." I heard the sound of movement saw her kneel down beside me at the edge of my vision. The place didn't smell green anymore—another bad sign, I was sure.

"Drothe," she said. It wasn't kind or coddling; it was a command. I looked up at her without thinking.

"Listen to me," she said. "Whatever you do, don't give that book to anyone."

"Except you," I gasped. "Right?"

She shook her head. "Not even to me. Hide it. Don't tell anyone where it is—that'll help keep you alive, at least for a while. I'd rather see Ioclaudia's book lost again than in the wrong hands."

I was about to ask what she meant when my leg spasmed. I winced, and when I opened my eyes, most of the color had washed out of our dream. The woman reached out and put her hands on my shoulders. The fingers didn't quite stop when they touched me, seeming instead to pass an inch into my flesh. Oddly, it didn't feel strange at that moment.

"Hide the book," she said, blurring and fading at the edges. "And keep it hidden."

Then I was alone in a silence that quickly turned into oblivion.

There was nothing gradual about it—no slow graying before my eyes, no buzz becoming a roar in my ears. One moment I was unconscious; the next, I was awake.

Everything was wrong. Instead of being cold, wet, and in pain, I was warm, dry, and lying in a soft feather bed. Crisp sheets covered me. My clothes were gone, replaced with what felt like a soft nightshirt. And I was alive. It was this last bit that surprised me the most.

Out of curiosity, I shifted my leg. A barely noticeable ache answered the movement. That wasn't right, either; the pain should have nearly driven me to tears. I pushed against the mattress beneath me with my left leg, my teeth clenched in preparation for the agony that would follow. A sharp burning answered the effort, but nothing more.

Glimmer—had to be. There was no other way I could be feeling this good.

Now I was really worried.

I kept my eyes closed and listened. The sounds of Il-drecca after dark came to me, but they weren't the usual cacophony of screams, drunken revelers, and rutting cats I was used to. Instead, I heard night insects, fragments of rough laughter, and the light tap of fingers on a drum somewhere in the distance. Whatever cordon I was in, it wasn't Ten Ways or the Barren, that was for certain.

I was about to roll over, when I heard cloth rustle and someone take a wet-sounding sip of something behind me. I froze, then forced myself to relax. Guard, nurse, or someone else? A glass clinked faintly as it was set down.

I took a slow, deep breath and was happy to find no hints of fresh greenery in the air around me. Still, there was something else in the air—something vaguely famil-iar I couldn't quite place. Basil? Crushed thyme?

I took another breath. Yes, it was definitely com-ing from the sheets. And I knew only one person who scented her sheets. Christiana. And that meant the other person in the room was . . .

"Damn it, Degan," I said, rolling over and opening my eyes. "Why'd you bring me here when you know I don't like—" And I stopped.

Jelem favored me with a sly smile. "I wasn't thrilled about having you here, either," he said. "But once my wife saw you bleeding all over the street . . ." He shrugged eloquently. "Well, it's not as if I have a say un-der this roof, anyhow."

Jelem was stretched out in a well-padded chair, his feet kicked out in front of him, crossed at the ankles. His dark hair was in disarray, and the long green and black kaftan he wore was uncharacteristically rumpled. A silver oil lamp sat on a table by his side, creating shad-ows around the room. Next to the lamp, a glass of wine glowed red from the flame. Above him, an open window revealed a fragment of the clear night sky.

I looked around the room. No, definitely not my sis-ter's house. She would never stand for the plain, white-washed walls—colored plaster was all the rage among the nobility now. Then again, she might forgive it, once she saw the woven cloths that had been hung at strategic spots around the room. Gold, green, crimson, and brilliant blue threads formed intricate arabesques and geometries, bringing color and grace to an otherwise unremarkable space.

I noted that neither my clothes nor any of the rest of my possessions were in ready sight. I turned back to Jelem to ask about them, when I noticed the battered, leather-bound book lying open in his lap. To hell with my clothes.

"Is that what I think it is?" I said.

Jelem glanced down at his lap. "This?" he said as he flicked a corner of a page. "If you mean, is this the waterlogged tome I've taken so many pains to dry properly, then yes, it is."

"Put it down," I said.

Jelem raised an eyebrow. "Excuse me?"

I ignored my muscles' complaints as I pushed myself into a sitting position and pointed at the book. "Put it down," I said. "Now." Dream warning or no, I hadn't slogged through sewers and fought White Sashes so Jelem could page through it at his leisure.

Jelem regarded me for a long moment, his expression fading from mild surprise to cool displeasure. Slowly, he closed the cover and set the book on the table.

"As you wish." Jelem picked up the glass of wine and sank back even farther into the chair. He took a long, lingering sip and held the glass up to the lamp's light. Then he smiled.

I knew that smile. He had something—something he'd found in the book. Something he wanted to trade for.

Fine. Let him smile. What could he have possibly found in just . . .

I looked past him to the window and the crisp, clear stars outside—stars that had been hidden behind storm clouds when I was last awake.

Oh.

"How long have I been here?" I asked.

Jelem's smile deepened at my tone. "A night, a day, and nearly another full night. It's almost Owl's day, and a new week, by your reckoning."

"Owl?" I echoed. Damn. Maybe he *had* gotten through enough of the book to find something after all. But what was he doing with it in the first place?

"Where's Degan?" I asked.

"He's been in and out—more like a worried hen than an Arm." Jelem took another sip of wine and looked at me. "You can ask me directly, you know. It's not as if I haven't already been insulted."

"Fine," I said. "What are you doing with the book?"

Jelem nodded. "Better. Simply put, you wouldn't let it out of your sight. You made Degan promise to leave it with you. He did."

"And you just decided to help yourself to it?"

"No one made me promise not to."

"I take it," I said, "that you found something interesting in there."

Jelem tipped his glass toward me in salute.

"And that it's going to cost me," I said.

Jelem set the glass on the table. "That," he said, "is entirely up to you." He picked up the book again. "I'm sure you'd be able to puzzle a fair amount of this out on your own, or pay someone else to do so, but that would take both time and trust. I doubt you have much of either to spare at this point."

I didn't bother denying it. He had me in a corner, and we both knew it.

"How much?" I said, steeling myself for what I knew was going to be a very large number.

Jelem surprised me by waving the idea away with a sweep of his hand. "Money? For this? Perish the thought. You already owe me, and besides, who am I to be greedy?" I was good; I didn't laugh in his face at that. "No," continued Jelem, "I was thinking of something of more immediate use."

"Such as?"

Jelem tapped his finger on the book meaningfully.

"No," I said. "Absolutely not. The book stays with me."

"You misunderstand," said Jelem. "I don't want the book—I'm not stupid, nor do I have a death wish—but I do want to know why you're so interested in it. You and glimmer don't usually mix, Drothe, especially when the glimmer's imperial, so I—"

"What?!" I said, throwing the sheets aside and swinging my feet to the floor. I stood, or at least tried to. My legs refused to bear my weight, and I only stayed upright by catching myself on the bed's footboard.

"Oh, be careful," said Jelem absently. "Your legs won't be able to hold you for a while yet. The healing glimmer used up most of the strength in the surrounding muscles to speed up your recovery. It should finish replenishing itself in a day or so."

"Thanks for the warning," I growled, clawing my way back to my perch on the bed. I took a deep, shaking breath and let it out about as smoothly as it had come in. "Are you telling me," I said, "that book is about *Imperial magic*?"

Jelem smiled lazily. "As far as I can tell, yes. And no. It—"

"What do you mean, as far as you can tell?" I said. "Either we can be executed for having that book, or we can't. You're the Mouth, damn it—is the stuff in there forbidden or not?"

Jelem sat up straighter in his chair and fixed me with a hard look. "I can tell you," he said evenly, "that this book was put down in that ridiculous mixture of termite tracks and rodent droppings you Imperials call writing; I can tell you that it's in a different dialect than you use today; and I can tell you that an imperial Paragon named Ioclaudia Neph wrote the book, mainly because she was kind enough to sign it. What I *cannot* tell you is what exactly Ioclaudia wrote about, because *someone* woke up in a foul mood and told me to put the book aside before I could finish."

"But if an imperial Paragon wrote it, what else would

it be about?" I said. Paragons were a select cadre of imperial magicians. By decree, they were the only ones allowed to work with Imperial magic.

"Not having finished it, I'd rather not hazard a guess."

I stared at Jelem and his smug smile for a long moment. The bastard knew more than he was letting on, and he wanted me to know it.

"All right," I said. "So if you don't want a book that may or may not be about Imperial magic, what do you want?"

"I already told you."

"Yes, but how does knowing why I want the book help you?" I said.

"Simple," said Jelem. "If I know why you're interested in it, I will know why others are after it. Kin and Imperial magic don't often cross paths—having that happen, and being involved in it, puts me in a rare position."

"You mean it'll give you leverage with whoever has the book in the end, be they criminal or imperial."

Jelem shrugged. "Something like that, yes. I've found that leverage is never a bad thing to have."

"That could be a hell of a dangerous lever," I said.

"A tool is only as dangerous as the man who uses it."

I leaned back into my pillow and considered. The offer made sense from Jelem's point of view; the more he knew, the more he could parlay it into an advantage. And, given the hints he'd just dropped, he had a fair start on the book's contents already. But that didn't help him unless he knew whom to play—or avoid—down the line.

As for my end—well, there was a hell of a lot to tell. What had started separately as a cleanup job and a hunt for a missing relic had become a twisted mass involving my sister, assassins, Gray Princes, a Kin war, White Sashes, and now, apparently, a long-dead Paragon and her notes on Imperial magic. I knew I could run most of it by Jelem without betraying either Kells or Degan, but that didn't mean I had to like it.

As a Nose, my instinct was to keep things close until I

had them figured out. Except, in this case, I wouldn't live long enough to do that unless I found out what I had.

Besides, I wanted to know *exactly* what all the fuss was about.

"Got any seed?" I asked.

Jelem reached into one of his sleeves and tossed me a pouch. I emptied two of the dark orbs into my palm, rolled them there briefly with my fingertips, and then took them into my mouth. They were superb.

"You have to keep this tight," I said. "I know I can't expect you not to use it, but it can't make the rounds. Understood?"

"Completely."

"All right," I said. And I told him. I talked about being sent to dust Fedim, the conversation above the sewer grate, the attempts on my life. I talked about the missing relic, the scraps of paper, Iron Degan and the Gray Prince and Ten Ways. I went over everything that impacted either Ioclaudia's book, Ten Ways, the fighting between Nicco and Kells—even my dream encounter with the Gray Prince. The only things I left out were my Long Nosing, my Oath to Degan, and my relationship to Christiana.

When I was done, Jelem remained silent for a long time, slowly swirling the last of the wine in his glass and staring at the light that gilded its rim. When he did speak, his voice was soft, as if coming from a great distance.

"The dream," he said. "The dream . . . disturbs me."

"You and me both," I said.

Jelem shook his head. "I'm not talking about the woman's warning, although I think you should heed her to be safe."

"Then what?"

Jelem looked up from his wine. "Dream manipulation is . . . Well, it's not done. At least, not that I've ever heard of. Not in the empire."

"But they do it somewhere else?"

"There are stories, told in the oldest *wajiq tals* in Djan—what you might call magicians' academies, though you have nothing to equal them here—of ancient masters who could step from one reality to another like we pass from room to room in a house. These studies were banned ages ago. The despots felt this power too closely mimicked the traveling of our gods, that it was a kind of blasphemy. It's said the first step to such travels was to be able to enter the land of another's dreams."

"Are you saying there's a Djanese *yazani* after this book, too?"

"No," said Jelem. "I'm saying that, if your dream was manipulated as you say, the person responsible has access to a form of magic banned in my homeland for generations. Whether your imperial glimmer can do such things, I don't know."

"But why all the dancing around?" I said. "Why not just use glimmer to find the damn thing in the first place?"

"Two reasons," said Jelem. "First, it's very hard to use magic to locate things. Unless you are intimately familiar with what you are looking for, the chances of finding something with a spell are minimal at best. You would do only slightly worse if you flipped a coin at every crossroads you encountered in the city. And secondly, if you suspected other potent magicians, as well as the emperor himself, were interested in the same thing as you, would you want to advertise your involvement in the first place?"

"You forget," I said, "I seem to have been doing exactly that all along."

"Ah, but you're a fool," said Jelem. "The people looking for this book know better. They've understood the stakes from the beginning, while you're just beginning to realize the risks now."

"So tell me why this book's so damn special," I said.

Jelem set his glass aside and opened the book. The bindings creaked in soft protest. "As I told you," he said, beginning to turn the stiff pages with disturbing disregard to their condition, "I can't be completely sure of the contents. It's in a strange script. I haven't had much of a chance to examine it. And, frankly, what passes for magical theory in your empire still puzzles me sometimes. Djanese magic is much less eccentric."

"Quit making excuses," I said, "and get to the point."

Jelem paused long enough to favor me with a dark look, then continued leafing through the book. "This is a personal journal. Part of it focuses on court politics, and part of it deals with glimmer. It's hard to say what's what. Ioclaudia skipped from topic to topic like an excited child—like so many Imperials, she obviously had no formal training in rhetoric—but when she does mention magic, it certainly seems to be of the Imperial variety.

"What's more, Ioclaudia Neph appears to have been one of the emperor's personal magical advisers—part of his inner circle. When he needed something, or someone, glimmered, she was one of the people he called. Information, punishment, defense, manipulation . . . She did it all for him."

I let out a low whistle. "That's one serious Paragon."

"When you cast for, and on, the emperor, you'd best be. But that's not the most interesting part."

"No?"

"No." Jelem was still turning pages, scanning over them as he went. When he reached the page he wanted, he brought the book to me.

"Here," he said. He handed it over and pointed to a portion of the page. "Read this section, here."

The book was in better shape than I had expected. I'd dealt with religious and historical texts that were more rot than book, and most of them weren't a third of the age of this one. Yes, there was water damage, both old and new, and some of the ink had faded, and the binding was loose, but the book was still in one recognizable, usable piece. Aside from the traces of Barren's mud still lingering in a few spots, I would have thought it had been residing in a library until now.

I tipped the book toward the light coming from the lantern. Jelem was right; Ioclaudia's hand had been atrocious. The ideograms looked to be a stylized form of ceph-ta, but they had been put down in a careless manner. I could barely recognize it as writing.

"Let's see," I said. *"I find I'm still having some problems with the third portion of the ... incantation. Could it be a centering issue? Perhaps, but I suspect it is more the nature of the spell itself. Hystia's Theorem states that ..."*

I looked up at Jelem. " 'Hystia's Theorem'?" I said.

"Patience," said Jelem. "Keep reading."

I repositioned the book in my lap. *"Hystia's Theorem states that while magic can be focused through the ...* fala n'arim*?"*

"It's a Djanese term. Keep reading."

"It cannot be used to effect the same. This is known. It is a Truth, handed down by the Angels, immutable as time.

"And yet, we have found flaws in the Theorem. While the fala n'arim *is the ideal lens, it might serve as a template as well. As a lens may be polished or faceted, so may it be altered to change its focal length. Is this the case for the* fala n'arim *as well? An imperfect analogy, I admit, but if it is so, then we can do much more than we thought. So much more than we were told we could. ..."*

I looked up. "All right," I said. "She's on the verge of something big, at least to her. Things aren't what they seemed. Great. What does it *mean*?"

Jelem took the book and returned to his seat. He stared down at the passage I had just read. *"Fala n'arim* is an old term in Djanese sorcery. There's no direct translation into Imperial, either, for the language or magical theory." He ran a finger absently along the edge of the book, then drew it hastily away.

"Fala n'arim," he said, "refers to the core of the caster, the very essence of the self. The great *yazani* of Djan have always written of shielding the *fala n'arim*, of keeping it pure and untainted. To bring power into it is to corrupt it, and therefore the man as well. It is one of our oldest precepts of magic.

"But Ioclaudia writes of *using* it as the focus for her

magic, of taking power into it and shaping it within. More, she even hints at using the *fala n'arim* to draw power from the Nether itself." Jelem paused and rubbed at his lower lip. "I suppose I can see it in theory," he said. "And it could give you access to immense power, but still, to—"

"Jelem," I said, "is the *fala n'arim* a soul?"

"For lack of a better term, yes." Jelem looked up at me. "Ioclaudia is talking about using her very being to tap directly into the power of the Nether. No gathering up the seepage like most Mouths, no constrained external taps—just Ioclaudia and the Nether."

"So that's what Imperial magic is—casting magic through your soul?"

"That's what Ioclaudia seems to be saying, at least as I understand it so far. There's still a great deal more to read."

I stared at the book in his lap. I wasn't much on theology, but you can't help but pick up some when you trade in stolen items. What little I knew was waving warning flags like crazy.

"She's talking blasphemy," I said. "*Big* blasphemy." Even the Angels had hesitated before they had divided Stephen Dorminikos's soul into three parts and set up the cycle of Imperial Reincarnation. No one messed with souls. It was the third Declaration in the Book of Return, just after, *Honor the Angels in all things* and *The Angels are the true successors of the Dead Gods*.

And then there was the whole topic of Imperial magic on top of it.

"That thing's a fucking death sentence twice over," I said.

"And a possible key to great power as well," said Jelem.

"No wonder those Sashes were after it." I ran my hand along my thigh, feeling a dull twinge where the sword had cut and gouged me. "We got lucky. This could have been far worse if they'd gotten away and told the emperor who had that book."

"Things still may be," said Degan.

I started and looked over to see Degan standing in the doorway, a canvas bag under his arm. Big men weren't supposed to move that softly.

His eyes had deep smudges underneath them. His clothes, while different from those he had been wearing in the Barren, still looked rumpled and hard worn. There was a dirty bandage on his left hand.

"The third Sash?" I said.

"Off into the night."

I closed my eyes. "Damn." Make that a death sentence thrice over.

Chapter Nineteen

"How'd she get away?" I said.

Degan, still in the doorway, shrugged. "It was either keep track of Larrios and the book, or kill her. Given how badly you said you wanted the book, I settled for shoving her into the basement and running Larrios down."

"That little bastard *ran*?"

"Like the wind," said Degan. "Well, the wind if it had a bad eye, a bad leg, and a couple of broken ribs. He ended up dropping the book rather than let me catch him."

"Where was I in all of this?" I had a vision of myself lying unconscious in the rain, a White Sash climbing out of the basement toward me, and I didn't care for it much.

Degan eyed me a moment. "You weigh more than I'd expect. Did you know that?"

"Oh," I said.

Degan nodded, then hefted the sack. "By the way, your clothes were ruined. I got these for you, instead." He tossed the canvas bag onto the bed. I opened it.

"You've got to be kidding," I said as I pulled out a scarlet doublet, the fabric pinked and richly embroidered with silver thread. A pair of matching knee pants followed, along with a set of cream-colored stockings. At the bottom, I found a linen shirt, complete with lace collar and cuffs.

"The Baroness Sephada sends her wishes for a speedy recovery," said Degan, a distinct twinkle in his eyes.

Christiana. Of course. I could see her cackling with glee as she went through Nestor's old things, looking for the least likely outfit to send my way.

Christiana . . . I looked up at Degan. The twinkle was still in his eyes.

"You couldn't have gotten me my own clothes?" I said instead of asking him about my sister.

"And how am I supposed to do that?" Degan wiggled his fingers in the air. "I know what it would take to get into your place, and I *like* having all my extremities and organs."

I sighed and looked down at the clothing in my lap. Then I held up the doublet and smiled. "Too big!" I said. "We'll have to find something else."

"Nonsense," said Jelem. He came over and gathered up the pile. "Ahnya can have these altered and ready for you in no time."

"You're a cruel man," I said sourly.

Jelem leaned in close. "I've been sleeping in a chair for two days because of you. This is only the beginning."

It was three hours past dawn when I left Jelem's via the front door, my features hidden beneath a great cloak. Jelem and Degan had left five minutes earlier, Jelem disguised as best we could manage to look like me from a distance. No one had melted from the shadows to follow them. I chose to take that as a sign that we weren't being watched, rather than as a comment on our meager efforts at misdirection.

I tugged yet again at the refitted doublet I was wearing. Jelem's wife had folded, cut, pinned, and stitched with amazing skill, but the clothes still felt like someone else's. As Degan had pointed out, though, no one would be expecting me to walk around dressed like *this*, so I was better off in them than in my own togs right now.

At least my boots had survived; otherwise, I would be scuffing about in too-big slippers, their toes stuffed with rags.

I had Ioclaudia's book with me, hidden beneath the

doublet and my cloak. By all rights, I should have been taking it straight to Kells—after all, he was the one who'd tasked me with finding it in the first place, and I *did* work for the man. But the fight with the White Sashes, not to mention the Gray Prince's dream, was still too fresh in my head to ignore. Until I better understood how Ioclaudia's journal fit into the war in Ten Ways, I wasn't going to give it to anyone. This wasn't something I could just set on the table in front of Kells, boss or no, friend or no. I respected the man, but that didn't mean I trusted him with a book on imperial glimmer—not when he was fighting for his organization's survival.

I kept my head down and my eyes to myself as I maneuvered through the morning crowds. The crush of Lighters slowed me down, but it also helped me blend in with the mob more easily.

I reached the edge of Fifth Angel Square and paused to buy a steaming cup of butter tea. I let my eyes roam over the crowd, looking for faces or forms that seemed a bit too busy being disinterested in me. The tea was good, full of butter and salt and mint. Warming. It would sit well with the five ahrami and small breakfast I had had earlier. I finished it quickly and moved back into the crowd.

I circled the base of Elirokos's statue three times, stopping to price carpets, haggle over a small bracelet, argue with a blind soothsayer, and admire a talented dancing girl with an unorthodox interpretation of the *a'Sakar*.

No one—there were no Tails, no Squinters, no Six-Foot-Gangs in sight. If anyone was following me, they were too good for me to see, let alone lose.

I went over to Mendross's stall.

"I'll be with you in a moment, sir," he said as he rushed by, a basket of lemons in his hand. He was just about to give the basket to a well-dressed woman when he stopped in midstride, turned, and stared at me. His eyes were still moving up and down my outfit when the woman behind him cleared her throat.

"My fruit?" she said pointedly.

"Eh?" said Mendross. Then he blinked and nodded. "Oh! Yes, my lady, of course." He spun around and handed her the basket, took her coin, and bowed his apologies, all the while still watching me out of the corner of his eye.

After she had moved away, Mendross turned and made an expansive gesture in my direction. "My lord!" he cried, loud enough to be heard three stalls over. "How good to see you! You must be here for those mangos you asked about last week, yes? Good news—they're in, just as I promised! I have them around back. Please, come see for yourself and tell me they are not the most succulent fruits you have ever tasted!"

I smiled and nodded and tried to play the part. Mendross bowed and scraped and ushered me toward the bright curtain that separated his inventory space from the front of his stall.

"I almost didn't recognize you," he whispered as he pushed the curtain aside.

"Glad to hear it," I said.

Mendross's second son was lying stretched out across three sacks in the back, asleep, a wax inventory tablet on the floor by his arm.

"Spyro!" Mendross snapped. Spyro snapped upright and began scrambling for the tablet. "Forget that and mind the stall," said Mendross. "And remember to push the plums—they're going soft."

The boy nodded and ducked out, barely sparing me a glance in his haste.

Mendross took one of the redder mangos, produced a small knife, and deftly carved out a long, wide wedge for each of us. He was right—they were delicious.

"So," said Mendross as he wiped a dribble of thick juice from his chin, "do I get to hear the story behind the outfit?"

"No."

"That embarrassing, hmm?"

"That unimportant," I said. "I need to know what you've heard lately."

Mendross settled himself on a small stool. "A lot. How much do you want?"

As tempting as it was to say, "All of it," I knew I didn't have that kind of time. I had been out of the game for more than two days—I needed the big picture first; the details could be sorted out later.

"Stick to Ten Ways," I said. "Plus anything you've gathered on Nicco. Or Kells." I paused to consider. "Or a scribe named Baldezar, for that matter."

"Haven't heard anything about any scribe, but where've you been that you need me to fill you in on the rest? It's all over the street."

"Just tell me," I said.

Mendross carved off another slice of mango. "Get comfortable, then," he said, and launched into his report.

It was ugly. Kin wars are always bloody, violent affairs, replete with ambushes in the street and bodies in the alleys, but this had gone well past that. Where past wars had usually been confined to byways and the dark of the night, Nicco's men were openly attacking Kells's in streets, markets, and squares, day or night, no matter whether the places were empty or full. No effort was being made to hide things from the empire, let alone give them a chance to turn a blind eye. Even worse, Rambles had supposedly told his people that any Red Sashes trying to interfere with the war were fair game. If Rags started going down to Kin gangs, it wouldn't be a question of if the empire stepped in, but, rather, when and how hard.

Iron Degan's and the Gray Prince's hands were all over this. It was turning out exactly as Degan and I had feared: Start a war, then draw in the empire. But what after that?

"What about the rest of the cordon?" I said.

"The Kin in Ten Ways are falling into three camps— for Nicco, for Kells, and for themselves. The last group is the largest. They've mainly been staying out of it, but some are starting to hire out."

"To?"

"Both sides, but Nicco's been picking up more."

"And Kells?" I said. "How's he faring?"

"That's the interesting bit," said Mendross as he reached above his head and stretched. A small cascade of cracks and pops erupted from his back. "Kells *should* be in the best position—he has Blue Cloak Rhys and Shy Meg at his back, along with a Ruffler called Mateo—but the street says he's barely holding on. Nicco's pouring Cutters into the cordon like crazy, but they aren't enough to explain why Kells's men are being rolled back night after night." Mendross leaned forward. "People are staring to talk about glimmer. Not just the stuff you can hire out on the street, but dangerous glimmer—things that take down men with a word, or shatters steel midswing."

"Has anyone seen anything?"

Mendross shook his head. "No, but there are whispers."

"I'll just bet there are," I said, remembering the body floating in my bedroom and the woman walking through my dreams.

I rubbed at my arm, trying to make the hairs on it lie down. The book beneath my doublet shifted at the motion.

"I need a favor," I said.

Mendross's eyes immediately became hooded. "Such as?"

I pulled out Ioclaudia's book. "I need you to hold this for me."

Mendross eyed the book but didn't touch it. "What is it?" he asked.

"Something I can't keep at my place," I said.

"Because someone may come looking for it there?"

"More or less."

"And what makes you think they won't come looking here instead?"

"Would you come looking for a book in a fruit peddler's stall?" I said. Especially, I thought, a book on illegal magic.

Mendross grunted and stared at the journal, thinking. "Who's after it?" he finally said.

I'd been trying to figure out how to answer that question since I'd walked up to the stall. Too much truth, and I'd walk out of here with the book still under my doublet; too little, and I'd be setting Mendross up for even worse trouble if someone came looking.

Halfway, then.

"Kells," I said. "Maybe another Upright as well."

Mendross's eyes didn't even flicker. "Two golden falcons now," he said. "And another two when you pick it up."

It was steep for what I had told him; not nearly enough for what I hadn't. I pretended to consider, haggled a bit to allay any suspicions, and finally gave in.

I handed Mendross the journal. He took it, turned around, and placed it in the middle of a pile of ledgers on his counting table.

"That's *it*?" I said.

"Which is more suspicious: seeing a book with other books, or finding one at the bottom of a barrel of figs?"

"But . . ."

Mendross held up a hand. "Don't worry. I'll find something better. This is just for now."

I left Mendross's stall with a basket of mangos—he insisted—and made another half circuit of the bazaar just to be safe. Satisfied, I gave the basket of fruit to a blind beggar at the edge of the square and headed for home.

My step felt lighter, and not just from a lack of coin after paying Mendross. For the first time in a long time, I had a handle on something. Yes, there were still any number of unanswered questions, but now *I* had one of the pieces of the puzzle. Hell, I likely had a key piece. And while that put me at risk, it also made me valuable. I might be captured, questioned, and tortured for the journal, but the odds of my being dusted out of hand had just gone down.

It was a strange kind of security, considering what having Ioclaudia's book likely meant for my long-term health, but in the short term, I'd take whatever I could get.

My good mood lasted until I turned onto Echelon Way and got within sight of my building. Then I noticed two things: First, that despite its being well into morning, Eppyris's doors were still closed; and second, Nicco had stationed two of his Arms—Salt Eye and Matthias the Brick—on either side of the shop.

I swore to myself and quickened my pace, pushing through the crowd. I hoped Eppyris's doors were closed because he'd followed after his family, and not because Nicco had forced him to shut down. It would be just like that ham-fisted Upright to punish me through the people under my protection.

I was ten yards away when Salt Eye did a double take and recognized me in Nestor's clothing. He stood up a little straighter, looked around for Matthias, failed to get his attention, and, with a shrug, began ambling toward me.

I threw the hood of my cloak back and gestured at Eppyris's shop. "This had better not be what I think it is," I said, pitching my voice to carry past the few people who still separated us.

"It's not," said Salt Eye. A smile formed across his jagged face as he came closer.

He was three paces away when the smile twitched and faltered. Then Salt Eye fell over. Behind him stood Fowler Jess, a long knife in her hand, the blade red and wet and shining in the morning light. Unlike Salt Eye, she wasn't smiling. In fact, she looked downright pissed.

Chapter Twenty

Our eyes met over the dying Arm. There were anger and murder and dark resolve in Fowler's face, but none of those inclinations seemed directed at me. Seeing her like that, knife in hand, standing over another man's body, reminded me of why I'd found her so damn alluring in the first place. Nevertheless, I let my right hand begin drifting toward my dagger.

Someone saw the body, saw the knife, and screamed. Someone else joined in. People began running and shoving and pointing.

Damn Lighters—just like them to ruin the moment.

I glanced away from Fowler in time to see Matthias get his throat slit from behind by one of Fowler's people. The woman winked at me and then slipped back into the crowd without a ripple.

Someone grabbed my arm. It was Fowler.

"Come on!" she said, pulling. I didn't move. She swore. "Nicco's got at least two more Arms farther up the street, and I don't like our chances against them in a fair fight." I stopped resisting and fell in behind her.

Fowler led me down Echelon Way to an alley called Chipper's Gap. Scratch was loitering at the entrance. He knocked over a stack of barrels as we passed, blocking off the alley mouth.

We turned into a doorway before the alley ended and followed a short flight of stairs down, cut back along a hallway, then ran up another set of steps. We came out among the leather hides and laces of Petrus the cobbler's back room. Then through another door, down more steps, and so on, weaving through a maze of connected cellars, gardens, and closely constructed upper stories until we paused inside a recessed archway at street level, four blocks away.

"I take it," I said, my hands on my knees, my thigh aching, and my breath coming in gasps, "that I'm no longer one of Nicco's favorite people."

"You think?" said Fowler. She was leaning against the opposite wall, head back. "Did your finely honed instincts tell you that, or was it my people saving your sorry ass that tipped you off?"

"A little of both," I said, "but I appreciate the asssaving more."

"Damn well better," she said. There was a strange catch in her voice, and I looked up to find her staring at me across the narrow space. "How long, Drothe?" she said.

"How long what?"

"How long have you been working for Kells?"

I froze. It was the last thing I had expected her, expected anyone, to say. Kells? How the hell had she connected me to Kells?

I blinked and tried to look more insulted than surprised. "What?" I stood up straight. "Where did you hear that?"

"Never mind," she said. "Just tell me. How long?"

"I don't—"

"How long?"

I glanced toward the street out of habit, then back down the hallway behind us.

Fowler tensed, likely wondering if I was going to run, or maybe remove a suddenly inconvenient witness. I shook my head to reassure her. She'd just saved my life and put her whole crew at risk in the process; I wasn't about to dust her. She was Fowler.

Besides, she knew, which meant other people did, too.

"How did you find out?" I said.

Fowler slapped me. Hard. "You just told me now, you son of a bitch!" she yelled.

I had stepped right into that one. Dumb. "All right, clever girl," I said. "Congratulations. You got me. Now, tell me how you knew to ask."

"Tell me how long, first."

"I'm the one who just had two Arms sent after him by Nicco," I said. "It's *my* turn to ask a question, so be patient and wait your turn."

I watched her jaw work for a moment before she gave a grudging nod.

"It's been coming from inside Nicco's organization," she said. "I only heard because of ... Well, we'll get to that in a minute. But word is he's decided you're a liability."

"I doubt he used the word 'liability,'" I said. "Liability" wasn't nearly colorful enough for what Nicco would be feeling when it came to me and Kells.

"Probably a safe bet," said Fowler. "Anyhow, from what I hear, some people are having a hard time believing you'd turn-cloak like that. Others are calling you a 'Long Nose' without batting an eye." Fowler paused to give me a caustic look. "But either way, Nicco's cut you loose, so it's open season on your ass. Good thing you weren't the kind to make enemies when you were under Nicco, right?"

"Yeah, good thing," I said drily. I'd been a Nose; part of my job, by default, was making enemies. "Any idea *how* the story got started? From inside, I mean?"

Fowler shook her head. "None. Like I said, I was lucky to find out it was going around when I did. If he hadn't broken into your place in the ..."

"Wait," I said. "Nicco broke into *my* place?"

Fowler looked up and down the street from the doorway. "I'd rather not talk about this here, in his territory, especially after what I just did to two of his people. Let's get out of here first, all right?"

I didn't argue. We headed out into the street. Fowler took us on a roundabout route, full of sudden turns and double-backs. Eventually, we ended up on a quiet side street in Rustwater cordon, just outside Nicco's territory.

"So, how long?" she asked again.

"I thought we were still on my turn," I said.

"Just answer the damn question, will you?"

I took a deep breath. "I've belonged to Kells since the beginning."

A brief silence, then, "You fuck."

It was about what I had expected. It's one thing to talk about the idea of a Long Nose, but quite another to find out someone you know has been lying to you from the day you met him. It's not personal, the lie, but people have a hard time seeing it that way. All they know is that you've been keeping something big from them for years. And with Fowler, it ran even deeper. Our occasional bedroom romps aside, she'd lost people keeping me alive. She'd put her life and reputation and crew on the line for me; in exchange, I'd hid who I was and what I did from her.

"Do you want out?" I said.

"I don't know. Maybe. Probably." Fowler swore and kicked at a stone on the street. "Dammit, Drothe, why'd you have to be a cross-cove?"

"I'm *not* a cross-cove," I said. "I came into Nicco's organization working for Kells, and I never turned on him. It only looks dirty from the outside. I'm straight — it's just the work that's crooked."

Fowler didn't seem convinced, but then she's never been one to appreciate a finely split hair. "I don't think Nicco's going to take it quite so philosophically," she said.

"We've already established that," I said.

"And I don't think you will, either, once I fill in a few details."

I glanced at her sidelong but kept walking. "Go on."

"The place wasn't exactly empty when Nicco came looking for you," said Fowler. "The apothecary was there."

"Eppyris?" I stopped in the middle of the street. "I thought he'd gotten Cosima and the girls out."

"The woman and the girls, yes," said Fowler. "But he stayed on."

"And when Nicco came?"

"He and his boys worked him over," she said.

There was more. I could feel it, hanging in the air between us.

"And?" I said.

Fowler cleared her throat. "When they were done," she said, "Nicco made him open the door to your rooms."

The door to my rooms. Oh. Oh shit.

"By the time I got to him," continued Fowler, "he was closer to dead than alive. We managed to get a carver in to sew him up and stop the worst bleeding."

"How bad?" I said.

"Between the beating and your ... and the traps. Crippled at least, maybe blind. I found out from a neighbor where the wife and daughters were. I had Scratch and Rook take him there after the carver was done."

"Will he live?"

Fowler shrugged.

I tried to imagine Eppyris without his apothecary shop, Cosima and the girls without him. It came all too easily. I pushed the images aside.

"How did Nicco get so close?" I said.

"What?" said Fowler.

"How did Nicco get so close to my place?" I said, my voice rising. "Where the hell were you and your people when all this was happening?"

"Don't," said Fowler. "Don't you *dare*! Yesterday, as far as I knew, you were still working for Nicco. If I'd known what was going to happen, I would have dusted the big bastard myself. But he was your boss—I didn't have any reason to stop him! We didn't know it had happened until they came out, wiping the blood off their hands."

"And you just let them walk?" I said.

"He was your fucking boss!" she said. "Maybe, just *maybe*, if I'd known you didn't actually work for him, and that you wouldn't cut my throat for cutting *his*, I

might have stepped in. But I didn't know that, so I stayed put."

"So you let Nicco just—"

"Damn it, Drothe!" said Fowler. "*You weren't home.* My job is to protect *you*, not everyone who walks in and out of the damn front door!"

I opened my mouth, hesitated, closed it again. Raging at her wouldn't solve anything. *I* was the one who had promised to keep Eppyris and Cosima and the girls safe, not Fowler. Me. And after all my promises and precautions and bravado, I still hadn't kept the Kin away. I hadn't kept Nicco away.

But I would handle that. Someway, somehow, I'd pay that bastard back. Revenge couldn't help Eppyris, and I knew it would supply no comfort to Cosima, but it was something Nicco and I understood. He had come after me because, in his eyes, I had betrayed him; I'd go after him not only to protect myself, but because he'd bloodied someone under my protection, in my own home. It was street justice, simple math that any Kin understood, and it needed to be settled. Instead of just dusting me, Nicco had gone out of his way to humiliate and insult me. If I ever wanted to be able to hold my head up among the Kin again, I had to address that fact—personally.

I started walking again. All of a sudden, the shaded silence of the side street seemed oppressive. I needed people around me.

"Is anyone watching Eppyris and his family?" I said. I wouldn't put it past Nicco to track them down, just to hurt me more.

"I have Rook hanging around their street," said Fowler.

"Put three more on them," I said, turning onto Tumble Downs. It was the main thoroughfare in Rustwater cordon, and we hit it right near the central square. There were people and traffic and shop fronts all around us, and I suddenly felt better for it. "And yourself," I added. "I want them well guarded."

"That doesn't leave anyone to cover you," said

Fowler, slipping closer to me so we wouldn't get separated by the crowd.

"I can handle myself."

"Right," said Fowler, "because that's been working so well for you up until now."

"With the number of Kin I have after me at this point," I said, "I may be better off without a slew of people trailing after ... Holy Angels!"

"What?" snapped Fowler, her hand immediately going to her knife.

I didn't answer. Instead, I stopped in the middle of the street and stared, ignoring the traffic that split and flowed and cursed its way around me. There had been a gap in the people a moment ago—a gap that had let me see a face. I stood and waited.

The gap came again. Yes. There.

I immediately began pushing my way through the throng.

"Drothe?" said Fowler from behind me, sounding more annoyed than anxious.

I ignored her. My whole attention was fixed on the tall, thin man standing in the open air of a street-side barber's stall. He had just gotten out of one of the wooden chairs. He was busy wiping his face with a towel to remove the last of the shaving soap.

"Baldezar," I whispered to myself, invoking the name to make it true. "Angels, let him be dumb enough to be standing there in the open."

As if in answer to my prayer, the man turned, a coin glinting in his hand as he reached to pay the woman who had shaved him. It was the Jarkman.

"Thank you," I whispered.

I quickened my pace, my hand going to the dagger on my belt as I dodged through the press around me. Behind, I could hear Fowler calling my name again. She sounded farther away.

Not far enough, though, as it turned out. As Fowler shouted out my name a third time, Baldezar's head snapped up and swung toward the street. I tried to duck behind a passing cart but wasn't fast enough. Baldezar's eyes grew wide as they lighted on me, and then he was off, sprinting down the street.

Idiot, I thought as I rushed after him. Idiot me for not giving Fowler a sign to keep quiet; idiot him for leaving the barbershop. There are very few places we Kin will not happily kill one another, but a barber's place of business is one of them. It's as close as our kind comes to giving sanctuary. The truce between the Kin and the Sisterhood of Barbers had been in force for almost one hundred and eighty years—ever since the Seven Months of the Razor, just after Isidore's death—and I wasn't about to break it for Baldezar, no matter how badly I wanted him. If he had stayed in the shop, I couldn't have touched him, but as soon as he hit the street . . .

I cursed almost continually as I dodged and shoved my way through the press of bodies. I could make out the back of Baldezar's head now and then, bobbing above the crowd even as mine stayed well below it.

He took his first right, then a quick left. I stayed with him and even began to close the distance. Baldezar might have the longer stride, but I could duck through the gaps in the crowd more easily. I allowed myself a feral smile. All I needed to do was keep pace. He was a scribe—how far could he run?

As it turned out, farther than I would have liked. Maybe it was all the stairs I'd just run with Fowler; maybe I was pushing too hard; or maybe Jelem's glimmer hadn't finished its job yet; regardless, by the time Baldezar began to show signs of wearing down, my left leg was stiffening up. I gritted my teeth and tried to keep pace. It only made things worse. Baldezar nearly fell as he turned onto an empty side street, but, try as I might, I couldn't take advantage of it. He might be weaving and stumbling like a drunk, but it was still better than the old soldier's limp I was forced to imitate.

That was when Fowler sprinted past me, arms pumping, hat jammed down firmly on her head, hair flying out from beneath it. I don't know how fast she was running, but, to me at that moment, it looked as if she could have given the wind a good race. I slowed further and admired the fit of her leggings as she closed on Baldezar.

When she came up behind him, she didn't waste time or effort. No tackling; no forcing him into a wall; no trying to trip him—Fowler simply drew her long knife and hamstrung the scribe with one smooth slash.

He went down on the pavement, hard and screaming.

I immediately picked up my pace again. The street we were on was narrow, with little traffic and few doors opening on it. What doors I did see were large, solid, ornate, and set into high walls. There was money here. That meant blood wasn't usually spilled on these paving stones, and when it was, the Watch didn't waste time getting here. This needed to be kept short.

Fowler was kneeling next to Baldezar as I hobbled up. He was doubled up on the cobbles, grabbing at his left leg and gasping through clenched teeth. There was blood coming out of his nose where it had smashed into the street, and he had a deep scrape on his chin and along the right side of his jaw. He had, however, stopped screaming. I chalked that last bit up to Fowler's threatening worse if he didn't shut up.

"This is all he had on him," said Fowler as she stood up. She handed me a knife and a small pouch of money, then glanced back down at Baldezar. "I hope you didn't need him whole."

"Just talkative," I said. I moved so Baldezar could see me standing over him. I liked to think it wasn't solely pain and blood loss that made him go pale.

"Go watch for Rags," I told Fowler.

"But—"

"Go."

Fowler muttered and cursed, but she went. As she did, I noticed at least three different heads poking out of windows set high in the walls. They vanished quickly.

"All right," I said, "I don't have time to do this how I'd like, so I'll give you a choice: Cooperate and I'll leave you for the Watch to find. Be difficult, and they'll trip over your corpse. Decide."

Baldezar opened his mouth, coughed, and turned his head to spit. Blood-tinted mucus came out, along with a tooth. "Drothe," he said, the side of his face still lying on the paving stones, "you have to understand, I didn't mean for it to happen. I just—"

"Corpse it is," I said as I drew my rapier.

"No, wait!" Baldezar held out a bloody hand. "What do you want to know?"

I showed my teeth in a manner too nasty to be called a smile. "Smart man," I said. "Start with the Blades and the forged letter from Baroness Sephada."

"That wasn't my idea."

"Of course not." I drew my rapier back for the thrust.

"No, listen!" Baldezar pushed himself up on his elbow. "When you came to my shop, I thought you were there for the letter I was copying for the baroness. When you showed me Athel's cipher instead, I panicked. I didn't know how you'd gotten ahold of it, if Athel was alive or dead, or how you were involved." Baldezar glowered. "All I *did* know was that you were toying with me, trying to make me nervous so I'd talk. I'm not stupid."

I forced my face to remain impassive even as what he was telling me sank in. Stupid? Baldezar had been too clever by half. He'd read more into our conversation than I'd had an inkling about. He'd been in on what was happening from the beginning, and I'd missed it completely! If anyone was stupid here, it was me.

"Then you came in with the forged letter," said Baldezar, interpreting my silence as agreement, "and I thought I was dead. I still don't know why you let me live, but I knew better than to give you a third chance. I was in over my head, so I ran."

"What about Lyconnis?" I said. "Were you just going to leave him for me in case I decided he was involved?"

Baldezar looked away and said nothing.

"The proud and mighty guild master," I said, "watching over his charges with courage and diligence."

Baldezar stayed silent.

"So what happened after I left your shop the first time?" I said.

"I went to see Ironius. He wasn't happy at the news."

I chuckled. "I'll bet." Ironius must have figured my visit meant I knew what was going on in Ten Ways—especially with Baldezar leaping to conclusions for him. And if *I* knew, then it followed that Nicco knew, too—or would, once I told him. Except I never had.

"So whose idea was it to put the Blade on me?" I said. "Yours?"

"No!" said Baldezar. "No. The plan was to lure you away and grab you. It wasn't until Fedim turned up dead and the book vanished that the decision was made to kill you."

He was lying, of course. Whether Ironius had wanted to talk to me or not, I would have ended up dustmans in the end. Sylos's message had confirmed as much. Besides, I couldn't see Baldezar forging Christiana's letter unless he thought I wasn't coming back from the appointment.

A sharp whistle interrupted my musings. I looked over my shoulder to see Fowler trotting toward us.

"Rags," she called out. "Five blocks and closing."

"How—" I began, but let the question go. This was Fowler; if anyone could recruit and organize a team of street urchins and beggars to watch our blinds on a moment's notice, it was her.

"Tell me when they're two blocks away," I shouted back.

Fowler nodded and went back the way she'd come.

I turned back to Baldezar. He was smiling. I showed my teeth again.

"Don't get cocky," I said. "There's still plenty of time for you to die."

It had all been premised on a mistake. Baldezar had panicked and leapt to the wrong conclusion, and then fed that conclusion to Ironius. They had sent Tamas, whom I had killed, which made things look even worse. From that point on, everything I had done—showing up at Fedim's shop, my growing interest in Ten Ways, turning up in Rambles's attic, the death of the second Blade—reinforced their initial conclusions. To them, I must have seemed one step ahead, always turning up or slipping away at the worst possible time, when in reality I was stumbling from one clue to another without knowing it.

And all because I hadn't been straight with Baldezar about why I was interested in Athel's slip of paper.

I couldn't help myself; I began to laugh. It was too ridiculous not to. I looked down and saw Baldezar's panic-stricken face, heard him babbling about it being a misunderstanding, and laughed even harder. Angels, but it hurt!

I dropped to one knee, gasping. The laughter finally trickled away, leaving an ache in my side to keep the one in my leg company. I felt drained, but strangely relaxed.

Baldezar was staring at me. Fear had been replaced by understanding on his face, and that was quickly giving way to disgust.

"You didn't know any of this before I told you, did you?" he said. "Not one part."

"No," I said.

He blinked. "You mean I . . ."

"Made it worse?" I said. He flinched, and I have to admit I enjoyed that. "I doubt you could have fouled up more if you tried." I levered myself to my feet, grunting at the effort. "Ironius is going to have a ball with you when he realizes what you've done."

"Ironius?"

"And his Prince."

Baldezar's face paled. "Prince? As in, *Gray Prince*?"

I smiled. "See, you didn't know everything after all."

"Drothe!" Baldezar's words came out quickly, tumbling over one another in his haste to get them out. "I didn't know there was a Prince involved," he said. "I swear it! Please, you have to—"

Another whistle. We both looked down the street.

Fowler was running toward us. "Rags a little less than

three blocks away and coming fast!" she yelled. "Must be at least a half dozen of them."

I turned back to Baldezar. "They won't bother you if you tell them we jumped you." I grinned. "Good luck with Ironius and the Prince."

"Wait!" he yelled. "Take me with you! I can tell you about the book."

I turned back just as Fowler came pounding up beside me.

"Tell me what?" I said.

"Take me with and I'll tell you."

I glanced at Fowler. She had her hand on her knees and was breathing heavy. "Are you on smoke?" she said in answer to my look. "I can't carry him alone, and you're having trouble fucking walking." She spit. "No way. We have to go. Now."

I turned back to Baldezar. "Tell me," I said, "and none of this gets back to Ironius."

"I need more."

"After what you just confessed to, you're lucky to be getting that much!" I said. "I *should* dust you and let the Rags clean up the mess."

Baldezar licked his lips and glanced down the alley, then back to me. "Make me your man," he said.

"What?" Fowler and I said at the same time.

"Take me under you," he said in a rush. "Be my boss and I'll tell you whatever you want to know."

"Your boss?" I said. "I'm no Baldober. Hell, I don't even have an organization!"

"Then start one with me," said Baldezar. "If you take me on, you have to protect me. You can't dust me without cause, and I can't betray you without knowing I'll be killed in turn."

I almost laughed at his naïveté. "You don't know much about how the Kin work, do you?"

"I know *you*," said Baldezar. "That's enough."

I stared at him while Fowler danced from foot to foot. She was staring down the alley.

"Drothe . . . " she began.

"Shut the fuck up," I said. Protection? *My* protection? I hadn't even been able to protect Eppyris and his family, and now Baldezar wanted me to watch over *him*? With what? I didn't have anything to offer.

Then again, did any Kin? Given the nature of our business, our lives, who were we to pretend to any kind of certainty? At best, we were lucky to fend for ourselves. And yet, that hadn't stopped me from staying secretly loyal to Kells for years, never mind invoking Nicco's name as a shield against the people in his organization. I was a Long Nose—if anyone knew about being in deep without any real support, it was me. Still, I had to admit that having that partial sense of protection had helped, and that I missed it now.

I reached my hand out, hesitated, and then finished the gesture. Baldezar took it in an awkward Clasp. And just like that, he was mine.

"We can do the pretty words later," I said. "Just talk."

"I don't know precisely what's in the book," Baldezar said, "but I know part of it deals with magic."

"I know," I said.

"*Imperial* magic."

"Know that, too."

Baldezar blinked in surprise. "So you know about the emperor, too?"

I let go of his arm. "What about the emperor?"

"From what I gathered, they plan on using the magic against him."

"*Against* him?" I said.

"Him, or the empire," said Baldezar. "It wasn't clear, but I managed to piece it together from bits of conversation Ironius let slip."

"Angels fuck me," muttered Fowler.

I took a step toward Baldezar, half in shock. "What are they—"

Fowler caught my arm. "There's no *time*," she hissed. "Listen!"

I did. I could hear shouts and yelling in the distance. It was getting closer. Rags.

"Damn," I said. I leaned down and handed Baldezar a small packet from my herb wallet. "Deer berries," I said. "They'll numb the pain."

Baldezar looked at the packet dubiously, then at me. "I don't think—" he began.

"If I wanted you dead, you'd be dead," I snapped. "I'm not about to waste time poisoning you."

Baldezar looked at the packet again and nodded.

"Very touching," said Fowler as she grabbed my arm. "Now, let's get the hell out of here before we all have a real reason to cry."

I let her hustle me down the street and around a corner. Behind us, I could hear Baldezar begin shouting for help. He was calling out to the approaching Rags, begging for someone to stop and help him.

"Think they'll let him live?" Fowler asked as we turned another corner.

"He's a scribe and a guild master," I said. "They have no reason not to."

"What about us?" she said. I didn't have to ask to know she was referring to the revelation about Ironius's plans for the journal.

"There's no 'us,'" I said. "You didn't hear anything."

"Drothe . . ."

"Get your ass back and watch the apothecary's family until this is over," I said.

"What about you?"

"I'm a Nose," I said. "When I hear dangerous things I don't like, I go see my boss."

Chapter Twenty-one

Kells wasn't at home. More specifically, he wasn't in Silver Disc cordon, or any of his other territories. He was in Ten Ways, directing the war against Nicco—personally.

"It's that bad?" said Degan.

"That's what I hear," I said. I had come looking for Degan after failing to see Kells, and had found the Arm playing two-man cabbat at Prospo's with Jelem. Degan was, of course, losing.

"And you need to see him right now?" said Degan.

"I do." Kells was the kind of Upright Man who worked best from the shadows, pulling strings and spinning plans; that he had taken to the streets, let alone the front lines, didn't bode well for our side.

Degan sighed and tossed his cards on the table. "Just when I was ready to make a comeback, too."

"Yes, of course you were," said Jelem as he raked the small pile of coins from the center of the table toward himself. "I can't tell you how grateful I am to Drothe for saving me from my imminent ... defeat."

"Business comes first," I said.

"Funny how your 'business' keeps interfering with *my* profits," observed Jelem, stacking his coins. "Especially since I'm still owed monies for working on a certain rope."

I stood up straighter. "I don't recall a whole lot of return on that yet," I said.

"Ah, as to that . . ." Jelem moved his glittering stacks aside and set his elbows on the table. "Give me six strands of your hair."

"What?"

Jelem snapped his fingers. "Just do it," he said, "before anyone comes wandering by."

I reached up and began plucking.

"Make sure they're long," said Jelem as he reached into the folds of his robe and came out with a length of knotted rope. Tamas's rope—no, I realized, *Task's* rope; there weren't any burned knots on this one.

"Watch for anyone who might notice us," he said as he took the hairs from me and carefully draped them in his lap.

"What are you doing?" I said.

"Keying the magic in this rope to you, of course."

"'Keying' it?" I said. "I haven't used a lot of portable glimmer in the past, but what I have used has never been 'keyed' to anything."

"That's because whatever you used was either harmless, or something you could physically control or avoid once it was activated. This is a *rope*. It bends and twists and wraps around things. The runes in it are activated when they strike someone. If you miss that someone, it's entirely possible it could swing back around and hit you. Unless, of course, you'd rather run the risk of knocking yourself unconscious with your own glimmer?"

"Keying it to me will be fine," I said.

I watched as Jelem plucked up a single hair and tied it around the first knot in an elaborate pattern. He began muttering to himself and making small pulling actions in the air.

Degan and I took up positions on either side of the table, settling into the casual slouch that is second nature to Kin who are keeping an eye out for something. I waved Cecil off when he came to see if we needed new drinks, while Degan placed himself between the street and the table whenever anyone walked past.

At last, the sounds stopped, and Jelem cleared his throat.

I turned around to find him sitting back in his chair, the rope coiled in his lap.

"It's done?" I said.

"It's done," said Jelem.

Jelem and I stared at each other.

"About the payment," I said at last.

"Yes?"

Crap. I hated doing this. It was embarrassing. "Nicco's cast me out, and all my hawks were . . ."

"You're broke," said Jelem.

"For the moment," I admitted.

Jelem nodded. "I expected as much. But fortunately for you, I've thought of a solution that doesn't involve money."

"No money," I echoed. I didn't like the sound of that.

"A favor," he said, the word sounding both silky and dirty in his mouth. "Payable . . . later."

"What kind of favor?"

Jelem raised his left shoulder a fraction of an inch. "If I knew that, it wouldn't be a favor—it would be a payment."

I gritted my teeth and looked at the rope, then at Jelem. I glanced over at Degan.

"Don't look at me," said Degan. "That kind of an arrangement makes perfect sense as far as I'm concerned."

I looked back at Jelem. He was sitting placidly, waiting, knowing he had me over a barrel. I needed any edge I could get right now, and that rope was one nice bit of edge.

"Fine," I said. "It's not as if I don't owe anyone else any favors, anyhow."

Degan coughed discreetly into his hand, hiding a smile.

"Excellent," said Jelem. He picked up the rope and tossed it at my head. "Here."

My eyes went wide. I tried to duck, but the rope uncoiled as it flew, and two of the knots hit my side.

Nothing happened.

"Well, that seems to have worked," said Jelem as he picked up his deck of cards and began shuffling them. "Good."

"It *seems* to have worked?" I said as I gathered up the rope. "You mean you didn't know if it would?"

Jelem squared the cards in one hand and then rotated them with his fingers so they cut themselves and restacked into a neat pile in his palm. He smiled and said nothing.

"Bastard," I said as I coiled the rope and tucked it in behind my belt to hide it from casual view. Jelem was still smiling when Degan and I walked away.

Kells had set up his operations base in the northeast corner of Ten Ways, in the remains of a small manor house. Like so many of the formerly fine buildings in the cordon, this one had been subdivided again and again by a succession of landlords and squatters, until it was little more than a maze of interconnected hovels and rooms, with new walls thrown up and old ones torn open, seemingly at random. Guessing by the traces of plaster and lumber I saw in the courtyard, he must have had his people tearing out some of the later additions to make it easier to move—and defend—inside.

"Wait here," said one of the Cutters who had escorted us in from the cordon. "I need to talk to somebody about you."

"You do that," I said. Degan merely grunted and studied the space around us.

It had been easier to get into Ten Ways than I had expected. There was open warfare in the streets now, with both Cutters and Rags running in larger packs. A couple of lone Kin were easy to miss, especially when everyone else was looking for bigger trouble.

And there was trouble aplenty. We'd come across three open street fights—two between different factions of Kin, and one between a small cohort of Rags and a squad of Nicco's men. Usually, I would have put the odds on the Rags, what with their being armed not only with blades but also with halberds and bucklers; but then, Nicco's people didn't usually go hunting with a Mouth in tow. A fistful of nails tossed in the air and a couple of spoken words were all it had taken to turn that battle. We'd found a group of Kells's men shortly after that and surrendered our steel in exchange for an escort to the Upright Man's headquarters.

"Good place for a dusting pan," said Degan after a few minutes.

I nodded. Between the high walls of the courtyard and the even higher windows on the second and third floors, anyone trying to take the place would be walking into a death trap. And that was assuming they made it this far. The piazza beyond the walls was even now being cleared of anything larger than a man's shoe, to remove any kind of cover or ammunition that could help an attacker.

It wasn't a good sign. It spoke of last measures and final stands. It spoke of Kells's losing.

Inside, the siege mentality was even more prevalent. Kin either hurried from place to place, readying themselves, or sat silently, waiting for the inevitable. There was none of the banter, none of the good-natured threats or bellicose bragging I was used to hearing from nervous Kin when a fight was brewing. There was only resignation.

The Cutter everyone in the patrol had called "Jock" came strolling back from the building, twirling his cane in his hand. "You're in," he said, pointing at me with the stick. "You're not," he said to Degan.

Degan shrugged, then went over and sat down against a wall. He was snoring before I was out of the courtyard.

I was led up two flights of stairs that felt like four, then down a long hallway. We stopped in front of a charred door. Through the soot, I could still see hints of fine carvings—flowers and leaves and a couple of bird wings. Jock rapped twice with his stick, paused long enough to give me sour look, then turned and walked away. I listened to his boots thudding hollowly on the wooden floorboards as he disappeared into the gloom.

I sighed and rubbed at the stubble on my face. How many days since Moriarty's? Since Christiana's? They were all blurring together, along with my thoughts. I blinked, slapped my face, and slipped two seeds. No help.

"Come," called Kells finally. I opened the door.

The curtains were drawn, the room lit by a scattering of candles. Someone must have found a stash of glassware in the house, because every candle was set in its own wineglass, creating small tulips of light. They flickered in constellations around the room, casting a patchwork of light and shadow that rendered my night vision useless.

Near the center of the place stood a massive desk that seemed more banquet table than workspace. A row of goblets had been placed along its front, each one slightly shorter than the last, forming a miniature stairway of light. Behind the candles, and almost hidden by the desk, sat Kells, the dark expression on his face made even more severe by the uneven light. His hands were before him, their thumbs tapping against each other slowly. Other than that, he didn't move.

I closed the door and was three paces into the room before I noticed the shadows behind Kells move. At first, I thought it was a trick of the light, but then I saw them shift again of their own accord. I stopped, peered, and was just able to make out a tall, dark figure behind my boss, his form hidden by a long, gray-black cloak.

My rapier was out of its scabbard in an instant.

"Good to see you, too, Drothe," said the familiar deep, smooth voice. The cloaked Kin stepped farther into the light, his face still hidden by the massive cowl.

"What the hell is *he* doing here?" I demanded of Kells.

"Drothe," said Kells, "put your blade away."

"Do you know who that is?" I said.

Kells arched an eyebrow. "Do you?"

The cloaked man hadn't moved.

"I know not to trust him," I said, gritting my teeth. "I know he led me to a pair of White Sashes who were more than ready to carve me into pieces, and I know he's too well-informed about happenings in Ten Ways to be true. So, yes, I know him well enough."

The figure chuckled, and even Kells gave the hint of a rueful smile. Their amusement didn't improve my mood.

A disturbing thought occurred to me. I gestured with my rapier toward the man. "He's yours, is he?" I said to Kells. "You put this walking bolt of cloth on my blinders to keep track of me, didn't you?"

"Hardly," said Kells.

"Then what the hell is he doing here?"

"Have a seat," said Kells, gesturing at one of the two chairs in front of the desk.

"I'll stand," I said. I did move to stand beside the chairs, though.

"Suit yourself." Kells came around the desk and perched himself on the corner nearest me. He paused a moment to openly study Nestor's hard-worn clothes, then shrugged.

"So, what have you got for me?" said Kells.

I looked at my boss for a long moment, then over at the man in the cloak. "I'm still waiting for an answer," I said.

"He's here because I asked him to be here," said Kells. "That should be enough."

"Not when he's been toying with me, it isn't," I said. "He's been feeding me information and steering me in Ten Ways since the beginning of this mess."

"Was any of the information I gave you wrong?" said the cloaked figure.

"That's not the point," I said.

"It's *precisely* the point," said the figure. "You may not have liked the results, but you can't say I didn't take you where you wanted to go."

"You could have at least said something about the damn Sashes!" I said.

"Would you have gone in if I had?"

"You son of a bitch!" I snapped. "You had no right to send me in there." I gestured at Kells with my free hand. "I work for *him*, not you, and I'll be damned if I'm going to stand here and tell tales in front of someone who nearly got me dusted."

"You'll—" began the figure.

"You'll do *what I tell you*, Drothe," cut in Kells. "And right now, I'm telling you to report."

I looked from Kells to the figure and back. What the hell was going on here? In all the years I had been reporting to him, Kells had always held our conversations in the strictest confidence. Even back when I'd been Nosing on the streets, before I became a Long Nose, he had stressed the importance of keeping our conversations private. Had my breaking my cover in Nicco's organization changed things that much? I couldn't imagine it; yet here he was telling me to spill in front of someone not in his organization.

It didn't make sense.

Kells stepped in closer and stared me in the eye. "I told you to report," he said. "Now do it."

And that was when I saw it—there, with Kells less than a foot from me, his breath in my face, his posture hard, his neck stiff, and his eyes . . . worried. They were wide and wavering and pleading. I watched as they flicked off to one side toward the cloaked figure now behind him, then over my shoulder.

Kells wasn't angry, I realized; he was scared. And he needed me to follow his lead.

I didn't hesitate.

"Go to hell," I said, stepping back and hoping I was playing it right.

"What?" said Kells.

"You heard me." I glared from him to the cloaked man. "I'm done answering everyone else's questions."

"Done answering questions?" said Kells. "You're a Nose, damn it—*my* Nose! Answering questions is what you *do*!"

"No!" I said. "Sifting information is what I do. Sepa-

rating rumors from leads is what I do. Putting my ass
on the line so I can get a better picture of the street is
what I do. And I do it for you, *not* him." I pointed at the
looming figure off to my right. "I'm not going to spill
anything until I get some answers about *him*; about what
the hell is *really* going on in Ten Ways; and about that
damn journal everyone wants!"

Kells stepped in close and raised a finger in my face.
"Your *job*," he snarled, "is to gather the pieces, *not* to
assemble the puzzle. If I wanted you in the middle of
things, I would have put you there. I didn't. So don't
complain when I remind you of your job. You seem to
need it."

"Wait," said the cloaked figure.

Kells winked. I pushed on, although I doubt I could
have stopped if I'd wanted to.

"You make it sound like I want to be here," I said.
"Like I enjoy having my ass kicked by more people than
I can count." I gestured toward the door and the cordon beyond. "I'm in Ten Ways because Nicco sent me
here, not because I wanted to come. And I *stayed* here
because I didn't want to see your organization go down
the shit hole. Not that it isn't on its way already, from
what I've seen."

Kells moved in even closer to me, the twinkle going out of his eye. "Are you saying I can't run my own
organization?"

This wasn't a ruse anymore, I realized, but I no longer
cared. It felt good to be saying this, to be laying it out
in front of Kells. I'd gone through too much in the past
seven years, let alone the past seven days, to be playing
games anymore.

"I'm saying you should have taken this seriously
when I first brought it to you," I said. "You knew Nicco
was going to come after you, but you had to try to play
games." I swept my hand toward the cordon beyond the
room. "Well, what the hell has it got you?"

"Wait," said the figure again.

"And what would you have done?" demanded Kells.

"How the hell should I know?" I said. "I've been too busy dodging White Sashes and assassins and Nicco's people to have time to consider tactics. Besides, I'm just a Nose—all I'm supposed to do, apparently, is listen to whispers and report. Angels forbid I get a clear idea of—"

"Wait!" The word exploded out of the depths of the cowl as if it were echoing up from a cave. Kells and I both stopped and looked at the cloaked man. He pointed at me. "You mentioned 'that damn journal,'" he said, his voice back to its normal coffee-dark tones.

"So?"

"Who told you it was a journal?"

Shit. "What?"

"No one's ever called it anything but a book, but you just said 'journal.'"

I stared at him.

"You have it, don't you?" he said.

I looked at Kells. He was watching me carefully, waiting, his eyes narrowed. At my look, his head gave a shake so subtle, I almost missed it from a foot away.

I looked back to the cloaked figure.

"I don't have it," I said, "but I think I know where it is."

"I'm sure you do," said the dark figure. "Now go and get it."

"Why?" I said.

"What?"

"Why is it so important to you?" I said. "Why should I make sure you get it instead of someone else?"

The dark cowl regarded me for a long moment. "I don't explain myself to minions."

Minions?

"Screw this," I growled.

Before Kells could react, I was past him, my left hand scooping up one of the lighted wine goblets. I slipped over the corner of the desk and deposited myself in front of the walking cloak.

"Enough games," I said as I reached up and grabbed

his cowl, shoving the candle forward and pulling back on the hood at the same time. "If you think—Angels!"

The cowl didn't move. Even though the edges of the hood crumpled and shifted in my hand like regular cloth, the cowl itself refused to shift back from his face. It was like trying to push over a brick wall wrapped in wool.

Worse, though, was the darkness inside the cowl: it didn't shrink from the light. Instead, a veil of gray-black shadows confronted me, shifting and rolling as if it had a depth greater than the hood that held it. I thought I caught a brief hint of chin here, a wisp of nose there, but I couldn't be sure. Somehow I knew that, even without the candle, my night vision would be useless—there was no piercing this darkness.

My stomach went cold and small.

The man in the cloak didn't move, didn't react at all. He simply whispered something, a word too low for me to hear. Then I was flying across the room, my ears ringing from the power he'd spoken. I hit the far wall, bounced off it, and met the floor face-first. I stayed where I landed.

I heard a voice, felt hands on me when I didn't answer. I wanted to respond but just ... didn't have the focus. Blinking was an effort at the moment.

I was put in a chair. I felt water on my face. That helped. Blinking became easier—then moving.

Then the pain came. I began to groan, caught myself, and gritted my teeth instead. Like hell I'd give him the satisfaction.

I lifted my head. Kells was prowling before the desk, anger and concern mixing freely on his face. Behind him, now seated in the big chair, was the cloaked man.

"Explanation enough?" said the latter.

There was only one explanation—for the cloak, for the darkness, for the glimmer, for Kells's reactions—and I didn't like it.

I'd known there was a Gray Prince involved; I simply hadn't considered that everything that pointed at one could just as easily point toward two. They did tend to keep track of one another, after all. And there was only one Prince *this* one could be. Hell, he'd been wearing his identity like a badge, and I'd been too dense to notice.

"Shadow," I croaked. "You're fucking Shadow."

The Gray Prince's cowl dipped in acknowledgment. "Just so."

Chapter Twenty-two

A Gray Prince—*the* Gray Prince, by some accounts. Nastiest of the nasty. Talking to me.

Crap.

And the other Gray Prince—along with Iron Degan—was on the other side of the war, with Nicco. Which put all of us lesser Kin in the middle between them.

Double crap.

"All right," I said softly, "I'm impressed." I hoped Shadow took the tremor in my voice as a sign of fatigue, but I wasn't counting on it. "But you still haven't answered my question: Why do you want the journal?"

Kells stopped his pacing before his desk, but I didn't look at him. I was focused on the shifting darkness inside Shadow's hood.

"You owe me an answer," I said, leaning forward in my chair.

"*I* owe *you*?" said Shadow.

"The way I see it," I said, "I've been dancing to your tune since the beginning of this whole mess. Tracking Larrios, fighting Sashes, getting the journal—it's all been for you, hasn't it?"

The cowl dipped once.

"And Fedim—that was you, too, wasn't it?" I said. "You're the one who gutted him in his shop and got me in trouble with Nicco in the first place."

Another dip of the cowl.

"So yes, I think I've earned something," I said. "I don't like being used, even if it is by one of you."

"You talk as if you haven't gotten anything out of it," said Shadow.

I laughed bitterly. "You mean besides beatings, blood, and seven years' worth of work in Nicco's camp down the sewers?"

"I mean a dead assassin floating in your bedroom."

That caught me up short. *Shadow* had been watching over me? I glanced over at Kells but got no help. He looked as surprised as I was.

"Task was out of your league," said Shadow. "Just as the next Blade would have been. And the one after that, if you somehow managed to live that long. I simply took the liberty of sending a message on your behalf."

"On my behalf, or yours?" I said.

"Does it matter?"

"It *matters* if it made things worse," I said. "It *matters* if people think I have the resources to find and float Task on my own. What the hell am I supposed to do when they send someone even better after me and you aren't around? Angels! Couldn't you just leave her with her throat slit in an alley and send a fucking note?"

"Has anyone put a Blade on you since?"

"That's *not* the point!"

"That's *precisely* the point!" said Shadow. "My removing the Blade sent a message: You have backing. *My* backing. And no one has tried for you since. So, say thank you and tell me where you hid the journal."

"I'm *not* yours," I said, "backing or not. So like I said—why do you want it?"

Shadow's hand formed itself into a fist. "You aren't as indispensable as you think, little Nose."

"Yes, he is," said Kells. I looked over to find his arms crossed and a hard expression on his face. "Drothe is my man, not yours, and I'll decide if he's dispensable. You and I may have a deal, Shadow, but it doesn't mean you can use my people however you please. You said yourself you're playing catch-up with Solitude in

Ten Ways—*you're* the one who needs *my* organization. If you want something done, you go through me, or it doesn't happen. The same goes for my people—*you ask me*. Understood?"

I bit my tongue, not because I wanted to kiss Kells for what he was doing—I did—but because he had just told me who the other Gray Prince was—the one who had Iron Degan in her pocket and had strolled through my dreams to warn me about the journal. Now I had a name to put to the face and the voice: Solitude.

For his part, Shadow sat silent for a long moment. Then he dipped his cowl ever so slightly. "Of course," he said. "My apologies if I overstepped."

"Tell Drothe what he wants to know."

"Very well," said Shadow, turning to face me. "You want to know why I want Ioclaudia Neph's book? Because Solitude wants it. Because she's wanted it for a while. And because if she considers it to be that important, I expect I'm better off with it in my hands than in hers.

"Solitude's smart. She knows if she makes an open move on Ten Ways, the other Princes will try to stop her. This cordon is too important for us to let any one person control. It's where Isidore got his start. It's the one cordon that has resisted control since he fell. To take Ten Ways is to achieve something only *he* has done. Can you imagine what it would mean for a Prince to take Ten Ways?"

I nodded. More than a few Baldobers and Street Bosses would give the Clasp to a Prince who united Ten Ways. And if she took down Nicco and Kells in the process? The power vacuum would only add to the swell.

"They'd be on their way to becoming the new Dark King," I said. I hadn't been mad.

"Precisely," said Shadow. "And I'm not willing to bend the knee to her, nor to anyone else. That's what worries me. Solitude knows one or more of us will move to stop her; yet she's going ahead, anyhow. That tells me she has an advantage—something she thinks will guarantee her taking Ten Ways. I think that something is the book."

I fought the urge to look away, to blink, to show any reaction at all. Shadow was more right than he knew, but I wasn't about to let him know that. Instead, I stared directly into his cowl, forced my voice to remain steady, and asked, "So how many other Princes *are* involved?"

"Right now, just Solitude and I."

"So if this is so important," I said, "why all the games? Why use me instead of sending your own people?"

"But you are 'my people,'" said Shadow. "Just as you are Solitude's, and the Dance Mistress's, and Ash Tongue's, too. It all depends on who is pulling the strings when. You don't honestly think every piece of information you sifted from Nicco's people and passed on to Kells was dredged up by your efforts alone? Did you ever consider the possibility that when you pulled strings to make Nicco's organization less stable, someone might have been pulling your strings in turn?" A dark chuckle came from within the hood. "You, of all people, should know that the easiest way to manipulate something is from the inside. I—we—just do it at a deeper level."

I'd always heard this was how it was supposed to work with the Gray Princes, but there's a difference between casual street speculation and knowing something for a fact. To hear it put so bluntly, so casually, sent a chill down my spine.

Shadow leaned forward on the desk, exposing the sleeves of a fine charcoal gray doublet beneath his cloak. "Now it's your turn," he said. "Tell me about the journal."

I looked into that midnight cowl and was tempted—tempted to tell him everything and let someone else worry about the book and Ten Ways and the war. If I talked, if I gave Shadow the journal, it would be done—no more running, no more puzzles, no more having to balance what I suspected against what other people knew. Let the Gray Princes fight it out—they were better suited to it than I. Let him thwart Solitude; I could just walk away and go back to being a Nose.

It was tempting, but I knew I couldn't do it. "Don't give that book to anyone," Solitude had said in my dream. "Not even to me." That didn't fit with what Shadow was saying. If she was so intent on using it, Solitude wouldn't have told me what she did. "I'd rather see Ioclaudia's book lost again than in the wrong hands," she had said. That was too big a gamble, even for someone as subtle as a Gray Prince; telling me that had raised the odds of my destroying journal too high for it to be a bluff.

Yes, Solitude wanted the journal, I realized, but not for the reasons Shadow and I had been thinking. I remembered what Baldezar had said about Solitude and Ironius, and a chill went through me. "They want to use it against the empire." I hadn't quite believed it then; now was a different matter.

"I'm waiting," said Shadow.

I glanced over at Kells. He was staring at me as well. No help there—or was there? How much did Kells really know? How much would he *want* to know?

I put on my best resigned face and settled farther into my chair.

"The journal," I said as I dug out a seed, "was written by Ioclaudia Neph. She was an imperial Paragon to Stephen Dorminikos back when he was still a normal person."

"It's that old?" said Kells.

"It's that old," I said.

"Have you opened it?" said Shadow.

"Of course I have! With everyone after it, how could I not?"

"And?"

"I'm no Mouth, so I can't say for sure, but the people I had look at it told me there was talk of glimmer."

Shadow's hand slapped down on the desk, making the candles flicker inside their wineglasses. "I knew it! What does the glimmer deal with? Did they say?"

"Yeah, they said." I leaned back farther in my chair,

letting the moment draw out. I looked from Shadow to Kells. I waited, then bit down hard on the seed. Kells nearly jumped at the sound. Perfect. "It's imperial," I said.

"Splendid!" crowed Shadow. "I'd only half—"

"What?!" Kells exploded, just as I'd hoped. "*Imperial* glimmer?" He spun toward the desk and almost climbed into Shadow's cowl. "You said those White Sashes in the Barren were looking for a relic, not a book on forbidden magic!"

"Relics come in all shapes and sizes," said Shadow. "This one just happens to be more useful than most."

"Relics are personal items used by the emperor," I pointed out. "This isn't a relic. I doubt the book ever came into contact with any of the incarnations."

"It deals with the emperor," said Shadow testily. "That's close enough."

"Nor do relics draw the interests of imperial Paragons," I added.

Kells's snowy brows descended into each other. "Paragons?"

"I can't imagine them not coming after it at some point," I said.

"*Paragons?*" said Kells. "Damn it, Shadow!"

I could almost feel the glare coming at me out of Shadow's cowl. I smiled at him.

"The *important* thing to remember," said Shadow pointedly, "is that *we* have the journal. If Drothe is right, the information in there could make Nicco and Solitude nothing more than minor annoyances."

"And what about the empire?" said Kells. "They're not going to just fade away."

"They might," said Shadow, "if we hand them the proper scapegoat."

"That'd have to be a damn big scapegoat," I said.

"My thought exactly," said Shadow.

I considered. "Nicco?"

"Solitude," said Shadow. "She's a bigger fish, and she's already after the journal. All we need to do is make sure the right words reach the right ears. Then, when the time comes, we arrange for her to fall into imperial hands."

I laughed. "Set up a Gray Prince, just like that? Forgive me if I doubt you—*even* you—of being able to pull that off. But let's say you do—she'd still talk. There's no reason for her not to."

"Not if she's dustmans."

"Not good enough," I said. "I can't believe the empire would be satisfied with one body and no book. I've been on the receiving end of some of their relic hunts, and this is a hell of a lot more valuable to them than a ratty old cassock."

"Then give them a few legitimate charred pages and a pile of bogus ash," said Shadow. "They'll put the pieces we give them together and come to the conclusion we want." He waved a dismissive hand. "Frankly, I think you're giving the empire too much credit."

"And I don't think you give it, or us, enough," said Kells, walking over to stand behind me. "Have you been by the Tower of Gonias lately? It's *still* smoldering, and the Whites and Paragons dragged that Mouth out of there during Theodoi's fifth incarnation, three hundred years ago! If they're willing to go to the trouble of making brick burn, let alone that slowly, just to make a point, I'm willing to bet they won't be put off by a corpse and a pile of charred paper.

"You may be able to vanish if things go wrong, but we can't. Not that well. I'm not going to tell my people to hunt down Solitude, watch half of them die in the process, and then take the imperial heat, just so you can come out of this with one less rival and a bunch of new glimmer at your fingertips."

Shadow stood up slowly. If it was meant to be intimidating, it worked. "It doesn't matter what you want," he said. "We have a deal. Solitude is in this. I'm in it. If you want to come out in one piece, you'll follow my lead. I know how to deal with Gray Princes—do you?"

"No, but I'm learning," said Kells.

"I'm sure you think you are," said Shadow. "Now . . ."

"I'm *not* finished," snapped Kells. Shadow froze, and for a moment I wished Kells hadn't decided to stand so close to me. "We cut a deal," said Kells, "but it didn't have anything to do with the empire or White Sashes or imperial glimmer. We agreed on three things: keeping my organization in one piece, rolling Nicco out of Ten Ways, and making sure Solitude doesn't establish a foothold here. You stick to *that*, you make sure *those things* happen, and I'll make sure you get the book when we're done."

"Don't be stupid," said Shadow. "If I get my hands on that journal, your problems with Solitude and Nicco are over."

"Maybe," said Kells. "But you promised to support me before the journal ever came up. Hell, *you're* the one who came to *me* offering help, not the other way around. You wouldn't have done that unless you needed me more than I need you."

"Believe whatever fantasy you like," said Shadow, "but you need me, Kells. Your men can tell you—Drothe can tell you—that if I leave now, you're doomed. Solitude has had more time to build ties, more time to lay groundwork, more time to import Mouths and get her plans in order. You're flailing by comparison."

Kells stepped past me and folded his arms over his broad chest. He planted his feet, straightened his back, and spit on the floor between himself and Shadow.

"I don't renegotiate in the middle of a fight," said Kells, "and have little use for cowards that do. The simple fact is, you get the book when my ass is out of the fire—not before."

I'm not sure what I expected—lightning to come down through the roof, Kells to be thrown about the room like a rag doll, or for the Gray Prince to simply walk over and casually eviscerate my boss—but none of those things happened. Instead, Shadow stood stone silent for a long moment, and then stalked past us.

"We'll finish this discussion," he said, "after you've had some time to see just how bad things can become." The door slammed shut behind him.

Kells let out a long breath. "Well, that didn't go as well as I would have liked." He walked over and settled into his desk chair with a small grunt.

"Now," he said, leaning his head back and closing his eyes, "why don't you tell me everything you've been holding back since you walked through that door? And it had better be good, because if it's not, you and that journal will become my peace offering to Shadow."

Chapter Twenty-three

I stumbled and caught myself on the banister beside the stairs. My left leg was numb, and my right felt like a pincushion. I ran a heavy hand over my face yet again—it still did no good.

How many hours had I been in with Kells? Judging by the light coming in through the windows a floor below me, it was a fair number. No wonder I felt like I'd been up for days—I had been.

I laid both of my hands on the banister and carefully guided myself down the last two steps to the landing. Then I sat on the bottom step, resting my head on my arms. It felt good, better even than the chair in Kells's office. Of course, that seat had been uncomfortable for other reasons.

I had told Kells what I knew about Ioclaudia's journal: the imperial glimmer, the talk about tinkering with souls to control the magic, the hunt by the White Sashes—all of it. The only pieces I danced around were the talk with Solitude in my dream and the fact that Jelem had been the one who had looked at the journal. The first piece I didn't want to share just yet, and the other I kept close for Jelem's sake. Bringing him to Kells's attention at this point would be far from a favor.

I felt guilty. Kells had stood beside me and told Shadow to go to hell when it came to using me. Shouldn't I return the favor by being completely up-front with him? I knew the answer, but I just hadn't been able to bring myself to do it—not until I learned more about the deal he had cut with Shadow. Aside from our both being on the Gray Prince's shit list, I didn't know where my boss stood with Shadow in the grander scheme. That bothered me, especially since I was starting to figure into it.

During my entire telling, Kells had sat unmoving, his eyes closed and his head back. He barely interrupted to ask questions.

"Well, you certainly know how to ruin a man's day, don't you?" he had said when I was done.

"You'll pardon me if I'm not too sympathetic," I said, "considering I walked in here to find you in Shadow's pocket. Never mind that he seems to have been using me for Angels know how long."

"He's using both of us," said Kells. "Just as I'm trying to use him. There's no surprise in that. And I'm *not* in his pocket."

"Oh, so where exactly does Shadow keep you, then?"

Kells cracked an eyelid. "You think you're the only one not happy with how this is turning out? Not only do I have Nicco and Solitude to contend with, but now I get to look forward to the empire knocking about Ten Ways, searching for a book on magical blasphemy. Recall what I said earlier: If the empire gets involved, we all go down."

"I remember," I said, "But you didn't answer my question."

"No, I didn't. Probably because I'm not sure anymore. Before you walked in here, I could have told you precisely where Shadow and I stood, but now . . . ?" He shook his head. "He's after more than just Solitude now."

"I suspect he always has been," I said.

"Very possible." Kells's hand crept up and began absently running along the edges of his mustache. "You think he's after the same thing as Solitude? Becoming the next Dark King?"

"Who the hell knows? I'm not even sure that's what she's after at this point. But Shadow? Yeah, I could see that."

"Is the journal safe?" said Kells.

"For the time being."

"Good." He rubbed his mustache some more. "We'll need to get rid of it, you know."

"Oh?"

Kells stared. "What do you mean, 'oh'? That thing is a lodestone if I've ever seen one."

"It's also the only thing that has been keeping me alive," I said. "As long as I have Ioclaudia's journal hidden away, Shadow, Solitude, and who knows who else won't lay a hand on me."

"You think so?" Kells crossed his arms. "What would you do if someone were keeping something from you? What did you do to Athel? These are Gray Princes, Drothe. This is the empire. They won't fuck around."

"I know that," I said. "But there's no good way out of this at the moment. The empire will lock me away for knowing about it, and I wouldn't be surprised if Shadow or Solitude dusted me on principle, once they have it in their hands. Keeping it hidden keeps me valuable. I like that."

"I don't," said Kells. "Too many people want it for too many reasons, and all of them will come sniffing around for you sooner or later. And since you're mine, that means they'll come to see me. That puts not just me, but the entire organization—*all* of us—at risk. I won't have it."

I swallowed and sat up straighter. "It's not your call," I said.

"Excuse me?"

"I'm the one with the journal," I said. "I'm the loose end they're all going to want to tie up. I'm not saying you won't take some heat, but most of it is going to fall on me. That makes it my decision, not yours."

Kells lowered his hand from his mustache. "Who the fuck are you?" He stood up. "*Who the fuck are you* to decide what's best for *my* organization? I'm losing a damn Kin war right now, and you tell me I don't get to make the call? You work for me, damn it—I'll tell you what to do and you'll do it!"

"Do what?" I said. "Give it to Shadow so he can kick Solitude's ass? Where does that put us once he's done? Under his thumb? Because we sure as hell won't be able to stop him after that. Or are you wanting to buy off Solitude instead? Give her both the book and Shadow on a platter? We know even less about her than we do about him!"

"At least we have a relationship with Shadow," said Kells. "He'll be grateful."

"Do you hear what you're saying?" I said. "You're willing to make"—I pointed at the closed door—"*that* the next Dark King?"

"Better the devil you know," said Kells.

"Excuse me, but weren't you the one who just told him to go to hell? I heard some pretty damn good arguments coming out of your mouth about why you *shouldn't* give it to him."

"Then maybe you also heard what I said at the end," said Kells. "About giving him the book after he pulls my ass out of the fire!"

"Your ass," I said. "Not mine. Not the Kin's."

Kells put his hands on the desk and forced himself to take a deep breath. "Think about it," he said. "Think about it like I have to think about it, Drothe. If Shadow *does* manage to save my ass, I won't be in a position to tell him no. The only reason I'll have an organization at that point is because of his help. I meant what I said: If he pulls this off, I'll give him the book. I gave my word, and I'll keep it."

"What about the empire?" I said. "What happens when *they* come looking?"

"He's the big fish," said Kells. "He'll draw the most interest. Besides, there's nothing that says Shadow will go down the same road as Isidore. He could surprise you and pull it off, you know."

Yes, he could, I realized. And that was what worried me.

Don't give it to anyone. Not even to me.

What Kells was saying made sense, except it felt

wrong. He was seeing the journal as a piece of swag—a problem that would go away once it was out of our hands. I knew better. There was too much in Ioclaudia's journal for people to simply forget about it. Nor would they forget about who else had had it—us, for example.

"You know that you and I will be the prime scapegoats," I said. "No matter what Shadow says?"

"I know," said Kells. "But it's going to take time to beat back Nicco and Solitude, and Shadow won't get the book until that's done. I figure that gives us some time to figure out a way to pin it on someone else."

I had made some noncommittal noises at that, which Kells had pretended to ignore. He wasn't expecting an immediate change of heart on my part, but he figured I would come around. I always had in the past. Except the past felt like a long time ago, now.

From there the discussion had turned to Nicco and Ten Ways and strategy, but not for long. I was too far gone to be of any more use, and Kells had sent me packing off to bed. I just hadn't realized how far gone I was until I had left his room.

I groaned and lifted my head off my arms. There were beds down there, I knew. . . . Rows of them . . . Only two flights down . . . Soft beds . . .

I was still thinking about those beds when I slid down onto the landing and curled up on the floor, happy just to meet the darkness.

I woke up to something hitting my foot.

I rolled over and looked up to find Degan standing over me. He had a short walking stick in his hand, which he was applying methodically to the sole of my boot. I also noticed I was in a bed in a private room. I didn't bother to ask how I'd gotten to this one, or how Degan had talked his way in.

"Let's have it," I grumbled. "You're only this annoying when you have bad news."

Degan slipped the stick under his arm. "The empire's closed off the cordon."

That was bad, all right. I sat up and winced at the pain in the muscles of my back. "Tell me."

"There are Swads at every gate into Ten Ways," said Degan. "At least a legion's worth. They're not letting anyone in or out—except the White Sashes, of course."

"Regular army *and* the Sashes?" I said.

"Word has it they've already started making forays into the cordon."

"Why?"

"Why do you think?"

My first thought was the journal, but that didn't make sense. Yes, the emperor wanted it, but surrounding Ten Ways wasn't going to flush it out. Besides, it would draw far too much attention to something he, of all people, wanted to keep quiet.

"The war," I said. "The emperor's had enough of Nicco's boys' playing Hunt the Rags. Now he's out to remind us who really owns Ten Ways." And probably bring it down around our ears. Markino was old—he wasn't in a patient or understanding frame of mind anymore. "How long ago did they surround the cordon?"

"About three hours ago. From what I heard, one moment, everything was normal—the next, there were Black Sashes everywhere. They sealed the place up in less than a quarter of an hour. No one had time to get out." Degan sighed, and I knew he was wishing he'd been there to see the execution.

"Three hours ago?" I said. "Why didn't you wake me?"

"I just told you—Ten Ways is sealed off. Where were you going to go? Besides, Kells said to let you sleep."

"Speaking of Kells, how's he taking it?"

"Out in the field, assessing the situation."

"Must be bad, then," I said, standing up. My left leg was stiff, but not nearly as bad as I'd expected. I was pleasantly surprised to find that my gait felt almost normal as I followed Degan out the door and into the hallway. Damn, but Jelem knew his stuff.

Dusk was settling outside the building. There were

candles aglow in the hallway, and someone had already gotten a small fire going in a brazier in the front courtyard.

Kells's people were on the move, rushing from place to place with a sense of urgency only desperation can bring. No one was saying it, but I could see it in their glances, hear it in their panting breaths. *The empire is here*, they were thinking. *We're going up against the Sashes just like Isidore did.* And everyone knew what had happened to the Dark King and to his Kin. No prisoners had been taken; no quarter had been offered; no deals had been cut.

This time wouldn't be any different. If anything, it might be worse.

"Come on," I said. "I need to . . ."

And I stopped dead in the courtyard.

Deals. The emperor hadn't cut deals last time, but that was because no one had had anything worth bargaining for. What could the Kin have offered him, then? Nothing.

But what about now?

"You need what?" said Degan.

I held up a hand for silence—for a moment to think.

The Kin had had nothing to deal with before, but, now, there was Ioclaudia's book. If there was anything that would catch the emperor's attention, anything that might convince him to walk away from the cordon and the Kin, a dead Paragon's journal might be it.

If it didn't bring him down on us harder, that is. There was always the chance he'd want to wipe out anyone who could have seen the book in the first place. But that would be a hell of a long list, and besides, if the Sashes were already in Ten Ways, he was close to doing that, anyhow.

It was a risk, but it was also a way out; and all it required was for me to betray Kells. And the Kin. And, in a way, myself.

It was a basic principle: Kin didn't go to the empire; we screwed the empire. We laughed in its face and pretended it didn't scare us. We were Kin. We were wise to the game and able to live outside the rules because we were smarter than that. The empire was a system to be used, a heavy hand to be avoided, sometimes even a pocket to be lightened; but it was never a cove to be trusted.

Nor was any Kin who went to the empire to be trusted, either. Turning rat meant becoming ostracized by the people who had once called you cousin or brother. If I managed to cut this deal, every door I had ever known would close, every friendly face I had once hailed would turn away. I would be dead to the Kin. No one would care why I had done it; all that would matter was that it had been done. I would have gone outside the organization, outside the extended family of the Kin—to *the empire*, of all places—to solve a problem. Even Kells wasn't considering what I was considering, and he had more on the line than I did.

Going to the empire meant not only being cast out, but also hunted, by the Kin. Why was I even considering this?

Because the alternatives were worse: Shadow as the Dark King, Kells as a lackey, and me under it all; or even worse, Solitude in charge, with Nicco at her left hand. Neither scenario appealed, and neither offered a very comfortable place for me once all the dust settled. Either I would work for a man I couldn't help but see as broken, or spend all my time trying to dodge the Blades Nicco would send after me in droves. And in the end, the Kin would be crushed by the empire, anyhow.

No, far better to be the Nose who had walked into the emperor's lair and saved the Kin, or at least tried. Even if they all turned their backs on me for doing it, none of them would forget me. I could live with that.

The only part I would regret would be having to betray Kells to do it, but I knew he wouldn't give his blessing to this. He'd already decided on Shadow, and I couldn't watch him follow that path.

"You need what?" repeated Degan.

"I need to get the hell out of this cordon," I said.

"Not that I'm arguing," said Degan, "but why?"

I stepped off to one side, away from the passing Kin.

"Kells wants to give the journal to Shadow," I said.

Degan drew back. "Shadow?" he said. "How did . . . ?"

"I just know," I said.

"And I take it you don't like this idea?"

"No. Nor do I want it to go to Solitude."

Degan stared at me. "Solitude," he said. "So she's the other Gray Prince involved in all this?"

"The one from the dream, yes."

Degan stared at me some more. "You know," he said at last, "I'm really starting not to like you. Not at all."

"Get in line."

"Dare I even ask what *you* want to do with it?"

I hesitated a moment before answering. "I want to give it to the person it belongs to."

"Ioclaudia?" said Degan. "That'd be a hell of a trick, considering . . . Oh. Not Ioclaudia. *Him.*"

"Yeah."

Degan considered. "Well, that *would* solve a number of problems at once."

"That's my thought."

"Assuming he lets you live."

"That's the hitch," I admitted.

"Do you have any idea how you might get the journal to the emperor?"

"I'm working on that," I said.

"Which means you don't have any ideas."

I shrugged.

"Well, one thing I know for sure," said Degan as he took my elbow and started leading me out of the compound. "You aren't going to find the emperor standing around here."

I couldn't argue with his logic. Instead, I handed Degan one of Kells's war cords and tied another on myself.

I steered us eastward into Kells's territory for a bit, then cut north. That would lead us into one of Nicco's strongholds, but our best chance of getting out of Ten Ways lay in that direction. The empire would be slow in closing down the Dancer's Highway, but, even if they did, there were broken patches of wall and several inviting drainage grates in that part of the cordon.

The streets were empty, or nearly so, with only a few Kin patrols, a couple brave or oblivious Lighters, and us. We dropped the war cords just inside the edge of Kells's territory, to better avoid being stopped once we left.

"So once we get out of here," said Degan as we crouched in the deeper darkness of an archway, "where to?" We could hear fighting a few blocks away.

"Christiana's," I said. "I need to get to court, or at least get word to the emperor's people, and she has the connections to do it."

"And you think she will?" said Degan. He sounded more than a bit dubious.

"Are you kidding? She'll balk and bitch and threaten, but she'll do it. How often do you get to do the emperor this kind of a favor? It'll do wonders for her at court. Besides, the idea of being able to put me over that big of a barrel, and the price she'll be able to ask for doing it, will be too good for her to pass up." I looked over at Degan. "What?"

He was smiling. "Just noticing the family resemblance."

"Bite your tongue." But I grinned, too.

The fighting wasn't getting any closer, so we moved out into the street. Four more blocks and we would be in Nicco's territory. From there it would be a zigzag path to the section of the Dancer's Highway I wanted to try. With luck, we'd be out of Ten Ways within the hour.

We'd gone maybe half a block when I heard a soft, metallic *ting* in the air. A moment later, a copper owl arced in front of me. It bounced on the street once, twice, before landing in a puddle of mud.

Oh, hell.

Degan was in front of me before the coin came to rest, his sword out. I didn't move. There was no point. I looked around Degan into the empty street and waited.

Shadow stepped out of a patch of his namesake, as if forming himself from the very darkness. Degan adjusted his shoulders and raised the tip of his sword to compensate for Shadow's height. Otherwise, he didn't move.

Shadow stopped five paces away. The dark cowl turned toward Degan.

"I'm not here for you," he said in his deep velvet and iron tones.

"I know," said Degan.

"You know who I am?"

"Yes."

"And will you move?"

"No."

Shadow crossed his arms. "Then we have a problem."

"One of us does," said Degan. "The other just has to figure out what to do with the body."

I reached out and put my hand on Degan's shoulder. "It's all right," I said. I looked past Degan to Shadow. "I'm too valuable to dust right now."

Shadow didn't dispute the claim. "Walk with me," he said instead. "We need to talk."

"What's to talk about?" I said. "I know what you want. I know what you can do to me. I'm impressed. But you're still not getting the journal until I say otherwise."

"You?" said Shadow. "I thought that was Kells's decision."

"We're still discussing that."

"I thought you might be too used to running on your own to go back to the leash. I see I was right."

"Clever you," I said. I moved to step around Degan and Shadow.

"If you want to get out of Ten Ways, I can help," said Shadow. "*If* you talk with me. If not, well"—he held up open hands—"the legions have closed the Dancer's Highway, and I have men at most of the other breaks in the perimeter near here. I'm sure you could still find a way out, but who knows what—or who—might be waiting on the other side?"

I stopped. The longer it took to get out of Ten Ways, the less likely I'd be able to get word to the emperor in time. That was, if Shadow even let me leave.

"Assuming we talk," I said. "What happens when I tell you to go to hell and refuse your offer?"

"You leave," he said. Shadow stepped back a pace and gestured down the street. "But at least walk with me and hear what I have to say."

Degan glanced at me, his eyes questioning. *Kill him?* they said. I shook my head. No. Talking would be marginally less dangerous than trying to dust him.

"All right," I said. "You lead. We'll be a step behind."

"The degan wasn't included in the invitation," said Shadow.

"Fine," I said. It was proper Kin protocol, anyhow. If Shadow walked alone during negotiations, so should I. Theoretically, he was treating me as an equal by doing this. I wasn't particularly flattered, given the circumstances.

"Follow by half a block," I said to Degan. He frowned but nodded. I set out with Shadow.

"You have to know that Kells will fall without my support," he said after a few paces.

"He hasn't been doing too damn hot with it. Your stepping away may help more than it hurts."

"We both know better than that. With the empire surrounding the cordon, Kells has no place to retreat. He might have been able to back out of Ten Ways and hold Nicco at bay before, but not now."

"It's a good thing he has such a stalwart friend in you, then," I said.

"I would be an even better friend if I had more resources."

"You know the deal," I said. "Save Kells and the rest of us first. Get the journal second."

"Except as you so adroitly pointed out, it isn't completely up to Kells, is it?"

"I'm Kells's man," I said. I didn't trust myself to say more.

"Yes, you are—and one of his most trusted." Shadow kicked idly at a small piece of timber in the street. It went clattering along ahead of us, stopped against a rain barrel. "Which makes me wonder why he would send you out of the cordon at such a critical time? You, the only man who knows where Ioclaudia's journal is hidden. That's quite a risk to be taking."

I stayed silent but let my hand brush against Tamas's rope on the back of my belt, just to make sure it was still there.

"A suspicious man," said Shadow, "might think Kells is scrambling to find a way out of our bargain. And a *very* suspicious man might think Kells has you working on a way to keep the journal away from me, at least until his plans are finalized. What would you say to that?"

"I'd say suspicious men spend too much time thinking," I said.

A low, rolling laugh tumbled out of his hood. "Maybe," he said, "but it's too late for me to get out of the habit now. So, instead, I'll share some of what I've been thinking. I can't see Kells having you destroy the journal — it's too valuable for that. Nor can you hide it indefinitely — sooner or later, someone will decide they'd rather it stay lost than end up in an enemy's hands. The easiest way to accomplish that is to kill you, but if that happened, Kells wouldn't have an out. Starting a bidding war for the book would be plain suicide. Which leaves you approaching someone on behalf of Kells behind my back."

"You've got me," I said, forcing sarcasm into my voice. "I'm planning to sell it to the emperor."

Shadow started laughing again.

We turned left onto a small side street, then right into an even narrower one. Darkness closed in tighter, seeping out of overhangs and recessed doorways. A baby began crying somewhere, its shrieks drifting down from the upper stories of a building. Someone swore sleepily, and a moment later the crying faded to soft whimpers. My nose detected faint hints of cat piss and mildew in the air.

"I don't like betrayal," said Shadow finally, his voice going flat. "Not when it's aimed at me."

"Who does?" I said. "But it's the risk you run when

you cut deals in the first place. Giving your trust means taking a chance it will be broken."

"Exactly."

Something about the way Shadow said the word made me stop in the middle of the street. It was too final; too pleased with itself.

Shadow stopped two paces farther along. He turned to face me.

"You have a choice," he said.

"What, between you and Kells? You aren't going to like that answer."

"No." The hood shook back and forth. "Between Kells and Baroness Christiana Sephada. Which of their trusts are you willing to betray?"

I felt my heart tighten in my chest. I stared, too shocked to hide it. We'd buried this deeper than deep. Only Ana, Degan, Joseph, and I knew. How . . . ?

"Come," said Shadow, reading my expression. "You aren't the only one who knows how to ferret out secrets. You have a history with the woman, Drothe. It's there to see if you look hard enough and haunt the right shadows. . . ."

Had he followed me sometime in the last week? How do you see, let alone hide, from a shadow?

"And it isn't something as simple as blackmail," he continued. "Blackmailers don't call on their victims the way you call on her. I don't know if she's your patron, paramour, or partner, and frankly, I don't care. What I do care about is that she means something to you. How much, I'm not sure, but we're about to find out."

I took a shallow breath even as my mind raced. "Patron, paramour, or partner," he had said, but not "family." That meant he didn't know all of it. There might still be a chance. . . .

"I'll make this simple for you," said Shadow. "If I don't get the journal now, not only will I cripple Kells and his organization—I'll also take my displeasure out on Baroness Christiana Sephada, widow of Baron Nestor Sephada, of Lythos. But if I do get it, well, then, everyone

remains happy, healthy, and whole." He made a sweeping gesture with his right hand, sending his cloak billow-
ing to one side. "There, that ought to be straightforward
enough for you."

It was. It meant I had only one choice.

Shadow had to die. Now.

Chapter Twenty-four

I slid the knife from the wrist sheath into my left hand and lashed out. At the same time, my right hand yanked Tamas's rope free, letting it uncoil like a whip.

Shadow was less than a pace from me, but he still managed to sweep the edge of his cloak up as my blade came forward. There was a moment of resistance before I felt my blade bite and bind in the fabric. I quickly drew my arm back to keep it from being caught up in the folds of the cloak. As the knife came back, I swung the rope forward.

I sent it in a wide arc, aiming for his waist. I'd never used the damn thing before, and I wasn't about to get fancy; I'd just take a shot at the center mass of his body and hope it worked.

Shadow was already stepping away. As the rope came around, he raised his cloak like a shield and spit out a string of sounds that reminded me of a drunk with a mouthful of food. When the rope connected, it felt like I'd swung an iron bar into a brick wall. The cord stiffened along its entire length, sending vibrations up my arm that nearly made me drop it. At the same time, I heard four distinct cracks as the runes went off. Shadow staggered back, nearly falling, and I lunged before I'd realized he'd moved out of range.

"Degan!" I shouted as I recovered and closed on the Gray Prince. "Degan, now!"

Shadow was good. He regained his balance even as

I came forward. By the time I was close enough to try for another strike, he had the edge of his cloak snapping and dancing before him, making it hard to find an opening. Shadow backed away and I followed. I needed to stay close, to keep this a knife fight; if I gave him enough room to draw a sword, I'd be in serious trouble, night vision or no.

I pressed hard. I slashed and stabbed with the knife, snapped the rope like a whip, and slashed again. The rope didn't even come close, but I got a certain amount of satisfaction seeing his cloak smoldering where the knots had hit it the first time.

All I needed was one gash, one deep *scratch*, and it would be done. The poison on the knife worked fast, and once Shadow was cut, all I had to do was fight defensively and wait for him to fall over. Except he was blocking every move with his cloak, and I was beginning to worry about the venom's being rubbed off by the fabric.

"You're a fool," said Shadow as I feinted right, then shifted left. He twisted and slipped his leg out of the way just before I could connect with the rope.

"Said the man without a weapon," I grunted as I dropped the rope, took a quick circling step, and grabbed his cloak with my left hand.

I had him.

Shadow laughed. His right hand swept past my face even as I was bringing my dagger around for the final thrust. I caught sight of a small stub of candle in his fingers, saw him crush it as it went past. Then my world erupted in agony.

Light as bright as day ignited in front of my face, shining through my night vision and into my head. Everything else vanished. There was only fire where my eyes had been — twin pools of sharp, merciless pain.

When awareness returned, I was screaming. I felt my hands clenched before my eyes, smelled the filthy pavement as it pushed up against my face. My mouth tasted like blood and sewage, and I spit to clear it out.

That was when I heard it—the sound of metal on metal, sword against sword. Degan and Shadow.

I drew my hands down and blinked experimentally. Bright amber specks and dark blotches floated before me, the whole thing edged with shifting rainbow highlights. The ghostly image of an elegantly gloved hand, fingers holding a bit of wax and taper, kept drifting across my vision.

And pain. Still lots of pain.

From somewhere in front of me came the sounds of shuffling steps, quick breathing, and the rasp and clash of swords. It didn't seem as fast and furious as I would have expected. Then I heard a soft, fading hiss. Degan cursed. More steps, another cautious pass of blades.

Was this the first clash, or had they been at it for a while? Pain can do funny things with time, but my guess was that I hadn't been out very long; Degan wasn't one to dally when it came to killing someone. Still, the longer it went, I suspected, the worse it would be for me.

I shook my head and knuckled my eyes. Spots and darkness.

I'd been blinded when using my night vision before, but never like this—never with glimmer, never this close, never so bright.

I heard another hiss. Degan grunted, and almost immediately there followed the ring of intense swordplay. Someone was pressing someone, but I had no way of knowing who. Worse, I could hear them getting closer. I quickly edged back, hoping that if I did inadvertently trip someone up, that someone would be Shadow.

A moment later, I heard Shadow gasp. I held my breath, waiting for the body to fall.

Degan sniffed. "Close," he said.

"Very," agreed Shadow.

They resumed.

Damn it! What the hell was going on? This should have been over already, which meant Shadow had pulled something else out of his cloak. But what? What was the damn hissing?

I needed to see. I needed to fix this. Now.

I rolled over onto my stomach and pressed my face to the street. It stank of mud and shit and rotting onions. I wrapped my arms around my head, shutting out the rest of the night. The stench intensified horribly; I nearly gagged, but I needed to keep all the light I could away from my eyes.

Darkness had been my balm that first night, when Sebastian and I had come home. Christiana had lit a lamp and been waiting, had met us as the door to the cabin when we threw it open. Sebastian hadn't warned me about the light yet, about what it would do to my eyes in the night; I had looked right into it and screamed at the pain.

It had been the darkness of the forest that comforted me, that helped bring my vision back, with Sebastian's coaching and my own concentration. I only hoped darkness would do it again now.

I blinked in the circle of my arms and stared hard. My eyes began to water from the smell of the street. The pain returned full force, filling my eyes, my head, my awareness.

Steel on steel to my right. A hiss. A yell.

I became aware of a new rhythmic pain, and realized I was hitting my head against the ground. I thought about stopping, but didn't dare. Each motion, each strike, brought a faint flare of orange to my vision. I dug my fingers into my forearms to keep them from scrabbling at my eyes, and I continued battering the street with my forehead. One more, I kept telling myself, one more. One more strike and I would either see or die — just one more.

And then, suddenly, a wave of color was before me — light and shadows, shapes and textures. I blinked and watched as the lines resolved themselves into an amber-hued sandal print.

Sight! And a raging headache behind my eyes, but, first and foremost, sight.

I unclenched my fingers and pushed myself up from the street, gasping to clear my lungs.

I saw Degan and Shadow almost immediately. They were less than ten feet away, limned in red and gold, blades at the ready as they measured each other anew. Degan held his sword in one hand, his hat in his other. He had the hat by its brim at chest level, slightly out from his body. I'd seen him use his hat once before in a fight to foul his opponent's blade, but that had been against seven men. That he was using it against just one didn't bode well.

Shadow, in turn, was holding a silvered piece of the moon in his left hand—light and fast and beautiful. The blade was slightly thinner than Degan's, and slightly longer. When the steel moved, the moonlight seemed to run along its length in gentle waves, lapping against the blue-black guard. It was Black Isle steel, just like Degan's, only of an even better temper, if the pattern of light was any indication.

Shadow's other hand was closed into a loose fist, but I could see tiny glints of metal showing between the fingers. The ends of throwing darts held against the palm? Brass knuckles in case Degan got close?

I squinted for a better look even as I gathered my feet beneath me. The movement caused my vision to blur. When it refocused, Shadow was in motion.

He stepped forward, blade lashing out to meet Degan's and drive it off-line. At the same time, his right hand came forward and threw two pieces of metal at Degan. I saw with amazement that they were coins— copper owls, by the look of them.

Degan twisted his body, bringing his hat around to meet the coins even as he tried to keep his sword in the line with Shadow's blade. On anyone else, it would have seemed graceless; on Degan, it looked like a practiced dance.

Their swords met, high and outside. At the same time, Degan scooped the coins from the air with his hat. An instant later, he twisted the hat to one side. Where two bronze owls had gone in, numerous lines and gobbets of molten metal came flying out. The shower of melted bronze sent up tiny spikes of steam where the drops hit the street.

Portable glimmer; the kind that would pass any Rag's inspection until it was used. And worse, it was the kind you could carry by the handful; which looked to be about as much as Shadow had.

I took a closer look at Degan. Yes, there was at least one set of burn marks running along the sleeve of his sword arm. I also noticed Degan's hat was pitted and showing wear—many more catches, and it would either catch fire or fall apart.

I scanned the street for my knife, saw it on the other side of the fight. So much for getting in a quick, poisonous slash. Nor was I sure enough of my night vision, or my aim, to try throwing one of my other blades. A wrong step at the wrong time and I could end up hitting Degan as easily as Shadow.

My rope, though, was closer. It lay in a dark puddle well behind Shadow, its knots bubbling and steaming in the water.

Staying low, I drew my rapier and quick-shuffled toward the rope. The world still seemed to fuzz and sharpen at random as I moved.

I stopped and knelt at the edge of the puddle. As my fingers quested out for the rope, my eyes lighted on Shadow's broad gray-cloaked back less than ten yards away.

I smiled. I didn't need perfect night vision or the steadiest feet or even the surest hands to deal with him this time. All I needed was to take a few quick paces and swing the rope. That much, I knew, I could do.

I was just closing my fingers around the rope when a boot stepped down on my wrist.

"*Ah-ah-ah,*" scolded a man's voice softly. "No time to play, Drothe—you're wanted elsewhere."

I didn't need to look up to know who it was.

"You have crap timing," I told Rambles.

"All part of my charm," he said. The boot shifted on my wrist. I winced. Something cool and hard laid itself across the back of my neck.

"Drop the tail," said Rambles. I let my rapier fall to the street. "Now," he continued, "leave the rope where it is and stand up. Slowly."

His boot lifted, and I brought my hand in toward me. I cradled it against my thigh as if he had hurt it more than he had.

I twisted my head to look up at him. The coolness on my neck was the forward edge of a short-bladed sword. A dark, self-satisfied smile was on his face. That was when it hit me.

"It was you, wasn't it?" I said. "You're the one who told Nicco I was working for Kells."

His smile widened. "It was either you or me. Lucky for me, you've been screwing up enough that I was able to make the story believable. Frankly, I'm surprised you're still alive."

Lucky? Believable? Rambles hadn't actually *known* I was working for Kells?

He thought he'd made it all up!

Oh, I was going to enjoy dusting this bastard.

The ring of steel on steel sounded behind me.

"We need to go," said Rambles, pressing harder against my neck with the sword. "Get up."

I started to comply, holding my left hand, seemingly limp and hurting, against my body. As I rose, Rambles took a step back to give me room. In the moment of his step, I felt the pressure of the sword ease off. That was what I'd been waiting for.

I lunged off the ground with both feet, driving myself upward. At the same time, I thrust my left elbow out. His eyes grew wide at my movement. They got even wider when my elbow drove into his crotch with the full force of my body behind it.

I ducked my head as I came up, but still felt a light cut slide across the back of my neck. It was worth it, though, to see Rambles collapse on the street next to me. I drew my boot dagger and gathered up the rope as he began to vomit on himself.

"I wish I could make this linger," I said. "Angels know you've screwed me over enough to deserve it, but I have more important business than you."

He blinked the tears from his eyes and rolled on the ground, drawn up into himself. Rambles looked at me, then past me. "Kill the fucker," he grated through his teeth.

"Kill him yourself," said a voice behind me. "I have orders."

Damn! Since when did Rambles run with a partner?

I rose and spun, lashing out with the rope. The woman was standing just beyond its reach. As the end passed by her, she slipped in neatly and punched me in the face. I staggered, brought my dagger up, felt it taken away. Then I noticed the white sash around her waist.

What the hell was a *Sash* doing here? Where were Nicco's people? Or even Iron Degan? If Rambles was going to have backup ...

She hit me again. Between her and what Shadow had done to my night vision, my head wanted to fall off.

I tried to back away. She grabbed my doublet, holding me in place, and brought her fist back yet again.

"Stop!" I said, dropping the rope. I held my palms out toward her. "Enough!"

The White Sash glared at me. "Hardly," she said, "but it'll have to do for now."

I looked up at her and felt a stirring in my memory ... A savage smile, cloak streaming out in midleap, her blade brushing me aside in the rain ...

"The Barren," I said. "You're the Sash who ambushed us in the Barren."

"And you're the fuck who helped kill two of my brothers," she grated. "Now, let's go."

She yanked on my doublet, pulling me toward her. She was tall, with broad shoulders, a narrow waist, and a hard presence—lots of muscle, lots of reflexes there. Her eyes were a pair of copper coins on a winter's morning, while her mouth seemed most comfortable set in a stern line of displeasure. The only thing remotely soft about her was her hair—a long auburn braid, the hair interwoven with a white ribbon edged in fine lace.

I remembered I'd thought her beautiful in the Barren, and she was. But it was the beauty of a finely swung sword, or a freshly frozen lake at morning. It was a beauty you knew better than to touch.

I glanced back at Degan. He was busy pressing Shadow, forcing him back, even as the Gray Prince reached into his pouch for more coins. I groaned. If there was ever a time to tap Shadow from behind ...

The Sash followed my look.

"That's a Gray Prince," I said. "Shadow. Think of the feather in your cap."

She bit her lip, then shook her head. "Orders," she said, and pulled at my clothing.

"Screw you, Sash," I said, digging in my heels. "I'm not about to—"

Her face was suddenly inches from mine. More important, though, I felt a firm, constricting pressure clamp itself around my balls through my pants.

"I don't give a damn about your friends right now," she snarled. "You'll move your ass, and fast, or we'll leave a few nonvital pieces behind." She squeezed to emphasize the point. "Understood?"

"Understood," I gasped.

She let go and spun me around, then gave me a shove. I would have bolted, except my legs were still shaky from her ... handling. By the time I caught my balance, I felt a hand on my shoulder and a blade at my back.

"What about me, damn it?" gasped Rambles from the ground behind us.

"Don't stand so close next time," she said. Then, to me, "Go."

I considered asking her what the hell was going on with Rambles but decided it would likely get me a punch in the kidney. Her being with Rambles meant she was most decidedly *not* going to be a shortcut to getting the journal to the emperor.

Instead, I took three dragging steps in the direction she was steering. Then I heard Degan call out.

"Drothe!"

I smiled and looked back past the Sash. Degan was stepping back from Shadow, as if to come after me. Shadow paused for a second as well to look our way.

"Stop!" shouted the Gray Prince.

Even better.

Both of them began to move in our direction, although not at a run. Each was eyeing the other as they moved, blades at the ready for any kind of treachery.

"Fucking brilliant!" muttered the Sash. Her fingers dug into my shoulder. At the same time, I felt a sharp spike of pain between my kidneys. "Understand this," she said as she prodded me forward. "I'll kill you before I let them have you, orders or no. So *move.*"

I moved. Part of me wanted to stumble, to drag my feet . . . to do anything to give Degan a chance to catch us, but the knife in my back argued otherwise. Then we went around a corner, and I realized that even if I could slow us down, it wouldn't matter.

In front of us, nearly filling the small street, was a patrol of Rags—waiting.

"There're two Crawlers behind us," said the Sash to the Rags. "I don't want them following me."

"Don't worry," said one wearing a commander's steel gorget. "We'll stop them."

"No, you won't," muttered the Sash as they parted and flowed past us, but she said it soft enough that only I overheard. There looked to be more than a dozen of them, but I knew she was right; at most, the Rags would delay Degan and Shadow, not stop them. That delay would be long enough for us to get away, though.

"Nice job, sending them off to die," I said as we moved forward again. "Is that standard procedure?"

"Shut up," she said. The pressure against my back increased.

"No, really," I said as we exited the street and cut across to a not-quite-parallel one. "That was well-done. I know some Upright Men who would have been impressed by that."

"Shut *up!*"

She steered us down a narrow side alley. I could almost touch the walls on either side.

I took a deep breath, let it out. "You know," I said, "if you ever get tired of working for the emperor, I can probably get you in with the Kin."

That did it.

She roared and shoved me toward a wall with her free hand, intending to drive me into it, quite likely repeatedly. I spun with the push, though, and lashed out with my fist. On the downside, the punch didn't land as solidly as I would have liked; on the upside, it hit her in the side of the neck. She staggered and started choking.

I bolted.

There was no way to get past her in the narrow space, so I headed in the opposite direction. I dodged piles of garbage and even kicked over a bucket of rainwater as I passed. Anything to make the footing worse and slow her down. Behind me, I heard cursing and the beginnings of a stumbling pursuit.

The alley exited onto the end of a rambling lane. There was a fence to my left; I headed right. After half a block, the lane widened enough to allow for a line of small trees down the middle. I cut to the left side of the avenue, hoping the trees would obscure me when the Sash finally came out of the alley.

Up ahead, I could see a corner wine bar, its light spilling out onto the street through the open door. A single table sat out under the trees. Even with the empire surrounding Ten Ways, someone was at the table, having a glass in the moonlight.

You had to admire the locals around here.

I swerved to give the table a wide berth and put on a last bit of speed. Around this corner, then a few more, and I'd be safe. After that, I could backtrack, help Degan, and deal with whatever came next.

Except what came next was a chair. It came flying in from the direction of the table, low and too fast for me to dodge. I leapt, anyhow, but the chair's legs got tangled with my own, and I came crashing down hard. Something beneath me snapped, and it took me a frightening second to realize it had been the chair, and not me, doing the breaking.

A large shadow loomed over me. I blinked in the light as my night vision faded. The shadow resolved itself into a man with heavy shoulders and an iron gray fringe of hair poking out from beneath a gray flat cap. He smiled, showing small, even teeth, and pushed the cap back with a thick-fingered hand.

"Good thing for me I decided to have a drink out under the stars, eh?" said Iron Degan. "Otherwise I might've missed you. Speaking of which . . ." He looked back down the street. "Where's your date?"

I groaned and began to gingerly shift myself off the remains of the chair. More aches and pains to add to the inventory, but nothing seemed broken or strained.

I rolled onto my hands and knees and ran a mental inventory. I was depressingly low on steel, which made the dagger at my belt the best option—not that any options are truly good when you're facing a degan. I groaned again and inched my hand toward the blade.

"Don't," said Iron without taking his eyes off the street. "I'd hate for you to end up worse than you already are, but you will if you try to use that steel."

I sighed, drew the dagger slowly, and tossed it at his feet. Damn degans.

I heard footsteps come running up, then slow, and finally stop. Hard breathing. I looked up. It was the White Sash.

"You seem to be light someone," said Iron.

The Sash gestured at me. "He took Rambles down in the street."

"And you left him there?"

"Considering Shadow and that other degan were coming after us, yes."

Iron straightened up at that. "Interesting," he said. "So who has Rambles now?"

"I sent a squad of Reds in," she said. "If he's smart, he got out of there while everyone else was busy."

Iron shrugged. "Nothing to do for it now," he said. "Rambles will come back or he won't." He bent down, laid a hand across my neck, and squeezed. I felt my head shift on my shoulders. "No running, now, you hear?" he said softly, as if cautioning a small child.

"I hear," I said as he half lifted, half guided me to my feet.

"I'll take him from here," he said to the Sash. "Best you fade."

"Hold on," said the Sash. Her voice was sharp. "We're done now, right? My end of the agreement is paid."

"Done?" said Iron. He laughed like a pile of rocks falling over—hard and blunt. "Not even by half, Lyria. You think bringing me this sorry mess of a Nose makes us even? Hardly."

"But—"

"No!" snapped Iron. "We don't discuss this here. I'll tell you when we're even, understand?"

The Sash—Lyria—crossed her arms and cocked a hip in defiance. "Pretty damn convenient for you, then, isn't it?"

Iron let go of my neck and stepped up to her. She was slightly taller, but it didn't seem to make a difference to him.

I knew better than to run. Iron was fresher than me; making him catch me again would likely only piss him off. Besides, the conversation was just starting to get interesting.

"Degans," said Iron slowly, "don't break their word. We don't rig a deal. And we don't stand being questioned. Understood?"

Lyria's lips pressed themselves into a narrow, blood-less line. "One more," she said after a moment. "I owe you one more favor after this."

"What you *owe* me," said Iron, "is your word. We'll see how long it takes to pay that back."

Lyria looked past Iron to me. "I owe my word to someone else, too," she said, running her hand along the white around her waist.

"That's between you and the emperor," said Iron. "But I don't think he's the one you ought to be worry-ing about right this instant, do you?"

Lyria's hand crept to her own sword, then fell away. "One more, degan," she said as she turned away. "Then my payback to you is done."

Iron watched her go, shaking his head all the while. When she was out of sight, he walked back over to his chair and sat down.

I stood watching where Lyria had been. Iron Degan had exchanged the Oath with a White Sash? What the hell could he have done for her? More important, though— what was she doing for him, besides grabbing me?

Iron Degan pushed a bottle of wine across the table in my direction. "Here," he said. "Have a drink before you say something stupid."

I took a pull at the bottle. The wine was red and soft and peppery. I swirled it around in my mouth, then spit it out onto the nearest tree.

Iron chuckled. "Prefer whites, eh? My father said to never trust a man who drinks whites."

"I don't drink wine," I said.

"Then I ought to cut your throat right now." He laughed and took the bottle back. More wine went into his cup, then into him.

"So," he said, staring into the cup, "how fares my sword brother Bronze?"

I fought to keep the concern off my face and out of my voice. "Fit. Dangerous. Probably on my trail," I said. I hoped.

Truth be told, with a dozen Rags and Shadow thrown

into the mix, I had no idea how Degan might be faring. I had seen him handle long odds before — but this? All it took was a lucky stroke or a random swing to change the equation. And Shadow probably still had some coins left over.

"As he should be," said Iron. "He's an Oath to uphold, after all." Iron raised his eyes at my silence. "Surprised I know? Heh. Well, I didn't until just now, but I suspected." He took a long drink. "Bronze bound to you, and me to ... well, someone else. No, I'm not going to enjoy resolving this one; he and I, we go back. Tell me, did he know I was involved in this before he took your Oath?"

I stared down at Iron Degan and made a show of crossing my arms. My back was beginning to ache where I had hit the street, but I leaned against the tree and tried to ignore it.

"Fair enough," said Iron. "Frankly, I'd be disappointed if you said. But you ought to know this: We degans, we don't fight one another — not if we can help it. If Bronze took your Oath knowing I might have to stand against him, then he's the one in the wrong. Win or lose, he won't be the Order's favorite son when this is done. Remind him of that for me, in case you see him before I do; and I pray you do."

"Same here." I glanced back to where Lyria had been. "So that's why you used her," I said. "By sending her, you wouldn't have to risk facing Deg — I mean, Bronze — when coming after me. Plus, who's going to argue with a White Sash? Everyone would assume she was on imperial business."

"They said you were clever. Aye, I used her for that, at least in part. As for the other reasons, well ... Let's just see how clever you turn out to be, hey?"

He drained his cup and set it on the table. "Now," he said, his voice turning crisp, "we'd best get a move on. Don't want to be late. You've been 'requested,' after all."

"Requested?"

"By the lady herself, lad." Iron Degan clapped me on the shoulder. "You're going to see Solitude."

Chapter Twenty-five

The house was large, well-appointed, and empty. Decorated with wrought-iron willow trees and laurel leaves, the gate to the street opened onto a summer garden not yet in bloom. A crushed-gravel path curved up from the gate to the front door, past budding trees and weed-crowded flower beds.

It was a gilt-ken—one of the fine, furnished houses that was rented out to country nobility when they came to court. These houses supposedly sat vacant the rest of the time, watched over by caretakers—except when the caretakers rented them out to well-heeled Kin. Gilt-kens usually played host to traveling games, flash whorehouses, or high-end cons, but I wasn't surprised to learn that a Gray Prince might hire one out for meetings as well.

Iron led me along the path. I blinked, rubbed my eyes, blinked again. It had taken a while for us to slink out of Ten Ways and get across the city, and somewhere along the way the sun had come up. Now, the morning light reflected off the gravel path, making my eyes sting and blur.

It was leftovers from Shadow's flash glimmer, I knew. While my night vision had come back, my eyes were still overly sensitive to light, much as they had been when I first got the gift from Sebastian. It would pass, I knew, but the question was how soon.

I blinked and squinted until we entered the shadow

of the main entry. Iron opened the doors without knocking. The foyer beyond was small, with a tiled floor and dark wood covering the walls. It was cool inside. The only light came from a pair of small windows set high in the wall behind us.

I sighed for the shadows and felt some of the tension drain out of my neck and shoulders. Then I noticed the woman in the archway across from us.

Solitude looked different in person than in the dream. She had traded in the close-cut jerkin and hose for an unremarkable blue dress, and her hair was falling casually to her shoulders. There were the beginnings of small lines at the edges of her eyes and mouth—from laughing or frowning, I couldn't tell—but the eyes themselves were still the same gold-sprinkled jade that would make any jeweler wring his hands in envy. Those eyes regarded me for a long moment before they turned to Iron.

"Well?" said Solitude.

Iron Degan stepped in close and spoke softly in her ear. Solitude's eyes narrowed in response to what he said, but otherwise her face stayed a careful blank.

When he was done, Solitude turned and led us deeper into the house, the charms on her dress and in her hair tinkling softly through the empty spaces. I couldn't help but notice that some of them were old pilgrim's tokens.

Of course—I should have guessed earlier.

We passed through three rooms, each larger than the last, each filled with furniture covered by cloths. The rugs had all been rolled up and set aside, and the drapes were still drawn across the windows. The place smelled of dust and disuse.

The fourth room we entered was smaller than the previous three. A pair of low chairs stood uncovered, a small slate-topped table between them. A book sat open on the table, with an extinguished taper next to it. One entire wall of the room looked to be made up of windows, given the size of the drapes and the amount of light leaking in beneath them.

Solitude settled herself in one chair. I moved toward the other.

"You'll stand," she said. There was no hint of warmth in her voice, none of the candor I'd experienced in the dream. She was all cold steel today.

I stopped and hooked my thumbs in my belt. Iron Degan took a position a few feet behind me.

"Well?" said Solitude after it became obvious I wasn't going to start.

"I don't have the journal on me, in case you're wondering," I said.

"Yes, I can see that. Where is it?" Her lisp, I noticed, became more pronounced when she was irritated.

"I didn't tell Kells and I didn't tell Shadow; what makes you think you're any different?"

Solitude leaned back in her chair and crossed her legs. They were nice legs. "They haven't got you. I do."

"Threats," I said. "How imaginative." I crossed my arms. "Let me explain something to you. I've been targeted by Nicco, cajoled by Kells, beaten by a White Sash, found a dead assassin floating in my bedroom, and gone up against Shadow face-to-face, all in the *past three days*! And those are only the highlights. So you'll understand if I don't give much of a damn for your threats. If you want to get your hands on Ioclaudia's journal, you're going to have to give me a better reason than, 'I'll make you bleed.' I've been bleeding since this thing started, and it doesn't bother me that much anymore. So offer me something besides blood, or shut the fuck up."

The room grew silent. I could hear the house settling, a temple bell ringing in the distance, Iron Degan shuffling his feet behind me. The last sound made me tense my neck.

Solitude didn't move. She sat watching, her body still. Except now, there was a hint of fire in her eyes.

"Ironius," she said at last, her voice making me jump, "leave us."

There was a brief silence behind me; then I heard Iron Degan turn and move away. His footsteps were far softer than I would have expected from someone his size.

"Never trust a sell-sword," pronounced Solitude once the door had closed behind him.

"Even a degan?" I said.

"*Especially* a degan. People who charge promises for their lives worry me. And people who can call those promises in anytime it suits them worry me even more."

"And yet you're working with one."

"Some worries are larger than others," she said.

I had to agree, but not when it came to Bronze Degan's promise. I'd seen what *that* had entailed, and I was still amazed. My worry with him centered around whether he was still alive; whether Shadow was dead; whether my sister was in danger. I wasn't worried about what I owed Degan; rather, I was comforted by the thought that he may still be out there, looking out for my interests.

Solitude gestured at the chair across from her. "Please," she said. I sat. "Tell me what you know about Ten Ways," said Solitude once I was settled.

"It's a shit hole," I said.

"And?"

"It's surrounded by imperial troops."

"And?"

"And there's a Kin war going on there," I said. "One you started."

Solitude didn't even flinch. "Good. Why did I start it?"

"You tell me."

She showed me a smile that would have made a razor seem dull. "It doesn't work that way," she said. "You spill what you know. Then I fill in the gaps."

"So you can keep back whatever you don't want me to know?" I said. "No. If you want to hear my side, I get to hear yours. All of it."

Solitude settled back and folded her hands before her face. I heard a faint clicking. It took me a moment to realize she was tapping at her front teeth with a thumbnail.

"Done," she said. "But you still go first. I need to know what Nicco and Kells and Shadow think I'm after in Ten Ways. You've been their main source on that count. I need to hear your version before you start adjusting it to fit my facts."

I pulled out a seed and rolled it between my palms. The combination of sweat and warmth released a burned, musky-sweet scent from the ahrami. I bent down and breathed it in, an old friend in a strange room.

This was the woman who had told me—in a dream, no less—to keep things close to my chest. I had to assume she played the same way. But there was a difference between being careful and being stupid, and holding out on a Gray Prince when she was willing to meet me halfway definitely fell into the stupid category. I doubt I'd get a better offer any time soon.

"All right," I said, still hunched over my hands. "You want to be the next Dark King. You needed the war in Ten Ways to pull Nicco and Kells in and get them reeling so you could take them down. From there, you're going to move into their territories, and then the rest of Ildrecca after that."

Solitude didn't move. "What about the other Princes?" she said. "They won't much care for that kind of a move on my part."

"That's why you want the book," I said. "It'll give you the power to roll over them if they decide to get in the way."

"Ah." *Tap, tap, tap*—the sound of a nail on a tooth. "And this is what you've told them?"

I put the seed in my mouth and clicked it against my own teeth. *Tap, tap, tap.* "More or less," I said.

Solitude smiled. At first, I thought it was in reaction to my imitation of her; then, she began to laugh.

"I could kiss you, Drothe," she said. "This is perfect!"

"Um?" I said.

"If Nicco, Kells, and Shadow think I'm after all of Ildrecca, they'll try to stop me outside of the cordon.

None of them truly *wants* Ten Ways, so they'll pull back and try to keep me contained. That means the cordon will fall even easier." A dark gleam entered her eyes. "And if the war doesn't go past the cordon's walls, then the empire will pull out, too. Once they're done wrecking the place, of course." She laughed again, clapping her hands together. "Oh, this is beautiful. I should be paying you to tell tales like this!"

I sat up in my seat, suddenly feeling far less clever than I had a moment ago.

"You mean this is all about *Ten Ways*?" I said. "The setups, the rumors, getting Nicco and Kells at each other's throats—even drawing in the empire—is all so you can take Ten Ways? You don't want to be the Dark King?"

"Hell no!" said Solitude. "I have enough headaches without *anyone* becoming the next Dark King, let alone myself. No, I just want the cordon."

I asked the obvious question—the one she was waiting for. "Why?"

"Are you sure you want to know?"

No. "Yes."

"I thought you might." Solitude smiled and leaned forward. "Because it didn't always used to be called Ten Ways," she said. "Because a long time ago, it was called Ten Wise Men."

I noticed that somewhere along the way I had chewed and swallowed my seed without noticing. I put another one in my mouth. "How long ago?" I said, starting to have a bad feeling.

"Right around the time Stephen Dorminikos became emperor," she said, "and before the beginning of the Endless Cycle."

"And why was the cordon called Ten Wise Men?"

"I think you're starting to suspect why," said Solitude. I kept silent, and she shrugged. "It was called Ten Wise Men after the people Stephen Dorminikos granted it to. He gave it to his Paragons—ten of them to be exact—so they could conduct research for him, uninterrupted."

"And one of those Paragons was named Ioclaudia Neph," I said.

Solitude nodded. "Including Ioclaudia. Who wrote a journal as insurance against her life, for all the good it did her."

"Insurance?" I said. "Why would she need insurance if she was working for the emperor?"

"Why does anyone need insurance when they work for someone of great power?"

"To protect them against that power."

"Precisely. The emperor didn't put them in Ten Wise Men to work on Imperial magic; he put them in there to work on soul magic. He put them in there to make him immortal." Solitude leaned forward and stared me in the eye. "The Angels didn't choose Stephen Dorminikos to serve as the Undying Emperor—he did. He charged his Paragons with finding a way to make him immortal, but it didn't work. For some reason, reincarnation was the best they could manage. So they broke his soul into three pieces and somehow arranged for those pieces to follow one another in a constant cycle. *That's* how Stephen Dorminikos Progenitor became Markino, Theodoi, and Lucien. The Angels had nothing to do with it."

My heart gave a flop, but I hardly noticed it. "And the Paragons?" I said, already knowing.

"Dusted. Them and everyone else in Ten Wise Men—servants, apprentices, bakers, everyone. All on the same night. The emperor surrounded the cordon, sent in his troops, and when they were done, he had the place burned to the ground. It's been rebuilt countless times since, and each time the name has changed slightly. But underneath it all, Ten Ways is still Ten Wise Men. And there are secrets buried there."

"Like Ioclaudia's journal," I said.

"Like Ioclaudia's journal," agreed Solitude. "Hers is supposed to be the most complete, but there are notes, fragments of journals, ancient runes, and circles of power still down there. And I want to dig them all up, which means I need Ten Ways."

I stared at Solitude, trying to wrap my mind around what she had just told me. If what she said was true, then the Angels had had nothing to do with Stephen Dorminikos's reincarnations. And if that was the case, then his whole foundation for sitting on the Undying Throne—being the chosen of the Angels, being an intermediary between Them and humanity, being guided in his rule by aspects of the divine—was all a construct, a hoax, a fucking *con*.

I felt my world starting to shift, and I didn't much care for it.

"How?" I said, scrambling for purchase. "How could anyone possibly set something like this up? The religion, the cults, the *sheer belief*. It's not possible!"

"Of course it is," said Solitude, her green eyes flashing. "How do you start a rumor on the street? You tell a few key people the tale you want spread, give them an incentive to talk, and step away. If done right, it'll take on a life of its own. Look at what I did with Nicco and Kells in Ten Ways—that was small-time.

"Now, think about what an emperor can do, especially if he has years to prepare. He could lay the foundations for a cult, create a corps of fanatics, indoctrinate the bureaucracy so it would be waiting for him when he came back. Stephen's Paragons didn't come up with the Endless Cycle overnight, and he didn't die the instant they worked the magic. There was time to plot, to lay groundwork, to make sure he would be reborn into an empire that was counting on his return as an article of faith. And when he *did* return?" Solitude spread her hands. "Everything was confirmed. The hardest part for Stephen was throwing down the First Regency when they decided they didn't want to surrender power to him. After that, it was just a matter of meeting the expectations he had already set."

I rubbed at my temples. The pain was back, but I knew it wasn't solely from my strained vision. "But why?" I said. "Why go through all of this just to keep the throne?"

"Why did Stephen kill his uncle and become emperor in the first place?" said Solitude.

"To save the empire," I said. Or, at least, that was the popular story. Now I wasn't so sure.

"Exactly," said Solitude. "He saved the empire, but he also knew that, no matter how good a foundation he laid, it would collapse someday. You know history — sooner or later, someone comes to the throne who undoes all the work of his predecessors. Have enough of them close enough together, and the empire falls." Solitude held up a finger. "Unless."

"Unless he stays on the throne forever," I said.

"That's the theory, anyhow. And so far, it's been working."

"But what about the Angels?" I said. "Stephen's been claiming to be their Chosen One since he came back. If They didn't set him up to come back, why haven't They cast him down?"

Solitude shrugged. "How should I know? I'm no theologian. Whatever They think of this, it's between Them and Stephen. For all we know, his creeping insanity is the punishment for blaspheming against Them, but I hope not. It's too damn tame for me."

I rubbed at my temples some more and reached for my herb wallet. It wasn't there. Of course. It had gone the way of my clothing seemingly so long ago. I pulled at one of the altered seams of Nestor's doublet and felt it give a little. I wasn't much longer for this outfit, either.

"Pardon my asking," I said, "but you have to understand when I say, where the hell are you getting all of this?"

"You mean, assuming I'm not making it up, or crazy, or both?"

"The thought occurs," I said. "Even you have to admit this isn't the kind of thing you find in any old history book."

"I have fragments of another journal," said Solitude. "Mainly bits and pieces, but enough to get a basic picture of what happened. The rest I've pieced together from ancient histories I guarantee you've never heard of, heretical theologies, and other sources. As you can imagine, information on this ... aspect ... of imperial history isn't thick on the ground. But it's there, if you know where to look."

"And you know where to look," I said, somewhat snidely.

"As do you."

I fidgeted slightly. She was right—it was easy enough for me to find out if she was telling the truth. I had Ioclaudia's journal; I could look it up. That alone made me more inclined to believe her, at least for the moment. The only problem was, if I started believing her, I would be buying into something far bigger than I had ever imagined.

That made me nervous. And suspicious. I was getting answers, but not the one at the core of everything—not the Why.

"What about Shadow?" I said. "How does he fit into all of this?"

Solitude's expression turned dark. "He doesn't," she said. "Or, at least, he didn't until recently."

"When he found out about the journal?"

Solitude didn't answer.

"You said you'd tell me all of it," I reminded her.

"When one of my people turned out to be a Long Nose," she snarled. I raised an eyebrow. "If you say *anything*," said Solitude sharply, "I'll have Iron bend you into interesting, complicated shapes."

I held up my hands. "Professional appreciation only," I said. Long Nosing against Solitude must have been a hell of a dodge. "How much does Shadow know?"

"Shadow knows the journal exists, but I don't think he's aware of its full implications. For him, it's a source of power, a potential guide to potent magic. I don't think he knows the imperial connection, but even so, the journal is too tempting a prize to ignore, and a bad enough threat on its own. Shadow with imperial glimmer is something I'd rather not contemplate. But if he gets his hands on Ioclaudia's notes and recognizes their true value . . ."

"He'll use them," I said. I didn't know Shadow well, but I'd seen enough in the meeting with Kells. He wouldn't pass up an opportunity to put himself on par with the emperor. "He'd tear Ten Ways apart to get the rest of the journals, and then he'd do it—he'd start another Endless Cycle, only for himself."

"Giving us two undying emperors instead of one," said Solitude. "One for the Lighters, and one for the Kin."

"Unlike you," I said.

Solitude's eyes narrowed. "What do you mean?"

"What the hell do you think I mean?" I said. "You tell me you want an ancient Paragon's journal, you tell me it holds secrets untold about reincarnation, and then you tell me you want to dig up Ten Ways to find whatever else you can about the process? Even if you don't want to become the next Dark King, you sure seem damn interested in finding out about not dying."

Solitude came out of her chair so fast, the tinkling of the charms on her dress formed a single multitonal note.

"Is *that* what you think?" she demanded. "That I want to shatter my soul so I can keep coming back to life? That I want to live as a fraction of myself for the rest of eternity?"

"Why else?" I said, prodding on purpose. "What's the point in finding the journal and taking over Ten Ways if you aren't going to use them? If you aren't going to reincarnate yourself?"

"Because knowing about something doesn't mean you have to use it in the same way!" she shouted. "Because magic can work both ways!"

I sat, staring at her, absorbing what she had said and what she had let slip.

"Shit!" said Solitude, kicking the table. It teetered and fell over with a crash. The marble top shattered, scattering itself across the floor. Iron immediately opened the door and stuck his head in. Solitude shooed him away with a gesture.

"This isn't how I wanted to broach the subject with you," she said. "Not until I knew where you stood."

"It's the emperor, isn't it?" I said, ignoring her complaint. "It's not about you or Shadow or the Kin—it's about *him*. You want to throw down the fucking emperor!"

"No," she said, shaking her head ruefully. "Rebellion is easy. It's been done more times than I can count. I want to *kill* him. Permanently. Forever. I want to figure out how the first Paragons made him immortal, and I want to undo it."

"You're insane," I said.

"You have it backward," said Solitude. "It's the emperor who's insane. All three incarnations of Stephen Dorminikos—Markino, Theodoi, and Lucien—are slowly going crazy."

"That's not exactly a revelation," I said. "Everyone knows each of them gets loose in the head as they get older. It's always been that way. That's why the next incarnation, or a Regent, is ready to step in and take over when the sitting incarnation passes fifty."

"But it's *not* harmless," said Solitude, "and it *hasn't* always been this way. The emperors have only begun to slip in the last two hundred and fifty years. Before Theodoi the Sixth, there weren't regular Regency courts, nor was the heir required to stay within a day's ride of Ildrecca. But after Theodoi went mad at the end of that reign, things began to change. The insanity has been creeping forward over time, coming on faster and running deeper every cycle."

I thought about what Solitude was saying, what I had read in the histories, what Lyconnis had told me about the Fourth Regency. If you looked at the history of the empire, as Solitude said, there *was* a pattern. The Regencies had become more common over time, and the various incarnations were less willing to leave the city than they used to be, both before and during their reigns.

Hell, stories were that Markino, Theodoi, and Lucien had even spent time together, back in the early days. That never happened now, though, not in public, and likely never in private, either.

"Before long," continued Solitude, "we won't be talking about paranoid or obsessive old men on the throne who drool when they talk. We'll be talking about three active, alert, clever men, each of whom has convinced himself that the other two are out to destroy him. I'm talking about paranoia, dementia, and God complexes, with an entire imperial structure in place to back the whole thing up. Each incarnation is at his predecessor's, or successor's, throat now more than they ever were during the first five centuries of the empire. It's only a matter of time before they begin to fight one another openly."

"Imperial civil war?" I said incredulously.

Solitude nodded. "A civil war with three emperors, each one returning from the dead, each one hungry for vengeance, each one able to raise and lead an army, again and again and again."

"But the empire has survived crises in the past," I said, though not with as much conviction as I would have liked. "The Reign of the Pretenders, the Bastards' Revolt, the betrayal of the White Sashes under Silverhawk—the Imperial Court kept going through all of it, without any version of Stephen on the throne. Who says they won't be able to handle a bent-headed emperor?"

Solitude crossed her arms. "Think about it," she said. "Even a 'bent-headed' emperor is still the emperor."

And people obeyed the emperor. Or, at least, they obeyed one version of him. But with three imperial camps to choose from, it would be chaos—unending chaos.

The world that had been shifting beneath me until now began to crumble. I could sense a tidal wave of events building beyond the horizon. When it hit, it would overrun everything and everyone in its path. Only a fool would be standing there, trying to build a dike when the wave broke.

"This isn't my concern," I said, standing up a bit too quickly. My vision flickered for half a heartbeat, then stabilized. I had my sister, Kells, and myself to worry about, not the empire. "I'm a member of the Kin—I'm in no position to oppose the emperor, let alone save the entire fucking thing. Let it fend for itself."

"Is that so?" said Solitude archly. She sat down and settled back into her chair. "I don't think so. You didn't sit on that journal just to save your ass, Drothe. If all you wanted was that, you could have given it to Kells or Nicco or Shadow or even me before this. It would have been easy, especially for you. But you didn't."

"We all make mistakes," I said.

"Yes, but it wasn't a mistake for you. Do you know why? Because, at some level, I think you want to be a player. You knew the journal was important, and you knew you could use it to make yourself important, too. Well, guess what, Drothe—it worked. You're in it, whether you like the final stakes or not. And I'm here to tell you it's too late to wash your hands and walk away."

"Watch me." I headed for the door, expecting Solitude to call out for Iron. Instead, I heard her sigh.

Then she said it. "Hypocrite."

That stopped me, although I didn't turn around. "What?"

"I've heard a lot of things about you, Drothe," said Solitude. "A lot of words used to describe you: tough, dangerous, relentless, clever. I've heard some less than pleasant ones, too. But there's one word I keep coming across that I almost never hear in relation to other Kin."

"You'd better not be getting ready to say 'honest,'" I said. "Even I won't buy that one."

"Not honest," she said. "Honorable." Solitude chuckled. "People actually call you honorable, Drothe."

Now I did turn around.

Solitude had her radiant smile on. "Imagine someone

using that word to describe one of *us*, the 'gutter crawlers.' I've heard nobles, soldiers, priests—even *merchants*, Angels help me—called honorable, but rarely a Darker, and never a Nose."

She stood. I watched her as she came across the floor, bits of marble crunching softly beneath her shoes.

"When someone chooses a word like that for a man like you," she said softly, "I have to wonder whether it's smoke or whether it's true. Are you honorable, Drothe? Are you loyal, not just to your boss, not just to your friends, but to the Kin? Because that's what it's about now. If you want to survive, if you want to hold on to the chips you have in the journal and make us take you seriously, then you have to admit that it's about more than what's in it for you. It's about all the Kin, be it keeping them alive, taking control of them, or even keeping the empire from wiping them out. The picture is bigger than you now; bigger than a single organization. I don't think you'd be here if you weren't interested in that. If it were just about you, the journal would have been sold or bartered a long time ago."

Solitude took a final step, bringing herself so close, we almost touched. She smelled of vanilla and cedarwood and summer wine. "What do you think?" she said.

I stared down into those green eyes and understood the stories about how she supposedly recruited all of her operatives on her own. She was good—*damn* good. And she was right.

I'd been—hell, still was—willing to go to the emperor to save the Kin. Even if it meant betraying Kells, being cast out, being hunted. It was what needed to be done.

But that didn't mean I had to give the journal to her, pretty speeches and green eyes aside.

"Even if you're right," I said, "and I'm willing to take one for the Kin, I don't see how giving you the journal accomplishes anything. If I want to keep the empire from wiping us out, I'm better off going directly to them. If the journal has everything in it you say it has, I ought to be able to cut a nice deal for both me *and* the Kin with the emperor. Giving it to you doesn't get either of those things."

Solitude nodded slowly. "Good," she said. "You see it."

"See what?" I said.

"The threat the empire poses."

"It's hard to miss when they surround an entire cordon and try to kill every Kin in it."

Solitude shook her head. "I'm not talking about Ten Ways, Drothe, nor even about what they did to Isidore. I'm talking about the emperor going mad—about the three incarnations going to war and dragging *every* aspect of the empire down with them. Including the Kin. You don't think we'll choose sides? You don't think that Gray Princes and Upright Men won't make deals with one emperor or another to benefit themselves? In a war that will be fought not just in the fields and forests, but in the streets of the empire, you don't think the various incarnations of Stephen Dorminikos will be able to overlook their distaste of us long enough to see the excellent tools we would make? Tools he could use and then discard, because after all, we're only Kin?

"No. This isn't about any threat to the Kin right now, Drothe—this is about what will happen to the Kin down the road. Fifty, one hundred, two hundred years from now. It's about the Kin surviving as an organization, as a way of life. If the empire falls, it will take the Kin with it. You can't have darkness without light, and you can't have the Kin without the empire. The great irony is, if we want to keep the empire, and therefore the Kin, alive, we have to kill the emperor to do it."

I was right; I hadn't liked where this was going. I swallowed and took another step back. Solitude followed me.

"Why should I care about what happens to the Kin in a hundred years?" I said.

"Why should you care about what happens to them *now*?" she replied. "You could have walked away anytime if you wanted to. But you didn't. Because you're

Kin. Because you're honorable. Because you care enough to see the bigger picture. That's why."

I stood there, not saying anything, my mind racing and blank at the same instant. There were so many things going through my head, I couldn't grasp any single thought on its own—except for one.

Solitude was right. Damn her, but she was right.

Chapter Twenty-six

I looked Solitude in the eye. She was smiling. It made her eyes sparkle.

Solitude was right. Maybe about the cause, maybe about the emperor—or maybe not. I needed to weigh that some more.

But she was definitely right about me.

I couldn't walk away, because there was too much at stake—too much that might, just might, fit together like she had said. History, I knew, was full of unlikely crap like that.

Dammit.

But just because she was right, and just because I knew I was going to help her, didn't mean I had to like it—or that I was going to make it easy for her.

"Being honorable's one thing," I said, "but bright and shiny feelings don't give me pull on the street or keep Blades off my blinds. If I give you that journal, I'll end up betraying Kells, snubbing Shadow, and risk pissing off the emperor. I'm going to need something besides a happy ending for the Kin to make it worth my while."

Solitude's shoulders drooped. "Money, Drothe? I had hoped for more than that from you. But if you—"

"I never said anything about hawks."

A small spark in her eyes. "A job, then?"

"I'm done working for other people," I said. "Too many compromises. And I don't want to be an Upright

Man, either." After working for Kells and Nicco, I knew I didn't want *those* kinds of problems.

"Then what?" said Solitude. "You can't tell me you want to go back to being a Wide Nose."

I walked over to the wall of curtains. I pushed them open slightly. As I'd thought, there was a wall of glass panes and doors on the other side.

The sunlight burned my eyes, but I looked out on the garden beyond the glass, anyhow. No one had been in to tend it, leaving it to become a bed of vivid green, cut through with a chaos of yellows, reds, blues, whites, and oranges. I suddenly wanted to punch out one of the windows, to banish the dust and closeness of the room with the smells of earth and growth and moisture.

I let the curtain fall back instead.

"I want you to cover my back," I said, not turning toward her. "I want the same protection you give your people, but without the strings. I want to know I have an organization behind me if I need it, but I don't want to be beholden to it. I want people to know that if they cross me, they cross you, but that when I talk, it comes solely from me."

I heard a gasp. "Do you hear what you're saying?" said Solitude. "No one has that kind of arrangement with me. Or anyone else, for that matter. No one!"

"If it makes it easier, I'll still work for you some-times," I said. "I just won't belong to you. Every dodge will be its own thing, a separate arrangement between you and me. Outside that, I'll be able to work with your people, but only if you agree, and they won't use me unless I give the nod."

I turned to face her. "I'm also going to need backing. Nicco's closed down or taken over my sources of money in his territory, and I haven't had my hands in any action on Kells's side of town for years. I have a few outside interests here and there, but not enough to let me operate on my own. I need more. We can work out the details after Ten Ways is settled, but know I'm going to need a cut of something down the line."

"You . . . " began Solitude.

"Have Ioclaudia's journal," I said. "The one thing you need to save the empire." The sparkle was gone from Solitude's eyes now, replaced by a much harder and colder light.

"What's the matter?" I said. "Is the cost of being honorable getting too high for *you*?"

Every line of her body went taught with indignation. *How dare* you *speak to* me *like that?* it said. But she stayed silent. And I knew that, at least for the moment, I had her.

I gestured at the empty chair amid the shards of broken marble. "Have a seat," I said. "There's more."

"How's the fit?" said Iron Degan.

"Not bad," I said, adjusting the hang of the doublet for the third time in as many blocks. "I think the last owner had narrower shoulders, though."

"Be glad we found you anything at all," he said. "Yours isn't the most common cut in the city, lad."

A new suit of clothes had been the last, and easiest, of my demands. Even so, Solitude had been fed up with me by then—she had told her people to find something for me as quickly as possible before practically throwing me out the door. "Quickly" had translated into secondhand drapes: a pair of dark breeches; patched stockings that had once been either yellow or white but were neither now; a worn linen shirt; and a doublet and slashed overcoat, both in a faded burgundy. Nothing fit quite right, and there were a couple of inhabitants left in the coat, but it was still a damn sight better than Nestor's hastily altered hand-me-downs.

On the upside, I still had my own boots, as well as a couple of replacement daggers and a surprisingly nice rapier they had managed to scare up in the house itself.

"Over here," I said, pointing to a blue and white striped canopy off to my right. Smoke flowed out from beneath it, carrying the smell of fish and oil and peppers.

"You hid the book there?" said Iron incredulously.

"No," I said. "I haven't eaten since last night. I'm hungry."

We were on the edge of Stone Arch cordon, still a good way from Fifth Angel Square. Iron looked around, taking in the late-afternoon crowds with one sharp glance. We were in Nicco's territory.

"Could half use a bite myself," said Iron, running his tongue over his lips. "Just stick close."

"Don't worry," I said. Iron was acting as both my backup and my handler. Solitude didn't want anything happening to me before I got the book, or me doing anything unexpected once I retrieved it.

Solitude had given ground on my demands grudgingly. Protection for Christiana had been surprisingly easy to arrange, although Solitude had wondered why I was so worried about shielding a baroness. She had been careful to point out that no one could *guarantee* protection from a Gray Prince, especially Shadow. I had learned this firsthand, of course, compliments of Task, but I had appreciated the honesty nonetheless.

My own protection from Shadow was a far dicier thing. Surrounding me with Arms wasn't tenable and likely wouldn't have done any good, anyhow. The best Solitude could do was let Shadow know I was under her wing now, and that any move against me would be a move against her. Since they were essentially on the verge of war already, I wasn't sure this would help, but there weren't a lot of other options.

There was a small line in front of the street vendor's stall, but we ignored it and moved to the front. A few Lighters muttered complaints, but a sharp look from Iron was enough to silence them.

The man bent over the charcoal grill was small, with the sandy skin and dusty hair of the steppes tribes. He was a blur of activity, turning hand-sized fish over the fire, chopping onions, mincing herbs, and pouring young olive oil into a hot pan, all while singing softly under his breath.

"Hello, Rall'ad," I said. "What's the catch today?"

Rall'ad's hands froze in midreach, one near the fire, the other over the cutting board on the table beside him. He looked up at me, his face pale.

"Please leave," he whispered in heavily accented Imperial.

I grimaced. Nicco—had to be. Word of my disfavor was all over the street, making even former Ears like Rall'ad eager to forget they knew me. Not that I blamed him—he had a wife and eight children to worry about. But I was hungry.

"Yellow salt skimmers today, eh?" I said, glancing into the bucket of gutted and cleaned fish. "Give us two. . . ." Iron tapped my shoulder and held up three fingers, pointing to himself. "Make that four of your best."

Rall'ad ducked his head in acknowledgment and dropped a small handful of red chilies into the oil in the pan. They immediately began to sizzle and spit.

Solitude and I had done our own bit of dancing over Nicco. Not surprisingly, I wanted him dustmans, both for what he had done to Eppyris and to get him off my blinds once and for all. Solitude had flat out refused. He was her main leverage in Ten Ways. Losing him would throw the cordon, and her plans, into chaos—or so she said. She had offered to talk to him instead, to make it clear I was off-limits.

I had laughed. Gray Prince or no, Nicco wasn't about to let Solitude get between him and his vengeance. She thought otherwise, though, and it had ended there. I got the feeling that she didn't much relish the idea of getting between Nicco and me, and that if there was going to be any resolution on the matter, it was up to me to find it—as long as it didn't interfere with her plans, of course.

Rall'ad tossed the pan a few times, then added a handful of chopped onions to the heated dance. The aroma burned my eyes and made my mouth water at the same time.

"If I'm seen talking to you, it could mean my death," Rall'ad hissed. He gave the pan two more quick tosses, then set it aside on the table. He picked up a bowl containing a mixture of chopped mint, parsley, garlic, and couscous. "Nicco has eyes everywhere."

"I know," I said. "I used to be one, remember?" The cook blanched. "Don't worry. If anything, Nicco will thank you for telling him I'm headed toward Five Pillars after this."

"And are you?" he said.

I smiled. "Careful you don't burn my fish."

"Never," said the Ear.

The worst sticking point between Solitude and me had been Kells. I wanted him left alone, or at least left alive, and his organization intact; Solitude, though, had rightly pointed out she was at *war* with him, thank you very much, and she couldn't just walk away. Besides, he was in league with Shadow, and how was that supposed to work?

Given how the war in Ten Ways was going, and given that Kells wasn't going to be able to deliver the journal after all, I didn't see his arrangement with Shadow lasting very long. I had said as much to Solitude, and also noted that Kells would be a wonderful counterbalance to the heavy-handed ally she had in Nicco. She had seemed intrigued by this notion, and while she hadn't promised to take my former boss on immediately, she had agreed it was worth considering.

It wasn't the arrangement I had hoped for, but it held out some hope for Kells. Not that it would do me any good; in his eyes, I would now be a cross-cove. He wouldn't know about the reasons or bargains or choices behind any of this—he would only know that instead of taking the journal to him, I had traded it for my life. He would only feel the stab in the back.

I wished there was some way I could explain away that disappointment, to make him understand why I was doing this, but any explanation would end up coming after the fact. It would come off as an excuse—and in a way, it was. Kells was one of the few Kin I looked up to, and my work for him one of the things I could hold up with pride. I'd stayed true in the midst of the enemy, even when it would have been easier to let go and just work for Nicco. To have made it through all of that, to have gone back to him with my head up, only to give him the cross now, even for the best reasons—it was almost too hard to swallow.

Almost.

Rall'ad pulled a fish off the grill, turned it on its back, and squeezed its stomach cavity open, forming a small bowl within the fish. Two spoonfuls of peppers and onions went inside, along with a handful of the herbed couscous.

Three more followed quickly. All were put on a trencher and handed over to us. No money changed hands, even though I tried to slip Rall'ad some hawks.

"It will only make it worse," he said. "Just eat and leave. Please."

I took my one, leaving Iron his three on the trencher, and we stood off to one side, scooping the fillings and flaky meat out with our fingers. The mint and the herbs cooled the bite of the peppers, letting the natural saltiness of the skimmer come through. Normally, I would have savored it; this time, I simply ate.

Iron finished before me and handed the wooden plate back to Rall'ad. I ate a last bite, threw the remains in the gutter, and pushed back into the street.

We were a handful of paces away from Rall'ad's stall when Iron said, "He was one of yours?"

"Used to be," I said. "Now he's too scared to look at me."

"You expected any different?"

I chewed on my mustache. "No, I suppose not," I said after a bit. "Still, it's hard seeing it end like this—watching myself being so hastily shoved aside."

"It never gets easier," said Iron. "Take my word on that."

I nodded, remembering what Degan had told me about his order—how degans sometimes served for years until the debt was paid. Was it easier for them, knowing they'd be walking away on their own terms, their deal kept, or did that make it harder? And what if the Oath required them to turn on their friends and associates? There was no one to blame except themselves and their honor. Even with Kells, I at least had the knowledge that I was saving him through my betrayal; the degans had no such luxury.

I shuddered at the thought. That was more weight than I would ever want to bear.

By the time we reached Fifth Angel Square, the crowds were out in force. Iron kept up with me far better than I would have expected, smoothly sliding his solid frame around knots of people even as I ducked behind and through them. I expected him to leave a wake of disruption behind him; instead, he left barely a ripple of notice.

As I walked, I looked up occasionally to catch a glimpse of Elirokos at the center of the square. The Pardoner's weathered statue still looked like a one-armed beggar to me, but now I found I could sympathize with his predicament. Battered, broken, his glory literally falling off him in pieces, he still stood tall and pointed the way to redemption. The carved souls under his care had vanished with his missing arm, but that didn't mean they were forgotten. I could see the weight of his burden reflected in the artfully carved lines of his face, the droop of his eyelids, the slight lean of one shoulder. If ever an Angel knew despair and failure, it was this one.

I nodded at the statue with a new appreciation. When this was all over, I decided, I would have to pay my respects at his shrine.

Mendross was in the middle of his closedown as I walked up. It was late enough in the day that most of the people who came to the bazaar to buy fruit had already been, so he was busy shifting bags, filling crates, and yelling at his son to do his share of the work. I could already see that the small handcart they used to sell their oldest produce on the street was nearly filled.

"Damn it, boy," groused Mendross, his tone grown casual from the nightly ritual. "If you don't move your ass, we'll never sell any of this. Anchaka's cart is already packed and away. If I end up with a pile of rotting— Sweet Angels and emperors, what the hell are you doing here!"

I smiled as the fruit seller caught sight of me and almost dropped the basket of dates in his hands.

"Being very unpopular with my former Ears, it would seem," I said drily.

Mendross licked his lips and glanced at the crowds creeping through the bazaar around us. "You have to leave," he hissed. "Now."

I crossed my arms and stared at the fruit seller. I was getting tired of everyone I'd known in Nicco's territory giving me the flick. Nicco might be after me, but it didn't mean I was poison to whomever I touched.

"I'll go," I said, "when I get the package I left with you."

Mendross looked at Iron and hesitated. As much as I would have liked to step off with the Ear, I knew Iron wouldn't stand for it. Instead, I nodded to let Mendross know it was all right to talk.

"That's just it," said Mendross. "People have been coming around asking questions about you." He set down the basket and stepped closer. "And about . . . *it*."

"About *it*?" I said. Who knew to ask Mendross about the journal? "Who's been asking?"

Mendross shifted his weight from foot to foot. "Tall cove, dark cloak." He swallowed. "No face."

Shadow? Shit!

"Did he ask you for it?" I said.

"No, no—just if I had seen you with it. And if I had an idea where it might be."

I let out my breath. "Who else?"

Mendross opened his mouth but didn't get a chance to speak.

"Well, there's always me," said Bronze Degan from behind me, "but I don't know if I count."

I spun around, a smile breaking across my face.

He was standing in the square, just outside the statue's shadow, a wicked grin creasing his own face. "After all," he added, "*I'm* not trying to kill you."

"Give it time," I said, laughing. I noticed he was wearing a new hat—deep red, like his doublet and pants—touched with a peach plume. I also noticed he was carrying a canvas sack.

"How the hell did you manage to get away from—" I said as I moved toward him, but a hand coming down on my shoulder interrupted me.

"Not so quick," said Iron, stopping me in my tracks. "We have an arrangement."

"I haven't forgotten," I said. I tried to shake his hand off and failed.

Iron nodded. "Aye. I just want to make sure *he* knows it," he said, indicating Degan with his free hand.

I looked from one degan to another. Neither was looking at me, and neither was smiling. My good mood, so fast in coming, died just as quickly.

Behind us, I heard Mendross making a hasty retreat into the curtained back portion of his stall. Lucky bastard.

"What arrangement?" said Degan.

"He's promised to give the journal to her," said Iron, taking his hand off me. "And I'm here to make sure she gets it."

"You mean Solitude?" said Degan.

"Aye."

Degan looked down at me, and then back up at Iron.

"I can't allow that," said Degan.

"What?!" I took a step forward. No one stopped me. I took three more, until I was right in front of Degan. "What the hell do you mean *you* can't allow it?"

"Do you know why Solitude wants that book, Drothe?" he said, almost patiently.

"Yes," I snapped. "Do *you*?"

Degan raised an eyebrow and said, so quietly that it barely carried, "So she can kill the emperor."

I took an involuntary step back. "You knew?" I said. "All this time, and you *knew*? You son of a bitch!"

Degan shook his head. "No. Not like that. I didn't

know what Solitude wanted to do. I didn't know how the book fit into it. I had my suspicions, but I didn't know for certain." He looked up at Iron. "Not until now."

"You know it's what needs to be done," said Iron.

"I know it's what *you* think needs to be done," said Degan. "I'm of a different mind on the matter."

"You're in the minority," said Iron darkly.

"Numbers have nothing to do with right or wrong!" snapped Degan. "An Oath's an Oath, whether you stand alone or you're backed by a hundred others."

"Wait a minute," I said. "An oath? As in, an *Oath*?" I scanned the bazaar, looking for large men with unique swords. Aside from the two near me, none were obvious. "Are you telling me there are more degans involved in this?"

"We're an old Order," said Degan, watching Iron. "Two hundred and eleven years since our founding. You don't think we've stuck around that long just to trade promises for service, do you? Believe me, there are better ways to make a living."

Iron moved a step closer. "That's enough, Bronze. Let's not talk out of school."

Degan chuckled drily. "No, *let's*." He dropped the canvas sack at his feet, leaving his own hands free. His gaze never left the other degan. "We degans have a 'higher' purpose—one we were founded to uphold. Except we can't seem to agree on exactly what that purpose is anymore. It seems things have gotten muddied over time. It *seems*," he said, his voice growing hard, "that some people have decided it's easier to become cowards than keep their honor intact."

"Don't confuse stubbornness with loyalty, Bronze," said Iron. "There's nothing cowardly in recognizing the truth."

"And there's nothing noble in destroying what you're sworn to protect!"

I felt my stomach drop. "You're talking about the emperor," I said. "The degans are fucking sworn to protect the emperor?"

"No," said Iron. "Not the emperor—the *empire*. There's a difference."

"Not in this case," said Degan.

"*Especially* in this case," said Iron.

"If you kill him, the empire will collapse," said Degan.

"And if we don't," said Iron, "it will eat itself alive."

Degan gritted his teeth and wrapped his hand around his sword's grip. "You don't know that."

I'd seen that look before. He wasn't going to give.

Crap.

"It's a moot point," I said to Degan. "I've made a deal with Solitude. For good or ill, it's going to her."

"No, it's not."

"You don't understand," I said. "I've—"

"No, *you* don't understand," he said. He took a deep breath and met my eyes. "I'm not giving you a choice in the matter. You're giving me the journal. Now."

I blinked. "Are you *threatening* me?" I said.

"No," said Degan. "I'm calling in your Oath."

And that was when Iron struck.

Chapter Twenty-seven

Iron surged past me, closing the distance between himself and Degan faster than I would have thought possible for such a large man. Degan caught the movement a fraction of a second later and began to draw his sword, but I could already see it was going to be too late. Damn, I had distracted him. Degan's blade still wasn't clear of its scabbard when Iron reached him.

Iron had come on empty-handed, opting for speed over carnage. Now, his left hand clamped on to Degan's right, stopping the draw in midmotion. At the same time, Iron's right fist connected with Degan's jaw, sending his head rocking back. Three more savage punches followed with smooth, precise rhythm—head, throat, stomach. Degan rolled with them as best he could, bending his body and shifting his shoulders and hips. This moved him enough to make the last two punches go wide, so that they skidded along his shoulder and ribs instead of crippling him.

People near us were starting to shout now, some pushing to get away, others struggling to move in and get a better view.

My right hand instinctively went to my rapier even as I skipped two steps back to clear space for the draw. Then I stopped myself.

Who exactly did I want to help here?

Iron was pulling his arm back for another swing when Degan twisted his body, bringing his left hand toward the other degan's face. Iron bobbed his head back. Degan's hand sailed past, and I saw Iron begin to smile. That was when Degan's elbow followed through and hit Iron's face with an audible *crack*.

The two men came apart, Iron staggering back from the blow, Degan using the moment to wrench his hand free from the other's grip. Then the steel came out.

Now the crowd surged as one, trying to get away from the bared blades. Merchants who had started announcing special fight prices now yelled for the Rags instead. Prigs and Palm Getters, who had begun maneuvering in for a choice lift, instead grabbed whatever spoils they could and faded away before things got truly dangerous.

And still I stood, hand on my own steel, unmoving. Try as I might, I couldn't persuade myself to step into the fight. I didn't care about Iron per se—he was just muscle, here to make sure I kept my end of the bargain. It was what he represented that gave me pause—my agreement with Solitude, the future of the empire, the security of my sister, and my own safety as well. If I helped cut him down, all of that went away. And, to be honest, I wasn't ready to break yet another promise so soon after making it—that wound was still too raw.

Except I had a promise to keep with Degan, too. No, not a promise—an Oath. One he took so seriously, he had fought Shadow to keep up his end. Could I do any less? Could I look him in the eye and tell him my word to Solitude was any more valid than his promise to me? Hell, this was *Degan*—was *any* promise more important than the one I had made to him?

Son of a bitch. If only it weren't the journal; if only it weren't the empire.

And still, damn me, I hesitated.

Degan and Iron moved farther away from each other and began circling, slowly. Degan's sword was longer than Iron's by a good hand span, but Iron's looked to be heavier and had a slight curve to it. Like Degan's, its guard was chased in the metal of his name, steel wrought with cold iron in a flowing, arabesque pattern.

I took another step back. Until I knew what I was going to do, I wanted to keep well away.

Degan reached up to feel his jaw, shifting it back and forth in his hand. He chuckled and spit blood.

"Did I loosen anything?" asked Iron. Degan's elbow had split the skin on his cheek. It was ragged and bleeding.

"Just the stones in my head," said Degan, smiling. "My teeth are all there."

"You're slipping, to let me get in that close, lad."

"Everyone gets one for free—that was yours."

Iron shrugged and took a small step forward. His blade slid a hand's breadth to the left. Degan countered by rotating the guard of his sword out and shifting his hips. Iron studied Degan for a heartbeat, then backed away.

"I remember that move from down in Byanthia," said Iron. "You used it against the duke's captain of the guard, didn't you?"

"The duke himself, actually," said Degan. Then, before the words had fully unfolded in the air, he was moving. Degan's feet became a blur, his sword a line of silver fire in the dying sunlight. Two quick steps and Degan's blade was inches from Iron, coming in a furious arc toward his shoulder. At the last moment, Degan compassed a small circle in the air with his sword's tip, turning the cut into a sudden, rising thrust.

Iron stepped back and dropped to one knee. His sword came up, catching Degan's blade along its edge. Steel hissed on steel as Degan's point slid over Iron's head. Then their guards met with a clang.

They were in close now; perfect dagger range, I noted, except neither of them had one to hand. Instead, Degan rammed his knee into Iron's chest even as Iron slammed the pommel of his sword down on Degan's opposite thigh, just above the other knee. Degan yelled, Iron gasped, and both men collapsed to the cobbles.

Degan moved first, rolling onto his hands and knees and levering himself upward. He met my eyes as he did, glanced at the sack he'd been carrying, then at me again.

I looked at the sack. It was amorphous enough to be anything. Had he already gotten what I'd come to fetch, to make sure I'd keep my end of the bargain? Was the journal in the bag, lying out in the middle of the street?

Unfortunately, there was only one way to be sure.

Iron was up and in an easy crouch as I began to move forward. Despite his gasping for air, his sword assumed a rock-solid high guard almost of its own accord. He glanced at me, then turned his full attention to Degan. Degan was on his feet now, obviously favoring the leg Iron had struck.

The sack lay directly between them.

"Leave it for now, little Nose," said Iron. Deep breath. "Plenty of time later."

"It's his property," said Degan.

Iron chuckled and took another breath. "That sure of your hold on him, are you?" he said. "He's given his word twice over, now, brother—both to you and to Solitude. Which one do you think he'll favor?"

Degan frowned. "Take the sack, Drothe," he said.

I have to admit, I was mildly surprised. It was good to know Degan had that much faith in me; that, or he figured he could just take it back again if he changed his mind.

"Leave it be," said Iron more forcefully. "Let it distract him."

I looked from one degan to another. "The hell with this," I said. I took my hand off my rapier and strode forward.

That was my first mistake.

Degan sprang to his left and stepped forward, using my body to shield himself from Iron's view. It would only provide a moment of cover, but for a degan, that would likely be enough.

Iron, for his part, shot to his feet, spinning in the opposite direction. As he turned, he switched his sword to his left hand, so that when he faced me again, he was able to redirect the momentum into a full-out lunge, blade already extended.

I started to back away from the lunge, when I felt a hand in the middle of my back. "Don't," said Degan in my ear. Then Iron's blade was arcing around my arm, its curve letting it slide past and come in at Degan at the same time.

I heard a grunt and the scrape of metal on metal behind me. Iron's face was less then three feet from my own, and I saw him clench his jaw. Then he was lurching forward into me.

To say I bounced off him would be putting it mildly. His body connected with mine and propelled me away as if I'd been thrown. At the same time, I felt Degan's hand shoving me, so that when I came to rest on the street, I was a good three to four paces away from them.

I rolled over and saw Degan with his free hand locked on Iron's wrist. He must have reached around me and grabbed it when Iron lunged. Iron was turning, trying to keep Degan's body between himself and the other's sword, even as Degan twisted and levered down on his wrist.

I looked away, scanning the street. There, five feet to my left, was the sack.

I practically fell over myself in my haste to get to it. I wanted to ask Degan how he had gotten the journal, ask Mendross what had possessed him to give it to Degan in the first place, but all that could wait. Right now, I just wanted to get my hands on the damn thing so I could get rid of it.

Except when I picked up the sack, I knew the journal wasn't in there. The heft was all wrong, and the mass inside too malleable when I lifted the canvas. Whatever was in there wasn't a book.

I reached in and gingerly pulled out a coil of knotted rope. Each knot had a small scrap of paper tied into it, and around each knot, I knew, though I couldn't see them, was tied a single strand of my hair.

Somehow, Degan had gone back after his fight with Shadow and retrieved the rope Jelem had made for me. That, or he had actually managed to pick it up without setting it off when he came after me. Either way, it couldn't have been easy.

Damn, but he was making this hard.

I heard a yell, followed by a flurry of sword strikes so quick they nearly blurred into a single, continuous noise. I looked up, ready to move.

Degan was pushing Iron back with a relentless array of cuts and thrusts, his blade whistling in the air before him. It was stunning; I'd never seen a sword move with that much speed and accuracy at the same time. Every action was precise, every attack flowing into the next with flawless efficiency. There wasn't a hint of uncertainty in any of it.

And Iron met each attack just as flawlessly, parrying Degan's blade the exact amount needed to keep it from touching him, but no more. Iron's defense never faltered, be it blade or body or foot—he was exactly where he needed to be to not get hit. But none of his counters worked, either. No matter what he tried, he couldn't turn Degan's attacks back against him.

It was a beautiful, daunting display. The only problem was, it was bringing them right toward me.

I hopped back two paces and was just deciding which way to leap when Iron suddenly stepped off to one side, practically turning his back to Degan even as he thrust his sword toward him. Degan bent his torso back and tried to step off as well, but not before Iron's blade slid along the top of his right arm. Degan's free hand slapped the sword away, revealing a long, shallow cut along his right shoulder and biceps.

The two men stepped apart and regarded one another. Then they began circling again.

My stomach lurched at the sight of Degan's wound even as my head recoiled at the thought of giving the book to him. Hell and damn.

I glanced at the bazaar around me as I coiled the rope and slipped it into my belt. Most of the crowd had dispersed, although there were enough people hanging back on the edges for someone to be making book on the fight. There was even a water seller moving through the crowd with his spouted pot.

I made my way around the edge of the fighting, trying to stay out of range of the degans while keeping my distance from the gawkers as I hurried back toward Mendross's stall.

The fruit seller had taken up a position before his partly broken-down stall, a solid-looking staff in his hands. Not a single fig was going to go missing if he had anything to say about it. Then I showed up, and his produce was forgotten.

"*Degans?*" he said, practically sputtering. "Degans are fighting over the book you gave me? The book you said *no one* would be looking for here?"

"I didn't think it would come to this," I said.

Mendross took a step forward, brandishing his staff for emphasis. "I heard the name 'Shadow,' Drothe. And 'Solitude.' Those are names I don't like hearing!"

"Join the club," I said. I stepped into his stall. Mendross hesitated a moment, then moved his staff aside.

"I want that book out of my stall," said Mendross. "Now."

"Do I look like I came over here to argue about it?" I said.

Mendross turned on his heel and shoved the curtain aside. "Spyro!" he yelled. The boy's head popped up from behind an opened sack of dates. His hair was mussed and his eyes only half open.

"Sometimes I think you'd sleep through the Angels' Descent, boy," snapped Mendross. "Get out there and make sure no one steals the stall." Spyro didn't quite fall over himself on the way out, but it was a close thing.

I followed Mendross through the curtain, glancing over my shoulder as I did. The two degans had come to grips again, each holding the other's sword arm with his free hand. Iron was pushing Degan backward toward a brass seller's stall, while Degan was busy trying to shift his weight and spin Iron into the stall instead. The curtain fell to block my view, and an instant later I heard the crash and clatter of a hundred incense burners and lamp holders being knocked to the ground. I wondered who had ended up against the table. Instead of looking, I turned back to Mendross.

The fruit seller was unceremoniously dumping a basket of figs out onto the floor. From the bottom toppled a cloth-wrapped bundle.

"Here." Mendross unwrapped the journal and held it out to me. "I don't want to know," he said as I took it. "Ever. Understand?"

I gave him a wry smile. "Trust me—I wouldn't do that to you."

"Hmm," he said. "Two days ago, I might have—"

We were interrupted by Spyro thrusting his head around in the edge of the curtain.

"Father!" he nearly shouted. His eyes were fully open. The significance of this fact was not lost on either of us. "You have to come out here!"

It was then I noticed the silence. There were no sounds of combat.

I dashed through the curtain, nearly knocking Spyro down in the process. I took two steps toward the street and stopped.

Degan and Iron were both standing in the middle of the square, weapons drawn, breathing heavily. Brass ware of every imaginable shape lay scattered about them, dully reflecting the day's last light.

Neither man was paying much attention to the other; instead, they were staring out at what was left of the surrounding crowd. Or, to be more specific, at the dozen or more men and women who had stepped out of the crowd, their weapons drawn.

At first, I thought they were Rags come to settle the disturbance. Then I noticed that the nearest one wasn't wearing a red sash; instead, she had a barely visible, dirty gold strip of cloth tied about her arm.

War colors. *Nicco's* war colors. Oh, damn.

I was taking a reflexive step back when a deep bass

voice I recognized boomed out across the street. It still had the power to freeze me in my tracks.

"I've got you now, you crossing little bastard!" thundered Nicco. Off to my right, the crowd parted, and the Upright Man stepped into the open space before the stalls.

At first I thought the war had been taking its toll on Nicco, what with his puffy eyes, tangled hair, and unkempt clothes—he looked as if he'd been dragged out of bed. Then I noticed Rall'ad standing behind him, and realized it was very likely the case.

The fish vendor saw me looking at him, smirked, and slipped back a little farther into the crowd.

Crossing little bastard; I'd sear his face on his own grill if I got out of this.

"It's going to be painful for you, Drothe," said Nicco, opening and closing his fists at his side. "*So* painful." He looked away before I could reply and addressed the degans.

"I've no quarrel with either of you," said Nicco, pointing to the two degans. "You want to fight in my territory, I'll overlook it. Hell, you can take this bazaar apart for all I care. My Arms won't lift a finger against you." He gestured at me. "But if you try to come between me and *that*, then we have a problem."

I took another look at the men and women Nicco had brought with him. All their steel was quality; all their faces were grim. More than one of them were wearing at least some sort of protection as well. Four sported steel gorgets; another two had leather jack coats; most had some sort of helmet; one even wore a well-oiled steel cuirass strapped to his chest. Armor wasn't usually worn on the street—that they had come this decked-out meant they had come ready for trouble.

I recognized some of the faces among them, too: Mythias, Seri Razor Edge, Gutter Janos, the Hell-and-Fury twins, the Cretin ... Some of Nicco's best muscle was here.

In a strange way, I almost felt honored at the talent he'd assembled, even though I knew it wasn't meant for me directly. What worried me, though, was that there might actually be enough deadly skill among the Arms to take both degans.

Iron took a slow, calculating look at the men and women surrounding him. Degan simply stared at Nicco.

"Well?" said Iron to Degan.

Degan didn't respond. He stood in the middle of the street, sword in hand, blood running down his arm. The silence radiated out from him, infecting the crowd until even the Purse Cutters and the water hawkers grew still.

Nicco met Degan's gaze. "Don't be stupid," said the Upright Man, his voice sounding like a shout in the stillness. "He's not worth it."

"Shows what the hell you know," said Degan. Then he moved, and the Cretin, who'd been a good four paces away from him, was falling over, Degan's sword already on its way back out of the Cretin's left eye.

In an instant, everything went from stillness to chaos. Knowing a bad situation when they saw it, the last of the crowd surged away from the imminent bloodshed. Two of the Arms got caught in the panicked tide and were swept away; the rest rushed forward to engage the degans. Iron laughed and waded in to meet three of the Arms outright, killing the front man with frightening casualness. When the remaining two shifted to keep him from joining up with Degan, Iron laughed again and waved them on with his free hand.

Degan hadn't even paused in his assault. Without looking down, he'd caught the guard of the Cretin's sword with his boot, kicked it up, and grabbed the weapon out of the air with his left hand. Now, with a sword in each hand, he was rushing Nicco.

Four Arms stepped forward to meet him. Degan cut with the left blade, parried with the right, feinted, and flicked the tip of his left sword. A gash appeared in the tallest Arm's throat, pulsing red as he crumpled toward the ground. Another cut, a thrust, a stab with each blade, and another Arm fell.

It looked like Degan was going to wade his way to Nicco without much effort. I smiled at the thought. Then another Arm rushed in from the side, forcing Degan to shift his guard and work against two fronts. His advance stopped.

Nicco had blanched at the sight of Degan bearing down on him, but now he had enough breathing room to think. He thought of me.

"Get the damn Nose!" Nicco yelled to the square in general. He began circling toward me.

I didn't need to hear him twice. Staying here only made me a target. If I wanted to do anyone any good, I needed to get out of this stall, preferably in a less than obvious fashion. The fewer people who knew where I was, the more damage I could do.

I drew my rapier and turned to duck back behind the curtain. That was when I saw Seri Razor Edge vaulting into the stall over a pile of crates, a nasty grin on her skeletal face.

Seri didn't say anything when she landed—couldn't, for that matter; she'd had her tongue cut out years ago. Rumor had it that her then-husband had done it because she had lied to him. Once she'd recovered, Seri had used the brace of long barber's razors she still wielded to carve him up and sell him for pig fodder.

Seri clicked the razors open and closed, open and closed, in a blur of silver steel. Even though I had reach with my sword, I thought twice about attacking her—I'd seen her take apart better swordsmen than I in a matter of seconds.

"Go ahead, try her," said a voice. I glanced right and saw another Arm, named Leander, standing outside the stall. He had a broad-bladed infantry sword resting across his shoulder—a souvenir from his days in the Imperial legions.

Two Arms versus me—I'd seen better odds at a fixed cockfight. If Ioclaudia's journal hadn't been filling up

my left hand, I would have tried a drop-and-throw with
my wrist dagger.

I saw the curtain shift slightly behind Seri, even
though there was no breeze. I resisted the urge to smile.

I looked over at Leander. "How much?" I demanded.

His eyes narrowed. "How much what?"

"How much to let me go?"

Leander looked at me, dumbfounded for a moment,
then laughed. "You mean how much to cross *Nicco*? I'm
not—"

That was when Mendross's staff thrust out through
the gap in the curtain. It caught Seri behind the ear with
an audible *crack*. Her knees buckled.

By then, I was already throwing the journal at Leander. I wasn't happy about it, and my gut tightened as
I did it, but it was either throw that or my sword, and I
needed the sword more just now.

The motion caught Leander by surprise. Instinct
made him block the book with his sword, which meant
he missed the rapier thrust I sent immediately after it.
My blade caught him at the base of the jaw. The tip bit
deep, his head snapped back, and he was dead.

I was still recovering from my lunge and turning to
thank Mendross when something collided with the side
of my head. My first thought was, *What the hell are you
doing, Mendross?* but as I staggered and fell, I saw Mendross still standing in the curtained doorway, a look of
surprise on his face. Then I saw Nicco step over me, and
I knew who had clicked me.

Mendross jabbed and swung with his staff, but the
stall was too narrow for him to be able to use it effectively. Nicco reached out and took the weapon away
from the Ear almost absentmindedly. He then grabbed
Mendross by the throat and began to beat him with his
own staff.

I pushed myself up off the ground. It bucked and
swayed beneath me, but I didn't have time to worry
about that right now. I reached for where my rapier had
fallen, missed once, twice, then got it on the third try. It

felt clumsy and heavy in my hand all of a sudden. That couldn't be a good sign.

Being this close to Nicco summoned a riot of emotions within me: fear, anxiety, hatred, panic, despair, even, oddly enough, elation. But underneath it all was a dark, seething need for vengeance — vengeance for Kells and his men; vengeance for the beatings I'd suffered; vengeance for what Mendross was suffering; vengeance for Eppyris and Cosima and their girls. I wanted vengeance for everything this bastard had put me through for the last seven years, for everything I had had to take because it was my job. Well, that job was done now, and it was time to take back my pride and pay him back.

I climbed to my feet.

As I rose, Nicco turned and let go of Mendross. Without the Upright Man to support him, Mendross collapsed to the floor. He was bleeding freely from more places than I could count, most of them on his head. When he fell, he didn't move. Nicco dropped the staff across him without a second thought.

I brought my rapier's tip up and got into the best stance I could. The world seemed to be leveling out a little bit, for which I was grateful.

Nicco grinned and slid into a wrestler's crouch, his hands out before him. He was wearing a pair of Meat and Greets — leather gladiator's gloves, their backs studded with iron, their palms and inner fingers lined with fine chain mail for grabbing blades. Looking at them, at him, I was surprised I was still conscious.

"Just us, little man," rumbled Nicco. "No degans, no Oaks, no Arms, and no fruit peddlers." He smacked his hands together, making them thump and ring at the same time. "I'm going to enjoy this."

"My thoughts exactly," I said, and I lunged. Nicco must have been counting on his intimidation to work on me like it had in the past, since he seemed genuinely surprised when I attacked. He jerked his body back from the thrust and barely got a hand up in time to knock the blade away. I advanced, pressing hard with two more thrusts and a low slash in quick succession. Nicco blocked them all, retreating until he felt one of Mendross's tables behind him. He blocked another cut, then lowered his head and hunched his shoulders. His eyes narrowed.

I knew that look. It meant I was about to be in trouble.

Before he could charge and use his greater mass to run me down, I stepped back and dropped to the ground. Two quick rolls and I was under a table and out in the square.

Nicco swore and came after me, throwing crates and baskets out of his way.

I glanced quickly around the square. Degan was backed up against the base of Elirokos's statue, holding off multiple Arms with his two blades. Iron had taken his fight on the run and was ducking in and out of stalls and behind tent backs, using the terrain to keep his attackers off-balance and in pursuit. There were more bodies on the ground than there had been last time I looked, but both degans also seemed to be sporting fresh blood themselves.

More important, there were no Arms in my immediate vicinity.

I gave a quick scan of the ground for Ioclaudia's journal. It was off to my left, not far from Leander's feet. Not in easy reach, but not too far, either. Then a crate landed between it and me, and I was forced to turn my full attention back to Nicco.

He was in the square before me, pawing at the air softly, waiting for his moment. I closed up my guard and reached for the fighting dagger at my belt. If Nicco got in past my rapier's tip, I'd need something to keep him at bay. The fingers of my left hand were just brushing the dagger's handle when Nicco made his move.

He reached out for my blade, trying to grab it and push it high as he came in low, his fist at the ready. My hand fell away from the dagger, and I danced back, pulling my rapier in and then thrusting it back out at his eye. Nicco had changed up the timing of his attack, though, slowing himself down after his initial reach. That meant I was backing faster than he was advancing. My tip fell short, waving weakly in the air. Nicco batted at the blade and came on.

I'd forgotten how long his arms were, how fast he was with his hands. Rapiers aren't very good for blocking punches in the first place, and with Nicco's being so adept at protecting himself, I was quickly finding myself on the defensive. It wasn't supposed to work that way; most times, three-plus feet of steel were enough to keep a brawler like Nicco at bay. Today, though, he seemed more worried about getting his hands on me than collecting a few stray stabs or cuts.

Worse, he was pressing me so hard, I couldn't find time to draw my dagger. If he got in before I got it out, I was done for.

Something needed to change.

Degan would have doubtlessly done something deadly and flawless; me, I leapt back a pace and squatted down in the street. I thrust my sword out in front of me, ducked my head, and laid my left arm over myself for protection. A second later, I felt an impact along my rapier's length. Then Nicco collided with me.

I was knocked sprawling on the cobbles. A sharp pain lanced down my right arm, running from elbow to fingertips and back. My rapier slipped from my hand with a clatter.

I sat up to find Nicco getting to his knees beside me. One hand was pressed against his right side. There was blood flowing out around his glove.

My left hand went for the dagger on my belt. Nicco leaned over and backhanded me. I fell back, sprawling, the dagger skittering away. I felt the knife taken from my boot, then a painfully heavy weight settle across my left arm just above the wrist sheath. I could feel the texture of the street pressing into my muscles.

Nicco leaned over from where he was kneeling on my arm. He was grimacing in pain, but still managed to summon up a nasty smile. "Out of toys, Drothe?"

he said. "I know you too well—know where you keep
all your sharps." He reached down and punched my
right leg, driving the knuckle studs on his gloves deep.
"Boot," he said. Then he punched my stomach. "Belt."
He rocked his knees back and forth on my arm. "Wrist.
Did I miss any?"

I gasped at each new torment but didn't cry out; I
didn't have the strength.

The rage was gone. I was hollow inside now, empty
of everything, save a growing sense of despair. Eppyris
and Cosima, Christiana, Degan, Kells, even Solitude—
I'd failed to keep my word to them, failed to deliver on
even one promise. I had thought that as long as I was out
in the street, as long as I had the journal, I could outma-
neuver everyone. That, even when cutting my deal with
Solitude, I could somehow sidestep the costs.

It was arrogance, pure and simple. I only had to look
around the square to see the consequences others were
suffering because of me: Mendross, beaten and bloodied
in his own stall; Degan fighting for his life against not only
half a dozen Arms but against Iron as well; Nicco system-
atically crushing or damaging those people or things I had
said I would serve; and all the others. I had been gambling
with other people's lives, and I hadn't even noticed.

Fucking Nose.

Nicco shifted his weight, releasing some of the pressure on my left arm. Blood rushed in, pricking and searing the new bruises. "We're going to have a nice, long
talk, you and I," he said. "*Very* long."

He looked around the square, making sure neither
degan was in a position to interfere, and then stood up.
My blade had caught him in the side near the hip, doing little more than cutting flesh and maybe scraping the
bone. So much for the hope of taking him with me.

Nicco reached down, gathered the front of my jerkin
in his fist, and hoisted me to my feet. I hugged my sore
left arm with my partially numbed right one. The action
caused my hand to brush against my belt and the coiled
roughness that resided there.

I felt a sudden surge of something. Not hope—not then, not yet—but maybe desperation; that, and a bit of darkest guile.

It was enough, though.

I let the fingers of my right hand trail slowly downward.

"Come on," said Nicco. He leaned his face close into mine, smelling of oil and olives. My fingers found their goal and closed around it as best they could. "I have three Brothers of Agony waiting to meet you," he snarled. "Each one ready to work eight hours at a stretch; each one ready to keep at it until I say it's over."

I looked Nicco dead in the eyes, then. I don't know what he saw, but it was enough to make him draw his face away from mine. I smiled a jagged smile.

Now. Now I could feel it coursing through me. Hope. And hate.

"I hope you paid them in advance," I said. Then I brought Jelem's coiled rope up between Nicco's legs. Hard.

Chapter Twenty-eight

There was a series of *pops* so close together, they almost sounded like one. Nicco's eyes opened wide and rolled up into his head. He fell over. I stood there, swaying on my feet, a smoking coil of rope in my hand. Then I bent down and wrapped the rope around Nicco's neck.

The knots in the rope were spaced just right for crushing a victim's throat—not surprising, considering Jelem's template had been crafted for an assassin. As I twisted and squeezed, I noticed that three of the paper runes weren't smoldering like the rest—they were still white and pristine. Glimmer to spare, then.

Nicco didn't put up a struggle; in fact, I don't even think he was aware he was dying. His face went blue, then purple, but I kept tightening the garrote until blood began to well around the edges. Even then, I didn't stop—couldn't stop. Deep down, I knew he was dead, but part of me kept saying, *Make sure. Make sure!* So I did, until my hands began to cramp up, until my arms were trembling with the effort. Even then, I had to consciously tell myself to ease up on the tension, to stop.

When I finally peeled the rope from around his neck, I had to wipe it on his clothes to remove the excess blood. I knew I should have felt something—relief, disgust, satisfaction—but all I could find was a vague sense of futility. Nicco was dead, but things hadn't changed—not in any way that mattered.

I straightened up to find the square empty of the living. It was thick with the gloom of evening now. I blinked and rubbed at my eyes. The darkness felt good.

I turned to go back to Mendross's stall and the book. Then I caught sight of Degan and stopped.

He still had his back to the base of Elirokos's statue, but now he was leaning against it in exhaustion. A half circle of corpses lay piled around him like some grisly barricade. Not one of the bodies groaned, not one shifted in pain, so thorough had been his slaughter.

Degan was covered in gore from the chest down and from his biceps to his fingers. His own sword hung limply in his right hand, and it took me a moment to make out a new cut that had laid that arm open between the shoulder and the elbow. He still had Cretin's blade in his left, but that hand was shaking visibly.

I looked around the square for Iron. He was nowhere in sight.

I coiled the rope carefully in my left hand. I retrieved my rapier and walked over to Degan. I stopped short of the ring of carnage.

"So," said Degan, his voice coming out low, flat, exhausted. He indicated Nicco's body with the extra sword. "How was it for you?"

My hand tightened around the rope until it creaked.

"You son of a bitch!" I said.

"Ah, straight to business, then." Degan looked down at his blood-slicked boots. He flicked a small bit of someone else's bone off the tip of his foot. "First, let me ask you something," he said, looking up and meeting my eye. "If I had simply asked you—after you cut your deal with Solitude, after you'd come here to deliver it into Iron's hands—to give the journal to me instead, would you have?"

I stared at him. I knew what I desperately wanted to say, but I couldn't bring myself to lie to him.

Degan nodded. "I thought as much. So, given that, you see why I had to invoke the Oath."

"No, I don't," I said. "You don't have to do this."

"Don't I?" Degan leaned his head back against the stone. "Why not? Because Solitude says so? Because Iron does? Because they think the emperor will somehow destroy an empire he's gone to amazing lengths to save?" Degan closed his eyes. "Why did you attack Shadow?" he said.

"What?"

"You heard me. Why did you attack a Gray Prince on your own?"

"Because he threatened Christiana," I said. "He threatened Kells, the organization, everything. Shadow was going to use them as leverage against me, and sooner or later, when I wasn't useful anymore, he'd make an example out of them. I realized the best chance for them was my dusting *him*."

"But you must have known you couldn't win," said Degan. "That you might have died even before I got there."

"I had to try," I said. "There wasn't any other option."

Degan smiled softly. "It's the same with me and the journal," he said. "I can't let them doom the empire just because they think the emperor is a threat. That's why I called in your Oath—because it's the only way to save both the empire and you."

"What do you mean?" I said.

Degan rolled his head back and forth against the granite, his eyes still closed—a tired man's head shake. "You don't think Shadow is going to give up on you, do you? If you haven't guessed, I didn't kill him. He's still out there. And he's not going to be happy with you when he finds out that not only did you attack him, but you also delivered the journal to Solitude. I don't care what she promised you—you can't hide from Shadow, Drothe." Degan opened his eyes and looked at me. "Unless . . ."

"Unless?" I said, knowing I was being led but not caring right now.

"Unless I take the book from you," said Degan. "Shadow knows you wouldn't be able to stop me if it came down to a fight. If I 'took' it—however that might end up happening"—a grin here—"he couldn't blame you for the book not making it to him."

"Maybe," I said, "but there would still be my having attacked him. And he'll be none too pleased with you, either."

"Leave that to me," said Degan. "He's not as good as he thinks he is."

"He was good enough to survive last time."

"He won't always have pocket change handy."

I crossed my arms. "So you're saying *he* was the one who got away from *you* after all the Rags were dealt with?" I said.

"Let's call it a mutual fade due to extenuating circumstances," said Degan. "Besides, I had to backtrack and get your rope for you."

I ran my thumb along one of the knots. "And you just *happened* to bring it to Mendross's stall to deliver it to me? Today? Right now?"

"If you stake out a place long enough, you're bound to get lucky. Besides, you tend to check in with your little fruit seller first and last when something is going down."

Was I that predictable?

"Yes, you are," said Degan.

I made a face. Then I sighed. "What now?" I said.

Degan pushed himself to a fully standing position. "I call in your Oath and take the journal," he said. "Nothing's changed."

"No, nothing has," said Iron Degan.

I spun around. Iron was stepping out from between two stalls. He was walking easy, his sword lolling in his hand. His shirt was soaked with sweat, and his short hair lay plastered to his head. There were two fresh cuts on his right forearm and a scrape along the knuckles of his left hand. Besides the split Degan had given him on the cheek, he had picked up a shallow gash along his jaw. None of the wounds looked serious.

I glanced at Degan. He was eyeing Iron, studying his condition. It was no great leap to figure he wasn't overjoyed.

Iron stopped outside the ring of bodies. "Has he told you what else happens if he succeeds?" he said to me. "About the consequences of his using your Oath like this?"

"Using it how?" I said.

"Bronze here is using the Oath you gave him to directly oppose the Oath of another degan—mine. That's a no-no."

"It's been done before," said Degan.

"Ancient history," said Iron, "and a different time. We don't do it anymore. But that's not the worst part, is it, Bronze?"

Degan stood silently, head lowered, staring out at Iron from beneath his brows.

"Bronze here took the Oath with you," said Iron, "*knowing* I was involved, and likely on the other side. By accepting your Oath, he set himself up to come into conflict with me." Iron now openly glared at Degan. "Not only did he walk into the problem—he helped create it. It's that last part the Order won't be able to look past."

"Which means what?" I said.

"Which means," said Degan, "that if I kill Iron and take the journal—in direct conflict to *his* Oath—I get cast out of the Order and hunted down."

"While if I kill him," said Iron, "he just has his name removed from the rolls, permanently. No Bronze Degan ever again. Well, that, and he's dead, of course."

"But degans must have had their Oaths conflict in the past," I said.

"That's not the point," said Degan, standing up straighter. He hefted both of his swords, then tossed the Cretin's aside. "It's about knowingly opposing a brother or sister and his or her Oath." A sneer entered Degan's voice. "It's about keeping the peace rather than keeping our promises."

"No, it's *about* loyalty," snapped Iron. "It's about following the traditions of the Order and *keeping your word* to those who have sworn to follow the same path as you!"

"My word is mine own to judge," said Degan. He switched his sword to his left hand and danced the tip in a small, intricate design. He frowned and looked up at Iron. "Believe me—if I could have found another way out of this, I would have taken it. But you're wrong, Iron—about the emperor, the empire, and what we need to do—and that doesn't leave me any other choice."

Iron stepped to more open ground, away from the corpses. He brought his sword up, the guard just below his chin, and saluted smartly. "To old times."

Degan stepped out past the ring of bodies. "It's been a pleasure," said Degan, though I couldn't tell if he was talking to me or to Iron. His salute was awkward in comparison to Iron's, slow and uneven in his left hand. My stomach sank.

Both men took their guards. Iron shifted his foot. Then he was dead.

I blinked. What the . . . ?

I can still see them: Degan, bent forward, his right hand on Iron's wrist, pulling on Iron's sword arm as his own sword slides beneath it. And Iron, his sword extended but off-line, his eyes narrowed in concentration, Degan's sword entering beneath his ribs and coming out somewhere between his shoulder blades.

For the briefest of moments, both men stood frozen before me, as still and imposing as Elirokos on his granite block. Then I blinked, or breathed, or the world turned again, and time resumed.

Iron smiled. He opened his mouth to say something, but only a faint sigh and some pinkish froth escaped. Degan grimaced and nodded in turn. Then Iron collapsed.

Degan levered his blade out of his sword brother and stepped back. He let out a shuddering breath.

"That was close." He mopped shakily at his forehead. "I was afraid he'd see it coming."

I gaped at Degan.

Degan gently wiped his sword on Iron's shirt and slid it home in its sheath. Then, with great reverence, Degan took Iron's sword and cleaned it on his own clothes. He dipped his finger in Iron's blood, dabbed a spot onto the sword's handle, another on its scabbard. Then he took both and stood up, sliding the blade home.

"Let's go," he said. "Now that we're done, I doubt the Rags will keep their distance much longer."

I fell into step behind him, still going through the combat in my head, still failing to fill in the missing pieces.

"I suppose that's that," I said.

"For me and the degans?" said Degan from in front of me. "Yes."

"So what do I call you now?" I said.

Degan didn't answer.

"What are you going to do with the journal once you have it?" I said.

"Destroy it."

"What?"

"What else do you expect?" he said, his voice growing tight. "As long as it's around, it's a threat."

"What about the emperor?"

"What about him? I don't know what he'd do with it, but even if it's locked away somewhere, it could still be used. Better if it's gone altogether."

"But not all of it deals with reincarnation," I said. "Hell, not all of it even deals with imperial glimmer! There's information on the beginnings of the empire in that book—from someone who saw it firsthand."

Degan spun around so fast, I nearly fell over. "It's not a relic to sell, Drothe! Not a game piece to trade. Not a history book to read." He gestured back at the square, back at Iron. "Do you think I did this lightly? I gave up my life for what that damn book could do, and now you try to tell me to trade it? To only destroy *part* of it? Have you even looked around to see the damage that it's caused?" He pointed over to where the journal lay, outside Mendross's stall. "That journal is *danger-*

ous," he said, "and not just to the emperor. It's going in the fire!"

"Because you promised to protect him?"

"Yes!" he said. "Because I *swore* it!"

"And what about what you swore to me?" I said. "You promised to help me and keep my best interests at heart. How the hell does making me break my word help you do that?"

"If you keep that book," said Degan, "you'll never know peace. Shadow will hunt you. The empire will hunt you. Hell, maybe even a degan will hunt you. Believe me, your 'interests' are far better served by having that thing go away."

"How fucking convenient for you that my 'best interests' coincide with your Oaths."

Degan straightened up. "What is that supposed to mean?"

"It means I trusted you," I said. "I trusted you not to take advantage of my Oath. I trusted that our friendship would count for something in all of this."

I didn't see him move; just felt the back of his hand across my face. I staggered back.

Degan's eyes were so bright, they looked feverish. *He* looked feverish. "You can say that?" he grated through clenched teeth. "After all this? After I took your Oath, knowing what it would mean for me? For Iron?"

"That's the point!" I said. "You *knew* what it would mean, but you didn't tell *me*. All I knew was what was hanging in the balance: Kells, the Kin, me, Christiana. From where I stood, owing you a favor looked pretty damn good. If you'd even *told* me what it would mean for you . . ." What if he had? Would it have changed things? Would I have put all of them at risk, just to keep Degan from going to war with his own order?

I wiped at the blood coming from my mouth and looked over at Iron's corpse. "Is that why you did this?" I said. "To be right when the rest of them were wrong? To be the degan who saved the emperor?"

"No."

"Then why?"

Degan looked past me and clenched his jaw. "He's the emperor," he said. "Without him, there's no empire. Maybe four or five centuries ago it could have worked, but not now."

"There might not be an empire *with* him, either."

"I can't believe that. Not now. Not after..." He trailed off, staring at the square; at what he'd done. And I knew at that moment that, for Degan, there was no other option. To admit otherwise would mean he had thrown who he was away for nothing; or worse, for me.

I couldn't ask him to do that—not after he'd already picked his path and sealed his fate.

"The book's going in the fire," he said. "Understood?"

I nodded. I knew why he had to do it—not for the emperor, or even the empire at this point, but for himself.

Degan put a hand on my shoulder. "It's for the best," he said.

"I know."

Degan nodded and turned back around. That was when I hit him in the back of the head with the rope.

I couldn't ask him to change his mind, but I couldn't let him destroy the book, either. And that meant I had to take the decision away from him, no matter how much it ripped me apart inside.

There was a small flash and a *pop*. Degan staggered a step, then fell. Iron's sword hit the paving stones with a clatter.

I could smell the bitter scent of singed hair as I knelt down next to my friend. "I'm sorry," I said, my voice almost breaking, "but I can't let it happen like this."

Degan was blinking rapidly, his eyes wide with surprise and shock. His mouth moved, but no words came out. I couldn't even be sure he was hearing me. Still, I reached out and pushed Iron's sword out of his reach, just in case.

"If it matters," I said, "it's not about the emperor or the empire—not anymore. If it were only that, I'd say to hell with it and toss the journal into the fire for you.

I could give a crap about Dorminikos compared to my Oath to you. But it's more than that. It's Christiana and Kells and the people *I've* sworn to protect. It's about the Kin being hunted down by the Whites all over again, just because a couple of us stumbled across the wrong piece of history. You were right when you said Shadow and the empire won't stop, but they aren't just going to come after me. They're going to come after everything that matters to me. And I can't let that happen—not even for you."

Degan's hand twitched feebly toward me. I pushed it gently aside.

"As long as I have the journal," I said, standing, "I have options and I have leverage. And right now, that's what I need. Destroying it would take all of those away."

I looked down at Degan. His eyes were still shifting, still trying to focus on me, but there was a hard set to his jaw. He'd heard me, I guessed, and still could.

"I'm sorry," I said again. "For breaking the Oath, for what you did for me, for . . ." I looked at the rope and threw it away. "I'm just . . . sorry."

Degan lay there and twitched and glowered. I turned away.

I looked around the square, wiped at my eyes, and looked again more clearly. I saw Spyro peering out from behind the curtain of his father's stall.

"Spyro!" I yelled. The boy's eyes grew wide, and he started to edge away. "Don't you dare run, damn you!" I gestured at Degan. "Come get him inside your stall. Now!"

Spyro came loping over. We half carried, half dragged Degan across the square. Degan mouthed silent curses at me weakly, but otherwise didn't put up a fight.

Mendross was peering out from behind the curtain when we arrived. His face was a mess—bloody and battered, the bruises just beginning to rise—but he nodded to me nonetheless. I nodded back, dropped all the money I had on me into a nearby basket, and gathered up the journal at Leander's feet.

On the way out of the square, I stooped to pick up Iron Degan's sword as well. I'd be damned if I was going to let it end up in some pawnbroker's shop.

As I ran into the evening, I could hear the Rags arriving in Fifth Angel Square. Their timing was impeccable, as usual.

The moon had set, and I could detect a faint brightening in the east as I entered the Raffa Na'Ir cordon. The streets were silent except for the shuffling and cursing that came from behind me.

I stopped at a crossroads and waited. My right hand fiddled with the handle of my sheathed rapier.

"Damn you, Drothe — I told you I couldn't make it all the way here," said Baldezar.

"And yet you did."

"No thanks to you."

I watched as the Jarkman came limping up. He was using a crutch, his left leg bandaged and bound between two wooden supports. It hadn't fully healed yet, and never would — not properly. Fowler's cut had done more than just bite into muscle; it had cut tendon and broken bone. Baldezar was a cripple now.

On his back, Baldezar wore a large satchel filled with pens and inks, along with parchment and jars of treatments for the same. I had not offered to carry it. This was one instance where I did not regret my part in the outcome of events. He had tried to kill me — hobbling about the rest of his days was a smaller price than I would have paid had things been reversed.

And yet, Baldezar still carried himself with arrogance. Head high, shoulders as far back as he could manage with his crutch; he was a master of his craft and his guild, and he wasn't about to let anyone forget it — even me. It was hard to feel pity for someone like that.

"The least we could have done was hire a litter," Baldezar said as he came up beside me.

"The fewer people who know you're with me, the better." It was why I had kept at least a block ahead or behind him on the way here and why I had not paused to speak with him until now. Here, the only eyes that would see us were indifferent to both the Kin and the empire.

Baldezar humphed and readjusted the pack on his back. "Now what?" he said.

"Now," said a smooth voice from the darkness, "you come with me."

Baldezar jumped and nearly fell off his crutch as Jelem slipped out of a doorway. I noted he had been standing in a place where I should have been able to see him with my night vision.

"Nice trick," I said.

"It's neither nice nor a trick," said Jelem. "It's hard work. And you should be grateful I came at all."

Jelem had been less than excited when I had found him earlier and demanded he find a safe house for me in the Raffa Na'Ir. His enthusiasm had dropped even further when I also told him I needed to collect Baldezar before we went to ground. In the end, it was only the promise of answers and more material rewards that had swayed Jelem to stick his neck out this far.

"Don't worry," I said. "I'm keeping close track of who does me favors anymore."

"That ought to be a short list, then, from what I hear," said Jelem. "Come."

I swallowed my retort and followed Jelem deeper into the Raffa Na'Ir. He doubled back on our path several times and paused twice to mutter glimmer into the night. Shortly after the second speaking, we arrived at a green door set in an otherwise unobtrusive mud-brick house. We passed through two rooms, out into an overgrown courtyard, and then into a separate, smaller outbuilding. It had once been a tack room, and a few harnesses and bridles still hung from dusty pegs in the walls. The place smelled faintly of leather.

Two tables, a pair of chairs, and a small chest occupied the space now, along with three tattered bedrolls piled up in the corner. A darkened lantern hung from a ceiling beam, and there was a scattering of candles about the room. Only one candle was lit. Two layers of heavy fabric had been hung across the single window to keep even that feeble light from escaping.

"There's only one door," I said. "That's no good if anyone finds us—there'll be no place to run."

"Run?" said Jelem. "You said you wanted someplace to hide from both the empire *and* the Kin. If either of them finds you, it doesn't matter if there are five doors, ten windows, and seven chimneys; you won't be going anywhere."

He had a point.

"How *very* reassuring," grumbled Baldezar as he limped over and settled himself into one of the chairs with a moan. "Very well," he said. "I am here." He gestured at Jelem. "*That* is here. What is it you want us to do, exactly?"

Jelem arched a dark eyebrow at Baldezar but remained silent.

I eyed both men, still hesitant, still unsure whether I could do this. It was desecration of a sort far worse than smuggling a holy tract or selling a talisman of belief. This was a desecration of the truth—of truths far older and deeper than I had any right to tamper with.

Except, as I had told Degan, there was no other choice—not after all of this.

I reached into my jerkin and pulled out Ioclaudia's journal. I set it on the table.

"What I want," I said, my hand lingering on the cracked leather of the cover, "is for you two to change history."

Chapter Twenty-nine

"What the hell is this?" said Solitude, staring down at the sheaf of papers I had laid before her.

We were in a curtained alcove off the public room of a tavern in Two Crowns cordon. Outside, the sun was shining, and people were just stopping in the taproom for their early-afternoon drinks. It was three days after the fight in Fifth Angel Square, and parts of me still hurt.

"It's Ioclaudia's journal," I said. "Or, at least, the most important parts of it."

"The 'most important parts'?" said Solitude incredulously. She was in browns today—leather doublet and skirt, tan shirt, rust shoes with bright yellow stockings showing beneath. As usual, she had a collection of charms hanging from her hair and clothing. I didn't see any pilgrim's tokens this time. "What happened to the rest of the journal?" she said.

I forced myself to meet her gaze. "I need it for something else," I said.

Solitude was out of her chair in an instant. "You *what*?!"

"It's the only way—"

"To what? Fuck me over?" Solitude flicked a finger at the papers. "You give me scraps while you keep the rest of the journal? That sure as hell doesn't sound like the deal I remember making with you!"

"Things needed to be adjusted," I said.

"Adjusted?" she said. "What the hell does that mean?"

I tapped the papers and dropped my voice. "It means everything in the journal about the emperor and reincarnation are in this bundle. You have what you wanted, what you said you needed to save the empire. The rest has to go elsewhere."

Solitude narrowed her eyes. "Meaning?"

"Meaning Shadow," I said. I didn't mention Jelem or the pages he had demanded in repayment of the favor I owed over Tamas's rope, let alone the notes he had taken in payment for working on the book itself. Given Solitude's mood, the fewer names mentioned, the better.

If I'd been expecting another outburst, I would have been disappointed. Solitude bit her lip instead and turned toward the curtain. "Gryph!"

The Arm standing guard outside the alcove stuck his head in.

"Clear the taproom," said Solitude. "I want everyone out—even the owner. This place is mine until I say otherwise."

Gryph vanished back through the curtain. A brief commotion sounded on the other side, then quickly quieted down.

"All clear," said a voice from outside the alcove.

"You leave, too," said Solitude. There were footsteps, then a door closing, then silence.

Solitude spun back around toward me. "What the *fuck* do you think you're doing?" she said. "We had a deal. You have no right deciding what to do with that journal, let alone breaking it up! You should have at least—"

"No right?" I said. "I have more right to that journal than anybody else in this damn city! I've sweat, bled, killed, and betrayed for that damn thing. While you sent out Cutters and tinkered with dreams, I was fighting Princes and Mouths and Arms in the street. I've seen people tortured and beaten because they were unlucky enough to be close to me. That journal is more mine than it is yours, Shadow's, the emperor's, or anyone else's. If there's anyone who's earned the right to make a decision about it, it's me!"

"And what was your brilliant decision?" said Solitude. "To give Shadow *Imperial magic*! You'll make him the most dangerous Kin in the city! And what's worse, when he starts using it, the empire will come down on all of us harder than a hammer on an anvil. Or aren't you worried about that? Maybe you're going to give some pages to the emperor, too, to cover your ass." Solitude threw up her arms in disgust. "You can't make everyone happy in this, Drothe. You shouldn't even try."

"I don't give a fuck about *anyone* being happy," I said. "If I wanted to cover my ass, there are a hell of a lot better ways to do it. I'm doing this because it's the best way to help you, to help the empire, and to keep the people who matter to me alive. That's *all* it comes down to anymore."

"And Shadow? What about when he starts bringing things down around our ears?"

I sat back in my chair. "He gets the journal, yes, but not enough to do him much good."

"What the hell does that mean?" she snapped.

"He's never seen the book," I said. "Never knew what was in it—just that you wanted it, and that it talked about imperial glimmer." I gestured at the pages in front of her. "When I had ... my people ... remove those pages, I had them alter the journal as well. Parts added, parts removed, new water stains—there're still notes on glimmer in there, but he'll be working a hell of a long time to make sense of it."

"And you think he won't notice?"

"My people are very, very good."

Solitude stared at me, her nails picking at the wood of the table. "Damn it!" she said at last. "We had a *deal*!"

"I kept as much of it as I could."

"You kept as much as you wanted to," she said. "There's a difference."

"The difference," I said, "is that I realized I had obligations to other people as well, and that they were just as important."

"How convenient—you get morals, and I get screwed."

I started to answer, but she held up her hand and continued. "No, shut the fuck up for a minute. I'm thinking." Solitude reached down, picked up the papers, and leafed through them.

"What about the people who did this for you? Do we have to worry about them?"

"You don't," I said. I expected Jelem to remain content, but Baldezar? He had information on me now, and I wouldn't be surprised if he became tempted to use it on me someday. The only thing that would likely keep him quiet was his own complicity in the whole affair. Falsifying part of a relic was heretical, after all, and for all his bluster, Baldezar was a coward at heart.

"And what are you going to ask of Shadow in exchange for the journal?"

"For him to walk away."

"From?"

"Everything that has anything to do with me."

"You think he will?"

"I don't have much of a choice," I said. "Like you said, I can't keep him away from anyone he wants to reach, so the next best thing is to get him to step away on his own."

"And if he won't?"

I shrugged.

"You expect me to believe you don't have a backup?" Solitude folded her arms. "There *has* to be more to it than that."

"That depends," I said. "Am I still yours?"

Now it was Solitude's turn to shake her head. "Not after this. I can't give you more than a clear path to the door, and even that's being generous. Given what you know and what you did, I should dust you right now."

"But you won't," I said.

"But I won't," she agreed. "You kept at least part of your bargain, and that counts for something. You could have given Shadow everything, but you went to a lot of effort to hide what you're giving me. Make no mistake:

I'm *not* happy about what you did—I'm damn pissed—but I'm not going to dust you."

"Thank you," I said.

Solitude waved an impatient hand. "Just get the fuck out of my sight."

I rose and was through the curtain and halfway across the taproom before she spoke again.

"Drothe," she called. "One last thing."

I stopped but didn't turn around. "What?"

"About Iron," she said. "What happened with him, really?"

I took a breath, let it out. "He tried to help me keep my word to you," I said. "For what it's worth, I didn't know I was going to do this until afterward. He died keeping his Oath."

Silence from behind the curtain.

I waited a moment longer, then continued through to the taproom, out the door, and onto the street.

The stairs at the back of the warehouse in the Barren creaked as I went up them. I pointedly ignored the week-old bloodstains my night vision picked out on the treads, just as I pointedly ignored the ghost pain that fired in my leg with every step.

Just like last time, it was dark; and just like last time, the place smelled of dirt and mold. But it wasn't raining now; nor had I been sent here by Shadow to find someone; rather, I was here to meet the Gray Prince. Alone.

That was the strangest part—not having Degan at my back. I'd felt his absence while coming through the Barren, and felt it even more now. It wasn't just the security of a strong arm and a ready sword that I missed, but the lack of his presence, his voice—even his dry sense of humor—that left me feeling exposed. It was as if part of my shadow were missing.

I had spent the past three days holed up with Jelem and Baldezar. My foray out to see Solitude had been my first major trip on the street since I'd killed Nicco.

Plenty of people wanted me dustmans for that, along with a host of other things. Now was the perfect time to settle old scores, especially with an out-of-favor Nose. But even with all that, I'd slipped out twice—the first to ask Fowler to track down Degan, and the second to learn that she hadn't had any success.

I still wasn't sure whether I was relieved at her failure or not. Part of me wanted to talk to Degan one last time, to try to explain, to hear him say he understood, or even for him to tell me to go to hell—just as long as I could apologize. But another part knew better; knew that no matter what I said, things were broken between us. And that part was glad I wouldn't have to go through the torture of trying to explain the inexplicable.

The blanket was still lying in the doorway. I stepped over it and walked a little over halfway into the room. I set down the bulky satchel I'd brought and pulled out the candle Jelem had given me. It was thick—about as fat around as my wrist—and heavy, made from a dirty yellow wax that looked like tallow but felt somehow softer to the touch. It was half as long as my forearm, with a clean-cut bottom and top.

I set the candle on the floor and pulled out my fire box. I sparked the tinder and lit it in short order.

The wick caught, hissed like an angry cat, and went out. I waited. Then, just as Jelem had said it would, the candle rekindled. The flame was small and yellow, with just the faintest hint of silver around the edges. If you didn't know to look for that trace of magic, you could miss it. I was counting on that.

I looked around the room: four windows, the one door, no chairs. I went back and retrieved the blanket, folding it as I recrossed the room. I stuck the journal inside the blanket so it couldn't be seen, then placed it under me as I sat down on the far side of the circle of light, well away from the door. I put the satchel containing Iron Degan's sword behind me, pulled out the bag of seeds I'd gotten from Jelem, and waited.

Shadow showed up an hour later, which made him

three hours early for our meeting. I didn't know whether to be flattered or frightened.

The candle, of course, had given me away. Shadow swept in without hesitation and walked straight toward me. As he moved, his cloak flared out and back, showing hints of a gray doublet and black jerkin, tall riding boots, and a silver-handled sword. His face was a veil of darkness.

I sat, motionless, my heart hammering louder in my ear with each step. When he reached the outer edge of the circle of candlelight, I spoke.

"That's far enough," I said.

Shadow took two more deliberate steps and stopped just inside the light.

"You're early," said Shadow.

"And you're not?"

"I wasn't the one who pulled a knife last time we met," he said. "I thought it best to come ahead and make sure you didn't have any surprises waiting for me."

"And maybe install a few of your own?"

Shadow waved a dismissive hand. "I think we both know that isn't necessary." The cowl panned back and forth, surveying the room.

"He's not here," I said, knowing the Gray Prince was looking to see if Degan was lurking in a dark corner. "Nor is anyone else. It's just you and me."

"Which effectively puts you at my mercy." Shadow crossed his arms, putting his right hand disturbingly close to his sword's handle. I remembered his taking on Degan and holding his own. I couldn't beat that, not straight on. "You must have something good, if you think you can talk me out of killing you," he said.

I made a point of digging out a seed and slipping it into my mouth. "What I have is Ioclaudia's journal. I want to talk terms."

Shadow threw his head back and laughed. "So you decided to do it after all," he said. "First you betrayed Nicco, and now Kells. Splendid! You're becoming quite the operator, Drothe. With a bit of money and time, you could make a reasonable Upright Man."

"If that's a job offer, I'm not interested."

Shadow's tone grew as serious as my own. "It wasn't. You tried to kill me. I can't let that stand. Showing any kind of leniency, let alone favoritism, would only undercut my reputation. And what are any of us but half action and half threat to begin with?" Shadow hooked his thumbs in his sword belt. "I can let the baroness live. I'll leave you alive, too, but there has to be a visible consequence—a missing finger, an ear, something small. And you have to leave Ildrecca. Five years, maybe seven—until people forget."

"It won't take them that long to forget."

"It will for me."

And there it was: This had become more personal than business for Shadow. My jumping him and getting away were eating at him more than the idea of Solitude getting her hands on something he wanted. Unless I could convince Shadow what I had to offer was more valuable than getting his hands on me, I wasn't going to get out of this in one piece.

I shifted on my seat, feeling the journal beneath me. "Have you forgotten what's in that book?" I said. "What I had to go through to get it?" I indicated the shadowy space around us with a sweep of my arm. "Degan and I fought White Sashes in this room. The empire has troops in Ten Ways because of it. Hell, I had to sneak through their lines just to get here. It's fucking *Imperial magic*! And now you're telling me that in exchange for something that will give you a stranglehold on the Kin, you're going to cut pieces off me and banish me from Ildrecca?" I let out a short, derisive laugh. "Something tells me I can hold out for more."

"You can hold out for whatever you want, Drothe," said Shadow. "But you need to remember something: Bargaining only works when both parties have something to lose. Whether I walk out of here with the journal, or you, in my hands, doesn't really matter. Either way, I'll be satisfied. And either way, I'll eventually end up with the book."

"And if I've made alternate arrangements for the journal?" I said.

"In case you don't come back?" said Shadow. "What are you going to do? Destroy it? Regrettable, but then no one else has it, either. Give it to Solitude? If you were going to do that, you would have done it already, and she would be here backing your play. Sell it back to the empire?" Shadow snorted a laugh. "We both know you stand a better chance with me than trying to deal with the emperor. No, unless it's destroyed, I'll find it. You've shown that that can be done, after all."

I looked up into the cowl. This was just about how I had figured it would play out: Shadow wasn't the kind to negotiate when he didn't have to—after all, he was a Gray Prince. We both knew the only real leverage I had was the book, and once that was out of my hands, all the power reverted to him. At least he was being honest about it.

The only thing that had gone my way so far was the fact that he hadn't tried to dust me the moment he'd walked into the room. And even that was dubious luck at best.

"I'm not going to offer again," said Shadow.

I sighed and shifted off the blanket. "I know," I said. I pulled out the journal and stood up.

Shadow chuckled. "Sitting on it this whole time? No one can say you don't have balls." He held out his hand.

"So that's it, then?" I said as I took a step forward. "For all the posturing and magic and mystery, you end up doing business like a common Cutter on the street? 'Give me the swag or you bleed!' I'd hoped for more from a Gray Prince."

"You get what you deserve," said Shadow. "For you, little Nose, this is good enough."

I stopped beside the candle. I looked down at the book in my hands, then up at Shadow. And met his gaze with my own.

He was smiling. It was a smug smile on a full mouth, with a dark spade-shaped beard beneath and a long nose

above. An otherwise round face was given a hard edge
by high cheekbones. But what struck me the most were
the generous laugh lines around his eyes and mouth.
Who expected a Gray Prince like Shadow to genuinely
laugh enough for it to show on his face?

I smiled in turn and watched Shadow's grin falter. He
could sense something had changed, but he hadn't figured it out yet. Hadn't figured out I could see him now;
that all the magic in the room had been burned up by
Jelem's candle.

"No," I said, "I deserve more." And I tossed the journal at him. My last glimpse of Shadow in the candlelight
was of his eyes going wide and his reflexively lunging
forward for the book. Then I kicked the candle over, and
the room went dark.

Chapter Thirty

I rolled to my right, getting out of any direct line of fire. The candle flame had been dim, but it was still going to take a moment or two for my night vision to adjust. I didn't want to be caught standing still, waiting to see my death coming at me.

That was assuming my vision *would* adjust. My stepfather had performed the ritual nearly twenty years ago; with magic that old, Jelem hadn't been sure what the candle would do to it. Like everything else tonight, it was a risk.

I circled two steps farther to my right in the darkness, silently drawing my rapier as I went, and waited. I could hear Shadow in front of me, muttering under his breath. Then I saw the hint of a gesture—an amber-hued blur several yards away that looked like a hand passing rapidly through the air. And another. And then, rapidly, I saw the image of a cloaked figure, crouched and gesticulating in the darkness, the rectangle of a book lying at his feet, all but forgotten.

The air before Shadow was empty: of power, of light, of threat. I slipped farther to my right, moving to circle behind, even as he reached to his belt and tossed a scattering of coins before him. They clinked on the floorboards, refusing to melt and burn as they had against Degan.

Shadow was no fool. As soon as he saw that his portable glimmer wasn't going to help him, he turned and

raced back the way he had come. I couldn't blame him; if
I were in a dark room with a man who put out the lights,
I'd want out, too. People don't set up situations like that
without a plan.

I flicked my left hand, felt the wrist knife drop into it,
and let fly. I knew better than to try to hit him—it was
dark, he was moving, and I was throwing left-handed.
The odds of my even bouncing the pommel off him were
negligible. But hitting the wall hard enough so the blade
made a loud noise against it, and then again when it fell
to the floor—that was another matter entirely.

Shadow skidded to a halt at the sound. In an instant
his sword was out, sweeping before, beside, and behind
him in a deadly circle. When no one tried to stab him, he
began backing slowly away, two steps at a time.

"It was the candle, wasn't it?" he said to the darkness.
"It interfered with the magic somehow." I could see his
cowl searching back and forth for any hint of motion, of
sound. His left hand made another pass in the air. Nothing happened. "And I can't imagine the darkness was an
accident, either. Which means you have a way of finding
me, yes?"

I stayed silent and adjusted my course so that I would
come at his back from an angle.

Shadow swept his blade through the air again and
shifted direction. Another cut, another direction, then
two more steps, a series of cuts that whistled as they
clove the air, then a dodge and a quick thrust across his
body.

I couldn't tell if it was a patterned drill or just a collection of random counters, but whatever it was, it kept
him—and more important, his sword—moving in an un-
predictable manner. He was doing his best to create a
wall of steel around himself; one I would have to breach
if I wanted to get this over with quickly.

And it needed to be quick.

I reached down and pulled out my boot dagger. As
much as I would have liked to dust him with a single
thrust, I knew it didn't always work out that way. Swords

like mine can wound just as easily as they can kill, but get in close with a dagger, and the odds of someone going home dead go way up—especially if one of the people can't see.

I dropped my sword's tip so that it just skimmed the floor. I came on.

Shadow was tending left, trying to get to one of the walls. His sword was still moving, his fingers still dancing. I slipped closer. Two steps more now, at most.

"Are you using the night vision?" he said as he cut a circle around himself.

I froze. His face was pointed directly at me. Then he looked away. I let out my breath.

"I've heard of it, of course," said Shadow, "but I've never known anyone who had it." His cowl shook back and forth. "If I'd only known . . . The use I could have made of you."

I stood up straight. "You used me enough as it was," I said. Then I dropped.

Shadow immediately threw a cut at where my voice had been. He was good; even crouched low, I felt the breeze of his sword's passing, telling me he had gone for my body and not my head—bigger target, better odds.

I did the same, only I pushed a thrust from down near the floor, low to high, right at his ribs. My sword connected, stuck and . . . bowed?

I felt the scrape of metal on metal down the length of my rapier, could hear a faint grinding as I twisted the blade in a move that should have stirred up his insides but only managed to pucker and turn the fabric of his doublet. Shadow let out a grunt but didn't fall or bleed.

Armor. Chain mail, by the feel of it, under his clothes.

Bastard.

I pushed my rapier's point deeper into Shadow's chain mail and lifted the guard above my head even as I lashed out at his leg with my dagger. Our blades connected at the same instant—my dagger with his leg; his sword with my rapier. It didn't go well for either of us. While I managed to lay open a sloppy gash above his boot, Shadow brought his sword down hard enough on mine to snap it in two. I'd been hoping the force of his cut would act like a hammer on a nail and drive my rapier's point through his armor, but, instead, my bracing the blade had simply made it easier for him to break.

Damn Shadow and his Black Isle steel blade, anyhow.

I leapt back, barely avoiding a blind follow-up, and scrambled away.

"Nice try," said Shadow. His voice was tighter than it had been a moment ago. "Lucky for me I'm not the trusting sort, eh?"

"What, you mean the armor?" I said as I slipped back across the room toward the satchel. "That just means I'm going to have to take you apart a bit at a time, starting at the edges." I tossed the remains of my rapier noisily off to my right.

Shadow's cowl swiveled toward the sound of the rapier's hilt hitting the floor, then came back in my direction. The fingers of his left hand were dancing again. He was favoring his right leg.

"You think so?" he said. He began cutting at the air around him, forming the deadly circle once more. "Considering you just lost your sword to someone who can't see in the dark, I'd say you have your work cut out for you."

I grinned darkly from across the room as I knelt down beside the bag and reached inside. "You got lucky," I said as my hand closed on the handle of Iron Degan's sword. I drew it out softly and stood up, hefting it. Iron's Black Isle steel practically danced in my hand. It was a heavier blade than I was used to, weighted more for the cut than the thrust, and slightly curved, but it would do. "I don't think I need anything more than a dagger to take care of you," I said. "Not in the dark."

Smiling, I turned toward Shadow and took a step. Then my smile faded.

There. A spark of light on the tips of his fingers, so faint it was barely visible even with my night vision.

I blinked. Had I imagined it? And if not, had *he* noticed it?

Shadow's fingers moved slowly, carefully. A flicker of ghostly light slithered along them, faded. Shadow chuckled, soft and low.

He'd noticed.

The magic was coming back.

Jelem hadn't been able to tell me how long the effects of the candle would last. It all came down to how long it burned and how much magic it ate up. The longer, the better. I'd been hoping to get a good three hours off it, but Shadow's early arrival had barely given me one. Which, it seemed, translated into less than five minutes of no magic.

I sprang forward, Iron's sword high, my dagger low, and ran at him. There wasn't time for quiet anymore—no knives in the dark, no circling for the perfect shot, no trying to make the bastard sweat like he deserved. It had become a simple matter of me getting to Shadow before the magic got to him. If I beat it, I had a chance—the darkness was still on my side, after all; if I didn't, well, like I said, I'd seen the bastard fight.

I was still three steps away when the fire bloomed in Shadow's hand. My heart sank and my eyes burned at the sudden light, but I kept coming. I yelled, just for the hell of it.

I don't know if it was the yell or the surprise of suddenly seeing me nearly on top of him, but Shadow staggered back. This was a good thing, since it meant that the whiplike tendril of flame he sent arcing out passed over my left shoulder, instead of hitting me square in the face. The bad thing was that I could still feel the heat of the fire's passage as it went by my ear and cheek.

I flinched, and that was enough to throw off my cut. Instead of coming down where Shadow's neck met his shoulder, the heavy blade dipped low, sloping toward his left leg. Shadow caught my sword on his own and used the impact to bring his own tip over and around, ready for a cut of his own.

I closed in fast, rushing to put myself inside the arc of his attack. Swords have more power near the point when swung, and getting past it would keep me safer. At the same time, I struck with my dagger, over and over, using short, underhand thrusts. I kept meeting chain mail with the point, but I didn't care; I just needed to stay in close, where my size and the dagger gave me an advantage. Even if I wasn't separating any links, I was driving the mail into him—hard. With luck, I'd break a couple of ribs and maybe even rupture something.

Shadow pivoted, trying to shift with my attack. I could feel the pommel of his sword hitting me in the back, but he didn't have the right angle to put any real force behind it. I pressed forward even harder and alternated my dagger thrusts—now low, now high, now from the side—to make it harder for him to catch my arm with his free hand. If I could get the blade under his arm, or even up along the side of his head ...

Then I saw his left hand come up and begin to pass before my face, just like before.

I turned and dropped away. An instant later, my shadow was projected on the floor in front of me by a brilliant flash of light from behind.

I felt burning—in my eyes, not on my face—as I stumbled away. It wasn't nearly as bad as it had been in the alley; I could still see the floor, still make out my hand in front of me, although everything seemed to be shifting. Amber mixed with yellow in my vision and ran across everything in waves, rather than the constant highlighting I was used to. It looked almost like ...

Oh.

I raised my eyes. The back wall of the room was on fire. Shadow's arc of flame must have continued past me and hit the old wood and plaster and lathe. It was no roaring inferno yet, but, judging by how quickly things were spreading, it wouldn't take too long to get there.

I spun around. Shadow was maybe ten paces away, bent over slightly, his left forearm pressed against his side. His sword sat ready in his right hand; in his left, near his chest, I saw the glint of coins.

"No darkness anymore, Drothe," he said in the glowing, growing light of the fire. "No glimmered candles." He straightened slowly and squared his shoulders. "My turn."

He took a step and I ran, not toward the doorway, but to the blanket I'd been using as a pad. At this point, only one of us was going to get out of here; heading for the door would only get me a sword—or something worse—in the back.

I cast the dagger away and swept up the blanket with my left hand. Turning, I was just able to avoid the first molten blob that came flying through the air. I shook out the blanket, shifted my hand, and spun the fabric twice through the air, wrapping it around my hand and forearm. That left a couple of feet of cloth hanging free, giving me a flexible wall of fabric to use either as a shield or a whip.

I swept another coin from the air with the blanket, then a third. Two more came after that, with Shadow right behind them.

He wasn't playing now. Shadow didn't set up out of measure and ease in, or play with my blade, or stand back and cast coins at me until I was a smoldering, exhausted mess; he came in fast, his sword a fire-tinted blur in his hand. A cut at my head, a second, then a switch to an attack on my outside line, followed by a thrust and then another slash, all in fewer heartbeats than it takes to tell. I caught the first two on my sword, got lucky when the blanket intercepted the next, barely backed away from the fourth, and watched as the last cut swept by, three finger breadths from my face.

I followed up with a counterthrust, but Shadow turned it aside almost absently and flicked a coin at my neck. I didn't have time to get the blanket up, so I instead rolled my head and neck away as best I could.

I felt a searing pain just inside the ball of my left shoulder. I screamed and backed away.

I crouched lower and extended the blanket out before me. The room was brighter now, and I was beginning to feel the heat of the fire as it ran up the wall. I
saw my right arm trembling in the wavering light. Part
of that was nerves, I knew, but part was fatigue as well; I
wasn't used to Iron Degan' sword, and even the addition
of half a pound of blade can make a big difference.

If this went on much longer, I wasn't going to be able
to maintain any kind of solid guard. Then again, if it
went on too long, we might both die when the roof collapsed, or the air ran out, or the heat cooked us. None of
the options appealed, but I wasn't sure what to do about
it at the moment—I was too busy being outmatched.

Then Shadow threw three coins at once, and I suddenly knew exactly what to do.

Three coins meant I couldn't dodge—not all of them;
three coins meant I had to commit to blocking them; three
coins meant Shadow was coming right behind them, counting on their threat to clear his way.

Three coins meant I had him—I hoped.

As the coins spread out and turned liquid, I fanned
the blanket out and up, catching them in its folds and
sending them off to my left. I let that action draw my
left arm back and turn me into profile. Then, I extended
my sword.

I'd seen Degan do this before, and had even tried it
myself once or twice. He called it a simple voiding of
the body; I called it damn slick. The idea was that you
got your body out of the way while you left your sword
in place, thus allowing your opponent to throw himself
on it when he attacked. Degan had made it look like
high art; the best I usually managed was a child's rough
sketch in the dirt. But it worked.

Usually.

I saw the flash and felt the breeze of Shadow's blade
passing through the space where I had been. Even better, I felt my sword bite—only it seemed wrong.

I looked down the blade, and my heart went cold. I
had extended Iron's sword into Shadow's path all right,

but I had forgotten about the curve in the blade. Where a rapier's straight blade would have planted its point in the middle of the Gray Prince's face, Iron's tip instead sloped off to my right. What should have been a killing thrust had instead ended up sliding past his face and coming out through the side of the cowl. I might have grazed a cheek if I was lucky, but I hadn't come close to stopping the Gray Prince in his tracks.

I pulled back on the sword, trying to turn a missed thrust into a savage gash to the face, but Shadow's left hand flashed up and grabbed the back of my right. Then he twisted.

Muscles and bones strained against one another along my arm, all of them turning the wrong way. The pain bent me forward, then down to my knees, my arm still straight out beside me. I felt my fingers loosen, felt Iron's sword taken from my grasp. It clattered on the floor. Then something hard—Shadow's sword pommel? The whole guard?—tapped me near the base of my skull.

I dropped to all fours, Shadow letting go of my arm at the last instant.

I heard a roaring, but only part of it was in my head. I glanced behind me. The back wall was now a sheet of flame. Overhead, above Shadow, the ceiling was obscured by a roiling black cloud. If it wasn't already burning up there, it would be shortly.

Shadow didn't seem to notice or care. His sword was extended, its point inches from my upturned face. Shadow reached up with his left hand and put a finger through the hole I had made in his cowl. He smiled. His sword didn't waver.

"Close," he said. He looked back down at me. "You should have just taken the deal."

"I still would have wound up dead."

Shadow shrugged. "Of course you would. You tried to dust me—that can't be tolerated. But at least it would have been, well, *fairly* quick. Now, though . . ." Shadow gestured at the glow of the fire behind me. "I hear the smoke kills you before the flames. Let's hope that's the case, for your sake." He shifted the sword so it hovered over my back, then raised it, ready for the crippling stroke.

Well, at least he wouldn't have reason to go after Ana anymore. That was something.

"Screw you," I said, and I braced for the blow.

Shadow's arm was just beginning to descend when something came flying out of the darkness and shattered against the back of his head. Brown and beige fragments bloomed around his cowl. Shadow staggered. His sword drove into the floor beside my feet.

Without thinking, I put my right hand up to his belt and came away with his purse. Shadow righted himself and pulled his sword free. He glanced at the doorway, then back at me—just in time for me to drag open the strings of the purse with my teeth and cast its contents full into his cowl.

Don't let them be keyed to him like my rope, I prayed to the Angels. *Don't let the damn things be keyed.*

Over the flames, I could hear the hiss of the coins as they hit the air, followed by a wetter sound as the molten metal found Shadow's face.

Shadow screamed and collapsed on the floor, clawing at the inside of his hood. I reached over and drew Iron Degan's sword to me. I stood.

Shadow's writhing stopped the second time I thrust the sword into his cowl. Then I looked up.

Degan was standing in the doorway. He had another piece of battered crockery in his right hand—he must have found a squatter's stash somewhere—and his bronze-chased sword in his left.

I laughed out loud and almost sat down on the floor. Degan, here, saving me again. Even after what I'd done. I laughed some more.

I hadn't even thought to hope.

Had he followed me, or Shadow? Part of me—the bit that housed my professional pride—hoped it had been the latter, but I had my doubts. If anyone could stick to my blinds without my knowing it, it was Degan. Not that I minded; not in the least.

The roof was burning now, and a fallen ceiling beam had split the room in two. There was a small gap at the far end, but the fire moving along the wall was close to reaching that area. Once it did, the opening would be too narrow, if not gone altogether.

I moved to go around, then paused as I remembered Ioclaudia's journal. It was lying on my side of the room near the burning timber, smoldering but not yet alight.

Degan followed my gaze. When I looked back at him, he shook his head and dropped the bit of crockery on the floor. Then he turned away.

"Wait!" I yelled.

Degan turned back around. As I watched, the smoke beginning to sting my eyes, Degan drew himself up straight and raised his sword to his lips. It was the same gesture he had made back in the Cloisters, when we had exchanged the Oath, except now he was staring straight into my eyes. He didn't blink as he kissed the blade, or as he flourished it in the firelight, or as he threw it onto the floor before him. He just met my eyes. Then Degan turned away and was gone.

It was over: the Oath, our friendship, his life as a degan. I knew it as sure as I knew my own mind. All the debts were paid for him, all the accounts closed. It was just as he had predicted: Binding ourselves with the Oath had broken everything else between us, and more.

I didn't move to follow him. I wouldn't embarrass him like that, wouldn't go after something that was already gone.

I was a Nose: I knew when a trail had run out.

The smoke was starting to fill the place now, making me cough, blurring my vision. I found my way to the journal and had to kick it away from the fire because it was too hot to touch. Its cover was more char than leather now, and one corner of the tome had begun to turn crispy black.

Which gave me an idea.

I smiled grimly in that small corner of what felt like hell and wrapped the journal in the blanket. It wouldn't do to burn it up—not just yet, anyhow.

I retrieved Iron's sword and laid it across Shadow's body. A few right words in the right ears, and the Order of the Degans would find the twisted remains of the sword here, along with Shadow's burned husk. Let them think a Gray Prince had killed their brother and kept the sword as a trophy—Shadow was certainly arrogant enough to make it plausible. It wouldn't ease Degan's conscience any, but it might keep his former brothers from hunting him down.

Not the parting gift I would have wanted, but it was the best I could manage.

I gathered up the journal and headed for the outside wall. I was on all fours by now, nearly blind from the smoke. I could feel cinders settling on me from above, burning the backs of my hands and neck, singeing my hair, smoldering my clothes. Those spots felt only a bit warmer than the rest of me at this point.

I reached the wall sooner than I expected and crawled along it until I was able to make out a patch of calm, shiftless black above me. I reached up, levered my torso over the window ledge, and let myself fall.

It was two stories down, but I wasn't about to complain.

Chapter Thirty-one

I stood loitering against a wall across the street from the Imperial cordon, trying to look casual. That wasn't easy, considering I had a dozen Gold Sashes staring me down.

The avenue that separated us was as wide as three normal streets and in impeccable repair. Along the west side, where I stood, ran residences with gated compounds, prosperous specialty shops, well-appointed taverns, and whorehouses of the best repute. On the east side stood the Wall, an immense line of red-and-white brick running more than a mile north to south, until it swept in a grand curve to meet the seawall that surrounded Ildrecca. Taller than any of the surrounding buildings, and thicker than most of them as well, the Wall marked the boundaries of Heaven on Earth, if you listened to the priests, or the playground of the pampered and powerful, if you had a more earthy bent. Either way, it wasn't the sort of place to let my kind in.

But that wasn't why the Sashes were staring at me.

I made a point of ignoring them and instead looked up at the sky. A dark smudge ran across the otherwise placid blue expanse. Ten Ways was burning, and had been for almost a day, thanks to Shadow and me. The blaze was contained—it turned out the legions were good for something after all—but there was ash settling all across the city, its pattern depending on which way the wind blew. A dark winter falling on the eve of spring.

I half wondered if the ash wasn't following me, making sure I didn't forget about how I had brought things to this point. Not that I would have forgotten, even under a clear sky.

The slam of the sally port in the gates across the street brought my eyes back down to earth. The Golds were at hard attention. A tall, familiar figure had just come out of the Imperial cordon. She was sporting a white sash around her waist and had ribbons running through her braid. Lyria.

She spoke to one of the Golds, who pointed in my direction. Lyria looked me over, frowned, then glanced at the folded piece of paper I'd had them deliver to her. *Concerning your Oath. Outside,* it read. No signature. She'd clearly been expecting someone else—a broad man with a big damn sword, a man by the name of Iron Degan.

I put an ahrami seed into my mouth and began walking away, up the street.

Footsteps came up behind me. I was just getting ready to turn around when I felt a hand grab me across the back of the neck. Another took my right shoulder and steered me into the wall. I bounced off it once, got shoved up against it again. The seed popped out of my mouth and went skittering away on the paving stones. I could hear laughter and jeers coming from the Imperial gate.

Lyria put her mouth up to my ear. "*No one* summons me out of the Imperial cordon, especially not a Crawler like you."

"Back off, Sash," I said into the wall. "I'm here as a favor."

"To whom, Iron Degan? Did he send you?"

"Iron's dead. I'm here as a favor to you, you stupid White." The pressure on my neck eased momentarily, and I twisted around and shook off her grip. She didn't bother to react.

"What do you mean, he's dead?" she said.

"What the hell do you think I mean?" I said, rubbing where my shoulder had hit the wall especially hard. "Dead. I'm sure you're familiar with the condition, at least secondhand."

"You're certain?"

"I saw him take the steel cure myself."

"Who did it?"

I shook my head. "Not important. What *is* important is that I'm here to help you."

"*You* help *me*?" Lyria stepped forward, forcing me back against the wall. "In case you've forgotten, you and your friend killed two of my sword brothers. The only reason I didn't kill you before was because of my word to Iron Degan." She smiled wickedly. "But now that he's dead, I suppose I'm free of that, aren't I?"

"That's just it," I said. "He's dead, but your word to him isn't; it's gone up for grabs."

Her back went as stiff as if she'd been called to attention herself. "What?"

That was more like it. "Your Oath wasn't just a deal with Iron," I said. "It was a promise to the entire Order of the Degans. If the degan who holds your Oath dies, the other degans are free to pick up the promise."

"You think I'm an idiot?" she said. "I know the terms of the bargain. My obligation ended when I delivered you!"

"That's not how I remember the conversation going outside the wineshop," I said.

Lyria's hand moved to the handle of her sword. She looked far too willing to use it at the moment. "I think maybe you're remembering wrong, Crawler."

I turned my head and spit into the street. Lyria puffed up even more.

"I don't misremember things," I said, meeting her eye, "especially when it comes to Sashes and debts."

She pressed against me further, holding me against the wall with her body. Under other circumstances, I might not have minded; there were some interesting things going on under that uniform. As it was, though, I didn't even have space to draw a decent breath.

"Are you threatening me, little man?"

"Not threatening; just telling. Iron's dead. Unless the degans hear otherwise, the Order's going to assume you still owe him. They'll come collecting, and I'm guessing they won't give you credit for services previously rendered. You'll get to start your debt from the beginning."

I watched as realization crept into her eyes, followed closely by fear. Whites were supposed to serve the emperor first, last, and always; owing anyone else service — especially someone like the degans — was strictly beyond the pale. I couldn't guess about the deal she had struck with Iron, but I could guess what would happen if she was found out: excommunication, banishment, possibly even a public execution for treason. Not things someone who had sworn her life and soul to the emperor would care to consider.

She needed to keep this quiet.

She needed me.

"And I suppose you can fix this?" she said sourly.

"I was the only witness, remember?" I said. "There were just the three of us there when you delivered me. If I tell the degans you cleared your debt with Iron, you'll be off the hook."

Lyria took half a pace back and crossed her arms. "And why should they believe you?"

"You beat the crap out of me and delivered me to Iron Degan," I said. "Plus, I'm Kin. Do you honestly think they'd believe I'd lie for a White Sash, especially under those circumstances?"

"And you don't think your volunteering the information might raise some questions?"

I sighed and closed my eyes. "You really don't understand how this works, do you?" Stupid Whites. I looked up into her eyes. Still smoldering but with a trace of interest in them, too, I noted. Good.

"Listen," I said, "I don't go to them — we wait for *them* to come to *you*. When they do, you tell them Iron and you are straight. When they don't believe you, you mention *I* was there. The degans hunt me down and ask me questions. After being vague with my answers and generally pissing them off, the degans scare me enough that I grudgingly admit that, yes, Iron said your debt was paid." I spread my arms and smiled. "Problem solved."

"And if they don't believe you were there?"

"I know where his sword ended up," I said. "They'll believe me."

Lyria studied me for a long moment. "How much?" she said at last.

"One service, payable to me—the same as you owed Iron Degan."

She shifted on her feet. "What service?"

I made a show of straightening my clothes. "Hit me."

"What?"

"We've been talking quietly for too long," I said. "Your friends at the gate are probably getting suspicious. Hit me, and I'll tell you the favor I want."

"No problem." I saw a blur, felt something hard connect with my jaw. I went down.

"If that wasn't convincing, I can do it again," said Lyria. She sounded far too pleased with herself.

"'S okay," I grumbled. I rolled over and looked up at her. No smile, but the sparkle in her eyes was all too evident. I ran my hand over my jaw, just to make sure it was still in one piece.

"Well?" she said as I climbed slowly to my feet. I hoped she was keeping her fists cocked just for show.

"Remember that book you were looking for in the Barren? The one you and Degan—excuse me, Bronze Degan—nearly killed each other over?"

"Ye-es."

"I want you to tell the emperor that it was destroyed in the fire in Ten Ways."

"*What?*"

"Don't worry," I said. "I have what's left of it. You'll have proof."

"*Was* it destroyed in the fire?"

"As far as you know."

Lyria ground her teeth. "I am not going to lie about the thing I was ordered to recover," she said. "And certainly not to the emperor!"

"You understand this is blackmail, right?" I said. "And that, for you to get what you want, you have to do what I want?"

"Yes, but I'm still not going to do it."

"Why the hell not?"

Lyria looked at me for a long moment, then turned and began walking away. "I can't," she said.

I grabbed her shoulder and swung her around. "You don't understand," I snapped. "You don't have a choice. It's me or the degans—it's that simple."

"No, it's not!" she said. "I've already broken the oath I took to the emperor once. I'm not going to do it again."

"Your *oath*?" I said. "Screw your oath! Let me tell you something about promises; they aren't blind, they aren't immutable, and they aren't fragile. I've seen more oaths and promises broken in the last few days than I want to think about, but I learned something about them in the process—you can't keep every one of them. No matter how hard you try, it's just not possible. So you have to choose, not only which ones you are going to keep, but *how* you're going to keep them. You have to look behind the words, behind what you want them to mean, and see what they're really about.

"It's easy to hold on to the idea of what the words meant to you when you spoke them, but that's not what it means to take an oath. A promise like that has to change as you change, and more important, it has to be able to adjust to fit whatever the world throws at you. The question isn't whether or not you keep your word; the question is whether or not you keep the intentions *behind* the words." *Even if your Order disagrees with you,* I thought. I understood that now. "If you walk away from me, you not only don't bring the emperor back the book he wants, you also put yourself in debt to the degans. You, a White Sash, trusted guardian of the emperor, will be beholden to *them*. You had an agreement with Iron Degan, but who knows what the hell *they* will ask you to do?"

Lyria looked away. I didn't bother telling her the degans essentially had a job similar to hers, only with a slightly broader focus. That wouldn't exactly help my case right now.

"Listen," I said, "you can draw this line now, after you've already crossed it once, and pretend you're pure, but we both know that's a lie. The degans will come collecting, and you'll be in it even deeper. Or you can do this one thing and walk away clean from any other obligations. Which one serves the emperor better in the long run?"

Lyria looked up at the walls of the Imperial cordon, seeing beyond the brick and mortar.

"Why do you want me to lie about the book?" she said.

"Because it's the only way to keep you and your friends from tearing apart the city—and some of my friends—looking for it. The only way they'll be safe is if the emperor thinks the book is cinders." *The only way your boss won't skin me alive for what I know,* I thought, but didn't say.

Lyria let out a slow breath. When she spoke, I almost couldn't hear her, it was so soft, so final. "Fine. What do I do?"

I reached into the satchel and partially withdrew the charred remains of the journal. There was just enough left to identify the book as Ioclaudia's, but not enough to be able to tell that pieces were missing. I'd burned it myself once I had gotten away from the warehouse.

"When the fire dies down in Ten Ways, you'll go back to the warehouse in the Barren where the other two Whites were . . ." I paused, the rest of the sentence hanging in the air between us. Lyria took a slow, dangerous breath. "Where your brothers died," I amended. "You'll find this book there, along with whatever's left of a body and a sword. Leave the sword, but take this. I'll make sure it looks as if the book was spared in the fire."

I slid the remains of the journal back into the satchel, then drew out a small cloth-wrapped case. "Here, take this, too. It might help you get in good with your boss."

Lyria reached for it, then hesitated. "What is it?"

"A relic," I said. *A bribe*, I thought. "The reliquary is a bit worse for wear, but the artifact itself is all right." *It's meant to keep you from being too pissed off at my using you.* I pushed it into her hands. "It's the pen Theodoi used to write the Second Apologia." *I don't need any new enemies right now.*

"How did . . . ?"

"Long story," I said. "You're better off not asking."

Lyria stared at the bundle for a moment, then carefully slipped it into her belt. "And after this, I never see you again, correct?"

"Not even in your dreams," I said.

"You'd better hope not," she said. Then she extended her hand.

I looked at it, surprised, and reached, out of habit, to exchange the Clasp. Except she wasn't Kin. Our fingers brushed, and then she was grabbing my wrist and using it to hold me while she drove her knee into my stomach.

I doubled over, collapsed to my knees, and started retching.

"Can't have it look like we're parting on good terms," explained Lyria coolly from above. "People might get suspicious." I watched her boots as she walked away.

If I'd had any breath left in me, I would have laughed. Instead, I gasped and watched my lunch spread itself across the cobbles.

I was just starting to suck air back into my lungs when a pair of soft brown shoes came walking up and stopped beside me. The legs sprouting out of the shoes wore faded red stockings.

"Still making friends wherever you go, I see."

I knew the voice. It was one I shouldn't be hearing. I pushed myself into a sitting position and looked up at Kells.

My heart surged in my chest at seeing him alive, but

I wasn't sure if it was out of joy or fear. He was healthy, hale, and even looked to have put on a couple of pounds. He was also smiling.

That couldn't be good.

My wrist knife was in my hand in an instant.

"Ah-ah!" said Kells, raising a scolding finger. "The Sashes are watching, and they tend to frown on what you're thinking about doing."

"Two Kin trying to kill each other in the street?" I said, rising to my feet. "What would they care?"

"We're Kin—they'll care, on principle, if nothing else." Kells looked me up and down. "Secondhand clothes, same old boots, a freshly bruised face—at least I know you didn't cross me for money."

"I didn't cross you," I said.

"No," said Kells coolly. "You abandoned me. You left me swinging in the breeze, at Nicco's mercy, trapped in a cordon surrounded by imperial troops. 'Cross' doesn't even begin to describe the totally thorough screwing you gave me."

I tried to meet his gaze but couldn't. I had an explanation, of course, but didn't offer it. No matter what I said, it would sound like an excuse. All Kells knew was that I hadn't followed his instructions, that I hadn't brought him the journal so he could hand it over to Shadow. Thanks to me, he was an Upright Man without an organization; a fallen Kin wandering the streets—just like me.

Kells didn't want excuses, and I didn't insult him by offering any.

"I swore I'd make you pay for that," he said. "Pay long and hard. And I will—don't worry—but not like you might think." I tensed. Kells sighed. "Come on," he said, stepping past me. "I'll buy you a drink."

I was so stunned, I simply stood there.

Kells stopped and turned around. "What?" he said, obviously enjoying my confusion. "You don't think I'd dust you now, do you? You're off-limits. If I even tried to touch you, Solitude would have my ass."

"Solitude?"

"How hard did that Sash hit you, Drothe? *You* were the one who cut the deal to get me out of Ten Ways, remember? Solitude kept her promise—she got me and half of my people out of there before the Imperials waded in in real force. I work for her now." Kells began walking again. I followed without thinking.

"*You* work for *Solitude*?" I said.

"Ironic, isn't it?"

"That's one word for it. I didn't expect Solitude to honor any part of my deal with her after what I did."

"You mean after you played her?" said Kells. "I wouldn't have, either, but she's a different creature. Even after you came up short, she stepped in and used your name to get my attention. Before I knew it, we were exchanging the Clasp. I can't say I'm thrilled at the terms, but I'm alive, and so are a lot of my people; I can't fault her for that."

"You can't fault *her*," I said. "But what about me?"

"As I said, you're off-limits."

We walked in silence after that, away from the Imperial cordon and into friendlier neighborhoods. Kells indicated a small café down a side street. We sat beneath the crimson-striped awning. I ordered a pot of coffee, currant-laced pastries, and a young sweet cheese for spreading. Kells ordered a pitcher of wine.

"You've heard about Nicco's territory?" said Kells after the food arrived.

"I've heard," I said, breaking open one of the pastries. It was more biscuit than pastry—dry and crumbly, but buttery sweet underneath the tartness of the currants. I spread on some of the cheese and found it overlaid the whole thing with a nutty smoothness. "How much of it did Rambles manage to take?" I said.

"About a third," said Kells, "maybe a little more. The rest is still up for grabs."

I grunted and had another bite. I would have been happier if Rambles had taken three feet of steel through his ribs instead, but life doesn't always work out that way. He had known the war was coming before anyone else; it must have been easy for him to position his people to take control once things went to hell—or maybe even before then.

No, Rambles wasn't stupid, but I was still going to need to kill the bastard one of these days.

Kells took a sip of wine and stared out at the street. He cleared his throat. "I heard about you and Degan," he said. "You seem to be on a roll with turning on people, if you don't mind my saying."

I didn't answer.

"Have you heard from him?" said Kells.

I thought back to the sight of Degan in the warehouse, of him turning away without a word. "No," I said.

"Are you going to try to find him?"

"No."

"Why not?"

"Do you think anything I could say would make a difference?" I said. "That he would forgive me if we could sit down over cakes and drinks and have a chat?"

Kells looked at the spread on the table and frowned. "No, he wouldn't."

"Nor will you," I said. "So why are you here? If you're not going to dust me, and not going to forgive me, then why? I can't believe that Solitude has you running messages to me—not after our last meeting."

Kells sat back in his chair. "To tell you you did the right thing," he said. "You bucked me and you conned Shadow and you played Solitude, and I don't think I could have done it, damn it, but you did. You put your head down and followed it through when just about anyone else would have walked. That's worth something."

"Maybe," I said, "but it's not enough. Not when I consider all the wrecked people I've left in my wake."

"I never said it would be *enough*," said Kells. "Just that it counts for *something*. That's the price you pay for signing on to a cause. The sooner you realize that, the better—for you and for all the people you'll end up using. And you'll use them, trust me. You won't have a choice."

"What about you?" I said. "Have you signed on for anything?"

"You mean with Solitude against the emperor?" Kells stared out at the street. I was surprised he knew about that, but only mildly. He *was* Kells, after all. "I don't know," he said. "I was ready to work under Shadow, but that was different—that was climbing into bed with a Gray Prince. This other thing is"—he waved his hand vaguely in the air—"bigger. I don't know." Kells glanced at me. I took another bite of my food. "Why, are you planning on starting an organization?" he said.

I nearly choked at the suggestion. "Me?"

"You ran a hell of a game all by yourself, Drothe. The street is talking."

"Me?" I said again, swallowing. I hadn't considered doing anything except surviving once I had gotten rid of the journal. That had been the final move, as far as I was concerned. "In case you haven't noticed, I'm on my own—no allies, no organization, no muscle. How the hell am I supposed to do anything?"

"How were you supposed to juggle two Princes, as many Upright Men, a Kin war, and the empire?" said Kells. "A lot of the Kin may not like you for what you did, but they respect you for it—now more than ever. You did something no one thought could be done. That counts for a hell of a lot, believe me."

I stared at Kells. Did people really think I'd had some sort of *plan*, that I had meant for things to turn out like this? I stared down at the crumbs of my pastry and shook my head. "Angels help me," I muttered.

"Let me ask you something," said Kells. I looked up. He was grinning.

"What?"

"How did it feel?" he asked.

"How did what feel?"

"Playing the Princes," he said. "Conning the empire; balancing Nicco and me; doing the *right thing*, at least in your own book. How did all of it *feel*?"

I looked into his eyes and saw a yearning there, a hunger to know what it was like to do what I had done—to beat the odds, to pick a side, to do something, right or wrong, for a reason. And I wondered for the first time how many other Kin—how many other *people*—felt that same yearning.

"It felt good," I said. "And it felt wrong. And it hurt, and it scared the hell out of me. And I still can't say whether it was worth it."

Kells nodded once, sharply. "Fair enough," he said. Then he pushed his chair away and dropped to one knee on the other side of the table. Before I could react, he had reached across and taken my hand in both of his. "In that case, you are my Prince, if you will have me."

I leapt back so fast, I nearly upended the table. *"What?"* I stammered.

Kells laughed. "Sorry. I couldn't resist." He gestured for me to sit, then did the same. "But you have to admit, it makes the point."

"What, that you're a twisted bastard?" I said.

"No, that the street has given you a promotion."

I gawped. I knew I should have said something—or run away and hid—but all I could do was stare at my former boss with my mouth open.

"It's true," said Kells. "Word has been going around about how a new Gray Prince is rising up from the ashes of the war, how he bested Shadow and Solitude and a host of Upright Men—me included—and is even now in the process of putting his people in place throughout Ildrecca." Kells took another sip of wine and then examined something in the bottom of the cup. He dumped the rest of the contents out on the ground. "Did you know people are already sporting your colors?"

"Colors?" I said. "I don't have any colors!"

"The street, and probably about twenty Kin wearing them, say otherwise. I hope you like gray and green, by the way." Kells poured himself more wine. "There are even whispers that Blue Cloak Rhys wants to meet with you. I'd recommend demanding a straight twenty percent off the top, by the way, since he's approaching you first, and then charging a higher cut for any Rufflers and Up-rights who come after. That'll make Rhys feel special—and put him deeper in your camp—while encouraging some of the fence-sitters to get on board sooner rather than later. You need to build fast right now."

"But I'm not a—"

Kells stopped me with a look. *"Yes, you are!"* he hissed. "You *are* a Gray Prince. The street says so, the Kin say so, and, based on how Solitude was talking about you, she's ready to say so as well. With that many people believing, it doesn't matter whether you agree with them or not, because they're going to treat you like a Prince. And so are the other Princes."

The other Princes. Shit. My stomach dropped even as I began scanning the street for likely Blades.

"Now you're getting it," said Kells. "I think Solitude is amused by the whole thing, but you can't expect that sentiment from everyone."

"Which means I need to recruit people and lie low. Fast."

"Hmm. Wish I'd thought of that."

I ignored Kells and continued to watch the street. Was that Purse Cutter looking at me strangely? And how about that beggar over there? Were they targeting me, or just checking out the newest Gray Prince?

Or was I being paranoid?

A woman with a child walked by and I caught myself following them with my eyes, my hand already on my dagger.

Okay, I *was* being paranoid.

I sat back in my chair and rubbed my face. A Gray Prince? Me? What the hell did that even mean? What was I supposed to *do*? The only firsthand examples I had came from a dream-walking woman who wanted to kill the emperor, and a glimmer-using schemer who had hidden behind a mask of darkness. Since I didn't exactly see myself wrapped in a dark cloak and holding vague, mysterious meetings in abandoned mansions, there weren't a lot of useful pointers there.

What *was a* Gray Prince, anyhow? The head of an organization that ran underneath other organizations. A Gray Prince was a Kin who worked past the street and cordon level, even past the level of the city. Looking at what Solitude and Shadow had wanted, I knew they thought broad. And big. And long-term.

And, I realized, deep down, they wanted to be as good as Isidore had been; as good as the man who had organized the Kin and made himself into the Dark King. Princes wanted to show they were kings.

Except I didn't want to be a king. I just wanted to be a Kin. Only I didn't seem to have much choice about that now.

I looked over at Kells. He was watching me, a hint of a smile on his lips, cold ice in his eyes. And I realized I didn't need to look to Solitude or Shadow or any of the other Princes, or even Isidore, for examples; I'd had one of the best organizers in the Kin as my mentor for years. And I still did, if I was lucky.

"The offer you made a few minutes ago," I said. "Is it still good?"

"It is. And it includes about a dozen of my people who are in Solitude's organization as well. We're yours, if you want us."

"I can't offer you anything right now," I said.

"You saved us; the least we can do is return the favor. Once you start having some stronger sway on the street, we can talk price."

I shook my head and looked out past Kells, at the street, and Ildrecca. Drothe, Gray Prince of . . . what? A Jarkman who'd tried to have me killed? A Djanese Mouth for hire? A handful of Cutters who were wearing colors I hadn't known I had? And now, thirteen Kin in another Prince's organization. What the hell kind of a start was that?

I shook my head and began to laugh.

"What's so funny?" he said.

"My 'organization,'" I said.

"What about it?"

"Almost half of them are Long Noses. Who the hell starts a criminal organization with a bunch of Long Noses and no money?"

Kells began to laugh as well. "Sounds like a perfect fit for you."

I nodded. "I suppose it does." I took a sip of cold coffee and considered. Yes. Those Noses would come in handy when it came time to bring Solitude to heel someday. After all, there was still an empire to save and the Kin to keep alive, and I'd be damned if I'd let her fowl it up.

When we left, Kells insisted on paying for the meal. It was only fitting, he said; after all, I was his boss.

Acknowledgments

This book began on a breakfast counter in Juneau, Alaska, and ended at a cluttered desk in St. Paul, Minnesota. It was more than ten years in the making. In that time, it has endured four moves, numerous jobs, unemployment, the birth of two children, voluntary and involuntary hiatuses, a leaky roof that killed the computer it was on, a pretty serious rapier addiction, and heaven knows how many other distractions.

When you spend that much time working on something, you end up telling a lot of people about it. Friends, family, coworkers, drunks in bars—sooner or later, everyone hears about the Book. Most of them are supportive; many are interested; some are even enthusiastic; but those aren't the people who make it into the acknowledgments section. That's reserved for the big money—the people who have, knowingly or otherwise, impacted the writer or the work in some important way. Even then, you can't remember everyone, but you can try your best.

Here's me trying my best:

First thanks go to the members of the best damn writers' group I could ever want to be a member of, the Wyrdsmiths (in all its various incarnations): Lyda Morehouse, Naomi Kritzer, Bill Henry, Kelly McCullough, Eleanor Arnason, Sean M. Murphy, Harry LeBlanc, Rosalind Nelson, and Ralph A. N. Krantz. Without them, this would have been a very different book, and not for the better. Next, a big tip of the hat to my beta readers, who helped provide a thorough polish and detailing, as well as a few key adjustments under the hood: David Hoffman-Dachelet, Stephanie Zvan, Tracy Berg, and Kelly McCullough.

Special appreciation to my editor, Anne Sowards, and my agent, Jack Byrne, for believing not only in the book, but also in me. Thanks to you both for all your hard work in making this dream come true.

And from farther back down the line, and in no special order, kind words to Larry Lindenbaum, my first honest-to-goodness fan (and a true friend); Roger Siggs, for first showing me how they did it with a rapier back in the sixteenth and seventeenth centuries; David Biggs, for helping me refine that knowledge; Robert (aka Dorian) and Muriel Jackson, for their belief; Barth Anderson for the last-minute produce consultation; and Dan and Katherine Kretchmar, for not minding that one of my villains shared their son's name.

A special nod is also due to all the folks who populated the =dwarf and =nomad lists back in the day. You guys were my first audience in a very wild, crazy, and creative time. A bit of Too Tall, Madam, the Pope, Andre, Spyder, Carlos, M the U, and all the rest will always be with me (no matter how hard I try to manage otherwise).

Big thanks to my family, who always made a point of asking how the book was coming, even when I didn't always want to say: my mom, Verna Hulick, who has always been my greatest cheerleader; my brothers, Nick, Ted, and David; and my sister, Nancy. And to all the family I inherited when I said, "I Do": Allene Feldman-Morris-Pine; Jerry Feldman and Al Morris (both fondly remembered); Stacy Fox; Ken and Gail Feldman; and Marmon Pine.

A tip of the hat to Evan and Cameron, who deserve mention, even though they excel at preventing me from getting work done. The closed office door means Dad is writing, guys!

Special thanks to my father, Nicholas Hulick. A hero is a hard thing to come by these days—I was lucky enough to grow up having one in my home. Wish you were here for this, Dad.

And, lastly, immeasurable thanks to Jamie, who listened and encouraged and supported and did so much more. If it weren't for her, I wouldn't be writing this, or much of anything else.